Praise for the novels of

"*The Secret Society of Salzburg* is a gripping, en............strength, filled with extraordinary characters and tender relationships. Renee Ryan reminds us that the universal languages of art, music and friendship bring light and hope amid even the most challenging of times. I loved every word."
—*New York Times* bestselling author RaeAnne Thayne

"*The Secret Society of Salzburg* is a powerful journey of bravery, secrets, and subterfuge. Renee Ryan is a brilliant storyteller and this book is definitely one you don't want to miss!"
—Madeline Martin, *New York Times* bestselling author of *The Last Bookshop in London*

"*The Secret Society of Salzburg* is a heart-wrenching yet uplifting tale about the importance of art and beauty in the darkest of times. Renee Ryan weaves a masterful story anchored by the unbreakable friendship of two extraordinary women. A must-read."
—Julia Kelly, internationally bestselling author of *The Last Dance of the Debutante*

"*The Widows of Champagne* is a heady concoction of everything I love about historical fiction—history, drama, and passion as effervescent as the resilient LeBlanc women and the champagne that bears their name. I highly recommend!" —Karen White, *New York Times* bestselling author

"The backdrop of the picturesque Champagne valley paired with the darkness of the German invasion helped this story come to life in a unique way. *The Widows of Champagne* will remind the reader of Kristin Hannah's *The Nightingale*." —*Booklist*

"*The Widows of Champagne* is a riveting novel of WWII France. Highly recommended." —Robin Lee Hatcher, Christy Award–winning author of *Make You Feel My Love*

"*The Widows of Champagne* will sweep you into a wartime story of love, greed, and how one should never underestimate the strength of the women left behind. I couldn't put it down."
—Donna Alward, *New York Times* bestselling author

**Also by Renee Ryan
and Love Inspired**

The Widows of Champagne

Visit the Author Profile page at LoveInspired.com for more titles.

The
SECRET
SOCIETY
of SALZBURG

RENEE RYAN

LOVE INSPIRED
Stories to uplift and inspire

LOVE INSPIRED®

Stories to uplift and inspire

Recycling programs
for this product may
not exist in your area.

ISBN-13: 978-1-335-42756-4

The Secret Society of Salzburg

Love Inspired
22 Adelaide St. West, 41st Floor
Toronto, Ontario M5H 4E3, Canada
www.LoveInspired.com

Printed in U.S.A.

For Mark.

After twenty-six years and counting,
you are still my first, my last, my always.

The

SECRET
SOCIETY
of SALZBURG

Chapter One

Elsa

August 1943. Salzburg, Austria.
Felsenreitschule *Theater.*

The black Mercedes-Benz approached the *Felsenreitschule* theater at a steady pace, giving the woman inside time to settle her nerves before stepping into the heavy August heat. It had been an exhausting two weeks for Elsa Mayer-Braun. The endless rehearsals, the physical demands on her body, the excessive stress to her vocal cords. Yet none of that compared to the torment unfurling in her own home, made worse by the escalating arguments.

She would not think about Wilhelm now. Nor would she dwell on the terrible things she suspected of the man she'd loved enough to marry. The pain was too great, the grief too real. And so Elsa sat very still on the worn leather seat, inhaling the soft floral scent of her perfume as it mixed with the

acrid smell of cigarette smoke left behind by the previous oc-
cupant. She would not think of him, either, or the way he'd
insisted she accept the loan of his state-sponsored car. The
generous offer, she was told with a hard clasp to her arm, was
one she would not refuse.

A chill crept along her spine at the memory of her husband's
cold, emotionless glare as he spoke those words in front of
his powerful friend. The glacial steel of Wilhelm's eyes had
been that of a stranger. The silent demand more threat than
warning.

If only Hattie were with her, sharing this moment, speaking of opera and art and very little else, certainly nothing of
the secret they shared. Perhaps then Elsa would feel less afraid,
and this terrible sense of foreboding would vanish.

But Hattie wasn't here. She'd been detained in London.
Elsa was on her own.

She stared straight ahead, speaking not a word, thinking
not a thought beyond what she must do tonight on the stage.
This would be her final opportunity to slip behind the mask
of Donna Anna in Mozart's *Don Giovanni*. Elsa's prior performances had captured high praise from the critics. *Unprecedented*, they wrote. *Matchless. Without rival.* Oh, yes. She had
much to be grateful for professionally, if not personally, where
the dual life she'd chosen required her to wear a different sort
of mask, with much higher stakes.

The Mercedes rolled to a stop.

Elsa flexed her fingers, lacing them together to make sure
her gloves fitted snugly, the way she liked them best. They
were new, a gift from her husband. Wilhelm had smiled when
he'd presented them as a peace offering last week after telling
her he would not be conducting *Don Giovanni* as planned. Pris-
tine and snowy white, the gloves were the color of a shroud.
She checked the fit again.

Biting back a sigh, she chanced a glance out the side window. A crowd had gathered along the curb, a river of faces swollen in anticipation. It seemed all of Salzburg had come to witness her final performance. Their voices tangled unnaturally, blending, until all Elsa could hear from inside her cocoon was a high-pitched buzz, much like the sound of bees in their hive. "El-sa," they chanted. "El-sa, El-sa, El-sa."

Something in their adoration was different tonight. Or perhaps it was Elsa who was different, making her feel like a guest in her own life. The throng pressed in closer, shoving at one another, throwing elbows, placing palms on the hood of the car, the roof, even the window that separated Elsa from their frenzy.

The driver—she didn't know his name—swiveled around in his seat. He wore a military uniform: SS, the hated enemy. The look in his eyes was not easy to read beneath the shadow cast by the bill of his hat. "Should I circle the block?"

It was too late. Elsa had been positively identified. Precious little could be done now but to accept her fate. "Retreat will only stir them up more."

"Then, I will drop you closer to the stage door."

She shook her head. "No, I'll exit here. I—"

The Mercedes began to rock. Fear skittered up Elsa's throat. She swallowed it back and forced herself to breathe. Perhaps she should issue the order for him to take a spin around the block after all. Impossible now. The choice was no longer hers to make.

Her fans continued closing in around the car, chanting her name, the earlier buzz of their voices sounding more like a roar. They wanted only one thing. A glimpse of the woman who carried the label of Hitler's favorite opera singer.

Elsa knew what was expected of her. She would give the masses what they wanted. She would smile and sign autographs and speak to a select few. No one would ever suspect how she used her elevated status within the Third Reich. Or that her notoriety had become both shield and sword against Nazi Germany's crimes against humanity.

She'd stalled long enough.

Scooting forward, she breathed slowly in, out. Then, with a flick of her wrist and a bold push, she exited the automobile in a rush. She'd moved quickly, and for a split second, the crowd froze. Elsa hardly noticed their shocked silence. Or the way the driver left his place behind the wheel to stand beside her in silent solidarity. Her attention was riveted on the long, narrow street. On the buildings themselves and the sea of Nazi flags waving their allegiance to a monster and his deadly regime.

Sorrow came fast and hard. Her beloved Salzburg had been infested with vipers, and stripped of her beauty. Her independence. Her dignity. With too many of her people treated much, much worse. People who relied on Elsa to be braver than she knew herself capable. Until a fortuitous meeting with a humble British civil servant, now her friend, ally and accomplice, a woman who had reached her own notoriety and fame with a very small push from Elsa.

The next ten minutes went by in a blur of flashing bulbs, garbled words of praise and more chanting of her name. No human deserved such earthly acclaim.

Despite the sticky, suffocating heat, Elsa shivered, fumbling her way through the riot of fans and journalists. Until finally, at last, she was inside the building, cloaked in shadow and the molten gold and orange light that played across the centuries-old stone walls. Only in Salzburg could an ancient quarry become the home of the greatest music festival in Europe. With its portico of arches on three tiers hewn into the rock, the former riding school for an archbishop's mounted soldiers was like no other theater in the world.

Elsa entered her dressing room and began the task of transforming herself into a woman bent on revenge because of a greedy man's selfish desires. She knew this character down to her bones. She *was* this woman. She finished her warm-up exercises and stepped into her costume, but there was still no sign of Wilhelm. She hadn't expected him to come, but she had hoped. So be it. She would face this final performance on her own, with no words of encouragement from her husband. No *Toi, toi, toi*—opera's equivalent of *Good luck*. Her punishment, she supposed, for refusing to believe his lies.

Of course, she had her own lies to protect.

Head high, she made her way to the stage, moving like a wraith through the darkened corridors, taking a position in the wings, concealed in shadow before she took her cue and rushed onto the stage. The mezzo-soprano singing Donna Elvira, a role out of her range, met Elsa's gaze. The bitter dislike was unmistakable, raw and blatant. Frieda blamed Elsa for many offenses. Her anger partly valid, mostly not.

With great success came enemies, some quite intimate. Wilhelm had taught her that.

The conductor took his place in front of the orchestra. He lifted his baton, and the overture began with a thundering D minor cadence. A short *misterioso* sequence followed, which led into a lighthearted D major *allegro*. The music changed, the singing commenced, and then it was Elsa's turn to hit her cue. She pursued the masked Don Giovanni onto the stage, clutching at his arm. She sang her opening notes. So caught up in Donna Anna's desperation, she didn't realize that the brilliant baritone playing Don Giovanni had gone unnaturally still and that she was singing alone.

She searched his face. Had he forgotten the words? It happened sometimes—rarely, but yes, it happened. She expected him to find his place in the melody, silently willing him to do so, right up to the moment she understood the expression on his face was one of terror.

Next came shouting in German, a sound that had no place in this opera. At the far end of the center aisle, soldiers stormed the auditorium. She recognized the uniforms. How could she not? These men were SS, an elite guard assigned to serve the secret police. *Gestapo.*

A rushing filled Elsa's ears as she watched the endless stream of soldiers marching into the building, perfectly matched in height, stature and soulless stare, like an army of ants. One by one, they broke off from the group in a precise, rhythmic tempo. Some took up position along the perimeter of the auditorium. Others lined up in the aisles and around the orchestra pit, cornering both patrons and musicians alike.

Elsa had witnessed this spectacle in other German cities, other auditoriums. She knew what came next. An arrest. She was not the only one to arrive at this conclusion. Gasps and murmurs followed. Tension, thick enough to cut with a blade, vibrated in the air.

Another group of hard-eyed men entered the building, three in total, wearing head-to-toe black. Their collars bore the SS runes, and the red armbands around their left biceps carried the Nazi swastika. The man leading the way caught her gaze. She knew him by sight and reputation. *Kriminaldirektor* Gerhardt Vogt. His face wore something she'd seen in others draped in the same uniform. Fanaticism. Bigotry. Hatred.

A dark premonition filled her mind as she watched the fiend take the stage, stopping only after he stood before her. Up close, his eyes were bluer, colder than she'd first thought, and he smelled of death. The scent made her frantic. She wanted to run, to vanish from the stage. *You're panicking*, she thought and lifted her chin, saying not a word. If nothing else, she would force the swine to speak first.

"Elsa Mayer-Braun." His voice held much distaste, as if the mere effort of stating her name was a personal insult. *"Du bist verhaft."*

You are under arrest, spoken with a Bavarian accent. The noise in her ears was deafening, an explosion of chaos and thought turned to sound. She choked for a moment, then stammered, "Wh-what is my crime?"

He closed the small space between them. "Treason against the Third Reich."

Chapter Two

Hattie

August 1934. London, England.
British Board of Education. Secretarial Pool.

Hattie Featherstone finished the document she was typing and pulled it free from the roller. Five more and she would be through her enormous workload, far and away ahead of her coworkers. It was no secret Hattie was the best typist in the building. She had an eye for accuracy and fast, sure fingers. Skills that came naturally, if not without a sense of quiet desperation.

Was she to be a civil servant the rest of her life?

Her artist's soul, inherited from her mother, cried *no*. Never. Hattie was barely twenty. She had plenty of time to escape the mind-numbing tedium of reproducing educational treatises in triplicate. Her current position was only a temporary pause, a way for her to cover her expenses so she could afford art classes as her mother had always wished for her. Classes, she was coming to realize, that were systematically slaughtering her desire to paint. Last night's critique had been especially brutal.

Her continued failure to succeed was like losing her mother all over again. Love of art had been their greatest bond.

A sob threatened to slip past Hattie's lips. She pressed them tightly together, sufficiently caging the emotion in her throat. No one in the secretarial pool could be allowed to witness her turmoil. They would ask questions and try to give words of encouragement. She didn't want their kindness. She wanted to be alone in her agony. It was easier that way. Even her older sister didn't know the depths of her disappointment. Vera would take on Hattie's failure as her own, as if she'd somehow failed her little sister.

Mouth grim, Hattie breathed in a slow, careful breath and turned her head to the right, then left, not really seeing her workspace but rather her painting of a pair of swans on a pond cluttered with lily pads in various forms of decay. The watercolor had been Hattie's best effort yet. Her fellow art students had agreed. Her professor at the Royal College of Art had not.

Derivative. Uninspired. Lacking imagination.

He'd driven home his point with harsh comments on her youth in his nasally, high-pitched voice. *You need to suffer, Miss Featherstone. Something devastating.* Surely losing her mother at the age of ten implied both suffering and devastation. *A heartbreak, perhaps. Then, in time, if you're very fortunate, your art will be sufficiently tolerable.*

Sufficiently tolerable. As if the best Hattie could hope to achieve was mediocrity.

Sighing, she lowered her head and studied her hands resting lightly on the keys of the LC Smith and Corona. The bits of paint buried beneath the unpolished nails and the charcoal smudged into the cuticles belonged to those of an artist, not a copying typist.

Of their own volition, her fingers rounded into fists, the knuckles turning bone-white, the nails digging into her palms. All the pain Hattie felt, all the anger and despair over yet another disparaging critique from a man who knew nothing about her or her past was there, in her tightly curled fingers. Why, *why* couldn't she translate her emotions, good and bad, raw and vulnerable, onto the canvas? What held her back?

More importantly, what was she going to do now that her confidence was all but gone?

She was going to keep painting, that's what. She was going to sit at her easel every night and paint until fatigue set in. Then, she would go to bed, wake up the next morning, head to work so she could earn her modest three pounds, four shillings a week and do it all again the next night. And the next. Until she found the missing link to success. It was a good plan. A solid plan.

She forced her fingers to unclench.

Her coworker called out her name, and Hattie braced herself. There would be a good reason for the interruption. There was *always* a good reason. Still, she felt a little annoyed at the pronouncement of her name in that whispery, sugar-sweet contralto. How was she supposed to finish her work with Iris Hughes pestering her?

Iris said her name again, with a bit more bite, and Hattie reluctantly lifted her head. Bright sunshine, thick with swirling dust, gushed in through a nearby window. The halo of light caressed Iris's pale blond hair in a golden glow that made her appear the picture of loveliness. It was an illusion. The woman's eyes, green flecked with gray, were sharp, and a ridge of concentration appeared across her forehead.

That ridge meant nothing but trouble.

"Yes, Iris. What is it you need?" She resisted adding *this time*. For some reason, the woman considered Hattie her subordinate. Not true. They held lateral positions, albeit in different divisions. She'd given up explaining this to Iris months ago.

The ridge on the woman's forehead dug deeper, another bad sign, but when she spoke again her voice was full of flowers and pleasantries. "Henrietta, dear, would you be so kind as to escort Professor Kremer-Lehman to the auditorium? She is waiting out in the hallway."

For a moment, Hattie could only stare at her coworker. The task was so completely unrelated to her job duties. "You wish for *me* to take charge of a guest lecturer?"

"Isn't that what I just said?"

What was Iris up to? She adored playing hostess to the visiting scholars.

"Kremer-Lehman has come all the way from Munich, or Vienna, or wherever, to give a lecture on German operatic history." Something passed through Iris's eyes, a look that read like judgment. "She brought her own equipment and will require assistance setting it up. You don't mind helping me out, Henrietta? Just this once?"

Speechless, Hattie blinked for several seconds. Odd, how long it took her mind to make sense of the situation, to understand that something about the guest lecturer had put off her coworker. "How many of the educators have signed up for the presentation?"

Iris gave a small shrug. "Fifty or so, likely no more than sixty. A hundred tops. But that's none of your concern. You've only to mind our visitor while she's in the building. Don't let her out of your sight until she is finished and gone."

It was an unusual request and even odder phrasing. Hattie nearly said no, then thought, *Why not?* She was nearly finished with her work, and it would be a nice distraction from her own dark thoughts. "Yes, all right."

"Brilliant. I knew I could count on you." When Hattie remained sitting, Iris huffed out a sigh. "Well? Come along."

Hattie scrambled out of her chair and followed Iris into the hallway. Their heels struck the parquet flooring in a synchronized, rhythmic staccato that seemed somehow rehearsed. It had always struck Hattie as peculiar how she and Iris, so different in sensibilities and attitude, moved with the same sense of purpose. There were other similarities. Nearly identical in height and build, they had the same gray-green eyes and wore their blond hair in a cascade of waterfall curls that hung past their shoulders. However, where Iris clearly spent her salary on fashionable clothing, Hattie invested in her art.

Still, when coworkers discovered Hattie had a sister working in the same building, they mistakenly assumed Iris was her sibling. They could not be more wrong.

Out in the hallway, Iris made the introductions with the simplest of words and very little eye contact. Hattie took inventory of their guest, estimating her to be somewhere in her late sixties, possibly early seventies. Why would this small German—*Austrian?*—woman with the bold slash of dark eyebrows need constant supervision? Dressed in a dark green tweed suit, cut on the bias and belted at the waist, she exuded both style and grace. Add in her perfectly coiffed hair, her delicate features, and Kremer-Lehman was the very definition of elegance. Beside her, Hattie felt unsophisticated and fundamentally average. *Like your art.*

Her mind immediately rejected the dismal thought.

Iris had stopped talking and was now tapping her toes in impatience. Hattie extended her hand and issued the politeness her coworker had failed to provide. "It's a pleasure to meet you, Professor Kremer-Lehman. I'll take good care of you while you are in my company."

The older woman took her hand, thanked her, then added in a lilting German accent, "I look forward to our time together, *Fräulein* Featherstone. And, please, call me Malvina."

"Only if you call me Hattie."

"Well, now that we all know each other…" Iris made a sound of dismissal deep in her throat, then turning her back on their guest in an openly rude gesture said to Hattie, "You may take over from here."

Hattie gave a little start. "Right. Of course. Please, Malvina." She reached out and relieved their guest of the larger of the two cases she carried. "Follow me."

They spoke about nothing of real consequence as Hattie led the way down the musty corridor. She was slightly embarrassed to view her workplace through the eyes of a guest lecturer. The British Board of Education did not keep a clean house. The air was thick with the putrid scent of mold and hundreds of old books no longer in use. Destroying books did not come easily to people working for the betterment of young minds.

It didn't take Hattie long to realize Malvina Kremer-Lehman was something of a surprise. Despite the double-barreled name, the woman was not, as she feared of a university scholar, frightfully dull. She was perfectly, utterly charming, and Hattie had much hope today's presentation would be far more interesting than typing educational discourses and treatises.

In the auditorium, she discovered the case she carried was a portable HMV gramophone. She was still staring in wonder when Kremer-Lehman set a stack of records beside the machine. "Are you a patron of the opera, Hattie?"

"I'm only mildly familiar with the art form." What knowledge Hattie possessed came from her brief walk to and from work. Twice a day, she passed by the famed Covent Garden on Bow Street. For ten months out of the year, the exterior of the Royal Opera House was plastered with posters bidding anyone who wished to spend one shilling and a half crown to come inside and dance.

But in the spring, the faded yellow notices were torn down and replaced with a list of the operas and accompanying artists scheduled to perform during the brief Grand Season. For three weeks, the sidewalks became practically impassable as devoted fans took up residence outside the theater. The patrons who could afford gallery seats only, which could not be reserved in advance, often arrived before sunrise to mark their place in the queue for that evening's performance. Few were able to stay all day. Most hired temporary camp stools to save their spot in the queue. It was all quite orderly and civil.

Such dedication had always fascinated Hattie, though not enough to join their ranks. Her free time was solely for her art. "Do you need anything else before we begin?" she asked.

"Perhaps a glass of water. If it isn't too much to ask."

"I'll fetch it at once."

After a brief detour, Hattie returned with the water and her sister, who'd come along reluctantly. Vera did not like her routine upset. Older by five years, she'd been more mother than sister to Hattie, supporting her when their father had followed his wife to the grave two years after her death. Though not a conventional beauty, Vera was pleasant to look at. She had a medium build, neither too thin, nor too thick. Her hair was an ordinary brown, as were her eyes. She had a slight overbite and, as some of their coworkers claimed, a very British face. Nevertheless, her frank, open expression called for a second glance. And it was then that a person discovered the kindness in Vera's eyes and her very pretty smile, so much like their mother's.

She was not smiling now. Perhaps her mood was due to the news out of Germany. Not two days ago, Adolf Hitler had abolished the office of president and declared himself Führer and thus no longer bound by laws of the state. Vera had been especially troubled by the news.

Hattie opened her mouth to reassure her sister, but Professor Kremer-Lehman—it was hard to think of her by her given name—began her lecture. She spoke with knowledge and the same passion Hattie felt for art, though she'd never been able to articulate her enthusiasm so well.

"Hattie, this is wrong," Vera whispered through clenched teeth. "We should not be here."

Her sister was only half-right. Iris had foisted her duty on to Hattie, and she was determined to discover what all the fuss was about for three weeks out of the year. "And yet," she whispered back, "here we are. Now, hush. She's getting to the good part."

Or so Hattie assumed, since the woman was positioning a record on the gramophone tray.

Always the rule-follower, which Hattie admired about her sister, Vera persisted. "This lecture is not for office workers. They will send us away if we are caught."

"We will not be caught. And, thus, they will not send us away." Finished with the conversation, Hattie leaned away from her sister and focused solely on the guest lecturer.

"It would be remiss of me to give a presentation on opera without also mentioning my favorite singer. Elsa Mayer-Braun is, while still rather young, a rising star among her peers. She also happens to be my niece." Kremer-Lehman said this with no small amount of pride. "You will now enjoy Elsa's interpretation of the final aria from *Madama Butterfly* by Giacomo

Puccini. In 'Tu? Tu? Piccolo iddio!' Butterfly tells her child not to feel sorrow over her desertion. She is letting him go to a better life, the one she cannot give him."

She placed the tonearm atop the record.

The music began. Then, a woman's voice filled the auditorium. Hattie didn't understand a single word of the lyrics. The language was completely foreign to her. Not German: she knew a spattering. Possibly Italian?

It didn't matter.

She took a quick inhalation, then stopped breathing altogether. Sensation after sensation rippled through her. Hattie could hardly catalog them all. Her stomach rolled over inside itself. Her heart danced. Her imagination soared. She closed her eyes and let the music thread deep into her soul, past the parts she knew well into the areas she hadn't let herself explore since her mother's passing, maybe ever. She could see Butterfly in her mind, a devoted mother preparing her child for her abandonment. Grief clutched in Hattie's throat. She closed her eyes and saw the woman's beautiful, tortured face twisted in grief as she sang to her child.

Something inside Hattie, something hidden and untouched since her mother's funeral, clawed for release. Her vision blurred, twisting, spinning. Feelings she'd shut tightly away for a decade awakened. Ten years of ignoring the pain that came from the abruptness of death.

She opened her eyes, and a shiver skittered across the back of her neck. The voice, so raw and vulnerable, broke her heart. Hattie had felt this burst of sorrow once before, as a child, when her mother still lived.

Time shifted and bent, transporting her back to her school days, when she was shown an illustration of a smug angel booting Adam and Eve out of Paradise. She'd been too young to understand the concept of sin or its consequences.

All she'd known was that the pair had been banished forever.

The unfairness had crushed the then five-year-old Hattie, and she'd wept bitterly, loudly, and then with much embarrassment when the other children laughed. She'd shared her anguish with her mother, who'd told Hattie to put her feelings on paper. She'd drawn the scene and had felt better for doing so. That same feeling of helplessness, the despair that she'd translated into her first real piece of art, was there in the voice of the singer. And Hattie must find a way to bring the drama and emotion to life on canvas. She would use oils, later, at home.

Now she simply listened. With her heart. Her soul. Every piece of her. Tears came. She didn't try to stop them. It was like losing her mother all over again and, yet, somehow having her back. She looked over at Vera and felt great satisfaction at the answering emotion spooling in her dark, expressive eyes. Her sister had been caught in the singer's snare. They held hands and listened.

When the music stopped, Hattie knew her future, her art, her very core would never be the same. She'd been transformed, reminded of the mother she hadn't fully grieved. And she owed it all to a woman she'd never met. A woman with a voice that transported the listener to a place where feelings of pain and sorrow, joy and hope, existed on the same plane.

It was a place where Hattie Featherstone wanted to live out the rest of her life.

Chapter Three

Elsa

August 1934. Salzburg, Austria.
Felsenreitschule *Theater*.

Elsa moved rapidly beneath a sky littered with gray clouds. She hurried through Salzburg's historic city center, past a trio of bicyclists and a harried mother herding her small child down the lane. The thick, humid air seemed to shimmer in anticipation of the inevitable soak. *Not yet*, Elsa thought, somewhat desperately. She was still two blocks away from the theater. A fat, wet drop hit her nose.

She quickened her pace, the sense of desperation moving from head to heart to feet. She could not arrive drenched to the bone. She must—*must!*—present a poised, self-possessed woman to the famous maestro, on this, their first official meeting. It was odd she'd never worked with Wilhelm Hoffmann before. He, being Richard Strauss's preferred conductor, and she the composer's ideal soprano. Their schedules were somehow always out of alignment.

Still, Elsa knew him by reputation. The Austrian-born conductor and opera impresario was a former singer himself, having started his career in the Vienna Boys' Choir. He'd married young but had lost his wife six months into the marriage, which had been some twelve years ago.

Brilliant, temperamental, driven by his own vision, Hoffmann was known for being hard on his soloists. It was said he could visually size up a singer within minutes and then, if he saw something he didn't like, insist on an immediate casting change. This was done, this ruining of a career, a life, all before he'd heard a single note from the voice itself.

A flicker of strong feeling moved through Elsa. She recognized the emotion as anger, sprinkled with bits of fear, a heady combination that sent her hurrying faster. Let Hoffmann take his look and make his judgments. He would find nothing to dislike. *If* she avoided the rain.

Thunder sizzled. Practically running, she cut through a small, wooded park, hardly noticing the variety of flowers perfuming the air. She was close now. Nearly there. She could see the theater up ahead, beckoning her to rush.

A young couple passed by on her left, staring into each other's eyes, paying her no attention. Elsa dodged out of their way. Then, to her surprise, she looked back, slowing her steps to watch the man absorb the woman into his arms, pulling her close, until two were one.

Something like loss clogged in Elsa's throat. She would never know that kind of all-consuming love for another. She'd made her choice years ago, at the age of thirteen, when her first vocal coach had warned if Elsa wished to find her place among the greats, she would have to choose opera over all other pursuits. And so, she had. Seven and a half years later, her heart belonged only to her art, a most demanding lover.

Tearing her gaze away from the happy pair, she set her eyes on the theater and resumed her quickened pace. She told herself she was grateful for her chosen path. She was something of a prodigy in the opera world, after all. Already, she'd sung the part of Anna in Strauss's *Intermezzo*, Butterfly in Puccini's *Madama Butterfly*, and the Queen of the Night in Mozart's *The Magic Flute*. She'd performed alongside the greatest talents in the world: baritones like Ezio Pinza and fellow soprano Iva Pacetti.

Head high, she entered the theater through the backstage door just as the rain let loose. She moved automatically toward the stage, then halted. She was not the first to arrive. The mezzo-soprano singing the lesser role of confidante to Elsa's Elektra stood alone, center stage, looking small and vulnerable, almost otherworldly. Arms outstretched, eyes closed, Frieda Klein appeared enraptured with some image only she could see. The small smile on her lips suggested she was happy with the vision. Frieda was beautiful when she smiled.

Charmed, Elsa smiled, too. She liked the other singer and considered her a friend despite the ten years that separated their ages. Suddenly, Frieda's arms dropped. Her head lowered, hanging limp, while she took a collection of long, audible breaths. Elsa's own smile vanished. She should not be here. She should not be witnessing this moment of private agony.

Elsa averted her gaze, her eyes watering, even as her heart filled with a need to right a terrible wrong. Frieda had yet to land a lead role in a single opera. Her failure wasn't due to a lack of talent or effort. She was one of the hardest-working singers Elsa knew.

Life was rarely fair, especially in the competitive world of opera.

She made to leave, then froze at the sound of heavy footsteps approaching. The echo of authority reverberated in each strike of heel to wood. The hitch in her breath told Elsa that Wilhelm Hoffmann had arrived at the theater and was heading directly for her. *Don't turn around*, she ordered herself. *Do not turn around.*

She turned. And nearly choked on her own breath.

He was magnificent. Nothing of what she'd gleaned about the man had prepared her for this version. She'd studied dozens of photographs. But the grainy images had failed to translate his height, or reflect the startling blue of his eyes, or the color of his hair, so pale it was nearly white.

Elsa let out a papery sigh. There was something in the storm of emotion raging through her she didn't immediately recognize, something dark, yet also compelling, a scorching realization her life would never be the same. *He will be my ruin.*

Fear swamped her senses, her mind, her heart. *Run. Run.* The word pulsed through her brain, shivered through her limbs. And still she stood, trapped in his gaze, unmoving.

Rescue came from Frieda, who rushed past Elsa. "*Herr* Hoffmann." She shifted to stand before him, reaching out her hand. "I'm delighted to be working with you again. The last time was quite exceptional."

With only the smallest turn of his head, he took a long, critical look at the mezzo-soprano. A small furrow of concentration appeared on his brow. "I do not know you."

Frieda blinked in surprise. "But..." she swallowed "...it was only last year. I sang the part of the maid in Strauss's *Intermezzo*."

"Yes. I remember. You were adequate. Now—" he made a dismissive sweep of his hand "—go away." He gave her a final, cursory glance, then abruptly turned his back on her.

Eyes wide, Frieda melted into the shadows, but not before

Elsa saw the angry bewilderment that flared on her face as quickly as it was smothered. She wanted to weep for her friend, but Hoffmann had returned his focus to her. "You are Elsa Mayer-Braun. The soprano *Herr* Strauss believes will bring his Elektra to life as never before."

Taken aback by the man's directness, Elsa could only nod her head.

"Come closer. Let me see you in the light."

It did not occur to her to disobey his request. As she crossed the small space, the gap between what she'd imagined this great conductor to be and the man who beckoned her forward expanded, changed, then morphed into something almost appealing. Almost, but not quite.

Something about him—his bold stance, that translucent stare—made her think he was not what he seemed. A man with secrets. He took her gloved hand, his eyes never leaving her face, and began gently rubbing his thumb along her palm. "I'm sure I do not need to tell you, *Fräulein*, that the success of this production rests solely on your shoulders."

No, he did not need to tell her this. *Elektra* was a one-act opera tightly focused on the main character. A challenge that promised great reward. "It is the role of a lifetime."

Still holding her hand, Hoffmann gave her a slow, satisfied smile. "I see you understand the opportunity you have been given."

"I do."

"You will work very hard in the coming weeks. Harder than you have ever worked."

"Yes."

"*Gut.* Now let me make my own promise. You will not take on this role alone. I will guide you every step. I will mold you and offer critique. When I am done, you will be more than you are now. More than you ever have been." She opened her mouth, but he wasn't finished. He tugged her closer. "We will try things on this stage, you and I. Some will work. Some will not."

She nodded.

"You will rehearse a minimum of nine hours a day."

Mesmerized by his touch, his voice, the things he was saying in that low, hypnotic tone, she nodded again. "I will give you twice that, if you ask it of me."

His smile came quick and dazzling. "If you listen to everything I say and work very hard and are at your absolute best, you, my dear, will come away from this experience a star."

She shivered almost sensuously. No conductor had ever spoken to her like this. Such arrogance, such expectations thrust upon her shoulders. Oh, how she wanted the picture he drew with his words. She wanted it more than air.

"Are you prepared to embark on this journey with me?" He leaned in close, so close she could make out the striations of gray in his pale blue irises. "Do you dare?"

"Yes. My answer is *yes*. A thousand times *yes*."

"Then, let us begin."

The rest of the day went by in a blur.

Rehearsals proved as intense and grueling as any Elsa had previously endured. She'd collapsed in her bed that first night, and then all the others that followed, exhausted and yet exhilarated. *Herr* Hoffmann kept their relationship professional throughout the first four weeks. Then, without warning, late in the afternoon during a dress rehearsal, he dismissed the entire cast. Everyone but her.

Alone, he searched her face. "You are tired."

Yes. She was tired. Tired to the bone, and with opening night a mere two weeks away, so tense she had to remind herself to support her diaphragm or she would miss hitting the high notes.

"You must take better care of yourself, Elsa."

There was something in his tone, something not fully kind, and she couldn't help but wonder. Was he worried about the woman or the singer? "I am trying."

He gave her a thorough once-over, head to toe to head again. "You have lost weight."

"Only a few pounds."

More staring, then a quick nod. "It's settled. I will feed you myself. Something of substance, I think. I know a place that serves hearty portions of sauerbraten. We will have a lovely time."

We. She tried out the word in her mind, rolling it around as she pictured the two of them together, outside the theater, sitting at a table, eating a meal at a restaurant that served traditional German beef stew. She liked the image that played across her mind. She liked it very much.

"Well, my dear?" He released her hands. "Are we making a dinner plan?"

"I suppose we are."

"*Gut.* Dinner it is. Not, I think, in your current state of dress." He looked down at her costume. She did the same. They both laughed. "Elektra has her charms," he said. "But, tonight, I wish to have the radiant Elsa Mayer-Braun all to myself."

It was the exact thing to say to send her dashing to her dressing room. Ten minutes later, clad only in a slip, she was frowning at her reflection. She could not make a simple decision. For most of her career, her focus had been solely on her voice. It wasn't that she didn't care how she looked, but what did appearance matter if her vocal cords failed her?

So this, right now, the open jars of cosmetics, the scrutiny of her features, the terrible rush of indecision with each sweep of the makeup brush, this was something new. Behind her, strewn on the chaise lounge sofa, was the entire contents of the personal wardrobe she kept at the theater. Nothing suited. Too many ruffles on this dress, not enough on that one.

A knock came at the door. She flinched.

"Just a minute." Mildly panicked, she surrendered to a solid green dress with blue trim. Feminine, a little dull, but still flattering. "I am ready," she called out. "You may enter."

The door swung open with a series of creaks and groans. And there he stood.

Elsa's pulse drummed in her ears. "Hello, Wilhelm," she said in a breathy whisper. It was the first time she'd used his given name.

An unhurried smile drifted across his lips. "Hello, Elsa."

He seemed taller. His face more aristocratic with that strong cut of cheekbones under the deep-set eyes. He was so appealing, so handsome, she wanted to rush her steps. She did not. A moment such as this required confident, liquid grace.

The restaurant was within walking distance. Wilhelm ordered for them both, then reached across the table and seized her hand. "Tell me about Elsa Mayer-Braun." He leaned forward, his eyes intent on her face, his gaze a silent caress. "I want to know everything."

Her stomach knotted. She felt the sudden urge to cry. Like any orphan confronted with this question, she was hit by all that she'd lost. Long-forgotten scenes from her childhood battered at her composure. She saw herself as a very little girl, seated beside her mother at the secondhand piano in her aunt's apartment.

She pictured her small fingers, miniature little starfishes, plucking away at the keys with far less elegance and finesse than her mother's long, slender ones. She could hear her early attempts at copying the notes with her voice, saw herself several years older, now sitting with her aunt playing complicated scales at a much grander instrument, singing them flawlessly.

There were no images of her father in her mind, only the two women who'd raised her. "I started singing seriously at thirteen." She worried her cheeks might crack from the effort to smile. "At sixteen, I earned a position in the choir of the Vienna State Opera. A year later, I debuted as a page in Wagner's *Lohengrin*. Then I—"

He stopped her with a hand in the air. "*Nein.* That is Elsa the singer. I want to know Elsa the woman."

The impulse to rush out of the restaurant was strong. Revealing her personal history to this man, still so much a stranger, felt impossible. She would do it fast. "I never knew my father. He died before I was born. My mother followed him to the grave when I was seven."

"You were orphaned young."

The normalcy in his voice gave her the courage to continue. Had she heard pity, she would have stood and walked away. From him. From the role of a lifetime. But she was not so foolish. "I was raised by my aunt. You may know her. She is a professor at the Royal Academy of Music in Munich and has lectured across all of Europe, but she started her career as a noted expert on German opera history at the Vienna Conservatory where you, yourself, studied."

Something emerged on his face, something not wholly nice, guarded, then it slipped away, leaving his expression unreadable. "Malvina Kremer-Lehman is your aunt?"

There was nothing outwardly suspicious about the question, but her heart started tripping. "She is my great-aunt. The sister of my mother's mother. She never married." A smile tugged at her lips as she thought of the older woman. Malvina had lived a full life, achieving enviable status in her field, all without a man by her side. She'd been the example Elsa had looked to when deciding to devote her own life to her art. "I am, as she puts it, her greatest achievement."

Malvina had made many sacrifices for Elsa, the largest of all when she'd agreed, as per her mother's dying wishes, to take her to a Christian church for her religious education. Malvina had never once wavered in her promise.

Eyeing her closely, Wilhelm said nothing for a very long moment. "Am I to understand your grandmother was also a Kremer-Lehman?"

The question was a telling one. "Yes, before she married Baron von Krauss."

"I see."

What, exactly, did he see? That her Jewish grandmother had married a German with noble blood? What would he think if she told him her father had also been an aristocrat, disowned by his very British father when he chose an Austrian wife with a Jewish mother instead of the peer he'd picked out for his son? Or that Elsa had changed her name for the stage?

She would never know what Wilhelm thought of these things, at least not that night. He steered the conversation to tomorrow's rehearsal. At her doorstep, he gave her the first of many kisses. As the final days of rehearsals drew closer, he showed Elsa great favor, in the theater and out. It was a whirl-wind of work during the day and romance in the evening. They spoke of Elsa's future, and soon he was rearranging her performances to match with his.

When *Elektra's* opening night finally arrived, Wilhelm came to her dressing room. He pulled her into his arms, kissed her tenderly on the mouth, then pulled her closer still. "My beau-tiful, talented Elsa." He whispered the words just above her ear, sending chills along her spine. "You will be nothing short of remarkable tonight."

She let his words settle over her, drawing strength from his confidence.

"Toi, toi, toi," he said, then added, "Before I leave you to prepare, I have a surprise."

Elsa's breath caught in her throat. Was this it, the moment he proposed marriage? It was too soon. It wasn't soon enough.

"I have scheduled you to sing a series of concerts in November. Seven performances, twelve songs each, with an entire orchestra backing you and, of course, me behind the baton."

A jolt of disappointment whipped through her. Wilhelm spoke of her career when she wanted to speak of love. She tried to smile. "Where will I be singing these concerts?"

"That, my dear, is the surprise. I have booked the Royal Opera House in London."

Her heart lifted and sighed, and all she could think was that Wilhelm had done this for her. He'd booked her to sing before audiences in the city of her father's birth. There was only one response she could give. "I suppose I should purchase rain gear."

Chapter Four

Hattie

Fall 1934. London, England.

Much to her delight—and relief—Hattie's art was transformed after hearing Elsa Mayer-Braun sing. She'd been given her mother back. But also, she'd found a part of herself she'd unintentionally buried for an entire decade. The soprano's voice unlocked hidden depths of feeling, and for the first time in her life, Hattie painted without restraint. No emotion was wrong. Especially not the darker ones.

She often worked deep into the night, sometimes until dawn. One such morning, barely a week after attending Kremer-Lehman's lecture, a bleary-eyed Vera joined her in the small sitting room of their shared flat. She took one look at the image on the canvas and said, "Oh, Hattie."

The way her sister said her name, coupled with that look

of complete awe in her widened eyes, had erased any shred of doubt. Hattie Featherstone had found her way, at last.

"Oh, *Hattie*," Vera said again, moving closer, angling her head in quiet contemplation.

In the ensuing silence, Hattie attempted to view her work from her sister's point of view. What she saw was the beauty and intensity her previous paintings had lacked. Only in this moment did Hattie understand her professor's harsh words. Here, in the image of a distraught mother, was the truth missing from her art. She'd painted Butterfly on her knees, in a floating garment of muted colors to reflect her inner turmoil. One of her hands reached for the little boy she was giving up, the child blindfolded, and so very far away, a blur in the distance. Butterfly's fingers were curled, as if clawing at the empty air, or possibly raging against the cruel forces, some of her own making, that kept her so thoroughly removed from her son.

Throughout the night, Hattie had wanted to cry for Butterfly, for that deserted child. And so she'd cried. Hot, wet, miserable tears. The music had been her guide. First, into the story. Then, into her past, to the day her mother had taken to her bed. The rapid decline into the dark, mysterious illness. Finally, into death itself. Followed by her father's inability to love her enough, the daughter who reminded him too much of the wife he'd lost.

"Hattie...how?" Vera extended her hand to the canvas much like Butterfly reached for her child. "How did you know to paint her like this? She's exactly how I pictured her in my head, without even realizing that's how I saw her."

"It was the music. No." She shook her head. "That's not right. It wasn't the music alone but also Mayer-Braun's singing. Her voice is still in my ears. I had to paint what I heard. The emotions I felt, and... I'm not explaining this well."

"Oh, but you are." Vera turned her head and captured Hattie's gaze. "It was not Mayer-Braun's voice alone, but the aria played a role, too."

"Honestly? I don't know for certain," Hattie admitted, somewhat flustered. "I've never heard an operatic aria before the other day."

"Then, it's settled," Vera said, the older, wiser sister in her voice. "We shall take it upon ourselves to explore how opera influences your art."

A grand idea, in theory. Unfortunately... "The season is over."

"No matter. We shall purchase a portable gramophone of our own and as many records as we can afford. It will require great economy from us both. But," Vera smiled a very fetching, very Veralike smile, "when has that ever stopped us?"

Hattie twisted around to stare at her sister. "You would do this for me? You would go without small little luxuries for the sake of my art?"

Vera looked at her strangely. "Goes without saying."

Hattie blinked at her sister. Awed and humbled and slightly guilt-ridden. Vera never failed to support her. Never. She'd stepped into the void left by their mother, and then by their father, without an ounce of hesitation or resentment, and it was long past time Hattie let Vera live her own life, on her own terms. "No, dearest. I can't ask this of you."

"You didn't ask, I offered. Truth be known, I'm not doing this only for you but for us both." She glanced at the painting, her eyes turning thoughtful. "I, too, have found a fondness for opera. I'm compelled to explore this new fascination for my own reasons."

"Which are?"

"Nothing I care to share just yet. I will. Eventually. When I am ready."

No amount of coaxing could convince Vera to explain herself. Hattie stopped trying and focused once more on the painting. Seeing a small flaw, she went to pick up the brush, made a few strokes, set it back in its cradle. Nodded.

An hour later, the sisters took themselves off to their jobs.

Thus began a new routine for both Hattie and Vera. During the day, they earned their modest salaries at the Board of Education. At night, Hattie lost herself in her art, while Vera secreted herself in her room. They scrimped and saved, skipped tea with friends and went without lunch twice a week. By month's end, they were in possession of an HMV portable gramophone and several vinyl records, many with Elsa Mayer-Braun's exquisite voice.

Hattie could no longer afford art classes. She didn't miss them much. She reveled in every new record purchase. As she listened, she saw entire scenes in her mind and painted them with wild abandon. She'd never felt freer or more connected to her mother. Overnight, she became a different person, more herself, an artist, an idealist. A dreamer. The air smelled sweeter. Colors took on shape. Shapes became sound.

In mid-October, Vera purchased a very fine Kirsten Flagstad recording of the Queen of the Night's famous aria from Mozart's *The Magic Flute*. After a short debate, the sisters agreed: Elsa Mayer-Braun's version was better. As if to reward their loyalty, the following morning when they passed by Covent Garden, a new poster caught Hattie's eye. Her feet ground to a halt.

Vera's own steps faltered. "What is it, Hattie?"

"Look." She pointed to the poster. "Elsa Mayer-Braun is to give a series of solo concerts next month. And Wilhelm Hoffmann will be conducting." What a boon. The man was considered one of the most gifted maestros in the world.

Vera's breath escaped in an enthusiastic burst. "We must attend at least one of the performances."

All record purchases were immediately suspended. More lunches were skipped. At last, at seven in the morning, on the day of Mayer-Braun's first performance, Hattie stood beside Vera outside Covent Garden. They gazed in stunned silence at the endless row of camp stools already arranged in a neat, orderly fashion along the sidewalk.

"So many of them," Vera whispered.

Hattie could only sigh. She estimated a minimum of fifty stools, each one marking a person's place in line, people who would purchase tickets ahead of them, thereby securing the best seats in the gallery.

"This is not good."

"No," Hattie agreed. "Not good at all."

Resigned to their fate, the sisters placed their stools at the end of the line. All was not lost. They worked close to the theater and were able to return at lunchtime with a brown roll and pat of butter each—the only meal they could afford. They sat on their hired stools, Vera eating and Hattie hoping she would gain a small glimpse of Elsa Mayer-Braun between rehearsals. On the calendar, winter was still a month away but today, at least, the milder autumn temperatures held firm, releasing the Featherstone sisters from the need to wear heavy coats. Lightweight jackets were enough to stave off the slight chill in the air.

They were alone in their ignoble position at the back of the queue, which suited Hattie. She'd brought along her sketch pad. Although she preferred painting with oils, it wasn't logistically possible when she was away from home.

From her satchel, she retrieved her pad and several compressed charcoal sticks. Closing her eyes, she called up the memory of her favorite aria from the second act of *The Magic Flute*, and soon her hand was gliding across the page.

She started with a loose, simple line sketch. Next, using the traditional back-and-forth method, she attacked the areas of high contrast, then strengthened the darker areas with thicker, broader strokes. She paused. The image was rough yet coming to life. A quick glance at one of the posters on the building behind her was all it took for Hattie to add Elsa Mayer-Braun's features to her rendering of Mozart's vengeful Queen of the Night. Next, she added emotion to the exquisite face: power, rage, the drive for revenge against her presumed rival.

Time passed, with not a single hint of the singer. Hattie hastily blotted the drawing, then stood and stretched out her legs, sketch pad dangling from her fingertips. The dominating facade of Covent Garden filled her gaze. While the building itself was technically the Royal Opera House in Covent Garden, somewhere along the way the name had been shortened.

"Hattie. Look. *Look.*" Her sister pointed to a spot down the sidewalk. "There she is. It's her. Elsa Mayer-Braun. And she's with a man!"

Heart leaping, Hattie swiveled her head in the direction Vera indicated.

"Who do you suppose he is? A friend? One of the musicians, perhaps?"

"That's Wilhelm Hoffmann." Hattie might have taken further note of the imposing figure, maybe wondered at his exceptional height and the proprietary way he held onto Mayer-Braun's arm, if she hadn't been so riveted by the woman herself.

The soprano was small—surprisingly so, given her large voice—and quite delicate, the genteel embodiment of femininity. She was also, as the woman's aunt had claimed, young, somewhere near Hattie's age. Her hair was the color of threshed wheat. Her eyes were, well...she was still too far away for Hattie to know their true color. The poster above her head suggested they were blue.

Mayer-Braun caught sight of Hattie staring and smiled warmly, a sure sign her character matched the loveliness of her voice. The angry emotions Hattie had just sketched were completely absent from that gentle expression. She couldn't help herself. Hattie smiled in return.

Without thinking too hard about what she was doing or the risk she was taking—no one save Vera had seen her art in weeks—she removed the drawing from her pad and took it with her as she approached the singer.

The masculine clearing of a throat had her reeling back, and she nearly dropped the impromptu gift she'd planned to offer her muse. She looked down, relieved to discover she hadn't smudged the image. She could feel Hoffmann's stare on her bent head. Her blood turned to ice. The sensation made her want to recoil, to hurry along without another word.

Something in her rebelled at the notion, some small part of her that had been critiqued too many times with unkind, harsh words. Hattie was more than mediocre, so much more. She was Caroline Featherstone's daughter, an artist in her own right, and this might be her only chance to thank the woman who'd unwittingly revealed the truth to her.

Jaw set, she lifted her head and looked straight into the man's scowling face. She knew him by his frown. He'd supplied not a single smile for the publicity photos. To say the conductor was an intimidating presence would be to miss the point entirely.

There was something in him that made Hattie uncomfortable, a smug superiority he allowed her to see quite clearly. She tried not to squirm as his cool gaze ran over her face, her hair, then slid to her simple two-piece gray woolen suit. There was cold knowledge in those calculating eyes as they took her measure, the same masculine dismissal she'd experienced in her art classes. This man seemed to understand everything about her, her lowly position in the secretarial pool, her lack of funds for a ticket beyond the unreserved seats in the gallery.

His attention suddenly dropped to the drawing she held, and this time she did rear back.

No. Hattie Featherstone would not be cowed. A surge of defiance lifted her chin, and she addressed her favorite singer directly. "Miss Mayer-Braun, I cannot express how lovely it is to meet you."

The woman's smile grew warmer still. "And I, you."

Emboldened by her kindness, Hattie took yet another chance. "I owe you my sincere gratitude. You have inspired me beyond my wildest hopes."

"I have?" She asked the question in heavily accented English. "How charming. You are singer of the opera, *ja*? Yes?"

"No. I'm a—" *Lowly civil servant? Aspiring artist?* Hattie didn't know what to call herself. "Perhaps it would be easier if I show you what I mean."

"Yes. You will show me, please."

The singer's enthusiasm gave Hattie pause. She took a deep breath, afraid she would unintentionally insult this gracious woman with her fierce drawing. Her sketch was raw, emotional, maybe too much so. Hattie wanted to retreat, to change her mind. It would be a simple matter of demurring. But the soprano was looking at her expectantly. And Hattie had spoken her truth. This woman had changed her life.

Courage, Hattie. The words in her head had her mother's voice.

Hand shaking, she handed over the drawing, then immediately thought better and pulled herself back.

"No, wait. Please." Mayer-Braun's expression was as gentle as her words. "You have come this far. You must not give in to nerves."

Such rare, unexpected encouragement. A reminder of her mother's unwavering support. And of Vera's. "The image is rough," Hattie said, trying not to sound too apologetic. "I only started sketching it an hour ago."

"I understand." Mayer-Braun smoothly took the drawing from Hattie's fingers and lowered her gaze. Seconds passed. When at last she looked up, there were tears in her eyes. "I hear the Queen's fury, but also her pain."

It was the perfect compliment. "I…" Words refused to find their way past her lips. She swallowed and managed to force out, "Thank you."

Too simple a response. Hattie wanted to howl at her clumsiness. Why could she not find the words to say what was in her heart?

The singer didn't seem to notice her inner struggle. "Come, Wilhelm. Come and see what it is I feel when I sing." She turned the sketch toward him. "Is it not remarkable?"

He gave the drawing a passing glance. Hattie herself had received a much longer assessment. "You have a talent, *Fräulein*." The heavy German *r* pealed beneath the word, adding a level of intimidation. "It is raw and unrefined, but I admit the talent is there."

"Do you have a name?" This, from Mayer-Braun, in a much softer voice.

"Henrietta Featherstone. My friends call me Hattie." Remembering she wasn't alone, Hattie linked arms with Vera and pulled her forward. "This is my sister, Vera."

"Hello, *Fräulein* Vera."

Blushing, Vera opened her mouth. Nothing came out.

Hattie continued for them both. "We had the honor of

meeting your aunt recently. She was very elegant, articulate and quite knowledgeable."

"Oh. But that is an excellent description of *Tante* Malvina. I must tell her what you said. She will like it very much. *Ja,* very much." The way Mayer-Braun's eyes lit as she spoke of her aunt betrayed deep affection that went beyond familial ties.

"Professor Kremer-Lehman played a recording of your aria from *Madama Butterfly*. My sister and I..." Hattie indicated Vera with a nod "...have been your devoted fans ever since. And, as I have tried to explain, quite poorly, really, your singing has become an inspiration for my art." *You gave me back my mother.*

It was true. Professor Kremer-Lehman had started the process with her lecture and portable record player. Mayer-Braun's exquisite voice had completed the journey.

"So now you sit outside the theater, drawing a picture of me as the Queen of the Night?"

Hattie smiled. The woman had such an uplifting effect. "Exactly so."

"It is time to say goodbye, Elsa. We have much to do before tonight." Hoffmann took her arm, tugged her to him. When she resisted, he said something in rapid, guttural German.

She held her ground, while he frowned in open displeasure.

"Please, Wilhelm." She spoke his name softly, almost tenderly, and like Hattie had done, he smiled in return. "One more moment. It is not so much to ask, no?"

He nodded, albeit reluctantly. Then, she smiled wider. He smiled back. Something rather intimate passed between them, and he slowly let her go. "Take your moment, if you must."

"I must." Turning back to Hattie and Vera, Mayer-Braun leaned in close, indicating they do the same. "You will come tonight and hear me sing. I'll reserve two tickets for seats in a very special place of honor. After the concert, you will join me backstage. Yes?"

They had barely time to say *Yes* and *Thank you* before Hoffmann swept the singer away with Hattie's drawing caught firmly in her grasp.

Hattie watched the two disappear through a side door into the building, her heart full. Elsa Mayer-Braun had liked her art, enough to keep the drawing without Hattie having to insist. Another unexpected compliment.

"I wonder," Hattie said to Vera as they headed back to work, "would it be in poor form to bring my sketch pad to the concert?"

Chapter Five

Elsa

November 1934. London, England.
Royal Opera House, Covent Garden.

Elsa entered her dressing room, head down, eyes fixed on the image of Mozart's vengeful Queen of the Night. She knew she was staring at a special piece of art, no matter the inferior quality of the paper. The drawing itself was good, very good. Dramatic, lifelike and far more powerful than a photograph. Elsa could hear the music pulsing off the page. It was her voice caressing the lyrics, gliding seamlessly up and down the octaves, liquefying the easy notes, bending the difficult high ones to her will until they fit smoothly within the melody.

How could a simple charcoal sketch evoke so much pain, so much sorrow and rage? Because this was no simple charcoal sketch. Henrietta Featherstone had seen past the costumes and set designs, past even the music and lyrics, and had exposed the very heart of the Queen's dark, tortured soul... The Queen's? Or Elsa's?

She tore her eyes from the page, looked back again and admitted that there, *right there*, in the features of her own face, was every unhappy emotion she had ever felt. The desperation to be better than her peers, the fear of falling short. The anguish over losing her mother, of never knowing her father. Even the quiet, often desperate, loneliness that was her constant companion.

This was Elsa's truth. Every raw, vulnerable piece of her that few met. Only Malvina, actually. Her aunt was her closest ally, and Elsa worried for her future now that laws in Germany barred Jews from holding civil-service, university and state positions. With no limits to Hitler's authority now that he'd appointed himself Führer, matters would only get worse.

Malvina would lose her job. If she hadn't already. At seventy-two, it would not be easy to find another. Harder still because she was Jewish. Even in Austria, where anti-Semitism was on the rise, a position that utilized Malvina's expertise would be difficult to find. Perhaps there was something Elsa could do. Or, possibly, Wilhelm. He was a powerful man. A good man.

She became aware of him standing beside her, his back ramrod straight, the strong and steady presence that had infiltrated her life so completely. He must have sensed her need for silence. It wouldn't last, this unusual show of patience. Wilhelm was not a man to let his opinions go unspoken. That much she'd learned since their meeting.

Had it only been three months? Elsa felt as if she'd lived half a lifetime in his company.

Now her mind was full of him and of their time together. He'd given her many gifts. Scarves to keep her throat warm.

Jewelry to adorn her wrists. Just yesterday, he'd emptied an entire garden of flowers and sent the bouquets to her hotel room.

He was courting her. She knew this. Felt it in her heart, saw it in his frank blue eyes when he smiled down at her from his great height. At first, she'd found the idea of his affection impossible, as if it were all some sort of a performance on his part. Wilhelm Hoffman was wellborn, connected, a brilliant maestro, sought after by many. What did he possibly see in her?

"Elsa." He took the sketch from her hand. Then, with only a brief glance at the image, he set the paper on her dressing table. "Elsa," he repeated, *"mein Liebling."*

Mein Liebling. My darling. A term he used when he meant to romance her. Something he rarely—never—did inside a theater where he was all business, no lightness or play. She stole a glance from beneath her lowered lashes and felt a little jolt in her heart. No, romance was not on his mind. But neither was work. Confusion stole her breath. She shifted to face him fully.

Their eyes met and held. A thousand wordless conversations started then stopped in the span of a single heartbeat. Elsa suddenly felt the weight of all the things she could not change. The unfair discriminations seemed to be getting worse. For Malvina, and others like her, targeted for their race and religion.

German leadership had taken steps against the Jews, boycotting their shops and businesses, publicly burning books they authored. Would the rest of Europe follow with similar policies? Would Austria? The Nazi Party wasn't large in her beloved homeland, yet it had successfully instigated a policy of sabotage and intimidation. They'd even pulled off a day of terror in June and had been behind the assassination of the Austrian dictator in July.

The tears rising in her throat were born of fear. Suddenly,

an uncomfortable desire to unburden everything on her heart surged into this strange, intimate moment.

Wilhelm's expression softened. Now there was romance in his eyes. But as he took her hands, apprehension welled inside her, prickled into her throat, and she turned her face away.

"You're upset. Is it the picture? Did that artist offend you in some way?"

"No." She whipped her gaze back to his. "It… No. The drawing is wonderful."

"Then, tell me." He spoke with the tenderness of a man who cared deeply for a woman. "What is troubling you?"

She had no interest in pretending. It was time they spoke openly about the world in which they lived. "What's happening in Germany, the rising anti-Semitism, the laws that are being passed almost daily. I fear it is only the beginning of bad things to come. Worse, there are Austrians who would wish to see similar restrictions placed in our country, on our people."

"Not all people," he corrected, his tone unreadable. "Just the Jews."

"Malvina." Her aunt's name rose in her throat like a sob. "She is Jewish."

"Yes." His agreement was shockingly calm.

Elsa slowly freed her hands and went to her dressing table. She spent a moment studying the sketch that had captured her very essence, the fear and indignation she hadn't understood fully until this candid conversation. She touched the image, her hot, damp fingers smudging the charcoal in several places. "I share Malvina's blood."

"No one but the three of us know that." His voice was no longer so calm, and Elsa wondered if she'd been wise to tell him her history, when he'd told her so little of his. "You were raised a Christian," he reminded her. "That is your truth, that is what the official records show."

"My faith doesn't change the fact that I am a quarter Jew."

"Elsa." He came up behind her, wrapped his arms lightly around her waist then captured her gaze in their shared reflection. "Your grandmother was Jewish, but your grandfather was not. Nor your father. Your blood is sufficiently diluted. That is what they will find, if anyone cares to look. You are safe."

She was safe, while others were not. People who could not hide their heritage behind a noble bloodline and a false stage name. The thought made her sick with guilt.

Stepping out from the cage of Wilhelm's embrace, Elsa glanced around the room, taking in all the small luxuries that came with her success. The jars of expensive creams and cosmetics, the exquisite costumes made specifically for her petite form. *To whom much is given, much is required.* Her mother had taught her that. "Surely, there is something I can do for Malvina. For others like her. I am not without connections."

He glanced at something on the dressing table, the sketch perhaps, and frowned. "In times such as these, it's important for you to make the proper alliances."

"The proper alliances?" she repeated, unsure what he meant. Did he question her choice of friends, many of whom the Nazis now targeted, or her desire, even need, for assisting others less fortunate than herself? "Leveraging my success to benefit others is not a bad thing, Wilhelm."

"You misunderstand me." He stepped toward her, his eyes soft, pleading. "We live in dangerous times. Europe is unstable. Civil war still brews in Austria. Even if none of that were true, you are famous. Known around the world for your voice and talent. Many wish to know you, to call you friend. Some are sincere. Some are not. A few, I fear, wish to do you harm."

He wasn't wrong. He wasn't wholly right, either. "I believe people are basically good."

"You have a generous heart, Elsa, and assume everyone you meet is the same as you."

Did he think her so young and guileless as to be ignorant of the evils in their world? The question rolled around in her mind, until she could not keep the words in her mouth. "You think me naive. I assure you, Wilhelm, I know the nature of men."

Better than most. Opera's demands, the politics and petty rivalries, even the tragic, unholy story lines had taken away her innocence.

"Perhaps you do understand, and yet you are too quick to see others in a favorable light. Take, for instance, that artist outside. You know nothing about her, and you still reserve her a special seat and invite her backstage." He paused, looked over at the sketch, shook his head. "She could be a danger to you. It would be a mistake to let her get too close."

His argument sent her back to the dressing table, to the drawing and the truth she saw in the bold lines and shaded planes. As she traced the image with her eyes, certainty took hold. "A talent such as this could not come from an ugly heart."

"Talent does not equal goodness."

"Neither does it equal cunning." *To whom much is given, much is required.* "*Fräulein* Featherstone has not yet found success, but that's not to say she isn't deserving of it. I can help her. I can introduce her to gallery owners. I know of one right here in London. He owns a whole stable of galleries here and across Europe, even a few in America."

"She will not thank you for your meddling."

Elsa wasn't looking for gratitude. "Her success will be reward enough."

"This predilection of yours to collect wounded birds and offer your help where it isn't always warranted or appreciated—" impatience sounded in his voice "—this will be your undoing."

"Or my salvation."

"How has your interference in Frieda Klein's life turned out so far?"

Elsa felt the familiar stirrings of guilt again. Through the years, she'd introduced her friend to composers, conductors, theater administrators, anyone with the power to place her in a starring role. Many had hired her, but never as the lead. "Frieda knows I have tried."

"She resents you."

Unthinkable. Elsa and Frieda were friends. They'd shared many evenings on the stage together, with Elsa always singing the better part. Her heart twisted. She could see it, then, so clearly. Everything Wilhelm claimed, all true. Frieda's dashed hopes had turned into something dark through the years, curdling into bitterness and, yes, resentment.

Elsa had failed her friend. "I will try harder." She said it as both apology and vow.

"She will only resent you more."

It felt, at once, like he was judging her. But the look in his eyes was tender. The answer came to her in that soft look. "Surely, Wilhelm, you could place her in a role."

"No." He made a sound of impatience in his throat. "I will not do this, not even for you. Elsa, please, do not look at me like that, with such disappointment. That woman is neither the talent you presume nor the person you want her to be. You have done what you can. Let it be enough."

How little he knew her. "It's not in me to give up on anyone, especially a friend."

An unhurried smile drifted along his lips. "My little optimist. You are too good by half."

She bristled at his patronizing tone. "I am no better or worse than the next woman."

"There you are wrong. You are the best of them all."

Elsa flushed at the compliment, spoken without an ounce of hesitation on his part.

"Come, let us not argue over these other women. Tonight's performance will be your greatest triumph yet. We have much to prepare." He reached out his hand, his smile as sincere as any he'd ever given her. This was the man she'd come to know in their most intimate moments.

Thoughts of resentful opera singers and aspiring artists and European politics fled from her mind. There was no music in her head, no thoughts of failing the people who needed her, no sound at all except the click, click of her heels as she answered Wilhelm's call.

She placed her hand in his. He kissed each knuckle, his eyes never leaving her face. A shiver slid along her spine. She felt suddenly hot, almost dizzy, her stomach looping into knots within knots. "You are trying to distract me."

His eyes glinted mischievously. "A lovely distraction, is it not?"

"Very."

"Elsa. Dear, sweet Elsa." He placed her palm against his heart, the beat strong and steady, a rhythm that instilled trust. "You must know, all this talk today, the advice, the warnings, this is because I want only to protect you. I want to keep you safe."

"I know, Wilhelm." He cared about her. She believed it. But did he love her? She'd barely had time to think the thought before he leaned down and placed his lips to her forehead, the tip of her nose, her mouth. The kiss was tender, full of promises still to be made.

She was utterly lost to his seductive charm.

He pulled away, then kissed her again, lingering. When he moved his mouth to her ear, it was to make a life-altering pledge. "I love you, Elsa. I have wanted you in my life from the moment we met." He lifted his head, keeping their faces close. "Will you make me the happiest of men and become my wife?"

She meant to say no, meant to say *This is all happening too fast. I need time to think.* The words were there, in her mind, moving up her throat, forming on her lips.

Rational thought nearly prevailed. Head nearly overruled heart. Ah, but her heart had the stronger will this day and spoke the words Elsa prayed she would not grow to regret. "Yes, Wilhelm. I will marry you."

Chapter Six

Hattie

November 1934. London, England.
Royal Opera House, Covent Garden.

Hattie and Vera arrived at Bow Street in their finest evening attire, which was to say their *only* evening attire. The dresses weren't new, nor had they been purchased in a department store or specialty shop. They'd made the gowns themselves. Vera, the better seamstress, had constructed a frothy, floor-length marvel in navy-blue silk. Hattie had gone with a pale, sea-foam green crepe de chine in an Art Deco–inspired shape that flared at the knees.

For added glamour, the sisters added elbow-skimming gloves and crushed-velvet capes. With their hair styled in fashionable finger waves, they looked quite elegant. That's what Vera claimed, anyway, a bit smugly, in fact, which had made them both laugh as they exited their flat.

With the Royal Opera House a mere block away, Vera slipped her arm through Hattie's. "What a lovely evening for a concert. Even the weather is cooperating."

Hattie's lips curved, and she nodded mutely, feeling an obscene sense of joy. Vera was correct. It *was* a lovely evening, not too cold, not too warm, while the sky above their heads had taken on a lavender-smudged hue somewhere between a slate blue and robust purple.

They made the final turn arm in arm, and up ahead their destination loomed. This was Hattie's first glimpse of the theater at night, and it was glorious. A goliath of marble and stone made even more dazzling by the theatergoers milling about at its feet. Hattie felt the urge to convey the scene on canvas or, at the very least, with her charcoals. It was not meant to be. After a lively argument with herself, she'd left her sketch pad at home.

She would have to store the image in her memory. The glitz, the glamour, the massive amounts of people who seemed to know each other intimately, it was all too much and yet, not nearly enough. The kaleidoscope of shapes and colors, the sound—so much noise—it all spun around in her head. There was an air of obscene wealth everywhere.

Hattie felt instantly the interloper. She and Vera both. They didn't belong amid this lofty crowd. They should be in the gallery with the other working-class patrons. Her steps faltered under the weight of that knowledge.

Vera's own steps slowed. "Hattie? Are you unwell?"

"I'm fine." But she wasn't, not really. She glanced into Vera's eyes, and in her sister's gaze, Hattie read the same feelings burning in her own throat: trepidation, nervous excitement, perhaps a little fear.

What did either of them know of this foreign world of tailored suits, silk gowns and mink stoles? The Featherstone sisters came from humble beginnings. Their father had been a teacher of modern literature at a private boys' school. He'd passed on his love of the written word to his oldest daughter. Vera was a great reader, though her idea of modern literature was a romantic novel that often began its life as a serial in a local newspaper.

Hattie admired that whimsical part of her sister's nature, so very different from the staid rule-follower. Oh, how she loved her sister. They could do this. Together. Smiling, she pulled Vera closer. "We are the very special, honored guests of Elsa Mayer-Braun. If anyone belongs at this concert, it is us."

"Well said, Hattie. I think I rather needed to hear that."

"I think I rather needed to say it." They shared a smile born from years of sharing hardship and loss. "Now, chin up."

The promised tickets were waiting at the box office, along with a handwritten note for each of them on parchment paper so fine as to be practically transparent. A faint hint of roses and lavender hovered on the air as Hattie opened her letter and read it.

My dearest Henrietta,
I am so happy to have made your acquaintance (that is the En-glish term, yes?). It is important for me to admit that I am quite mesmerized by your portrait of the Queen of the Night. I have spent many minutes dissecting the image with my eyes. I hope someday to review how you came to choose this character to me-morialize, and why you thought to give her my face. We will not do this tonight. Tonight is for the music. Another time, we will discuss the art. Now I must go. I am told it is time to rehearse. Your friend, E.

Hattie gave a swift, happy gasp and read the words again, twice over, landing each time on *Your friend*, as if Mayer-

Braun considered Hattie on an equal plane. In that moment, it was worth it, all of it, the skipped lunches, the canceled art classes, the economizing.

She read the letter again, starting back at the beginning. *My dearest Henrietta…*

Vera's voice stopped her halfway through. "Oh, Hattie, can you believe it? Elsa Mayer-Braun enjoyed meeting us and is looking forward to renewing our acquaintance backstage after her performance." With great care, Vera tucked her own note into her handbag. "I'm so happy we came tonight. I had several moments of thinking we shouldn't."

"Me too," Hattie admitted. "What a large mistake that would have been."

"Quite."

They looked at each other, so alike yet not. Sisters, always, but one favoring their father, the other resembling their mother. A smile passed between them and then, arms linked once more, they strode onward, weaving through the maze of theatergoers, up the stone steps, through the front doors and straight into the foyer, where the noise level was even more pronounced than out on the streets.

Caught up in the swift-moving crowd, there was only time for impressions as they bobbed along, pushed past concessions, the other vendors, until they were standing on the main floor of the domed auditorium.

"Magnificent," Hattie whispered, craning her neck left and right.

Everywhere she looked her eyes met gold filigree and plush red velvet. Four tiers of boxes curved around the perimeter of the theater, rising up and up, and up higher still, to the very top of the dome, where the gallery of unreserved seats held massive amounts of dedicated fans jostling for position at the rail.

An usher met them at the edge of the aisle and handed them a very plain program—no drawings, no artwork, only bold typeface that included the name of the theater and the date and time of the performance. Such a boring keepsake, Hattie thought.

She and Vera had barely found their seats in the center of the third row when the houselights dimmed, once, twice, three times. A collective hush fell over the audience.

Wilhelm Hoffmann appeared at the front of the orchestra pit, formally attired in a black tuxedo with tails. The air seemed to instantly chill, and Hattie was unable to prevent a small shiver as she watched the maestro step onto a raised platform.

Elevated above the rest of the orchestra, he bowed to the audience. The corresponding applause was as profound as his arrogance. There he stood, basking in the adulation, his eyes sweeping coolly over the audience. His gaze landed on Hattie for a beat, nothing more than a single tick of the clock, but there was a sudden hardness to his jaw that wasn't there before, an edge of temper. His attention left her an instant later, but Hattie felt it again, that unpleasant roll in her stomach, the sense that Wilhelm Hoffmann was not a man she wished to know well.

He gave the audience a final nod of acknowledgment, then swiveled around to face the orchestra. Hattie had never been happier to take in the view of a man's—*this* man's—back.

With a flourish, Hoffmann raised his baton, instruments poised at the ready. The music began, slowly at first, building theatrically up and over the notes, back down again.

The curtain rose, a slow ascent, and then Elsa Mayer-Braun glided into view, her steps as smooth as liquid gold. An explosion of applause guided her across the stage. She stopped in the center and gave her first full smile to Hoffmann. There was something secretive in her eyes, mildly intimate, and very, very feminine, as if he were the very air she breathed. Unease flashed through Hattie, gone as quickly as it came, and yet she felt a sting of trepidation for the singer.

The soprano gave her next smile to the audience, which had them surging to their feet, Hattie and Vera included. Mayer-Braun hadn't uttered a word or sung a single note, and already she held her fans in the palm of hand.

Such poise, such self-possession.

The applause slowed, and the audience sat, and only then, as silence fell, did the singing begin. Beautiful, each note more glorious than the one before it, followed by another even better.

For two hours, Hattie lost herself in the music. Each song, though chosen from a different opera or composer, seemed to meld perfectly into the next. She heard a faint touch of melancholy that went straight to the heart. The roots of a memory stirred, a bittersweet reminder of a time with her mother, the two of them looking at a piece of art in a museum, her mother pointing out the proper use of perspective or how to identify the brushstrokes unique to each painter.

It hurt to travel through that memory, and yet, she craved the experience, needed it. Tears sprang to her eyes. Hard to know if it was the tenderness of Mayer-Braun's voice or the tenderness of the memory that sent them running down her cheeks.

When the singer launched into a series of familiar hymns, beginning with "Amazing Grace," the song sung at Caroline Featherstone's funeral, Hattie sensed someone reaching for her hand. She looked over at Vera and felt, rather than saw, her sister's fingers twining through hers.

That was Vera, an anchor in a storm, *her anchor*, through their mother's illness, her passing and the very rough days afterward. Had she ever thanked Vera? Did sisters need to say the words? Of course they did. Hattie would say them again, tonight.

The performance ended, and the audience surged to their feet again, this time with cries of "Brava!" Mayer-Braun took five curtain calls. During the final one, she looked down to where Hattie and Vera stood, clapping wildly. She waved. They waved back.

The evening only got better from there.

As if their roles had been switched, Hattie guided a very nervous Vera backstage. She immediately spotted Mayer-Braun standing among a group of musicians. Much to her relief, Wilhelm Hoffmann was nowhere in sight. The singer turned her head, and Hattie saw, with even greater relief, genuine pleasure on the soprano's face.

She started toward them.

Vera let out a soft mew of alarm and grasped hold of Hattie's arm. "You do the talking."

"That's silly. She invited us both backstage. We should *both* do the talking."

"I wouldn't know what to say."

"Compliment her performance."

There was no more time for arguing. Mayer-Braun arrived and, smiling fondly, greeted them like old friends with an embrace and a kiss on both cheeks. "My two favorite Londoners. The beautiful Henrietta." She took Hattie's hand, then reached for Vera's. "And her equally lovely sister. I'm so happy you came tonight."

Vera said one word. "Hello."

Hattie managed a bit more. "Thank you for the wonderful seats."

"Did you enjoy my little concert, then?"

So many ways to respond. Hattie was no expert. She had

no intelligent, witty remark to make. She only understood how the music made her feel. "Your voice is the light that cuts through shadow."

Mayer-Braun stared at her for a very long moment, a sparkle of tears glittering in her eyes. "Oh, my dear, dear Henrietta. You have given me the greatest of compliments. Now come with me, both of you, and let me introduce you around."

There were so many people to meet, too many. The litany of names flew in and out of Hattie's head the moment she heard them. Vera seemed equally overwhelmed and soon became quite agitated. She excused herself to sit on a piano bench out of the flow of traffic. Once settled, she appeared content to watch from the sidelines.

"Now, Henrietta, I wish to—"

"Please, call me Hattie." At Mayer-Braun's arched eyebrows, she added, "I insist."

"All right, but only if you will call me Elsa."

"Done."

"Excellent. Now, *Hattie*, there are two very important people I wish for you to meet. I would not be here tonight without their support."

Elsa drew to a stop beside two well-dressed gentlemen. Both wore wedding rings. The younger, a clean-shaven fellow somewhere in his midfifties, smiled warmly. The other man, older, sixty at least, had a droopy mustache, a floppy mop of gray hair and a very stern-looking face. "Hattie Featherstone, this is Mr. Geoffrey Toye." Elsa indicated the younger man with a jerk of her chin. "Mr. Toye is managing director of Covent Garden's Royal Opera House. And this elegant gentleman is Sir Thomas Beecham, the artistic director."

Sir Beecham addressed Hattie first, with nothing more than a nod; not rude, precisely, but not overly polite, either. In the next instant, he excused himself, leaving Hattie and Elsa alone with Mr. Toye.

Undaunted, Elsa continued. "I believe, Mr. Toye, you will remember I told you about my new friend. She is the artist of the sketch I showed you this afternoon."

"Ah, you are *that* Miss Featherstone." He eyed her with interest, as if trying to work something out in his mind. "It is a great pleasure to meet an artist of your talent, and so young. Like our Elsa."

Hattie was unsure how to respond: no man had shown such open admiration for her work. Or remarked on her youth quite so openly. "I…that is…thank you."

"Do you have your own studio, Miss Featherstone, or do you work out of a gallery?"

He thought she was a professional artist. Stunned, Hattie turned to Elsa, wondering what the soprano had told him about her. Not much, surely, since she'd shared nearly nothing of herself. "I… No, Mr. Toye. I don't have a studio of my own." *Yet.* "In truth, I'm enrolled at the Royal College of Art and have been for the past two years."

She didn't add that she'd quit attending because she'd been unable to pay the tuition.

"Ah, the RCA. You chose a fine institution for your training." Mr. Toye nodded in approval. "Very fine, indeed."

They discussed the college, the names of her professors, then nothing of consequence after that, and soon enough Elsa was steering Hattie away to make more introductions.

She smiled a lot, nodded even more, until the evening was over, and she was back in the tiny flat she shared with Vera, declaring, "I must hear Mayer-Braun sing in a complete opera."

Vera matched her enthusiasm over the idea.

"What's more," Hattie said, warming to the subject, "I

should like to watch her perform at the Salzburg Festival. It's the one event she never misses. Isn't that what she said?"

"That's exactly what she said."

If Elsa Mayer-Braun was guaranteed to sing in Austria, then to Austria Hattie must go. To Vera, she said, "I intend to travel to Salzburg next summer."

Vera's response was, naturally, "You can't go alone."

"Of course not. You're coming with me."

Money, of course, would be their greatest challenge.

They stayed up late working out their expenses. Roughly at first, then in ruthless detail. It could be done, but just barely. At least their passports were current. They would travel third class, through Belgium, Germany and on to Salzburg via Munich. They were British citizens, after all. Certainly it would be safe for them to make such a journey despite the political unrest on the Continent.

When the conversation waned, Hattie made the decision to tell the singer of their plan. She would deliver the letter directly to the theater herself. *Dearest Elsa,* she wrote. *My sister, Vera, and I are determined to hear you sing in a proper opera during the Salzburg Festival. We are quite dedicated in our quest to do so next summer.*

It was a rather bold statement and possibly—probably—unattainable, but in a flurry of hope and a good dose of whimsy, Hattie dropped off the letter anyway.

To her delight, Mayer-Braun wrote back the next day, her letter ending with the lovely promise: *If you succeed in coming to the festival in my beloved Salzburg, then you shall have tickets for everything I sing.*

That, Hattie decided, was all the invitation she and Vera needed to put their plan in motion.

Chapter Seven

Elsa

August 1943. Salzburg, Austria.
Felsenreitschule *Theater.*

Elsa held the stare of evil. The Gestapo agent did not disguise the truth of his nature. He let her see the depravity of his soul, the Nazi uniform only one slice of the vicious whole. She could feel *Kriminaldirektor* Vogt's malicious spirit like a snake coiling around her. She wanted to shrink back.

She did not.

Where was Wilhelm? His absence was glaring and hinted at abandonment. Or, worse, betrayal. Surely not. Surely, her husband hadn't turned her in to the Gestapo. Such a thing could not be. There was tension between them, yes. But they could have not fallen so far away from where they had started. She would not believe that.

This was not a time for speculation about her missing husband.

From center stage, she felt eyes on her, appraising her, wondering what she'd done. Her hands began to shake and a shudder rolled through her. Yet Elsa refused to look away from Vogt's cold stare. Even as she stood before him in her costume of layers upon layers of lacy, cream-colored chiffon, it felt good, somehow powerful, to gaze into those hard eyes and know she was on the right side of history. God was ultimately in control. Good would prevail.

Elsa had no regrets. She'd done her small part to save lives. She'd been caught, arrested for treason, but she knew others would rise in her stead and take her place in the battle against tyranny. Hattie would see to that.

Hattie. At the thought of Elsa's closest friend, the fear came fast and hard, scorching through her mind until all that was left was the charred remains of what had once been rational thought. She must get word of her arrest to Hattie, who would take the information to her contacts in the British government. Lives would be lost if the news failed to reach her friend.

Panic made her flinch.

Vogt misunderstood her reaction. That smile of satisfaction returned, curling his lips into a sneer. "Do you deny this charge?"

Silence was her greatest weapon, her only weapon. A charge of treason in Nazi Germany was the equivalent of a conviction. There would be no trial. Not a legal one. No pleading before a fair court. Only interrogation, followed by sentencing. And death.

"You have nothing to say in your defense?"

Words were useless. Words could not save her. She exhaled a long, terrified breath and thought again *Run, Elsa. Run.* And go where? She was surrounded by SS soldiers. She could feel them at her back, to her right, her left, hovering in the shadows like monsters preparing to pounce on their prey.

"Well, Elsa Mayer-Braun?" He spoke her name with complete and utter loathing. "This is your last chance to answer to the charges against you."

She stood tall, held Vogt's stare and lifted her head a fraction higher. "I have nothing to say."

Her answer infuriated him. His hand shot up and grabbed her chin, his grip bruising. A pleading noise slipped out of her before she could pull it back.

His smile came again, more vicious than before. The expression of a viper.

She caught Frieda giving her a sidelong look. Smugness there. Disdain. Wilhelm had been right all those years ago. Frieda resented her. More, she hated Elsa.

Enough to turn her in to the Gestapo?

She felt tears running down her cheek, a fast-flowing river, though she didn't remember the first gush. Slowly, she became aware of the other people on the stage. Their murmurs had stopped. The silence beat heavy in Elsa's ears. She was surrounded by men and women she thought her friends. Not so. There were no friends in Nazi Germany, only people to suspect. She was alone. Completely, wholly alone. Not even Wilhelm stood with her. Her husband's absence was the greatest betrayal of all.

"Very well." Vogt's hand fell away. "Since you refuse to speak in your defense, you will do so at the *Polizeistation*. Seize her."

In a move so fast her vision blurred, one of the soldiers wrenched her hands apart, dragged them around to her back and snapped shackles on her wrists. Another barking command from Vogt, and Elsa was shoved forward with the flat of a hand. The heavy skirts of her costume whirled around her ankles as she stumbled across the stage, past her fellow singers.

They watched her, eyes wide, lips pressed tightly together, saying nothing in her defense. Their abandonment caused her more pain than the metal at her wrists. Even the conductor averted his gaze, here only because her husband had placed him behind the baton. Evidently, his loyalty to Wilhelm did not extend to her.

She was given another push and practically fell down the stairs. Years of stage training helped her maintain her balance. Head high, she set her eyes on the outer doors and strode past the orchestra pit and up the center aisle of the auditorium.

Audience members fidgeted in their seats. This was not the show they'd come to see. Still, she felt their gazes follow her, heard their quiet murmurs, a noise that hummed low and sinister in her ears.

In a moment of weakness, she glanced to her right, at the faces, the ones that didn't turn away. Many shared her terror, others her shock. But in some she saw the glint of condemnation, as if they'd always known she would be branded a traitor.

Here, too, she was alone. But then, a woman draped in fine jewels and silk organza met Elsa's gaze. There was outrage on her face. She attempted to stand, this stranger with courage in her eyes. Hope flowed through Elsa—there was still good in her fellow Austrians—and was quickly lost as a masculine hand yanked her would-be ally back into her seat. Feeling the sting of rejection, Elsa cut her eyes away and pulled herself together.

Swatches of memories traveled through her mind, faces of the many she'd saved in her work with Hattie, and then she was outside in the hot, sticky air, gasping for breath.

The guard gripping her arm dragged her away from the theater toward a familiar black Mercedes-Benz waiting at the curb. The same but different from the one loaned to her earlier in the day. Different because this vehicle belonged to *Kriminaldirektor* Vogt. Elsa's stomach became a nest of withering snakes, her eyes watered, her head ached, and all she could process, all she could think, was that once she was inside that car, all was lost. There would be no escape.

Vogt reached for her arm, his grip that of iron.

Searing resentment wanted to reveal itself, but Elsa knew if she surrendered to the urge, the Gestapo agent would think her weak. So she ignored the pain shooting up her arm and stood with her head high, carefully thinking of nothing at all.

"Your defiance will prove your doom, *Frau* Hoffmann."

She flinched at the use of her married name, uttered as if it were something vile. Had Wilhelm been arrested, too? For what? He'd played no role in her activities.

A gleam of satisfaction lit in Vogt's small, ratlike eyes as he swung open the car door and shoved her into the back seat.

Darkness shrouded the interior, and Elsa's mind raged with the same boiling fear she'd felt inside the theater when Vogt climbed in after her and settled on the seat beside her. Panic scurried up her throat. She forced it down with a hard swallow and looked out the window. She concentrated on the twists and curves of their route. Seven blocks north, a turn to the right, another to the left.

The vehicle came to a sudden halt. Elsa recognized the building. The cloister had once belonged to Franciscan monks before the Gestapo requisitioned it for their Salzburg head-quarters.

She was yanked out onto the street, surrounded again by SS soldiers. Vogt snapped his wrist in the air. "Take her to Interrogation."

Though full of people, the streets stood empty of allies. None came to her rescue as she was dragged into the build-ing. More twists and turns down dark, eerie corridors. Finally, she was thrust inside a holding cell, her hands still secured at her back. The room was small and barren but for a metal table and two ladder-back chairs. She took one and considered the dull light spilling from the dingy fixture overhead.

Vogt made her wait. Minutes became hours. Elsa shifted in her chair. She shifted again and again. With her hands bound behind her back she could not find a comfortable position. The more she tried, the harder the chair became.

Her body understood what her mind could not comprehend. *This is the end.* Pain shot up her arms. Eventually, they grew numb. Her eyes lowered. She forced them open. Sleep beckoned. She fought it off, fearing what would become of her if she let down her guard.

Lord, she prayed, *I need Your strength. Your courage.*

More time passed. Hours, minutes, an entire day? She'd lost track. Her bladder filled to bursting. This quiet torture, this agony, she knew it was part of the interrogation. Her mind battled with indecision. Give in to sleep? Or stay awake? Sleep would restore her. Animal instinct begged her to relent, to close her eyes. Sleep could prove her ruin. Ultimately, her body made the choice for her. The moment her lids fell to half-mast, she was startled awake by harsh light in her face and a solid slap to her cheek. She shook her head to erase the stars playing before her eyes.

Just as her vision cleared, Vogt, in full Gestapo uniform, including billed cap atop his head, took the chair across from her. Malicious intent clung to him. Elsa could hardly breathe under the weight of it.

He carefully set a thick file on the table. Elsa saw her name on the tab. Her hope caved inside itself, like dirt pouring in a hole, because that was when she knew the truth.

It didn't matter how she answered this man's questions. She'd been found guilty already. The proof, whether real or contrived, was in that dossier. The rest would be for show.

She had one thought: *It's over.*

All she could do now was pray to her Lord and Savior and beg that death came quickly.

Chapter Eight

Hattie

November 1934. London, England.

Several nights following Elsa Mayer–Braun's concert at Covent Garden, a minor disagreement occurred between the Featherstone sisters, their first in months. The last had been over Hattie's desire to quit art school after an astonishingly vicious critique. Vera had insisted Hattie ignore her professor and continue her training despite his disapproval. At the time, Vera had been right.

She was not right now.

She claimed that the evening spent at the Royal Opera House had been so absolutely perfect that any attempt at recreating the experience would prove a massive disappointment. While Hattie agreed Elsa's singing had been beyond compare, she disagreed that a second showing would somehow fail to satisfy.

"I am determined to attend another concert before Elsa leaves London. Even if that means watching from the very top of the theater in an unreserved seat in the gallery."

Hands fisted on her hips, Vera's mouth turned down at the edges. For one horrifying second, Hattie thought her sister would raise her voice or stomp off in a huff or something equally terrible. Vera, being Vera, did none of these things.

She became the voice of reason. "I understand your wish to hear Elsa again. But I'm afraid you're forgetting one very important element."

"I don't believe I am."

"Attending another performance will require purchasing another ticket, which will require money. Money we could be—*should be*—saving for our trip to Salzburg. No," Vera said and held up a hand, "don't interrupt me. I already know what you're going to say. And you're wrong. Traveling to Salzburg to hear Elsa sing in a complete opera is entirely different than attending her concert here in London."

"I don't see how."

"Well, then, you're just being stubborn."

Hattie dug in her metaphorical heels with renewed vigor. "As are you, Vera. As are you."

"No, I'm being sensible. Pause a moment and think, Hattie. At the festival, we will have access to all manner of operas, some of which will be performed by the greatest singers in the world, Elsa being only one of them. We may hear Ezio Pinza sing in *La Cenerentola* or Elisabeth Rethberg take on the role of Mimi in *La Bohème*. Should I go on?"

Hattie sighed. "No, Vera. There's no need to say more. You have struck the winning blow. There will be no more trips to Covent Garden this week."

"You're disappointed." Vera touched her arm, squeezed

gently. "But you will thank me when we are in Salzburg and sitting in the famous *Felsenreitschule*."

Hattie bit her lip, released it, sighed again. "I'm sure you're right."

They hugged, each needing to end their disagreement on a peaceful note. Then, with nothing more to say, they retreated to their individual domains. Hattie to paint, and Vera to do, well, whatever it was she did when she was locked behind her closed bedroom door.

Her sister had become quite secretive, which had Hattie thinking about the time just after their mother died. Vera had discovered romance novels thanks to a friend who'd sneaked her one after school. She'd spent hours in her room consuming the book. Clearly, that's what she was doing now, reading, most likely, and probably a romance novel.

Hattie woke the next morning feeling groggy and out of sorts. She'd dreamed of her mother, then of opera, then of her mother singing opera, which had been both ridiculous and absurd. Caroline Featherstone had been gifted with many talents, but singing had not been one of them. In that, she and her youngest daughter were the same.

Hattie sighed—she'd been doing a lot of that lately—and took in the dull, gray light creeping across her bedcovers. Dawn was at least an hour away. She closed her eyes and attempted to fall back asleep. It was no use. Too many images chased around in her head. She tried to separate them, or at least place them into manageable categories, but there were too many, each one begging to be brought to life beyond the confines of her mind.

So be it.

Shoving herself out of bed, she wiggled her toes into a pair of ratty slippers and padded over to her easel. She painted the strongest of the images in her head, Carmen singing "Habanera." Elsa's version had been especially dramatic, but Hattie thought the courtesan should be older than her friend, the facial features more earthy and exotic.

She became utterly absorbed in the process of painting the tragic courtesan, completely unaware of time passing until Vera popped her head into the room. "Oh, Hattie. Please tell me you didn't stay up all night painting again."

"I didn't stay up all night painting again." Brush still in hand, she checked the clock on her bedside table. "It's only been an hour." And she was feeling the tendrils of exhaustion that had been missing when she'd left her bed.

Sleep beckoned—how utterly inconvenient. If she and Vera were to make it to Salzburg in August, Hattie had to provide her share of the money to cover their expenses. That meant trudging off to work and sitting at her desk in the secretarial pool. An hour later, she was dutifully banging away on her typewriter.

She was suddenly so very tired of the never-ending routine of her life. She wanted more. A purpose, one that incorporated her passion for art. But what? Her head grew dizzy, spinning wildly. The heat didn't help. The room had few windows to begin with, and all of them, she noticed rather mournfully, were closed. By midafternoon, the uncirculated air turned rancid, the putrid odor of too many perfumes gone sour. Worse even than the cloying scent was the sound of lacquered fingernails striking typewriter keys.

The constant pecking sent Hattie's head spinning again.

She had to get out of this room. Glancing at the stack of documents awaiting her attention, she sighed. And, really, that was quite enough of that. Lost in the tedium, she didn't immediately hear her name. It came again, louder and more impatient. Iris, who else?

"Hen-ree-etta." Her coworker snapped out each syllable

in a fast staccato, sharp as glass. "Did you not hear me? I said you have a visitor."

"A what?" Hattie looked up from her typewriter. "A visitor?"

"Isn't that what I said?" Iris drew in a long, audible breath, looking completely put out. "He's waiting for you in the lobby of the building."

He? Hattie blanched at the impossibility of a male visitor come to see her. She didn't know many men and certainly none who could afford to leave their jobs in the middle of the day. Blinking in confusion, she stood and cautiously looked around, as if the answer to this baffling turn of events hung in the silted air. No answer was to be found, of course.

With nerves pulled as tight as violin strings, she joined Iris in the doorway. "Do you know who he is? Did he provide a name?"

"No."

"No, you don't know who he is? Or, no, he didn't give his name?"

"Both, neither." Iris pretended grave interest in her manicured fingernails. "He may have told me his name. I really don't remember."

"That's marvelously unhelpful."

Iris shrugged in her careless way.

Hattie barely had time to form a puzzled frown before the other woman was striding down the hallway. Clearly, Hattie was meant to follow. At the edge of the lobby, Iris gestured vaguely to her left. "There he is. Over there. The one holding the sad little gray hat."

Hattie tried not to sigh. Why did Iris have to be so contentious? Half the men in the immediate area carried gray hats.

"Well, anyway," Iris said, spinning around, "you'll figure it out."

Hattie didn't bother watching her coworker saunter off. She was too busy searching the lobby for her male visitor. She caught sight of a possible candidate in a tweed jacket that marked him as the quintessential academic. Perhaps he had information about one of the documents she was meant to type today. She motioned to him to gain his attention.

His eyes met hers without an ounce of recognition. Clearly, not her visitor.

She continued searching. No one seemed familiar. Then, she saw him. Her heart leaped in her chest. What could he possibly want with her? And how—*how*—had he found her? She hadn't told him where she worked. Had she? No, only where she took art classes. She'd been too embarrassed to inform him of the rest. "Mr. Toye? Mr. Geoffrey Toye?"

The managing director of the Royal Opera House closed the distance between them. "Ah, Miss Featherstone. So delightful to see you again. So delightful."

He appeared sincere and was looking at her with interest. Not masculine interest. She might be young and inexperienced, but not *that* young and inexperienced. No, the man had something else on his mind, something important by the serious look in his eyes. "I'm surprised to see you, Mr. Toye. Do you have business at the Board of Education?"

That seemed the most likely of explanations.

"I'm here on Elsa Mayer-Braun's recommendation. She speaks very highly of you, Miss Featherstone, and is a great admirer of your art, as am I." He shifted his hat from one hand to the other, his very *black* hat. "Talent such as yours is rare and doesn't come along very often."

This was the second time he'd complimented her art, with equal amounts of enthusiasm.

"I'm flattered." And very much confused. Mr. Toye did not strike her as a man who would journey ten minutes by foot simply to compliment her. "How did you know to find me here?"

"Ah. That. It wasn't so hard. Once I put my mind to the task." He smiled, a rather sheepish grin that didn't fit with his expensive clothing or confident manner. "I started at the Royal College of Art. A few inquiries later, and here I am, come to make you an offer."

"What sort of offer?"

"An arrangement, if you will, regarding the upcoming opera season. Sir Beecham and I have decided our programs lack a certain...panache."

I'll say.

"While Sir Beecham is still on the fence, I am quite certain you are up to the task."

He was looking at her expectantly, and she looked right back, unable to form her scattered thoughts into a coherent stream of words. Her mind was caught in a tangle of shock and questions. So many, many questions. "Are you asking me to design the programs?"

"Not precisely, no. Sir Beecham requires a bit more convincing yet. You will need to produce a minimum of three samples for his review." Mr. Toye continued talking, speaking quickly, gesturing calmly and occasionally smiling as he explained what he wanted from her.

Hattie attempted to keep up. But her mind was reeling, and her hands were shaking so hard she had to clasp them together at her waist. Disjointed phrases came to her in a rapid-fire sequence. *Ten illustrations in total...one featuring Covent Garden itself...* On and on, he spoke. *Short notice...printer's tight schedules...pay you handsomely...*

At last, he drew a breath.

"Well, Miss Featherstone? Is this an opportunity you would be interested in pursuing?"

Her mind could hardly focus. "When would you need these sample illustrations?"

"Friday next." He listed the sum he would pay her—enough to cover two train tickets to Salzburg—and the amount she could expect to receive for the rest of the drawings, should Sir Beecham give his approval.

Hattie did her best to cipher the meaning of what this man was saying. The potential future that stood before her was staggering. Money, prestige, a chance to prove her merit as an artist. It felt like a dream or another transformation, as if her former life were separating from what it once was and becoming a newer, brighter existence. A world of creative endeavors and art commissions.

"What do you say, Miss Featherstone?"

Hattie wanted to say yes, but she couldn't. Not yet. It went against her nature to accept his offer without addressing the uncomfortable truth. "Mr. Toye, you understand I have never done this type of work before."

"I'm aware you lack professional experience, as is Sir Beecham. Which is why I've requested a minimum of three samples before we move forward with a formal contract."

A formal contract. The man was serious. He was really, truly offering her this chance. She simply had to agree to his terms. Very fair terms, at that. Still, she hesitated. "Why me? Surely there are a hundred more seasoned artists you could hire."

"True, but none of them come highly recommended by Elsa Mayer-Braun. Although," he leaned in closer, as if sharing a secret meant only for her ears, "even had she not spoken so fondly of you, I have seen your work. Your vision is very much my own."

It was exactly the right thing to say to erase her indecision. "When you put it that way, then yes, Mr. Toye. I shall have the samples ready for you by the end of next week."

They shook hands, their palms barely touching.

Mr. Toye gave her the rest of the details she would need to complete her initial sketches, including the name of the opera he wished her to illustrate, how to contact him should she have any questions and where to deliver the final drawings.

Hattie smiled a lot as he spoke, nodded even more, even as her mind kept hooking on one humbling, salient point. He was offering her this incredible opportunity because Elsa had recommended her. The soprano had risked her reputation for Hattie, a virtual stranger, on nothing more than a hastily drawn picture ripped from her sketch pad.

Tears of gratitude burned in her eyes, and a hard lump lodged in her throat. She wanted to laugh. To cry. To shout for joy. Elsa's generous nature was so like her own mother's, so like Vera's.

Three incredible women had given something of themselves for Hattie to chase her dream. They'd provided their support, all because they believed in her and her talent. Because they were good and kind of heart, and one day, Hattie vowed, she would be more than a receiver of so many blessings. She would be the giver of them, too.

Mr. Toye finished his instructions, placed his hat upon his head and bade Hattie a very hearty farewell. She watched him exit the building, then, only once he was gone did she begin winding her way through the dusty corridors, straight to Vera's office in the textbook department where she worked as a translator of German tomes. Mostly self-taught, Vera had studied very hard to learn the difficult language and all its nuances.

She was very clever. Hattie should tell her sister that more often. Right now, though, her head was full of her own stunning news. She had much work ahead of her, and she would need to purchase a recording of *The Marriage of Figaro*, the opera she was to illustrate for Sir Beecham's approval.

Stopping outside of Vera's office, she knocked on the doorjamb. "Shall we head to Oxford Street after work and visit the record store?"

Vera set down her pen, frowned. "We suspended all purchases, so, no, I don't want to go to Oxford Street after work. It will only depress me."

"You will change your mind once you hear my news." Hattie told her sister about Mr. Toye's visit, the grand opportunity he'd offered and how much he was willing to pay for the initial three sketches and the additional amount should she land the job.

Eyes wide, Vera picked up her pencil, set it down again, then shot out of her chair. A second later, she was around her desk and tugging Hattie into her arms. "What happy news."

"If I am to illustrate scenes from *The Marriage of Figaro*, I should hear at least one aria from the opera. Perhaps two. Maybe three. Four. No, five. Five, at the very least."

She was babbling. It was hard not to: her excitement was impossible to contain, as was her trepidation. So much relied on her getting the first set of illustrations right. She couldn't let Mr. Toye down. Or Elsa. Or Vera.

Or, she realized, herself.

Seven days later, on the morning she was scheduled to deliver the initial sketches to Mr. Toye, Hattie stood shoulder to shoulder with Vera in their tiny kitchen, each of the three finished pieces spread before them.

"They're really quite good, Hattie. The best you've ever done." Still gazing at the drawings, Vera nodded to herself. "You're going to get the job. I just know it."

They would discover if she was right soon enough. "I must thank Elsa Mayer-Braun for recommending me."

"Yes," Vera agreed. "You must."

"How? She's already left London for Scandinavia." Sweden was the next stop on her tour.

"You could write her a letter."

An excellent idea, except for one small, tiny, insignificant detail. "Where would I send it?"

"I'm sure Mr. Toye will know."

And, of course, he did. He cheerfully provided a forwarding address. It had helped her cause that he was pleased with her illustrations. "Wait here while I show these to Sir Beecham."

"You wish to show them to him now?"

"We're on somewhat of a tight schedule. It's imperative we settle this matter today."

Mr. Toye returned within ten minutes, with Sir Beecham in tow, who told her, "I am very happy with your sketches, my dear."

Happy enough, it would seem, to add a twenty percent bonus on top of the amount Mr. Toye had originally offered. Hattie left Covent Garden in somewhat of a daze. She was a professional artist, with a paid commission, half of which was currently in her possession. She and Vera could afford to attend the Salzburg Festival. And they had plenty of time to make new evening gowns.

Later that night, flush with satisfaction, Hattie sat down to write to the woman who'd been the cause of her good for-tune. At Vera's suggestion, she went with a formal tone, one professional artist to another, but after her sister went to bed, Hattie immediately had second thoughts. The words didn't sound like her own.

She started over.

It took her several tries, but she eventually found the right tone to express her gratitude. She ended the note with the news that she and Vera would indeed attend the Salzburg Festival that summer as planned. To her delight, Mayer-Braun wrote back the following week.

> *My dearest Hattie,*
> *I am so very pleased to hear of your success and, better still, that we will meet again. I look forward to renewing our acquaintance when you arrive in Salzburg. Please tell me where you will be staying. I will make sure your tickets are waiting for you at the front desk.*

Hattie paused. How generous. How kind. She continued reading.

> *I end this letter with some happy news of my own. When next we meet, I will be a married woman. Wilhelm Hoffmann has asked me to marry him, and I have said yes.*
> *Your friend, E.*

Hattie stared at the words, forcing her mind to comprehend what she'd just read. Elsa was to become Wilhelm Hoffmann's wife. His *wife*. Her reaction was surprisingly strong, visceral even, and not altogether pleasant. A white-hot pressure spiked through her that felt very much like dread. What was her friend getting herself into, marrying such a proud, superior man? He had to be at least a decade older than Elsa, but that wasn't what bothered Hattie.

It was the man himself. Twice she'd encountered him, and only one of those times had he spoken to her directly. He'd been complimentary about her art, albeit grudgingly so.

His affection for Elsa had not been grudging, quite the opposite, in fact. So why did Elsa's news come as such a shock? Because Hattie had read something shadowy in Hoffmann.

Arrogance and superiority, but also something else. Something darker. No. She had to be wrong.

What did she know of such matters, of men? She'd misunderstood the scowls and black looks. It was concentration she'd witnessed in the man's eyes, not malice, nothing nefarious. It was Hattie's own insecurities that had led her to misread his behavior.

Yes, she decided, she'd misread Wilhelm Hoffman.

He would make Elsa a fine husband. Very fine, indeed. Hattie spent the rest of the night convincing herself it was true.

Chapter Nine

Elsa

July 1935. Salzburg, Austria.
Hotel Sacher.

Elsa greeted her wedding day from the top floor of the Hotel Sacher. Originally, she'd taken up residence in the three-bedroom suite for practical reasons. Salzburg Cathedral was a short ten-minute walk away, half that by automobile.

There was also the problem of overzealous journalists, some of whom had come from as far away as America. Apparently, the engagement between the "Salzburg Songbird" and Austria's most celebrated maestro had created something of an international sensation. The adoring public wanted to know every detail of their romance.

Elsa was no stranger to attention, especially from the press. She submitted to the intrusion on her personal life with a stoic shrug and practiced smile. Her patience, however, had run out two days ago, and here she was, alone in the enormous suite.

With not even Malvina for company, Elsa was regretting her decision. She was too alone with her thoughts. *Love. Marriage.* These were only words to her. She had no personal example to draw from. Her parents had been happy, blissfully so. That's what she'd been told, what she'd come to believe. But the tales were stories built on Malvina's memories.

Would Elsa's marriage fall short of her own lofty expectations?

An absurd concern. Wilhelm was decent. He was good to her, kind and as eager to marry her as she him. Once he'd issued his proposal, hadn't he found a small pause in their schedules and seized upon the two-day break before rehearsals began for her next performance? He'd even taken over the wedding plans so that Elsa could concentrate on her singing.

Of course, he'd applied his trademark efficiency to the task, handpicking the church, the minister, the flowers, even the cake. He'd created the guest list and had designed Elsa's wedding dress, a snow-white, frothy confection with acres of lace. Her only job was to show up at the cathedral, recite her vows and sign the official marriage documents. Simple.

A queasy sort of dizziness rose in her head that sent her in search of running water to splash across her face. That done, she donned a robe, shoved her feet into plush slippers and wrapped a scarf around her neck despite the summer heat. Two days off did not mean she could be careless with her health. A summer cold would throw off her performance schedule.

Stepping out onto the terrace, Elsa breathed in the still morning air, already hot and weighted with humidity. She looked to the sky next. A bank of slow-moving, pink-tinged clouds swathed the perfect yellow ball of the sun in a misty cloak.

Breathing in the scene, Elsa cupped her hands around the

bronze railing and leaned forward to glance over the Salzach River forging its way through the heart of the *Altstadt*—the Old Town—with its many domed rooftops, towers and spires. This was Salzburg, home, her home, where she felt the most like herself.

Would she still feel the same later tonight when she stood in this very spot next to her husband? Or would the view look different once she was married to Wilhelm?

It was a fanciful thought. Elsa should be fanciful on her wedding day. Smiling, she returned to the suite and invested five full minutes in dressing before admitting defeat.

She could not do this alone. The dress was too complicated. She stood there in her slip, staring, blinking, wishing again she'd spent the night in her own home.

A delicate knock told Elsa her worries were over. She let Malvina into the suite and almost immediately found herself encircled in her aunt's arms. She wasn't sure which of them initiated the hug, nor did she care. She needed to lean into the comfort of her aunt's embrace. "Thank you for being here."

"I would wish to be nowhere else." Malvina stepped back, and Elsa felt pleasantly warm as they stood facing each other in the bright, cheery sunbeams streaming in from the balcony.

But then, she looked closer and felt the first stirrings of concern.

The strain of the past year had left its mark on her aunt's face. Fresh lines showed around her eyes and mouth, harsh reminders that Malvina had not come to Salzburg for Elsa's wedding alone. Circumstances far more sinister had brought her back to Austria. In a matter of a few short months, Elsa's aunt had endured the loss of her job, her dignity and her German citizenship.

The politics of evil men: that was why Malvina was in Austria. It was all so unfair.

"Elsa, my darling girl. What is this? Tears? On your wedding day?" Malvina smoothed her fingertips across Elsa's cheek. "You should not look so sad. This is a day for happiness, unless..." Her hand dropped. "Are you having second thoughts?"

"Of course not. Wilhelm is my destiny." Elsa laughed a little. Attempted a smile. Failed miserably. "I was thinking about Adolf Hitler."

"You must not think of that hateful man. He does not belong here, in this room, on this blessed day."

"No. He does not belong in this room." That didn't stop Elsa from worrying over what the little tyrant would do next. His fanaticism was growing worse, stronger. Soon, Jews would lose all their rights. Possibly even their lives. "Something must be done to stop his madness."

Before he annexed Austria and brought his hatred across the border. There was already a groundswell of support. Anti-Semitism was spreading far and wide. Even the opera world had suffered its sting. Forced resignations were becoming more frequent. Singers, composers and musicians were losing their jobs, leaving the country, some disappearing altogether.

"That is a worry for another day. Now," Malvina said as she took Elsa's hand, "time is slipping from us. Let's get you into your wedding gown."

They entered the bedroom. The light was stronger here, and as Elsa scanned her aunt's face in the bold light, she saw the ravages of the past year far better. "Have you considered moving to another country? England, perhaps? You could apply for a position at—"

"I could never call England home." Malvina's eyes burned with regret as she took the dress from its hanger and brought it to Elsa. "Besides, the British have strict immigration laws. It is a country of transit only. A month visit is all that is allowed.

Now, enough of this depressing talk. I mean it, Elsa. No more. I will not be the cause of sadness on your wedding day."

Elsa gazed down at the miles of satin and lace. A surge of guilt and concern for her aunt slipped through her. Something had to be done to keep Malvina safe. Her mind working on the problem, she absently stepped into the dress, moved to the full-length mirror and faced her reflection while Malvina tackled the infinite row of buttons at her back.

Elsa's eyes began to burn.

Malvina was Elsa's family, her only family, as much a mother to her as her own had been. She owed every bit of her success to this woman's love and support. She'd done her best to pass her blessings on to others. Frieda Klein was only one of them. There had been others, and, of course, there was the aspiring artist from England. Hattie Featherstone was a kindred spirit.

An idea formed in Elsa's mind, a way to put her aunt out of harm's way. It would require planning—which she could do— and money—which she had—and the assistance of a woman she hardly knew. Ah, yes, the one unknown.

"There." Malvina secured the final button. "It is done."

Not yet, Elsa thought. *But soon.* "Well?" She turned away from the mirror and spread out her arms. "How do I look?"

"Like a bride. You are very beautiful, Elsa. So much like your mother on her wedding day." Something like sorrow came and went in the older woman's eyes. "And now, it is time for me to give you some advice about marriage. Oh, I know what you are thinking. An old, unmarried woman like me could not possibly know of such matters."

"You have witnessed many marriages."

"It is true, I have, and I can attest marriage is very hard work."

"I am not afraid of hard work, *Tante* Malvina."

"This is not the same as preparing for an opera. You will

need to make sacrifices, the kind that will change a life, or rather, two lives. Yours and his."

"I am no stranger to sacrifice."

Malvina nodded. "Then, all that is left is for me to ask, do you love him?"

A sweet, liquid longing slid through her. "I do love him. Oh, Malvina, I do. Wilhelm is my destiny."

"So you have said." The worry in Malvina's eyes turned to something else, something closer to fear. She wore the new emotion on her entire face, across her body, in her slumped shoulders. "He is older than you, married once already and more experienced about the ways of the world. He is not, I fear, an easy man. No, not easy at all."

She knew this about Wilhelm. "I am aware of Wilhelm's faults. He loves me. That is what matters. I do not doubt his devotion."

"What of children? Have you spoken of having children with him?"

Yes, Elsa had broached the subject only last week. He'd taken her face in his hands and, smiling softly, had said, "Now is not the time for babies. You are on the verge of becoming the most celebrated soprano of your generation. Under my guidance, it will come to pass within a few short years. Then, once your name is linked with the greatest sopranos of both past and present, that is when we will discuss the possibility of a child."

His words had echoed what Elsa wanted for herself: fame, international acclaim. But now, with Malvina looking at her expectantly, she had doubts. It was Wilhelm's wording, she realized, the lack of a definitive answer. The promise only to discuss the *possibility of a child*.

She was putting too much stock in a few words. Nerves, she told herself; that was the source of her hesitancy. Elsa and

Wilhelm would have a baby, one day. "I'm young yet. There is plenty of time for children in the future."

"You are comfortable waiting? This is your wish, to put it aside for now?"

"In the plainest of terms, yes."

Malvina nodded a second time, and almost, nearly smiled. "Then, I wish you much success and happiness. What next? Ah, yes. The veil."

They arrived at Salzburg Cathedral a half hour before the ceremony. The journalists and photographers had been herded into a cordoned-off section of the main courtyard. *So many of them*, Elsa thought, as she took a few careful breaths before stepping into the flashing lights.

She answered no questions, made no direct eye contact, but walked quickly, keeping her footsteps light. There was only time for impressions as she and Malvina passed the Maria Immaculata column, the cathedral arches, the statues of the four evangelists—Saints Matthew, Mark, Luke and John—and the pediment representing the Transfiguration of Jesus. The artists' work was incomparable. No wonder the cathedral drew so many visitors every year.

Finally, they entered the building and were shown to a small antechamber off the vestibule. Silence hung heavy in the air. Nerves wanted to take flight in Elsa's stomach again. She blamed the sensation partly on concern for her aunt's future and partly on Malvina's marriage advice and the talk of children. So caught up in her thoughts, the sudden knock on the door startled her.

"I'll see who it is." Malvina went to the door and cracked it open.

Elsa thought she heard a familiar masculine voice. Then, Malvina was stepping back, and the door was opening wider, and there he was, her groom, standing on the threshold, dressed in a perfectly tailored tuxedo, his back straight as a ship's mast. Confused by his sudden appearance, Elsa scanned his face.

The answer simply wasn't there, not in his eyes, nor his features, nor his perfect posture. In all their acquaintance, Wilhelm had never been this unreadable. It made her voice falter as she said his name. "Wilhelm, what is it? Has something happened?"

He said nothing, just continued staring in that unfathomable manner. Time seemed suspended. Seconds went by uncounted. And still, he remained silent.

"Wilhelm?"

He took a step closer, and now she saw it. It was quite astounding, really. Her groom looked...vulnerable. "I'd like a word with my bride." He glanced briefly at Malvina. "Alone."

Malvina opened her mouth, no doubt to argue, but Elsa shook her head.

"I'll be right outside." She left without another word.

Alone with her groom, Elsa stood very still, very attentive, and waited. Wilhelm moved a step closer, his expression easy to read now. Whatever had brought him to this room, he was not here to call off their wedding. There was love in his eyes.

His heart belonged to her. It was enough. It had to be enough. Of course it was enough.

"What is it you wish to say, Wilhelm?" Perhaps, finally, he wanted to speak about his first wife and the tragedy of her death. This would not be the time Elsa would have chosen for such a conversation. Still, she lifted a hand to the lapel of his jacket, running her fingers down the material. "Whatever it is, I will listen."

"It is my greatest wish to keep you safe. You know this, Elsa? Tell me you know this."

Her answer came without reservation. "I know it."

"I have done what I can to secure our future. I can only hope it is enough." Before she could ask him what he meant, he pulled in a deep breath, released it slowly and gave her the smile that had won her heart all those months ago. "You make a very beautiful bride."

Love and hope blossomed in her heart. Malvina had said Wilhelm was not an easy man. With her, he was. "You make a very handsome groom."

"I have something for you. A gift." He stuck his hand into one of the inner pockets of his coat and pulled out a small box. "Go on. Open it."

Surprised, she curled her fingers around the soft velvet. The look in her groom's eyes stole her breath. It was the look of a man in love. With trembling fingers, she flipped back the lid and gasped at the emerald pendant winking up at her.

"The necklace belonged to my mother. It now belongs to you."

Blinking rapidly, Elsa concentrated on the exquisite green gem. On the black velvet box. On anything but the fresh ache in her chest. Silently, she handed him the necklace and turned to face the mirror. "Will you help me with the clasp?"

She lowered her head and waited.

He hesitated. Then, coming up from behind her, he shifted the veil aside and fastened the pendant around her neck.

When she lifted her head, she caught his gaze in the mirror and knew she was making the right decision. She spun around to face him directly. "I love you, Wilhelm."

A strangled sound whipped from his throat, and with a single swoop, he roped her tightly against him. "And I you, Elsa."

The embrace was short. "Ready to become my wife?"

A nod was all she could manage.

"I will meet you at the altar."

He was gone a second later.

Malvina returned almost immediately. She searched Elsa's face. "All is well?"

"All is well."

Elsa accepted the bouquet of flowers Malvina presented to her, and together, they left the antechamber. Malvina took her trip down the aisle first, settling in the first pew.

Taken aback by the sheer number of guests, Elsa paused. A low buzz filled her ears. She recognized many, though not all. Some of the guests were close colleagues, devoted opera patrons, a few she would even call friends. But there were also dignitaries and their wives. Every Austrian political party was represented. Social Democrats were in attendance, Pan-Germans, Communists and, shockingly, some from the National Socialist Party—Nazis.

Wilhelm had invited these people to their wedding. Why? What purpose could have called for such a varied guest list that included Nazis? Elsa had never known Wilhelm to be political. She thought of his words from moments before. *My greatest wish is to keep you safe.* And *I have done what I can to secure our future.* Was that his intent?

Make friends with all so that none were their enemy?

Elsa set her eyes on her groom, and her mind filled with him. He stood with confidence. Her doubts crept away as words passed between them. Promises were made, the kind that would take a lifetime to keep.

He stretched out his hand. The silent call was familiar, expected, a part of their routine. Elsa's heart took an extra hard beat. Her stomach performed a tumble. Then, the music changed. And her head filled with one lone purpose: to answer her groom's summons.

Chapter Ten

Hattie

July 1935. London, England.

The morning after Elsa's highly anticipated wedding, Hattie sat with Vera at their ridiculously tiny breakfast table. Both were eager for details of the event. "I must learn all there is to know," Vera announced. "What she wore, the style of her dress, the length of her veil. What flowers she carried. Was the cake two tiers, or three? I'm sure it was all very romantic."

Hattie hoped so, for her friend's sake. Still, she felt a quiet, lingering sense of dread. She could not get out of her mind the impression that Wilhelm Hoffman disapproved of not only her but most people. Was his devotion to Elsa bigger than his disdain of others? Did he treat her in the way she deserved? Hattie had to think yes. Elsa would not have married him otherwise.

Despite her concerns, her curiosity was piqued. "I'm off to the newsstand."

She returned twenty minutes later with five different papers, including *The Tatler* and *The Times*. All of them covered the wedding, some in greater detail than others, though not on the front page. That was reserved for news from Germany, none of it good. Hattie worried the political unrest would prevent her and Vera from traveling to Salzburg. "Well?" Vera asked. "Are you going to hoard all five of those papers or share one of them with me?"

"Oh, right. Sorry. Here." Hattie spread the offerings on the table between them.

They read in silence. All five publications agreed that the romance had been swift, a whirlwind. Those same newspapers could not, however, agree on when the relationship began. One writer claimed the pair had first been seen together in 1933, at a restaurant opening in Vienna. No, it was in Munich. Possibly Berlin. At a charity event, a party. Two claimed it was at the Salzburg Festival a year ago. Another said it was when Hoffman conducted Elsa in *Elektra*.

"There seems to be little consensus," Vera groused. "Except that their marriage is the perfect pairing of talent and beauty."

"We should send our congratulations." If only Hattie knew where the two would honeymoon, if at all. That was another point the papers could not agree upon. "I suppose we'll have to wait to do so in person."

Three days prior to their trip to Austria, on the fifteenth day of September, devastating news came out of Germany. The Nazis had met in Nuremberg to pass anti-Jewish racial laws, effectively barring Jews from marrying Aryans, holding citizenship or flying the German flag. It was as if they were systematically erasing an entire race of people, one terrible law at a time. Their ideology wasn't even logical.

How could every Jew be bad and every Aryan good? Besides, weren't Christians and Jews interconnected? *Israel's history is our history,* Hattie's mother had said whenever the subject arose. *We have been grafted into the Jewish community, not the other way around.*

Hattie blushed to think how ignorant she'd been to the significance of the Nazi Party's rise to power. And still so naive to what was really happening in Germany. She rectified this immediately, purchasing as many newspapers as possible and doing her best to educate herself.

Her art suffered in the process. There were only so many hours in a day. Not that anyone was clamoring for her work. Mr. Toye had mentioned commissioning her again for a series of Christmas-themed concerts, but he hadn't done so yet.

"Do you think all this political unrest in Germany will prevent our holiday?" Vera wondered. "Our route takes us through Cologne, Frankfurt and Munich."

Hattie shrugged. "I suppose it will depend on how Austria responds to the enactment of the Nuremberg Laws."

"So we wait and see."

A few anxious days later, they discovered the festival would go on as planned.

"Our holiday is safe," Hattie announced, though not without some trepidation over what they would find in the foreign cities. She and Vera traveled by night, third class.

The weather was fine for the ferry crossing. Hattie peered up at the inky fabric of the sky dotted by a million stars and prayed for safe travels. Unfortunately, the weather turned nasty in Brussels just as they boarded the train that would take them to Cologne. Soaked through to the bone, and happy for the warmth of the compartment, they'd barely settled when the whistle blew, and the wheels chugged along the tracks.

The wind outside quickened, scratching against the windowpanes like tiny claws. Not a good omen for the rest of their trip. Then again, it was only water. Their clothing would dry, and they certainly weren't the only ones miserable.

There were quite a lot of people on the train, which was surprising to Hattie. In London, the cars would have been mostly empty at this hour.

A vacant space opened across from them, very quickly taken up by an attractive couple, both only a few years older than Hattie. They had glossy black hair and dark eyes and were dressed in very fine quality clothing. The woman wore what appeared to be real jewelry—no paste for her—which begged the question, why had they chosen to travel third class, and at night?

Hattie received her answer when Vera struck up a conversation with the pair. Abraham and Rebecca Boscowitz were not a couple, nor were they married. They were brother and sister, traveling to Munich to join their parents and three younger siblings. Neither gave a reason for why they had to leave Cologne and, in fact, smoothly turned the conversation back to Vera.

"What brings two British girls to Germany?" Abraham asked.

"We're heading to Salzburg," Vera said. "For the annual music festival."

This seemed to cause him a moment of anxiety. His heels started to bob up and down and his eyes darted around the crowded compartment, never quite finding a place to rest. "You're not worried about crossing the border?"

Vera exchanged a look with Hattie. "Should we be?"

"Austria is no friend of Germany," he said, his restless gaze bouncing between them, over to other passengers, while his feet continued their odd, disjointed dance. "You should not have come. The border will be difficult to cross, possibly even closed."

His sister placed a calming hand on his knee. "The border will not be closed for them. Only for people like us."

Hattie looked from one to the other. *"People like you?"*

"Haven't you guessed?" Rebecca spoke in a low whisper meant only for the four of them. "We're Jews."

"Jews can't leave Germany?"

"Oh, we can leave." Abraham's tone was full of bitterness. "In fact, the Nazis want us gone. Their policies are clear. No," he said, shaking his head, "leaving isn't the problem. The problem is where would we go?"

"Any number of places, I would think," Hattie said, while Vera added, "England, perhaps?"

"Not without a visa, and good luck getting one of those from your government." Hattie heard the tremble in Abraham's voice, just barely noticeable, but there. "Not without proof of a job and a place to live. Money also, always that, as evidence we won't become a burden to the system. Once we secure those small things, sure. We can relocate to England."

That couldn't be right. No, Hattie wouldn't believe it. Surely, the British government was sympathetic to Jewish refugees, especially German Jews seeking asylum.

The thought had barely formed when she heard a series of purposeful footsteps approaching their seats from the front of the train. In the next instant, a porter appeared. Skeleton-thin, with a large Adam's apple and ruddy skin, he looked from Hattie to Vera, then reached out his hand. "Your tickets and passports, please."

The request was spoken in heavy German. More proficient with the language than Hattie, Vera presented her documents first, Hattie a few seconds behind her.

Seeming to study the documents longer than necessary, he asked without looking up, "What is the purpose of your trip?"

Vera answered for them both. "We're on holiday."

"Your final destination?"

"Salzburg," Hattie blurted out. "For the music festival."

"Very good." He handed them back their documents.

The Boscowitz siblings were up next. Sitting closest to the aisle, Abraham was required to show his documents first. The young man hesitated for a split second, just one, which proved a disastrous mistake. The porter narrowed his eyes.

As if seeing something Hattie could not, he gripped the young man's arm and yanked him to his feet. *"Du kommst jetzt mit mir."*

Hattie understood enough German to make out the porter's meaning. *You're coming with me now.*

Years seemed to fall from Abraham's face. "Wh-wh-why? What have I done?"

The porter spewed a stream of angry German too fast for Hattie to interpret properly. She caught some of the words... *schmutziger Jude...übel riechen...*

She gasped at the slurs and shot a glance to Vera, who looked at her in return, her eyes very direct, her message perfectly clear. *Stay silent.*

An impossible request. If Hattie remained silent, wasn't she as bad as the porter? A man who seemed to have a problem with Abraham merely because he was a *Jude.* A Jew.

Then again, what would she say? And why wasn't anybody else stepping forward? She looked around the compartment. All heads were down, eyes cast on the floor or out the window. Meanwhile, the porter was still shouting at Abraham.

Something must be done.

That was the thought tearing through Hattie's mind, drawing her to the edge of her seat, her feet finding purchase, her knees straightening.

Vera took her arm and held her steady. "No, Hattie," she hissed. "Stay out of it."

Hattie tried to shrug off her sister's hand. She had just managed to free herself when Rebecca jumped to her feet. *"Lass ihn in Ruhe."* Leave him alone. *"Er hat nichts falsch gemacht."* He has done nothing wrong.

More angry German from the porter. More protests from Rebecca.

More passivity from the other travelers.

Hattie swallowed against the thickness in her throat and looked to Vera again. Her sister's transformation was remarkable. While Abraham took on the look of a scared youth, Vera seemed to have gained every one of his lost years. She looked older suddenly, her face lined and fatigued, more parent than older sister.

Something changed between them, and a distance that had not been there before filled the moment. They sat, saying nothing, as angry German mixed with a young woman's pleas and the aching, terrible sobs of a young man who'd lost his dignity inside his fear.

"Vera, please," Hattie whispered in harsh undertones. "We must do something."

"No, we mustn't."

They hesitated too long. The porter dragged away the siblings. Hattie watched them go with something like revulsion. Vera, wiping quickly at her eyes, turned her gaze away. A moment of indecision seemed to pass over her.

Hattie seized on it. "We may still intervene."

"Intervene?" Vera snapped out the word. "You would have us arrested, too?"

"No. I…that is, I think—" She swallowed. "We're British."

"That makes us foreigners," Vera reminded her. "On temporary holiday, traveling third class. We have no power, no connections, no money."

Vera was right. She hated it, but she was right.

"You've read the newspapers, Hattie. You understand what's happening in this country. This is not our fight. You must leave it alone."

Hattie turned her head to look out the window. Under the black, moonless sky, with rain cutting tiny rivers down the glass and blurring the view, Germany appeared gray and bleak, as gray and bleak as her own heart. If this wasn't their fight, whose was it? The other passengers had been equally silent. It had all happened so fast. A single hesitation, an angry porter with hate in his heart, and two lovely people were gone. Taken away to who knew where.

"Hattie, please. I know you're upset. But let us try to put this unpleasantness behind us and enjoy our holiday."

Taken aback, Hattie looked at her sister. Unspoken words hung between them, black and heavy like the scenery passing by outside the window. Something new had crept into her relationship with Vera. She'd always known Vera to be a timid sort, or at least shier than most, but this insistence they remain passive in the face of gross injustice, when everything in Hattie cried out to act—it was shocking. Disappointing. Unexpected. And…

Wise. Something their father would support.

Hot, helpless tears slipped from her eyes. Hattie had never missed her mother more than in this moment. She swiveled and looked at her own watery reflection in the window. A sunken version of herself stared back. "If only it would stop raining."

"It will," Vera said softly, apologetically. "When we arrive in Salzburg, I promise we will be met with clear, blue skies."

"I'm sure you're right." Hattie closed her eyes. Her mind was with Abraham and Rebecca and what terrible fate awaited them when the train stopped in Munich. Deep in her soul, she knew she'd failed them.

Next time she was confronted with gross injustice, she would not fail. She would not remain passive. She would not allow anyone to hold her back.

No. Next time, Hattie promised herself, she would take a stand.

Chapter Eleven

Elsa

August 1943. Salzburg, Austria.
Gestapo Headquarters.

Every one of Elsa's prayers went unanswered. Death did not come. Pain and fear were her only companions, and the desperate need to know the name of her betrayer. Whenever she asked herself that question, the only face that came to her mind belonged to her husband.

The burden of her regrets sat heavy on her chest. And yet, she could not regret marrying Wilhelm. She had loved him once. Part of her still did. Why would death not arrive and release her from this misery and fatigue? The shackles at her wrists carved bloody lines into her flesh. She would not cry out. She gathered her strength and made herself hold *Kriminaldirektor* Vogt's stare.

A fruitless endeavor. The bill of his hat concealed his face.

All but the curve of his weak chin invisible to her. Suddenly, in a jarring move, his hand reached up. A beat later the hat rested beside the file, wrong side up. Elsa stared at the wretched thing, her mind unable to focus, even as her thoughts filled with the ridiculous image of an upended turtle.

She caught Vogt's eye and knew she ought to turn her head, so he didn't see her smiling.

"You smile now, *Frau* Hoffmann, as if this is some sort of game." Vogt slapped his open palms on the table and rose slightly, leaning forward so their noses nearly touched. "You will *not* be smiling once I am through with you."

No idle threat. Elsa saw the truth of his words in his reptilian eyes.

Dread unfurled in her heart and down her limbs. The numbness that had crept in from sitting in one position for hours shouted at her to shift in her seat.

She remained perfectly still. A small defiance that brought no reward, not even to her pride. She felt as if she were perched on a ledge, crawling on hands and knees, leaning over the craggy edge, welcoming the plunge.

Vogt flipped open the file.

Elsa snapped to attention.

The interrogation began without prelude, without pleasantries. Setting a pair of spectacles on the bridge of his nose, Vogt leveled a gaze. "Elsa Mayer-Braun, also known as Elsa Hoffmann, wife of *Herr* Wilhelm Hoffmann, and…" He rummaged through the stuffed dossier, as if searching for a specific page. "Elsie Marie Westaway. These are your names and aliases?"

Elsa tried to respond, but her words came out as a muffled sob. The Gestapo knew her birth name, the one she'd changed before taking her first role on stage.

"Lord Robert Westaway was your father, is this correct?"

She didn't answer, didn't move, didn't lift her eyes to meet his.

He continued to turn pages. "Your father was..." more page-turning "...British. An earl stripped of his title. Disowned by his family for marrying Katarina Wittenmyer, daughter of Baron Ernst Wittenmyer and Sarah Kremer-Lehman, a full-blooded Jew."

Elsa wanted to defend her father, her mother, herself, knowing the effort would be pointless. Men such as Vogt were not interested in the truth. They were no better than thieves, stealing hope and distorting facts to fit their narrative.

Monsters, all of them, this one among the worst. Elsa could hardly breathe under the weight of Vogt's evil nature. The air had a different quality with him in the room.

He continued peppering her with questions at a machine-gun pace.

Blinking, she crossed and uncrossed her legs, trying to look at Vogt without actually looking at him. He was a small, ugly little man with a hooked nose, pallid, unhealthy skin, and tiny eyes that darted over her face, her hair, up and down the costume she still wore. Donna Anna's nightclothes were meant for the stage, not interrogation. Made from layers of creamy white lace overlaid with more layers of lace, the garment was a frothy, angelic ensemble with strategic rips at the shoulder and waist, meant to suggest a betrayed innocence.

When Vogt's eyes dropped to the low neckline, Elsa had a sudden, terrible urge to slap that smug look off his face. He stood up without warning, moving so fast his chair went careening onto the cement floor in an earsplitting clatter. "You will stay here."

She almost laughed out loud. Where did he think she would go?

The light snapped off, and the world went black. Elsa let out a cry, slumping forward in her chair. Alone in the dark, her pulse raced faster, faster, then slower. Slower. Fast, slow. Fast, slow. Her thoughts blurred. Her mind lost track of time.

Her head lulled.

The walls seemed to close in around her, almost lovingly, like her own mother's arms when she'd fallen and hurt her knee. Seduced by the comforting sensation, so real in her mind, Elsa shut her eyes. Lowered her head. *Bang.* Her nose connected hard with the table. The tinny taste of blood washed down the back of her throat.

What did it matter? Sleep took her.

She dreamed of Don Giovanni. His face belonged to her husband. Wilhelm reached out and beckoned her to him. A silent call. Sweet. Alluring. Their hands touched. She felt a moment of peace, of rest.

The light snapped on.

She sat up with a jerk, blinking away the flashes of light swimming in her blurred vision. Her gaze cleared, and she was looking into a hard expression. Not Wilhelm's, someone else's. "Who are you?"

"You know who I am."

She didn't.

"I am *Kriminaldirektor* Vogt, the man who arrested you."

She blinked, remembered, then fought to forget.

"Do you know why you are here, *Frau* Hoffmann?"

I am here to die. The words rattled in her head. *Please, Lord. Call me home. Let me die.*

As if sensing her resolve slipping, Vogt changed tactics. "You can save yourself, *Frau* Hoffmann. All I require is your full cooperation."

She said nothing, except the one question she couldn't help. "Has my husband been informed of my arrest?"

There was a long pause, but no answer was given.

Vogt continued his interrogation. He never once touched

her or applied physical violence, nothing so obvious. He asked the same nonsensical questions. What is your name? Who was your mother? When did she die?

Question after question after question. And then, suddenly, Vogt was back on his feet, the chair clanging to the floor again. Her ears ringing.

The lights went out, plunging Elsa into darkness once again.

She sat unmoving, not knowing how long, breathing in the scent of her own blood, her own indignity. That, she thought, was the cruelest of Vogt's brutality, forcing her to relieve herself where she sat.

He returned in another blast of light.

She stared at him through the hazy curtain of her fatigue, gray on gray, shapes and colors smudged into a kaleidoscope of spins and pirouettes. Shadow and light, one and the same.

"How did you become acquainted with Henrietta Featherstone?"

Elsa answered without hesitation. "I don't know this woman."

"You are lying. At the time of your first meeting, she gave you this."

He pulled out the sketch of her as the Queen of the Night. How could he have possession of this? Wilhelm. He'd been there when Hattie gave her the drawing. He knew where Elsa kept it, knew how much the image meant to her.

Oh, Wilhelm, how could you?

The pain of his betrayal crawled through her limbs, curled in her lungs, stole her air. This would be how she died. Her body simply giving out.

"You find this amusing?"

She hadn't realized she was smiling.

"Again, I ask. How did you become acquainted with Henrietta Featherstone?"

There were advantages in not speaking. Elsa had learned

this in German drawing rooms. She'd developed an ear, listening to what was being said and what was not being said. Did Vogt know how much she could tell of the loyal Nazis who were not so loyal?

He asked her about Hattie again. And again. More questions about her mother, her father. Back to Hattie. They went through this pattern for hours, all night and into the next day. Elsa forgot where she was, her own name, why she was shackled, then remembered everything, only to forget it all again. Remember. Forget. Remember. Forget.

She thought she might be losing her mind.

This time, when Vogt jumped to his feet and made for the door, Elsa followed his departure with her eyes, peering hard at his retreating back, willing him never to return. The sound of a familiar voice had her leaning to the right, just a little—and there. Out in the hallway. A split second. That was all it took for her to meet the eyes of another prisoner.

In shackles, just like Elsa. But not like Elsa. The guilt that showed in the tortured expression sent her heart pounding against her ribs. To be so wrong about a person. And yet. Now, thinking back to the beginning, to today, to all the times in between, she realized the warning signs had been there all along.

She'd been too naive to see them.

Chapter Twelve

Hattie

September 1935. Salzburg, Austria.
Salzburg Festival.

Hattie startled awake at the feel of a light touch to her arm. "Huh? What?" She looked around, unable to comprehend her strange surroundings. A train. She was on a train, that much she remembered. "Where are we?"

"Munich."

"Munich?" she repeated, the word not fully registering in her sleep-soaked brain.

"We switch trains here." Vera's tone was softer even than her touch, her way of apologizing, Hattie supposed, and she felt her cheeks burn with annoyance.

"Hattie, did you hear me? It's time to disembark."

Reluctantly, she looked at her sister and received another shock. Vera's face seemed to have changed overnight. It was pale and stricken now, and Hattie swallowed back her irritation because she knew her sister was suffering.

The incident with Rebecca and Abraham had left them both reeling.

How could we have been so cowardly?

Vera seemed to share her shame. She closed her eyes and sighed heavily. That sound, that defeated, awful sound stirred something inside Hattie and made her feel deep, horrible, awful regret. Tears formed, threatening to spill. She didn't want to cry. She wanted to be strong.

How could she be strong? Nothing made sense anymore. Injustices were allowed to thrive in this country. They were not only allowed, they were put into law. And the rest of the world looked away. *Why?* Hattie wanted someone to explain it to her. Anyone. God, the universe itself.

Vera put a hand on Hattie's shoulder. "Let's go."

Somehow, Hattie managed to stand. She glanced out the window and saw that Germany was still the same drab gray as her mood. Gray sky. Gray platform. Gray depot. Gray figures moving at a speed two times slower than normal, as if they were wading through a waking nightmare. This was not a scene she wished to paint, ever.

"You go first." Vera stood in the aisle, patience personified, waiting for Hattie to take the lead. She grabbed her bag and hurried ahead of her sister.

Standing on the platform next to Vera, she stared, speechless, at another scene she wished never to paint. Blood-red Nazi flags were everywhere, whipping in the wind. Hattie's eyes went from one black swastika to the next. All she saw were a bunch of broken crosses and a once-godly nation in decay.

Worse than the flags were the soldiers themselves. They were everywhere, swarming the train platform, the depot. Their uniformed presence announced that Germany was a military state now. The rest of the passengers seemed to comprehend their new reality. Heads down, they hurried along, never making eye contact with the soldiers or each other.

Hattie could feel their desire to be left alone, to go unnoticed. She could feel their fear, and at once she understood Vera's desire to remain silent.

"I didn't understand," she said under her breath. "I thought I did. I thought I knew what was happening in Germany. But I didn't understand." She shook her head. "I do now."

"I wish it were not so, Hattie. I wish that every man, woman and child could have their very own happy ending. I wish that evil didn't exist. But it does."

Especially in Germany, Hattie thought, wondering where all the heroes were.

A sobering silence carried them to their next train and throughout the final leg of their journey. They arrived in Salzburg by midmorning, Hattie more determined than ever to find a way to fight the evil sweeping across Germany. She would do her part to fight injustice, someday.

In the meantime, she would attempt to enjoy her holiday.

As if to nudge her along, the weather broke in a spectacular, sudden wiping away of rain clouds and gloom. The bright, shining sun glittered over the entire city and the snow-capped mountains beyond. Mozart had been born here, and Hattie could all but see his characters milling about the narrow lanes and broad squares. Entire scenes from *Don Giovanni*, *The Magic Flute* and even *The Marriage of Figaro* came alive in her mind.

Her fingers itched to create.

She would start with charcoal—she'd packed her sketch pad—and save the more elaborate details for oils on canvas when she returned to England. Her melancholy lifted, nearly disappearing altogether when they arrived at the Hôtel de l'Europe with its manicured grounds, large statuary and land-scaped walkways.

Inside, the gilded decor was equally enthralling. So much gold, everywhere. Flower arrangements and potted plants sat atop tables or rested beside intricately patterned rugs. But the real stunner was the airy, delicate chandelier above their heads. The clear glass and crystal rosettes twisted around a metal frame in such a way as to give the illusion of a float-ing waterfall.

Vera spun in a circle. "I can't believe we are to enjoy such grandeur." She took another spin, giggling like a schoolgirl. "I'm so glad we splurged on this hotel."

"As am I." Everywhere she looked was a treat for the eye.

Best of all, a letter from Elsa awaited them at the front desk.

Hattie skimmed the contents, then passed the paper to Vera, who read the entirety aloud. *"My dear Featherstone sisters,"* she began. *"At last, the great moment of our reunion has arrived. I am pleased you plan to stay in my beloved city for an entire week. As promised, I have reserved tickets for you both, starting with tonight's performance of* Madama Butterfly. *I will think of my lovely British friends in the audience as I sing. Then, you will come backstage, and we will have ourselves a proper hello. Until tonight! Your friend, Elsa."*

Vera looked up. Hattie smiled. "What a lovely way to start our visit."

After an afternoon of exploring the city, they left for the theater dressed in their best evening gowns. Hattie wore a sleek blue creation that skimmed her curves and flared at the knees. Vera picked a floor-length gown in shimmering gold that had a modest neckline but dipped low at the back. The dress was quite daring. She looked lovely. Hattie said as much.

Vera's pace slowed. "Is that your way of saying you aren't angry with me anymore?"

Hattie shook her head. "I'm not, you know. Well, not anymore."

"Truly, Hattie? All is well between us?"

Not fully. A rift had been carved into their relationship, and she wasn't sure how to bridge the gap, or even if she could. "I understand why you encouraged me to remain silent on the train."

"Understanding is not the same as forgiveness."

No, it wasn't. "It's a start."

"You're dancing around the issue, and that's not like you."

There was a chip of ice in Vera's delivery, and Hattie found herself sighing. "We're sisters, Vera. You know I don't like us being at odds."

"And still, you keep me at a distance and avoid a direct answer to my question. Do you forgive me, Hattie? Yes or no? I need to hear you say the words."

Hattie wanted to sigh again, but two times was twice too many for one conversation. "Yes, Vera. I forgive you. Now, can we put this behind us and enjoy our evening?"

"I'd like that."

The temperature still a bit frosty between them, they navigated the crowded streets and entered the *Felsenreitschule* and almost immediately came across Malvina Kremer-Lehman strolling alone in the promenade. She wore an elegant, navy-blue gown with a fashionable fur stole wrapped over her shoulders.

In an uncharacteristic move, Vera boldly recalled herself to the older woman. "*Frau* Kremer-Lehman. Malvina. Here we are. Over here."

"Vera Featherstone? Why it is you, and Henrietta. Hattie. What a wonderful surprise. Elsa told me you would be in attendance tonight, but I never thought I would run into you like this."

Vera greeted the older woman with a kiss to each cheek, then went on to explain how they'd only just arrived in Salzburg that morning. "It's rather poetic, don't you think? That we have come all this way to hear your niece sing in the role that turned us into her devoted fans."

"I'm so glad."

They chatted a while longer, and then it was time to find their seats.

"We shall meet again," Malvina promised. "After the show."

Hattie watched the older woman head to her seat, thinking something had changed. She was as charming and pleasant as ever, but there had been a sadness in her subdued manner.

Elsa's singing reduced Hattie to tears.

As expected, Wilhelm Hoffmann conducted from a raised platform in the orchestra pit. Even though she'd witnessed him wield the baton once before, it was still a revelation watching him now. The economy of movement was like nothing she'd seen in other maestros, almost imperceptible at times, yet he managed to pull forth the best out of his musicians and singers.

There was clearly a reason for his fame, and for Elsa's sake, Hattie hoped her first impression of the man was wrong. There was a moment in the final aria when Elsa's eyes connected with Hoffmann's, and Hattie knew she was looking at a woman deeply in love.

If someone as kind and generous as Elsa Mayer-Braun found the man worthy of her affection, then Hattie would do her best to see him in a more favorable light.

When the opera came to its mournful conclusion, she knew she'd just witnessed a once-in-a-lifetime performance. She was still wiping her wet cheeks as she and Vera found their way backstage. A host of well-dressed patrons crowded the tiny area, but Elsa was nowhere to be found. "I wonder," Vera said on a sigh, "if we missed her altogether."

Just then, a door swept open, and the singer stepped across the threshold, trailed by a small entourage of well-dressed men and women. Hoffmann wasn't among them, but Malvina was beside her niece. Again, Hattie thought the older woman looked unusually small and fragile.

Elsa, however, glowed from within even in a simple, pale green dress that could have been purchased in any number of dress shops. Her face was scrubbed free of its heavy stage makeup. The bare skin only added to her fresh-faced beauty. "She looks so pretty and happy," Vera remarked.

Malvina said something to the singer, and then Elsa was looking their way. Her face brightened even more, and she hurried over to greet them. As if rehearsed, her entourage peeled away, one by one, all except Malvina, who kept pace with her niece.

A heartbeat later, Hattie found herself encircled in Elsa's arms. Then it was Vera's turn. Then they were smiling and laughing and talking over one another.

Beaming, Elsa took each of their hands. "I'm very much pleased to see you both."

"Thank you for the tickets," Hattie and Vera said in unison, and all three of them laughed again. Malvina merely smiled.

Elsa reached out to hook her arm through her aunt's. "You remember *Tante* Malvina."

"Our paths crossed earlier." Hattie smiled at the older woman. "Lovely to see you again."

"You as well. And you, Vera."

Her words unlocked Vera's jaw. "Professor—I mean… Malvina. I've been hoping to ask you about the history of *Madama Butterfly*, namely the circumstances that brought the American soldier to Japan in the first place."

They fell into a complicated discussion about the story's timeline and how it fit within historical events. At some point, they switched from English to German, and Hattie lost much of what they said. Elsa, however, appeared enthralled, and though she didn't join in the conversation, she listened intently.

Hattie took the opportunity to look around, noting the differences between this theater and the Royal Opera House. Perhaps she would draw a singer standing in the wings, about to take her place on stage. She had the entire image in her mind when suddenly she felt eyes on her. It was an odd sensation that had her sweeping her gaze in a wider arc.

Her breath stalled in her throat. Wilhelm Hoffmann stood in a spot against a far wall, his eyes narrowed ever so slightly. Now that he had her attention, he looked her up and down. Then, frowning, dismissed her in favor of conversing with the man beside him.

Hattie's fingers tightened on the program in her hand. She looked down at her feet, took a quick breath, lifted her head again. Now both men were looking in her direction.

No, not in *her* direction. Elsa's. Hattie was merely in the way. Except, when Hoffmann moved away, the other man continued staring at Hattie. She couldn't think why a well-dressed, handsome man in his early thirties would study her so intently, as if she were a math equation needing to be solved.

Well, two could play at that game.

Shadow and light played across his face, cutting sharp angles and deep planes across the handsome features. He had a dark, turbulent edge. Not sinister, exactly. More mysterious. She immediately wanted to draw him. He'd make an excellent villain with all that glossy light brown hair, aristocratic cheekbones and square, masculine jawline.

"You know, Hattie dear," Elsa leaned toward her, "I am feeling rather ignored."

Jolted by the reprimand, Hattie eyed the soprano, then let

out a sigh of relief as she realized Elsa wasn't referring to her. She was watching her aunt and Vera with a soft smile.

"It's as if," she continued, "you and I no longer exist."

Hattie took in the bent heads. "They do seem rather engrossed in their conversation. And I have failed to congratulate you on your marriage. Let me say it now. Congratulations, Elsa. I wish you many years of happiness with *Herr* Hoffmann."

"Thank you, my friend."

"Is married life everything you hoped for?"

Elsa gave a delighted laugh. "More. Wilhelm is a very attentive husband."

Her eyes had taken on a dreamy look that left Hattie fumbling for something to say. She blurted out the first thing that came to mind. "Oh. Well. Lovely." She took a breath. "Now that you are married, what should I call you?"

"You will continue calling me Elsa, and I shall continue calling you Hattie."

"Well, that was easy."

Elsa reached down and squeezed her hand. "Matters are always easy between friends."

They shared a smile that bridged time and distance and their short acquaintance.

"Shall we leave them to it?" Elsa hitched her chin toward Vera and Malvina.

It was Hattie's turn to laugh. "I doubt they will miss us."

Still holding her hand, Elsa asked, "How is your German?"

"I get by all right."

"Well, then, let me introduce you around. There is one person in particular I wish for you to meet." She tugged Hattie a few steps. "You will like him, I think. He is very handsome, and you have much in common."

"Him?" Hattie's voice cracked a little. Surely Elsa wasn't playing matchmaker.

"A fellow British citizen who happens to own art galleries. Ah, but first," Elsa said and pulled her deeper into the crowd, "here is my cast mate. Hattie, this is Frieda Klein. She sang the part of the American wife, Kate Pinkerton."

Hattie recognized the mezzo-soprano, mostly because she still wore her costume and heavy stage makeup. It was hard to tell her age under all the paint. She was older than Elsa, that much was obvious. By a few years or a decade, Hattie couldn't determine. "You were very good tonight, Miss Klein."

The mezzo-soprano accepted Hattie's compliment with a small nod and an even smaller smile. There was a sort of cold reserve in her manner that made Hattie, a woman who hated awkward pauses, scramble to say more. "I believed you, or rather, I believed that Kate Pinkerton considered Cio-Cio-San—Butterfly—her bitter rival. I especially loved the way you—"

Hattie broke off, realizing she'd lost the singer's attention. Then, without a single word of goodbye, Klein walked away, leaving shocked silence behind her.

Oh, my. Hattie had never been treated with such blatant hostility.

Trying not to cry, she turned to Elsa. "Did I…did I say something wrong? My German is rusty, I know…but I…" She trailed off, suddenly having to swallow the hard, painful lump that appeared in her throat.

"You said nothing wrong." Elsa's smile seemed forced, her eyes thoughtful, her face tight and awkward, as if she was trying to make sense of her cast mate's behavior. "It's just Frieda. She can be…abrupt."

That was one way of putting it.

"And now," Elsa shifted her gaze, sighing heavily, "Oliver is gone from his spot. No matter, we will track him down. Are you game for an adventure?"

With her heart still thumping hard and her cheeks still burning, Hattie didn't think she was up to meeting a handsome gallery owner. *But if not now, when?* "Why not?"

"Excellent."

Hattie followed Elsa, her own steps unusually slow and heavy. They never found the mysterious gallery owner, but Elsa introduced her to Ezio Pinza and Amelita Galli-Curci and many other great opera singers, plus a few musicians and devoted patrons.

Back in their hotel room, she and Vera deemed the night a grand success.

Hattie didn't mention rude opera singers or dismissive conductors or missed opportunities to meet gallery owners. Instead, she pulled out her sketch pad.

While Vera chattered away about Japanese history and how much she adored Malvina, Hattie drew Don Giovanni. She gave the opera lothario glossy light brown hair, aristocratic cheekbones and a square, masculine jaw.

Chapter Thirteen

Elsa

September 1935. Salzburg, Austria.
Home of Wilhelm and Elsa Hoffmann.

My plan will work. Those were the words that echoed in Elsa's head when she left her bedroom in search of her husband. *My plan will work*. It had to work. Malvina's safety, her future happiness, possibly even her life, were at stake.

My plan will work.

The details were nearly fully formed in her mind. Only a few items were left to consider, none of which Elsa had shared with Wilhelm. She wasn't sure why she kept her plan from her husband, only that some instinct warned this was something she had to do on her own.

The fewer people who knew where she sent Malvina, the better.

Wilhelm hadn't seemed to notice Elsa's secret plotting. He'd been preoccupied. As one of the main conductors of the festival, he had a terrible amount of responsibility with as many as four performances a day. Elsa hadn't wanted to add to his burdens.

That's what she told herself, anyway.

This morning, he'd risen early. He'd sat on the edge of their bed, kissed her on the forehead and told her to go back to sleep. "You had a restless night, all that tossing and turning and mumbling in your sleep. Another hour in bed will restore your strength."

Restore her strength? Elsa didn't feel frail or weak. She felt afraid. For Malvina. For Austria. For her and Wilhelm. Nevertheless, she'd obeyed her husband's request and had stayed under the covers. Not to rest but to think through her plan to ship Malvina off to England. Her aunt would be in good hands with the Featherstone sisters.

Assuming they agreed to Elsa's plan. Surely, they would agree.

Elsa could not, would not, watch Malvina become a shell of herself in a country heading down a similar path as in Germany. Too many Austrians failed to see Hitler as a threat.

Elsa was not so foolish.

Where was Wilhelm?

She wandered through the house by way of the outer rooms, never penetrating the grander spaces. She resisted the urge to call out for her husband. She'd heard him leave the house. She had not heard him return.

Emotions whirling, Elsa pulled her robe tighter around her waist. She craved a cup of coffee. Or a cup of tea. She could have neither. Caffeine compromised a singer's vocal cords, so she settled on hot water with a touch of lemon.

Cup and saucer in hand, she moved into her private sitting room off the kitchen. Morning light breached slits in the thin curtains, changing shadows into soft, warm colors. The room was her domain and had been redecorated solely for her comfort. Elsa ran her finger along the edges of a table, across the rim of a decorative bowl, and tried to find pleasure in her surroundings.

Her mind was too full of Malvina. What if Elsa put all the pieces in place and she couldn't get her aunt to leave Austria?

Perhaps she should bring Wilhelm into her confidence. No. He already considered Malvina a liability to Elsa's career. He'd insisted the older woman move into Elsa's former home instead of here with them. He'd blamed the need for the physical separation on a wish to be alone with his wife of only two months.

Elsa worried it was more than that. She worried Wilhelm had a shade of anti-Semitism in his heart. Needing to hear her aunt's voice, she picked up the telephone. Malvina answered on the third ring. "Good morning, *Tante* Malvina."

"Something's wrong."

"Nothing's wrong." Elsa clutched the phone tighter in her grip. "I just wanted to hear your voice."

"I'm coming over."

"No, please, that isn't necessary. I have to begin my morning vocal exercises." It wasn't a lie. She'd stayed in bed too long and should have started already.

"I'll help you with them."

"You know I like to do them alone."

Another pause. "If you are sure…"

"Very sure." They spoke a few minutes more, with her aunt doing most of the talking and all of it about those lovely Featherstone sisters. Elsa's knees buckled with relief as she returned the receiver to its cradle. As she dressed for the day, her mind stayed on her aunt. *My plan will work.*

How she would miss the older woman. Sending her away would hurt. She closed her eyes and saw the slim, serious girl she'd once been, a ghost of her former self, sitting at the piano, her aunt next to her, always there, always guiding her. Elsa let out a sob.

What would she do when Malvina was gone from her life? *You have Wilhelm.*

He was good to her. Good for her, handling her schedule, organizing her life. She sighed. Just once, Elsa would like him to ignore routine and timelines, as he'd done on the day after their wedding. They'd enjoyed breakfast on the terrace, then a walk along the river beneath the music of wind rustling through the trees.

Maybe when the festival was over. Perhaps then Wilhelm would relax and become the man she'd married. Or, maybe, there was time yet this morning for a stroll through the streets of Salzburg. If only he would return. She glanced at the door, willing him to appear.

The door remained firmly shut.

The clock told Elsa she was woefully behind schedule. What would a few more minutes matter? Giving in to temptation, she shot out her arms, spun in a circle and let dreams fill her head. Dreams of what life would be like once she and Wilhelm had a child.

They would dote on her—oh, let it be a girl—and Elsa would sit at the piano with her daughter showing her how to complete simple scales, up and down the octaves, slow at first, then quickly, expertly, as her mother and Malvina had done with her. She opened her eyes, banishing the images. No. She would not bring a child into this unsafe world, where uncertainty reigned.

She'd dawdled long enough.

Her voice was an instrument that required tuning, refining. Repetition was key. Posture crucial. She shook out her arms, let them hang loosely by her sides. Planted her feet. Unlocked her knees. Breathed. Easy, slow, deep, one inhalation at a time.

It was all wrong. She could hear her breath. The tension underneath.

She closed her eyes and leaned against her diaphragm. If she wanted her voice to reach the back of the theater and up to the top tier, it was imperative she use her belly to push out the notes. *Focus*, Elsa told herself.

Her fans deserved her best.

She thought of Hattie, then, and her sweet, shy sister, and breathed. Elsa didn't know Vera well, but she'd made a friend in Hattie. How far could she push that friendship?

Her mind was drifting. *Focus*.

She began again, this time becoming aware of where her voice resonated naturally throughout the range of notes within each octave. She breathed in, exhaled, moved on. She yawned, hummed, proceeded to lip trills, then pretended she was blowing bubbles under water. Deep breaths, she reminded herself. Lips soft. No pursing.

She rolled her *r*'s next. The open vowels followed, beginning with the *e* and moving through the other four. She played around with the order, then moved into a two-octave glide, keeping the volume soft. The sound of the door opening did not stop her. Nor did the purposeful footsteps that came next. Then, Wilhelm moved into sight.

Elsa felt the constriction in her throat, pushed past it, continued her scales.

Her husband watched her, eyes unreadable. He wore a black shirt over perfectly tailored charcoal pants, no jacket, no hat. Casual and elegant, approachable, just a normal man comfortable in his own skin, moving through his own home.

This was her favorite Wilhelm. Not the famous maestro, not the manager of her career, but a man, just a man. Still singing, she pressed her hand to her stomach and shifted to face him fully. So handsome, so sure of himself. And hers. All hers. The newness and wonder had not worn off. Elsa doubted it ever would. One day, they would make a child together. *Their* child. Equal parts her and him.

She continued up the octave, back down again.

This pleased Wilhelm. The smile he gave her was tender and intimate. She nearly stopped and would have, had he not wound his wrist in the air to indicate she continue.

Accustomed to following his direction, she navigated the octaves, eyes locked with his. They stood there, her singing, him watching and listening, and Elsa felt tears start in her eyes. Tears of joy, of resolve, of setting aside her doubts. She'd married Wilhelm for a reason. Her happiness, her future, her very life began and ended with him.

At last, he lifted his hand, gave it a flick, lowered it with a snap.

She went silent.

"Very good." He approached her, approval in his eyes. She was in his arms a second later, wrapped inside his solid embrace, her face upturned to receive his kiss.

Their lips met for a long, endless moment.

Pulling away first, Wilhelm placed a hand on her cheek. "Hello, darling."

Her stomach rolled over. "Hello." In moments such as these, she knew he loved her, with as much of himself as he was capable of giving another human being. "I missed you this morning."

His hold gentled, but she sensed a fierceness in him, and she thought to pull away. He tightened his hold. "I had an appointment."

"So early?"

He didn't answer, lifting his hand to her cheek instead, up to her hair, stroking gently in a paternal gesture she found annoying. She was not a child. "Your voice never ceases to amaze me, even as you curl your way up and down the scale."

Elsa tried not to flinch. His compliment was as patronizing as the brush of his palm. Scales were not meant to impress. They were not beautiful or lyrical. And she did not need this false praise. She was not his protégée.

She was his wife.

There was a reason for his empty words, though she wasn't sure she wanted to know it. "You flatter me."

"I speak truth."

"Thank you." She couldn't find any more words to add, and so she gave the same ones twice. "Thank you."

He kissed the top of her head, the gesture more parent than husband. She frowned. "Who did you meet this morning?"

"Alfred Frauenfeld."

Elsa's breath came in snatches. "You...you spent the morning with the leader of the Austrian Nazis? Why, Wilhelm? Why did you go see this man?"

"Erich Kleiber has resigned from the Berlin State Opera."

She knew this. She also knew why. It was Kleiber's way of protesting the Nazis' judgment that Alban Berg's opera, *Lulu*, was degenerate and thus banned from the stage.

At least someone in the opera world had taken a stand.

Elsa wished it had been her husband. Instead, Wilhelm was making friends. "I made my case, and *Herr* Frauenfeld has agreed to recommend me to replace Kleiber."

Wilhelm wanted to head the Berlin State Opera and, literally, work for the Nazi regime? "I don't understand. How can you want this job?"

"It would only be for a year and put me in the perfect position to move over to the Vienna Philharmonic. Think of it, Elsa. This would mean stability for us both. As my wife, you would be the lead soprano in every production I chose."

Elsa had to rein in her shock to speak. "But I don't want to live in Berlin."

"The decision is not yours to make."

Elsa stared at her husband, speechless. He looked into her—right into her—as if he knew what was in her heart and didn't care. They stayed like that for a long, long time, then he shot back his shoulders and asked, "Are you finished with your exercises?"

It took her a moment to process the question. "Nearly."

There was a hint of disapproval in his eyes. "Finish," he told her. "Then we will celebrate our good fortune with lunch at the Hotel Sacher."

Their good fortune? He meant his own. "I have plans with Malvina." It wasn't technically true, but Elsa desperately needed to see her aunt, needed to find a way to understand her husband, a man she thought she knew.

"Cancel them."

Elsa saw it again. That hint of disapproval. The same shift in his eyes whenever she mentioned Malvina. Suddenly, the job in Berlin became secondary to a larger concern. "You don't like her." As soon as she spoke the words, Elsa knew them to be true. "What is it about Malvina that always puts a scowl on your face?"

"You ask the wrong question."

"What question should I ask, if not that?"

He widened his stance, clasped his hands behind his back. "It's dangerous to stay in close contact with a woman such as your aunt now that the Nuremberg Laws have been passed."

"Those laws apply only in Germany," she reminded him.

"Hitler will soon annex Austria. He has been very clear on this point, and when he does, we will become German citizens, bound by German laws."

Understanding dawned, and with it came bone-deep sorrow. "And this is how you justify applying for a position in Berlin?"

"We must be on the right side of history, Elsa. It is wise to consider the future."

How could aligning themselves with Nazis be wise? "What if you are wrong? What if Austria isn't absorbed into Germany?"

"Elsa." Wilhelm's voice softened. His manner followed. And then he stepped to her with the look of a man who cared deeply for her, his wife. She thought she might be sick. "Annexation will happen, and when it does, Malvina will be a danger to you, to us, to all that we've worked to build together."

The crack in Elsa's heart spread wider still. This man she'd married, how little she knew him. How little she wanted to know of him. "Malvina is my aunt. Have you forgotten this? We are family. I share her blood."

"Laws are being passed that will deem your blood sufficiently diluted."

She remembered he'd said something similar in London.

"The longer you keep Malvina close, the worse it will be for you."

How could such words come out of her husband's mouth? "What would you have me do?" A sob clogged in Elsa's throat. "Dump her out on the streets?"

"There are plenty of places we can send her."

We. The word did not fill her with hope, only a question. Was he worried about her, or himself?

"You mustn't worry yourself over this, Elsa. I will find the perfect solution to the problem of your aunt."

Elsa absorbed his words. Did this man, her husband, who claimed to love and admire her, think so little of her? Did he think she was some sort of empty-headed diva incapable of anything more complicated than hitting a high C?

Who was this controlling man who made deals with Nazis, who wanted to align himself, and *her*, with monsters? Wilhelm was supposed to be her husband, her defender and protector, but now, as she looked into his eyes, all she saw was a man who'd taken over her career, her future, her life. And she'd let him. She'd given him that all-consuming power without a fight, even laying the question of having a child in his hands.

Now, he offered to solve the *problem of her aunt*. It was too much. She needed to get out of this house, away from Wilhelm. Far, far away. She headed for the door.

"Where are you going?" he demanded.

She kept walking.

"Elsa." He came around to stand in front of her. "You will not leave this home until we've sorted this out."

"Get out of my way, Wilhelm."

He refused to budge. "I only want to protect you, you see that, *ja*? You understand."

"Oh, I understand."

"Then, tell me where you are going."

"To see Malvina."

"I'll come with you."

"No." She pushed around him.

"Elsa." He reached for her. She sidestepped him and headed to the door. "Elsa," he said again, more forcibly, with far less tolerance than before.

She kept walking.

"*Elsa*. You cannot walk away from this discussion."

Oh, but she could. And she did.

Even though tributaries of tears ran down her face and her heart had shattered into a million pieces, she opened the door, stepped across the threshold and kept walking.

Chapter Fourteen

Hattie

September 1935. Salzburg, Austria.
Salzburg Festival.

The Featherstone sisters' time in Salzburg flew by in a flurry of opera and musical concerts, often three in one day. Life became a series of late nights and early mornings that Hattie deemed worth every minute of missed sleep. She lived in a wonderland of exquisite music and endless inspiration, requiring her to purchase a second sketch pad.

On day five of their visit, Elsa performed in a matinee of *The Magic Flute*, followed by a private dinner party at her home. Much to Hattie's delight, she and Vera were at the top of the guest list. An honor she could have hardly fathomed four months ago.

Now, as she stood in the main salon, watching Hoffmann's solicitous behavior toward his wife, Hattie wondered at the tension. Had the couple argued? She hated seeing her friend unhappy. And, yes, Elsa was unhappy. Her husband was harder to read. The maestro appeared absolutely enthralled by his wife, but something seemed off in the performance.

And that was just it. Hoffmann was putting on a show. He leaned down several times and said something in Elsa's ear. She turned her face up to his, nodded and then smiled.

She, too, was acting.

As if sensing her watching them, Hoffmann looked over at Hattie. Something was there in his eyes, a ruthlessness, just a flash of it, but Hattie had to shove down a jolt of distress. She looked away and caught another man watching her. She knew that face. She'd sketched it a dozen times since the last time their eyes had met.

He gave her a brief nod.

Air tightened in her lungs, trapping her between breaths, and her hand instinctively flew to her throat. The quick, nervous touch of her fingers forced out two fast breaths. Then another. It wasn't until Vera's voice broke through the drumming in her head that Hattie was fully released from her frozen state.

"Malvina is motioning for me to join her." She touched Hattie's arm. "Do you mind if I have a brief chat with her? I should like to ask her about the difference between a tragedy and a comedy. I'm unclear on the finer points."

Hattie shook her head and said, almost absently, "Go on. I'll be all right on my own."

As Vera trotted off, Hattie briefly shut her eyes, battling a sudden, compelling need to sketch the stranger again. It was those tiger eyes and the sculpted features. No, it was him. Tawny and golden. Something about the way he held her gaze. It felt almost too intimate. She slowly became aware of people moving around her, laughing, congregating in tiny little groups, someone coming toward her. Elsa. With a genuine smile on her face, her first of the night.

"Hattie, darling, I have a rather important request to make."

Happy for the distraction, she widened her smile. "Whatever it is, ask and it's yours."

Elsa paused, turned thoughtful, spoke again. "Have tea with me tomorrow at your hotel."

Hattie blinked in surprise. Elsa Mayer-Braun wanted to take tea. With her. It felt a little like being invited to tea at Buckingham Palace, only better. "I would like that very much."

"Marvelous."

Now that that was settled, she said, "I have a question for you. Elsa, who's that man over there?"

"Man? What man?"

"The one standing by the piano." Hattie went to point him out, only to discover the stranger had disappeared. "Oh. He's gone."

"We have stumbled into a mystery. How intriguing."

Hattie looked around, spotted him again. "There he is. By the buffet table."

Elsa gave a delighted little laugh. "Well, well. How fortuitous. That is Sir Oliver Roundel, the gallery owner I mentioned the other night."

That name. It was familiar to her. But...how? "He's British?"

"Very."

Hattie would have guessed Austrian, or German, though now that she looked again, she could see he had the look of a British peer, the aristocratic features, the elegant suit, the polished shoes. She suddenly felt out of place in her homemade gown and jewels made of paste.

"I'd hoped he would accept my invitation." Elsa gave another happy little laugh. "And so he has. Let me introduce you."

Giving her no chance to protest, Elsa drew Hattie through the room, filling her in about the man as they went. "Oliver and his brother own art galleries all over Europe and one or two in America. I've only met the brother once, in London. Simon is his name. He has some other job. Oliver is the face of the business, I think. He does all the traveling."

Trying to keep up with Elsa's dissertation, Hattie dragged in a sharp pull of air, cast a quick glance in the man's direction, and then she was standing in front of him, and she could see the vivid color of his eyes and smell his pleasing scent. Leather, wood, spice.

Unfortunately, he was not alone. Hoffmann had joined him.

Elsa made the introductions, starting with her husband. "Wilhelm, you remember *Fräulein* Featherstone."

He inclined his head, his gaze no warmer than the last time they met. Unpleasant man, Hattie thought. Icy, frigid. A little scary.

"And this gentleman," Elsa said, steering Hattie slightly to her left, "is Sir Oliver Roundel." *Roundel. Roundel.* Again, Hattie thought she'd heard the name before. It circled around in her thoughts, a shadowy mist, a distant memory. "Oliver, it brings me great pleasure to present my very good friend, Henrietta Featherstone."

He smiled at Hattie, with none of the coldness Hoffmann had directed her way. "Miss Featherstone, a pleasure and, might I say, at last."

So, he *had* been staring at her. "I can't imagine why."

"Can't you?" He gave Elsa a quick glance. Something shifted in his eyes, as if he were trying to work out the final piece of a deceptively tricky problem. "I have been wanting to make your acquaintance ever since I saw your sketch of Elsa in *The Magic Flute*."

Her art. He was interested in her art. She should be flattered. She *was* flattered. And mildly confused. "You showed him the drawing?" she asked Elsa.

"Didn't I tell you? No matter." She gave Roundel a meaningful look. "Well, go on. Tell Hattie what you thought of the drawing."

He suppressed a grin. "I liked it. Very much."

"There. That is done." Elsa beamed like a proud mother. "Oh, Wilhelm, my dear, look. *Frau* Warwick is regaling *Herr* Krauss with her opinions again. I believe he is in need of our rescue."

Hoffmann had no time to respond before Elsa swept him away.

Alone with Oliver Roundel—*Sir* Oliver Roundel—Hattie attempted to continue their conversation with what she hoped was a level of sophistication. There was one problem. She couldn't think of a thing to say. He stood too tall, too proud, too much like a member of the British aristocracy, and she was… Well, she was a lowly civil servant.

There was her opening. "You are wondering how a woman of Elsa Mayer-Braun's status and reputation could become friendly with a mere copying typist."

"Actually," he said, amusement dancing in his eyes, "I was thinking how much you favor the beautiful soprano."

Heat rose to Hattie's cheeks, her mind hooking on one word. *Beautiful.* Beautiful? He thought she was as beautiful as Elsa?

"I've embarrassed you."

"Not at all." Except that yes, he had. "I…" *Think, Hattie. Think of something witty to say.* "You own art galleries. Of course, you do. Elsa said so. In Europe and America, I believe?"

He gave her that smile again, the one that held the impression of secrets and mysteries, and Hattie thought her heart might break a rib if it kept pounding so hard. "My brother and I own seven galleries in Europe and two in America. New York, to be precise, both on the Upper East Side."

"So many?" She took another assessment of the handsome face, the perfectly cut tuxedo, the tiger eyes that appeared too predatory to belong in the art world. Sir Oliver Roundel didn't look like an art dealer, or an opera enthusiast, despite his expensive clothing and sophisticated manner. The man was too, well, masculine.

Then again, what did Hattie know about men or art dealers or men who were art dealers? "Are you at the high end of the market?"

It would stand to reason a peer of the realm would cater to his fellow elite.

"My little shops are not auction houses, if that is what you're asking."

It wasn't, not really.

"I sell works by the masters, when a special piece comes along. But mostly, I am in the business of connecting talented artists with interested buyers. Think of me as a broker." He gave her a wry smile. "Do you frequent art galleries, Miss Featherstone?"

"Of course. Well," she amended, "admittedly, more so when I was attending art school. Students are required to frequent as many galleries as possible. It's a must if we are to learn our craft."

"And where, Miss Featherstone, did you attend school?"

"The Royal College of Art."

His eyebrows lifted. "And were you a good pupil?"

"I was. Absolutely. One of the best in my class." Look at her, embellishing the truth beyond all recognition. She snapped her mouth shut, the disastrous critiques from her professor coming to mind. *Derivative. Uninspired. Lacking imagination.* Even now, the words still had the power to hurt. "Enough about me. I believe you were telling me about your galleries and why you have so many in Europe."

"Was I?"

It was Hattie's turn to lift her eyebrows. "I would think it's difficult to conduct business on the Continent, what with the volatile political climate such as it is."

There was a long silence, and Roundel's eyes narrowed slightly over her face, as if taking her measure, but then, his expression cleared. "People still crave beauty during volatile times. Perhaps even more."

He spoke very softly, and for a moment Hattie didn't understand his quiet tone, then she realized he was being careful with his words, here, where surely there were a few Germans milling about, possibly some who sympathized with the Nazis.

She bit her lip, wishing she had never brought up the subject. With a kind of desperation rising in her throat, she scrambled to cover her mistake. "I assume expanding into so many cities a worthy endeavor." And that wasn't what she'd meant to say at all. "That is, you must meet all kinds of interesting people. Some, I would think, very powerful and connected and..."

She let her words trail off because that wasn't what she'd meant to say, either. Perhaps she should just stop talking. *Yes, Hattie, excellent plan. Brilliant.*

Roundel didn't speak right away, and for a minute she thought he would simply leave. But then he swallowed and smiled—really smiled—and there was a sort of satisfaction in his eyes that hadn't been there before. Hattie felt as if she'd been given a test and had somehow, astonishingly, passed. "Men such as me, with businesses that have international appeal, expand beyond the shores of England for all sorts of reasons."

"Even in times such as these?"

"*Especially* then."

Hattie found herself staring again, trying to decipher the meaning behind his words, sensing he was saying one thing and meaning another. "All right, then. I shall ask. Why are *you* in the business of owning galleries?"

"I enjoy art. And..." he took a sip of the sparkling liquid in his glass and stared at her meaningfully "...I also enjoy finding new talent."

Hattie couldn't help but feel anticipation building inside her. The sensation began in her toes, moved to her stomach, paused, then alighted into a million little pings of awareness along her spine. "Have you discovered any new talent lately?"

"I believe I have. A very gifted young artist with a love of opera."

Her. He was referring to her.

"Aren't you going to ask me the name of the artist?"

How could she? When she felt as if she'd wandered into someone else's big moment?

"Miss Featherstone, may I be blunt?"

She nodded.

"I would like to see more of your art."

Her throat cinched on a breath. This man, this gallery owner, wanted to see more of her work. It was her experience with Mr. Toye all over again, only grander, better.

"Would you be amenable?"

Her palms grew clammy, and her fingers found the edge of her wrap to begin tugging at a stray thread. "I would, yes."

How she managed those three words she would never remember. "Yes," she said again. "Yes, yes, yes."

He chuckled. "One *yes* will do."

She tried to laugh with him. The sound came out tortured.

"Shall we say next week? When we are both back in London. Wednesday, at noon. Is that time and day acceptable?"

She nodded, coming up with the most expedient set of directions in her head that would take her from the secretarial pool to...where, *exactly*, was his art gallery in London? Had he told her? Had she asked? She couldn't quite place it in her mind.

"I will come to you, of course. All I need is the address of your studio."

He'd just made the mistake Mr. Toye had. She considered how she might correct him, but his eyes were probing her face, and she felt sure he sensed her embarrassment.

"I see I've tripped into it but good. You don't have a studio, do you?"

She'd regained some of her dignity under the softness of his smile. "I don't, no."

"Ah. Give me the address where you keep your art. I will come round and have a look."

Did he realize he'd just invited himself to her home? Whatever would he think of the tiny flat she shared with Vera? An odd, furious sense of pride came over her. She might be from humble beginnings, with few possessions to speak of, but that did not make her unworthy of this chance to become more. She forced a small nod, shaking loose her hesitation, and opened her mouth to give him her address.

"Forgive me, Miss Featherstone. I'm pushing. It's a disastrous habit. My brother, a diplomat to his core, points it out all the time. When I see something that I want, I can be very single-minded and very rude."

Hattie took several steadying breaths. "Not *so* rude. Just—" another breath "—unexpected."

"A diplomatic answer. Simon would approve." The boyish smile he gave her made her head grow light. "Here." He dug into an inner pocket of his jacket. "Take my card."

With a shaky hand, she curled her fingers around the scrap of embossed card stock.

"At your earliest convenience, ring me at the number listed below my name, and we'll set up a time and place for me to view your work."

"All right."

Hattie's breath caught in her throat, and she became aware of Elsa standing beside her. The soprano had returned, without her husband. "You look very serious." She bounced her gaze from one to the other. "Have we come to an agreement? Are congratulations in order?"

"Not quite," Roundel spoke for them both. "Although, I'm confident we'll come to one soon. For now, I bid you lovely ladies farewell." With a smooth bow of his head, he stepped away, but not before he looked Hattie straight in the eye and said, "I will anticipate your call, Miss Featherstone. Do not let me down."

"I won't."

As she watched him disappear into the crowd, Hattie could hardly believe her good fortune. What were the odds that the owner of art galleries all over Europe—and two in America—would want to see more of her work beyond a hastily drawn charcoal sketch? The math made her head spin. "Thank you, Elsa. You did this."

"I merely made the introduction between two people, each in need of the other."

"It was more than that." So much more. "I'm in your debt. How will I ever repay you?"

"That is not necessary, except, perhaps…" She paused, turned thoughtful. "There is one thing you can do for me."

"Name it."

Elsa looked over at her aunt with a pain so real Hattie felt it in her own skin. She knew her friend's request had something to do with Malvina. She also knew she would do whatever Elsa asked of her. "Go on, Elsa. Make your request."

The other woman's stance changed. She glanced around the crowded room, her eyes darting between the patrons, singers and various musicians as they melted in and out of groups. What was she looking for, or who?

Eventually, her gaze landed on her husband, and she stiffened. "This is not the right place to ask. At tea. Tomorrow. That is when I will make my request."

They set the time for three o'clock the following afternoon.

Chapter Fifteen

Elsa

August 1943. Salzburg, Austria.
Gestapo Headquarters.

The war Vogt waged was subtle, vicious and effective. He came at random intervals, asked his endless questions, left, only to snap the light back on just as Elsa was beginning to fall asleep. Half in a dream, half out, she thought she might be going mad.

She couldn't take the rounds of questioning anymore. Over and over. Her back was on fire, and she was tired, so tired.

Treason.

The charge floated through the fog in her brain, and she shut her eyes, remembering the look on her betrayer's face. Remembering how it had started between them. The happy times. The bad days. The bitter reality of a relationship gone wrong.

This time, when Vogt returned, he set down a cup of water just within her reach. She wanted that water. Holding her gaze, he unbound her hands, secured them again in front of her. She was not so stupid as to refuse the offering. Ignoring the pinpricks of pain in her bruised wrists, she wiggled her numb fingers and reached out, cradled the cup between her palms. It took her three tries to secure her grip. Finally, she took a sip, then a gulp. Another. Too fast. Too fast. Her stomach rebelled.

Sitting back, Vogt watched her struggle to keep the contents of her stomach in place.

The man was a monster.

Elsa took another sip, slower this time. Vogt pulled off his spectacles, such a normal, everyday gesture. Yet, she felt pure rage as he went about cleaning the pieces of round glass at a slow, steady pace. Or perhaps it was the water roiling in her belly that was making her sick with fury. She set the tin cup on the table. Her hand shook so hard, water spilled out.

Vogt referred to a new page in the file. He lifted the paper for a better look, set it back down. "How are you acquainted with Henrietta Featherstone?"

Elsa looked over his head, focusing on a stain imprinted in the wall. Had he asked this question before? Had she answered? "She is a loyal patron of the opera."

"Liar." Vogt jumped to his feet and grabbed her by the hair. He yanked, hard.

Stars exploded in her vision, temporarily blinding her. It felt like her head was on fire. Her cry of pain was instinctual.

Vogt let her go. Face blank, he straightened one sleeve, the other, then sat back down. "Let's try this again. Henrietta Featherstone. How did you first meet the British operative?"

British operative? Hattie, a spy?

"What about Oliver Roundel? When did you first become involved with him?"

She said nothing.

"You choose to be difficult." He returned to the dossier, turning pages without any discernible pattern. The randomness tested her sanity. "What is your connection to Malvina Kremer-Lehman?"

In this, it would not do to lie. "She was my grandmother's sister."

"She is your aunt."

"Yes." Easily verified in the documents he had beneath his hand.

Vogt looked back at the file, a frown creasing his brow. "Are you in contact with your aunt still?"

"I have not seen her since 1935."

"Another lie. You met with her in London, in January of…" he referred to the page he'd pulled out "…1936."

She pondered the advantage of truth over more lies. It was evident he had information about her comings and goings long before the war. "Yes, that's right. It was 1936." But it had been February, not January, or was she remembering that wrong? "My head, it hurts. I need a moment to think."

She reached for the water cup.

He slapped it to the floor. "Did you travel with *Fräulein* Featherstone to Munich in 1939, for the Wagner festival?"

"Our countries were at war in 1939."

"The festival was held two months prior to the declaration of war."

"What do I know of politics?" The words sounded like a question in her head. They came out as an accusation.

Eyes narrowed, Vogt searched for and found a page in the file. "You began assisting German Jews seeking asylum in England in 1936."

He had his dates wrong. The first had been Malvina, in 1935. "No."

"Are you aware *Fräulein* Featherstone is a part of a secret cell of operatives who help Jews escape Germany?"

Of course she was aware. Elsa and Hattie were the organizers of the operation. "I am not aware of this secret cell you mention."

The lie came easily to her lips, even as her mind raced over the years, recalling the many times she and Hattie had met in safe houses in Germany and Austria, each one set up by Elsa herself. The interviews. The many refugees they'd helped. The ones they'd failed.

"You realize, *Frau* Hoffmann," Vogt said, directing the weight of his hard, merciless gaze on her, "collaboration with the enemy is a criminal offense punishable by death."

Silence was her only weapon.

"This will go better for you if you explain what you know about *Fräulein* Featherstone's movements in and out of Germany."

To do so would be to incriminate her friend and herself. "*Fräulein* Featherstone is a renowned artist of much acclaim throughout Europe. That is all I know."

"And yet," he said, consulting his dossier, "many of her showings corresponded with your performances in the same cities."

"Not true."

"All true." Without further checking the file, he rattled off the list of their meetings before the outbreak of war, and after in the neutral zones. He had times, dates, addresses, names of their accomplices.

But how? How could he know all this?

Elsa's betrayer. It was the only answer that made sense. She'd seen the features washed in guilt. Painful memories swarmed her. All the days and nights they'd spent together. So many happy times, and then not so many. Was Elsa the only one with these memories?

Was she the only one with regrets?

She attempted to cross her legs, tried to flex her toes. Failing at both tasks, she fumbled for composure. Nearly found it.

Then, Vogt leaned closer, his cigarette breath hot and rank as he lowered his voice to a harsh whisper. "The Führer knows how you use his favor."

Elsa swallowed against a hard, painful lump.

Vogt sat back. "Who are you working with in Germany?"

She said nothing.

"Give me their names."

She would not.

"You will betray them. If not here, then…" As he trailed off, Elsa knew she should turn away, pretend grave interest in the table, the floor, her feet, but she couldn't. She wouldn't. She must be strong. She must hold Vogt's stare until he said the words that would seal her doom.

"So be it." He pushed back his chair and stood. Taking up the folder, he headed for the door, paused, then glanced over his shoulder. "Your trial will be held in Berlin, two days from now. I suggest you prepare your defense. The judge is not a patient man."

He smiled at her then, a wide smile that revealed stained yellow teeth. Elsa watched him yank open the door, and again she caught sight of the other detainee in shackles.

She called out a name. The slow turning of a head, the meeting of eyes. Something there, Elsa thought, in that wide, terrified gaze: shame, but not an apology. No, not an apology. She said the name again, but the door was shut, and the room dark, and she was completely, utterly alone. Elsa let out a choked sob that left her gasping for air.

The weight of her own head was suddenly too heavy for

her neck to bear and plopped to the table with a hard, painful crack.

The trial in Berlin was only a formality, this much she knew. The judge and his council would deem her guilty. Would they shoot her, hang her or haul her away to one of their death camps? Whatever her fate, it would not happen until the Nazis made an example of her before their kangaroo court.

The Führer knows how you use his favor.

No, she would not die before one, final humiliation in Berlin before a packed crowd.

It was only when a tear ran down her nose and pooled onto the table that Elsa realized she was crying.

Chapter Sixteen

Hattie

September 1935. Salzburg, Austria.
Hôtel de l'Europe.

Hattie placed the final pin in her hat and stepped back from the mirror, scrutinizing her reflection with her critical artist's eye. Not completely awful, she decided. The glory of her outfit was the revers, the part of the garment reversed to display the lining of the lapels. It was a complicated feature, and Hattie had suffered several misfires in the construction process. She was unreasonably proud of the result and indulged herself with another, longer look in the mirror.

The same old Hattie stared back at her. She may have earned a tidy sum for her commission with the Royal Opera House and currently entertained the promise of something bigger, but she was still a humble civil servant at heart. She envied no one, and when something lovely caught her eye or she wished for a trip to, say, Salzburg, she economized.

Even if I become flush with the spoils of success, I will not change who I am.

For now, she would enjoy taking tea with a woman she admired greatly, who had a request to make of her. "Well?" she asked Vera, turning away from the mirror. "How do I look?"

"Very elegant and smart."

"Exactly what I was going for."

They entered the hotel's restaurant and discovered Elsa was already seated at a table with her aunt. The two looked completely at home in the elegant surroundings, an elaborate tea service set between them. As Hattie followed Vera through the restaurant, she noticed gold seemed to be the predominant color here, as was the case in the lobby. It was everywhere. In the chandeliers, the sconces, even the walls themselves. There was so much gilt it hurt her eyes to take it all in.

Elsa stood and greeted them with her usual kiss to each of their cheeks. "I'm so glad to see you." With a dramatic sweep of her arm, she directed them both to sit.

Hattie took the chair closest to Elsa, wondering at the strain she saw in her pretty features. It was not the look of a happy newlywed. A smudge of dark shadow had taken up residence under her eyes. What had Hoffmann done to her? That was the first thought that came to mind. Hattie hoped it was an overreaction on her part.

"Well, now," Elsa said, offering a smile as she took over the role of hostess. "How do you take your tea?"

"Cream, one sugar," they said in unison, earning them a delighted laugh.

Still smiling, Elsa poured the steaming liquid. She dropped a single cube of sugar into each cup and then added a thin stream of cream, lifting the small pitcher expertly high and then low before placing it back on the tabletop.

It wasn't long before Vera and Malvina fell into one of their academic discussions, this one about Mozart and his childhood antics. Hattie lost interest almost immediately and turned to Elsa. Her eyes were fixed on her aunt, and there was great love in her gaze. But also great concern. She was nearly shaking with it.

Hattie set her hand atop Elsa's. They shared a sad smile, then Hattie sat back. They discussed the weather—too hot—the various operas the Featherstone sisters had attended—brilliant, all of them—and their upcoming travel plans.

"We leave for London tomorrow." Hattie couldn't keep the forlorn note out of her voice.

Part of her never wanted to leave Salzburg. Part of her wanted to return home at once, to her simple life, and her art and the possibility of showing her work to a gallery owner in the business of making careers. For an instant, Hattie felt a rush of impatience, as if she'd been gone from all that was familiar for a hundred years. So much had happened. She was changed, by the music, the incident on the train, her friendship with Elsa. She wanted to tell the singer all of this. She simply didn't know where to start.

Talk turned to their childhoods, and Hattie discovered they shared a similar heartbreak. "How old were you when your mother died?"

Elsa sighed, and there was a painful, raw sadness in the sound that Hattie understood in the depths of her own soul. "I was seven. And you?"

"A bit older. I miss her every day."

"I feel the same. I learned my love of music from my mother." Elsa told Hattie about her memories of sitting at the piano, picking out tunes with her mother guiding her hands. "And you? When did you discover your fondness for art?"

Hattie's early childhood was a composite of impressions that included security, love and frequent visits to the Albert Memorial. "I remember staring up at Queen Victoria's beloved husband. My father identified the famous poets and architects surrounding the statue. My mother pointed out the painters and sculptors and then took me to museums to show off their art."

"What a wonderful collection of memories."

"It really is." Hattie had decided that if Prince Albert had found the pursuit of art noble and right, then so would she. "That began my love affair with art. And, I suppose, it was also the beginning of my quest for a purpose."

"Oh?"

She shrugged. "I always felt a strong sense of unfairness that Albert died young. It's not natural for someone to leave this world before he completes his good works."

"No," Elsa agreed. "Not natural, at all. I suppose we were both fortunate. Unlike your queen, neither of us were left completely alone. You had your sister. I had Malvina." She smiled fondly at her aunt, and her usual cheer was gone, replaced by something fiercer. A secret resolve.

"We are blessed in our family."

"Very. Your sister has found a friend in my aunt." Elsa took a deep breath. "Let's take a walk, shall we?"

"All right." Hattie followed Elsa through the terrace doors, out onto balcony, down the steps to the walkway along the river.

Their route was clogged with tourists and festivalgoers. Many recognized Elsa. They stopped her, asked for her autograph or if they could take a picture with her. The singer handled the attention with grace, but Hattie could feel her impatience. She suggested they head back to the hotel. "There is a secluded courtyard on the east side of the building where we can speak privately."

"Wonderful idea." Elsa allowed Hattie to direct her to a bench near a tall hedge. Once there, they sat side by side, their gazes locked on the river below the terrace, carefully speaking of nothing that truly mattered.

Again, Hattie could feel Elsa's agitation. Her face wore a series of unhappy emotions. Worry, fear, anger, all mixed into a slight furrowing of her brow. What had put that look on her friend's face? Her husband?

Something dark moved through Hattie.

She wanted to ask about Elsa's life with the temperamental maestro but wasn't sure she should. For all their friendliness, they didn't really know each other. Hattie tried to smile, to reassure the other woman that whatever had put that sorrow in her eyes, all would turn out well. But she didn't know if that was true, and she'd caught the change in Elsa now that they were alone. Exhaustion slumped her shoulders forward.

That she could remark on. "You seem tired, Elsa. It must be hard singing every night, sometimes twice in a day when there is a matinee scheduled. But, I think, it's a good life?"

"A very good life. I am happy with my choices." Her words didn't ring true.

Hattie shoved aside thoughts of her friend's husband and addressed the reason Elsa had asked her to tea. "You have something you wish to ask of me."

"It concerns my aunt."

A kind of sickness rose in her throat as something terrible struck her. "Is she ill?"

"No, no. Nothing like that. But the situation is dire, and I find myself in somewhat of a predicament because I…" She considered something in silence, something that dug the lines of worry deeper across her forehead. "I am not in a position to provide my aunt with a place to live. There are reasons."

Again, Hattie thought of Hoffmann. They'd barely interacted, and yet none of what she'd learned of the man was overly positive. She'd seen his possessiveness with Elsa and wondered what he thought of her closeness with her aunt. Was he jealous? "Go on."

Elsa looked over her shoulder, as if fearing someone was listening. "How much do you know about what is happening in Germany?"

Hattie's mind immediately went to the incident on the train. She thought of Abraham Boscowitz and his pitiful sobs, of his sister, Rebecca, and her pleas for mercy, of the porter and his terrible threats and expletives spat in angry German. As she relayed the memory to her friend, a sense of revulsion showed in Elsa's eyes, and Hattie felt the same loss. The same sorrow, and anger. So much anger. "I believe," she said carefully, "these are dangerous times for the German people."

"Yes. Although," Elsa said and shut her eyes then put her slim fingers to her face, pressing them against her forehead, "not all German people are in danger."

"Not all, no. Only people deemed unworthy, by both sentiment and now law," Hattie said softly, realizing she and Elsa had begun speaking in whispers. "People like Rebecca and Abraham Boscowitz."

"And Malvina."

Hattie gasped. "Malvina is, she is—"

"They took her job at the university, eliminating her ability to earn a living, to have a home." Elsa shifted in her seat. "That is what it means to be Jewish in Germany. Did you know this? Do they speak of these things in England?"

"Not enough," she admitted. "Appeasement is the official policy. Most Londoners are insulated. They don't speak of the troubles on the Continent. I'm afraid I was one of them. Until this trip." Until she'd witnessed the indignity firsthand. "What really upsets me, I mean, *really* upsets me, is that no one raised a fuss when the porter carted off the Boscowitz siblings. Not even me." She looked to Elsa, waiting for her condemnation, her judgment. "I wanted to intervene. Vera stopped me."

Elsa nodded. "Your sister understood the danger, perhaps better than you."

Hattie wasn't sure she agreed. Even now, knowing the danger, she wondered if she'd made the decision of a coward. "If good people don't stand against tyranny, who will?"

"It's a question I ask myself every day. If not us, who then will stand?"

Hattie sensed something bigger was happening here, something more than friendship: an alliance, a promise, a plan. "Go on, Elsa. Make your request. You have done so much for me. Let me return the favor. Ask anything of me."

"Is it truly that easy?"

Easy, simple, right. Good for good. Blessing for blessing. It was the only way Hattie knew how to live, the way her mother had taught her daughters how to live. And, she believed, the way Elsa herself lived. "A wise woman once said matters are always easy between friends."

Elsa's eyes filled with gratitude. "Oh, Hattie. I do adore you."

"And I you." She looked around, saw that they were still alone in the courtyard. "Now, about your request…"

The prompt earned her a sigh.

"Elsa?"

"Malvina is nearing her twilight years, but when I think of the young men and women, the children…the babies." She shook her head, losing herself in the injustice. "What life will they have if the Nazis have their way?"

"None worth living."

"No. But that is a conversation for another day." Elsa took Hattie's arm. "I am sending *Tante* Malvina to London. Money won't be an issue. I will see to that myself. Will you see her settled and that her paperwork stays up-to-date and keep me informed if the situation changes?"

"Consider it done, all of it."

Elsa nodded, let Hattie go. Her face was pale, but relieved. "How soon will Malvina arrive in London?"

"As soon as her papers are in order. There are travel arrangements to make, which I will do on my end, and lodging in London once she arrives."

"Which I will take care of on my end."

Elsa smiled, and something passed between them, an understanding, a promise. "I'd hoped you'd say that. But, Hattie, I must warn you. There is no telling how long she will be forced to stay in London."

"We'll figure it out as we go," Hattie said, her mind made up.

They agreed to share with each other any issues that arose. A quick hug, a promise to stay in close communication, and then they were heading back into the restaurant, Elsa's steps a little lighter. Hattie's a little heavier. Her friend was putting a lot of trust in her. When it was time to say goodbye, Elsa made a final request that included both Hattie and Vera. "Come and see my last performance in *The Magic Flute* tonight."

It was all very ordinary, this invitation, as if she were asking them to join her bridge club. Hattie knew Elsa was really offering them a chance to say goodbye before they parted for what could prove months, possibly much longer.

How far they'd come, Hattie thought, in so short a time, from devoted fans to friends and, now, allies.

After the performance, when Hattie and Vera were ready

to leave the theater, Elsa pulled Hattie into a fierce hug. "I shall remember your kindness, always."

"And I shall remember yours." Good for good, blessing for blessing. "Vera and I will show your aunt all the sights London has to offer. She will be very busy and have very little time to miss her beloved niece."

It wasn't true, but Hattie sensed Elsa appreciated her attempt at levity. "I am confident my aunt will be in good hands with you and your sister."

"I vow before you now, Elsa. Malvina will be safe in our care." Hattie was quite sincere and quite committed. And nothing would stop her from following through on her promise.

Chapter Seventeen

Elsa

November 1935. Salzburg, Austria.

Elsa flinched at the shrill sound of the train's whistle and wrapped her coat tighter around her waist. Neither she nor Malvina spoke. They simply stood on the platform outside the first-class carriage, facing each other. The brittle wind struck their faces, while hot steam poured out of the locomotive's underbelly and snaked around their ankles.

Melancholy and sorrow filled the air.

The other travelers moved past them with purposeful strides, hurrying, rushing and generally giving the moment an added sense of urgency. There was so much to say to the woman who was more mother than aunt.

The words would not come. The tears easily made an appearance.

No, Elsa would not let emotion win over logic.

It had to be done, this awful farewell. Keeping her aunt close would not keep her safe. Sending her to London would. It helped knowing she would be met by the Featherstone sisters at the train station. Elsa didn't know if she could part with Malvina any other way.

"You have everything you need?" she asked, straightening Malvina's collar, smoothing down the lapels of her jacket. "Your travel documents, money, jewelry?"

"I have everything."

"Your work permit, do you have that in a secure place?"

"I do."

"Good." Although the British government didn't ordinarily hand out visas to Jewish immigrants, Malvina was a distinguished scholar, and Elsa had been able to secure her aunt a research post at a London university through a network of contacts, starting with Oliver Roundel and ending with the gallery owner's brother. Simon Roundel worked in the British Foreign Office, doing who knew what. He'd talked about his job in the most general sense when she'd met him in London last year.

For his part, Oliver had been a fount of advice, and Elsa had followed his instructions down to the last detail. She'd purchased Malvina a first-class ticket on each leg of her aunt's trip to ensure easy entry into each country. Only travelers in third class were processed as foreign immigrants. Malvina's route would take her through Zurich, on to Paris, and from there, Brussels, ending finally in England. The journey would take three times longer than if Malvina traveled through Germany. But after hearing Hattie's story, Elsa wouldn't think of sending her aunt into what amounted to enemy territory.

"You will let me know when you've arrived in London?"

"Stop fussing, Elsa. This is not my first trip to England."

"I know. I know." Still, Elsa worried. How could she not?

The skin beneath Malvina's eyes was purpled with fatigue. Sorrow etched in the lines around her mouth.

Malvina patted her cheek. "This is not an easy goodbye for either of us, so let us keep it brief. Kiss each of my cheeks, Elsa, say *auf Wiedersehen* and know that I will return to Salzburg once rational minds prevail."

Elsa wasn't certain that would ever happen, certainly not soon. The Nazis were gaining power in Germany and, as Wilhelm had warned, would absorb Austria eventually. Now that they'd legally defined a Jew as anyone with three Jewish grandparents or someone with two Jewish grandparents who identified as a Jew, meaning they attended synagogue, it was best Malvina leave the Continent altogether.

At least Elsa was confident she'd chosen their allies well. Hattie and her sister, with their good hearts, and Oliver Roundel, with his close connection to the British government through his brother. Malvina's escape to a new life would be a success, and so Elsa's heart stopped beating too fast, and her breathing calmed, and with deep affection, she placed a tender kiss on each of her aunt's cheeks. "Take care, *Tante* Malvina."

"You do the same, *mein Schatz*." Malvina cupped Elsa's cheek. *"Auf Wiedersehen."*

"Auf Wiedersehen." Good-bye. *"Für jetzt."* For now.

As she watched her aunt board the train that would take her to Zurich, Elsa made a promise to herself. Someday, somehow, she would return to this train platform and welcome her aunt home to Salzburg. She prayed it was soon, for all their sakes. For the sake of others.

Agitated, feeling bereft, Elsa went straight to the theater. Matters were still cool between her and Wilhelm, but their marriage was young. He was making an effort to find common ground again, and so was she. Tonight's performance was their last in a seven-night run of Richard Wagner's *Tristan and Isolde*. Elsa would sing the lead, and Wilhelm would conduct.

In the meantime, he had a meeting with government officials, something about organizing a special concert for Austrian dignitaries visiting from Vienna. Elsa wasn't entirely sure which ones, or if she even cared. She simply wanted to lose herself in the music.

It was early yet, several hours ahead of tonight's performance. No matter. She would put the extra time toward warming up her vocal cords. Better than sitting at home, worrying about her aunt, or her marriage, or her husband and his determination to make questionable alliances. Elsa didn't like this new tension that had seeped into her marriage.

Perhaps, with Malvina gone, Wilhelm would feel less compelled to befriend Nazis, and they could find their way back to a more peaceful existence. A happier one, before politics had become a third member in their marriage.

Mind on her fragile relationship, Elsa entered the darkened auditorium with her head down and a fresh hole in her heart. Already she missed Malvina. She knew she'd done the right thing, sending her aunt away. She prayed that rational minds would prevail, but she feared it would take a war for the rest of the world to understand what was happening in Germany under Nazi rule.

Elsa did not wish for war. War meant loss and death and starvation and other unspeakable atrocities. At least Malvina would not be one of the casualties.

"What are *you* doing here?" The words came from deep within the shadows, spoken in a familiar voice laced with resentment. "Is this your doing? This shame I am forced to endure?"

Shame? What was Frieda talking about? "I'm sorry. I don't know what you mean."

"Don't you?"

Blinking rapidly, Elsa stared at the mezzo-soprano, willing her to provide information that would unravel the knot of confusion in her own head. But when the other woman continued frowning, with that bitter twist of her lips, Elsa's patience snapped, and she felt a shocking urge to slap the scowl off the woman's face. "No, Frieda, I don't know. Why don't you enlighten me?"

"Your husband demanded I come for extra training. He said my voice was flat last night."

Frieda *had* been flat, but she was wrong in thinking Elsa had mentioned this to Wilhelm, or he to her. He was the conductor, completely in charge. Elsa had no more say over what occurred on the stage—or off—than Frieda did. "I know nothing about this additional rehearsal."

It wasn't unusual for a conductor to expect perfection from his singers. Rehearsals were often called for this purpose. Why had Wilhelm failed to tell Elsa about this one? Had he lied?

Shocked at the implications, she looked around, searching for her husband. The area felt barren and cold. And there was something else, something chilling and unnerving vibrating from Frieda as she moved closer to Elsa. "He's not here, as well you know." Frieda spit out the words in an angry staccato. "And now I see why. *Herr* Hoffmann sent you in his place to further my humiliation."

"That's not why I'm here. But," she ventured, cautiously, not quite sure she should continue, but again: Frieda had been flat. "I don't mind running through our scenes together."

Frieda snorted, the sound crude and lacking any musicality. "As if you have anything to teach me. You are still a girl, a child, barely out of the schoolroom."

The woman's bitterness was so strong, so ugly. Elsa had hoped for more from someone she'd once called friend. "I'm not your enemy," she said, willing Frieda to hear her sincerity. "I'm your friend."

Owl-eyed, Frieda's expression turned blank, placid even, but fury radiated from her, shown in the way her hands balled into fists. "You are no friend of mine."

Her words were not gentle, but a slap, an assault. "What did I ever do to turn you against me?"

"You exist. That is enough."

Elsa fell back a step, opened her mouth, shut it. The taunt was unnecessarily cruel. Her heart cinched with a mixture of shame and fury. Fury at Frieda, but mostly at herself for allowing the hope that they could find a way to bridge their differences and return to the friends they'd once been. "I'm sorry. I..." she bowed her head "...I'm sorry."

"Sorry? You're *sorry*? That's not good enough. You think I don't know how you go behind my back and speak to the conductors and the composers about me? You think I don't comprehend how you undermine my chance at earning better roles?"

"It's true. Yes, I speak to many people about you. But I say only good things, Frieda. Only good. I try to get you parts."

With a loud hiss, Frieda pushed her. *"Lügnerin."* She pushed Elsa again. "Liar. Liar."

"It's the truth."

Frieda came at her again, hands up, fingers curled, as if she meant to scratch Elsa's face.

Elsa lifted her own hands to ward off the attack. "Stop this. Frieda." She grabbed the woman's wrists. Held on tight. "Listen to me. Stop. Take a breath. Please. You must try to calm yourself."

The other woman sneered. "I'm calm."

Now who is the liar? "I am not your enemy."

"You are the worst of all who wish me ill." She yanked

her hands free, poised for another attack. "You are the enemy within."

Elsa's pulse flailed wildly through her veins. She braced for Frieda to come at her again, feet flat and wide, hands up.

But Frieda surprised her and stayed back. Breathing hard, she asked, "Why, Elsa? Why do you persist in ruining my life?"

"I care about you. I do," she added when Frieda scoffed.

"Your arrogance is astounding."

"Wanting to help a friend is not arrogance."

"I don't want your help, Elsa. I don't want your friendship." Frieda's words were clipped, controlled and very, very angry. "I only want you to leave me alone."

"I only ever meant well. I still mean well."

"If that's true, if you really mean me no harm, then do as I ask and leave. Me. *Alone.*"

Frieda hated Elsa. It was there in her furious eyes. There would be no reasoning with her now, no changing her mind.

Elsa shouldn't be surprised. Wilhelm had warned her this would happen if she didn't stop interfering in Frieda's career. He'd been right. And she'd been wrong, terribly wrong. She shouldn't feel this devastating sense of defeat, this unconscionable hurt. She shouldn't feel as if she'd lost a dear friend.

But she did.

The worst part, the very worst part, was that she only had herself to blame.

Chapter Eighteen

Hattie

November 1935. London, England.
Home of Hattie and Vera Featherstone.

Hattie spent the first two weeks after returning from Salzburg consumed in her art and very little else. She'd lost her ability to focus and had suffered several reprimands from her supervisor. She did her best, but it was hard to care about typing educational documents when she'd had an entire week of exquisite music and private dinner parties at Elsa's house.

The images in her head wanted—needed—to be put on canvas. Every night, Hattie forced herself to eat dinner before losing herself in her work. At first, she'd kept to fictional scenes. But then, other images called to her, and she found herself painting those. Elsa standing in the wings of the *Felsenreitschule*, head down, poised in a moment of contemplation. The train station in Munich, the scene neither dark nor light, but gray on gray, except for the hideous, menacing Nazis flags, oversized and oppressive. Abraham's tragic face.

The trip to Salzburg had changed Hattie in ways she couldn't put into words. She explored her new feelings in her art, the good and the bad, the ugly and the beautiful. But whenever she felt the nudge to take her career to the next level, she hesitated contacting Oliver Roundel. She told herself she didn't have enough material to show him. Or reasoned, if he was really interested, he would find her as Mr. Toye had done.

A faulty argument, and one that skimmed the real source of her resistance to picking up the telephone. Hattie simply wasn't ready. Allowing the gallery owner to view her work would mean allowing him to see inside her soul, to the hidden parts she barely understood herself.

What if he dismissed her work and thus dismissed her along with her art?

Hattie couldn't bear that. She couldn't bear to hear the horrible words that would label her an impostor, a fraud, her art substandard—contemptible, clichéd, boring. Then again, he could find her work worthy. *You will never know if you don't ring him up.*

Vera cleared her throat. "Hattie, did you not hear me?"

She looked up from her uneaten food, wondering how long she'd been staring at the congealing meat. "I… No. I'm afraid I didn't."

"I have news."

Probably something to do with Malvina. Hattie had brought Vera into her confidence almost immediately. Their shared concern for the older woman had helped heal the rift that had not fully vanished, though neither spoke of it openly. In typical British fashion, they kept most of their conversations light unless, of course, they were speaking about Malvina and her situation.

Hattie had no idea how Elsa would secure a work permit for her aunt, but her friend hadn't seemed concerned about it, so Hattie wasn't concerned, either.

"Hattie!"

She set down her fork and knife. "I'm sorry, Vera. You were saying?"

"I was telling you about my news."

Hattie angled her head and gave Vera her full attention. "I'm listening."

Vera paused, chased her gaze around the room, nibbled on her lip. "I'm proud of you, Hattie, for chasing your dreams. You've inspired me, more than you can possibly know."

The words were tossed out nonchalantly, but they hit Hattie with a force of deep gratitude. "I couldn't have done it without you. Your support...it means everything to me."

This made her sister's mouth twitch, that perfect line of lips cracked briefly into a smile that she quickly pressed away, and the distance was back between them. "You're my sister," Vera said simply. "It's what sisters do."

"Well, yes, but it's more than that. You created a safe haven for me to create, both emotionally and physically. If I haven't said it before, I'll say it now. Thank you, Vera."

Her sister brushed off her gratitude with a wave of her hand.

"I mean it."

"Yes, yes, Hattie. I know. And you're welcome. Of course, you are. And I hope you will call that gallery owner very soon. But that's not why I have brought up the subject of your art."

"No?"

Vera looked at her for a long moment, a million thoughts moving swiftly behind her dark eyes. This was Vera's worried look. Hattie had learned to recognize it years ago. "As I already said, you've inspired me, and I've finally, after much consideration and prayer, taken your example to heart. I have quit my job at the Board of Education."

"What? No, Vera. Don't tease me." Words tumbled out of her mouth as soon as she could think them. "I... I have only been offered one commission, with no promise of another."

"You'll get another." She gave Hattie a meaningful look. "Once you make that call."

"And if I don't? Or if I do, and he hates my work? Then what? I don't make enough money to support us both while you pursue..." She paused, frowned. "What is your dream, Vera? You haven't told me, have you? How can I show support if I don't know what I'm supporting?"

"Well..." Vera stood and absently gathered up their plates, set them in the sink. "I have taken a position at Brooks and Baker Publishing. They own several magazines and a small but prestigious book imprint. The pay is slightly more than I make now. I will start at one of the women's magazines, with the promise of moving into the fiction department if I prove myself."

"It sounds like a perfect fit." Vera was very good with words. "But are you sure this is what you want?" It was a big step. She'd worked at the Board of Education for nearly five years. Taking this new position would mean giving up her hard-earned seniority.

"It's a risk, I know. But as Mother always said, we can't soar if we don't leave the comfort of the nest."

Hattie jumped to her feet and gave her sister a fierce hug. "Then, soar, baby bird, soar."

Vera was, indeed, put to work at a women's magazine mocking up advertisements. Hattie thought this the wrong position for her sister. Vera was far too academic for the likes of what amounted to cutting and pasting pictures to a grid.

Even Vera thought she'd made a mistake and came home

after the first day utterly defeated. "The situation is as bleak as the London weather in January," she'd complained. "Why did I leave my civil-service job?"

"It's only been one day, Vera. Give the job a week, and see if things don't improve some. After all, the pay is good, exceptionally good, and you're situated close to home." Which meant no additional cost to commute.

The next day, Vera came home no happier. "No one can pretend I'm good at my job. I make the silliest mistakes, and I can never seem to measure up illustrations where they belong."

"Give it one more week," Hattie suggested, not sure why she insisted on this, only knowing that Vera deserved a chance to find her calling as Hattie had found hers.

"Yes, all right. One more week."

After the extra week Vera's spirits seemed to improve. And then, everything changed. She came home from work, all but rushing through the door, sounding breathless, excited and very unlike herself. "I have had a stroke of real luck."

Hattie turned from her easel, eyebrows lifted.

"We've been running a series of articles—well, questionnaires, actually—asking our subscribers if they are the Best Friend type or the Little Sister type or the Woman He Wants to Take Home to Mother type, that sort of thing. Anyway." Vera took a fast breath. "We've been short-staffed lately, and Miss St. James, my boss, asked me, rather desperately, if I would write up a short vignette about each type of woman going on a first date."

"That sounds like…" Hattie couldn't think of a word.

"A really terrible idea? I agree. I mean, what do I know about dating?" What did either of them know? Hattie worked in a secretarial pool—all women—and Vera worked for a women's magazine, with mostly female coworkers. Not exactly a wellspring of opportunities to be asked out on a date.

And the sort of men they did know were as broke as they were or focused on their careers and uninterested in pursuing anything beyond a pint at the local pub.

"So I said, yes." Vera laughed. "I would do it. I thought this might be my last chance to save my job, and anyway, I mean, how hard could it be to write one tiny little article?"

"Very hard?" Hattie suggested. She couldn't think of any worse task thrust upon her. And she typed educational essays in triplicate all day long.

Vera laughed again. "Not even a little bit. Well, not after I decided to turn the article into a piece of fiction. I actually had fun with it."

Vera would. She was a voracious reader. She'd read all sorts of books from Beaumont and Fletcher to Dickens, Brontë and Austen. Even Balzac at far too young an age, and Dumas. But mostly she loved her romantic novels, and surely, that interest had given her some vital material for an article on dating.

"Miss St. James read the piece without comment, which was very disturbing, then she looked up and said, 'Let's send this to the fiction editor, shall we?' and, just like that, she picked up the phone. I heard her say to whoever was on the other end, 'I am sending you an article. Let me know how you like it' and off it went to Mr. Rupert on the fifth floor."

Grinning madly, Vera stopped talking.

"And...?" Hattie prompted.

"*And*...he liked it, and then... Oh, Hattie, and *then*, Miss St. James suggested I try writing a short story, something I have been doing for quite some time now."

Hattie had a moment of revelation. "Wait. Just wait a minute. Vera, is that what you've been doing all this time holed up in your room while I've been painting?"

Vera flushed. "Well, yes. You've been so engrossed in your art, and I was slightly bored at first, not sure what to do with those free hours at night. I started writing to fill the time and, really, to see if I could do it."

"Why didn't you tell me?"

"I wasn't sure I was any good."

"How could you not be any good?" Hattie asked, genuinely surprised. "You are the smartest, most talented woman I know."

"You have to say that. You're my sister."

"I have to say it because it's true."

They grinned at each other, their smiles carbon copies, the one trait they'd both inherited from their father. And just like that, the distance between them became a little smaller.

"Apparently, Miss St. James agrees. I took one of my stories to her this morning, about a young woman working in translations at a university, who meets a visiting professor, and, well," she said, blushing, "the plot wasn't very original, but she bought it on the spot. She paid me eight whole guineas and asked for more."

"Vera, this is wonderful news."

"She even suggested possibly trying my hand at a monthly serial." Vera bounced on her toes, and Hattie thought, *Who is this animated woman? What has happened to my very proper, very staid, rule-following big sister?* "If a serial is well received, it is often picked up and turned into a novel." A dreamy look filled her gaze. "Wouldn't that be something?"

"It would, indeed." Hattie hugged Vera. "You know what this means, don't you?"

"It means we can find a larger flat and, if nothing else comes around, move Malvina in with us temporarily."

Of course Vera would think of someone other than herself during a personal windfall. "Well, yes. That. What a wonderful idea." Brilliant, actually. "But also, Vera, you are now a published author. Father would be so proud of you. Nearly as proud as I am."

Vera beamed. "Would you look at us. Ordinary British girls, office workers, no different than a thousand others in this city, and yet, *we* are realizing our dreams. Can you believe it?"

It was Providence. And their own hard work. But also, Vera had been brave enough to try. Hattie would follow her sister's lead. She dug out Oliver Roundel's business card and made the call she'd been putting off for weeks.

He showed up on her doorstep two days later, on Sunday afternoon, looking sophisticated and completely out of place on the threadbare carpet beneath his feet. She opened her mouth. Nothing came out. She was glad her sister wasn't home to witness her embarrassing reaction to the man. Hattie had left church ahead of Vera, who'd stayed behind to speak with the vicar about Malvina's arrival, or more specifically about potential lodgings for the older woman.

"Good afternoon, Miss Featherstone."

"Hu… Hullo." A deep, spreading warmth moved from her lungs and clogged in her throat, and she was back to staring. It wasn't merely that the man was handsome or so obviously worldly or even that he held her future in his hands.

No, it was those clever eyes—she'd forgotten how penetrating his gaze could be—and that beautiful voice. When Sir Oliver spoke, his perfectly pitched baritone melted over her like thick syrup.

"May I come in?"

"Oh, yes. Please." She motioned him into the flat.

The door shut behind him with a soft click. Hattie felt his eyes on her and stepped very slowly away, remembering how Elsa always took her time crossing even the smallest of spaces.

At last, Hattie made it to her destination and paused before the row of paintings she'd set up in the sitting room. "These are the most recent of my paintings, each one inspired by my trip to Salzburg. Well, except for this one. It was the first. The others, I have organized by theme…" She was aware she was speaking too fast and then took a breath and started again. "There are more. Most of those were inspired by recordings… I have become quite a collector… One purchase turned into two…and another…and…"

Stop babbling, Hattie. Let your art speak for itself.

She swallowed back her nerves, then felt them rise again because Roundel was staring at her paintings, moving closer, fully absorbed, and Hattie could see the emotions passing across his face, the ones she'd felt as she'd put paint to canvas.

He moved closer still, his gaze riveted on a particular painting, her first attempt after meeting Malvina: Butterfly on her knees, reaching for her child in the distance.

Hattie was so consciously set to hear criticism she nearly apologized for wasting his time. It wasn't his expression that held her tongue, stunned and raw with a little flash of wonder, it was her own awe at seeing his reaction. She watched his astonishment turn to pleasure then to calculation, and Hattie knew her life had taken another dramatic turn.

Roundel blew out a long breath, just as she breathed in one of her own. She caught a hint of bergamot and amber: the scent would always remind her of this moment. Of him. The smell of success. That would be how she would describe the aroma to Vera later.

Closing her eyes, Hattie wrapped her arms around her middle, feeling the slow burning joy of her dreams coming true. Roundel said not a word, but Hattie felt as if everything were happening at once and to someone else.

He started speaking finally, very low, and she could just make out some of the words. *Remarkable. Exquisite. Better than I'd hoped. An easy go of it, praise God.*

Hattie forced down the nervous laughter bubbling in her throat.

At last, he turned to face her, and this time when he spoke, it was loud enough for her to hear her life transform. "We'll schedule the first of three exhibits here in London, after the holidays, possibly as early as January, but probably not. We'll move on to Berlin and Munich, respectively. Paris, next. Stockholm after that." He began to move between the paintings. Then, standing directly in front of Butterfly, he nodded decisively. "This is your star, your centerpiece. We'll show at least twenty additional paintings besides this one, and twice that in sketches."

He spoke decisively, with a clear voice. Hattie stumbled to an oversized chair and quickly sat down before her knees gave out.

He came to stand before her. *He's so handsome* was all she could think, his hair cast golden brown in the beam of light streaming in from the narrow window behind him. Tall and straight and tanned and worldly, the face of a fairy-tale prince offering far more than his kingdom. He was offering her a chance to have her own kingdom. "This is more than I can take in. I… I don't know what to say."

"Say that you want this as much as I do." He crouched in front of her so that she no longer had to crane her neck to look into his eyes. "Say that you will allow me the honor of launching your career. Say, Miss Featherstone, that you will give me exclusive rights to introduce your art to the world."

She held his gaze. He didn't move a muscle or make a sound but simply waited for her take a long breath and say, simply, "Yes."

After he left, and Vera arrived home, and Hattie prattled on and on about the meeting with Sir Oliver, she went to her room and penned a letter to Elsa. She started with Vera's news, then her own. But, after much debate with herself, she decided to hold off posting it until after Malvina arrived so that she could include that news as well. *We settled Malvina into a hotel room for now but have already begun plans for a more permanent situation*, she wrote.

With the vicar's assistance, Vera had located two possible flats, both considerably larger than the one they shared now. All that was left was to agree on which one they liked best, sign the lease and make the move to their new neighborhood.

There was also the matter of convincing Malvina to join them, which added up to too many unknowns. Hattie shared news only of what was already done. *I quit my job as a copying typist so I can prepare for my first exhibition. To celebrate, I spent the rest of the day with Malvina. We visited Buckingham Palace and Whitehall and Westminster Abbey.*

Malvina had asked if the abbey was Protestant or Catholic and had shared with them Elsa's upbringing and the promise that she'd made Elsa's mother. *Tomorrow, while I paint, Vera and your aunt will attend the local synagogue.* It had been Vera's idea after hearing the story of Malvina's personal sacrifice for her niece. *Then they will explore as many libraries as they can fit into a single afternoon.*

Hattie finished with a promise to keep Elsa informed about Malvina's living situation. She posted the letter on the twentieth day of November and went to work at her easel.

Her first showing was in less than three months.

Chapter Nineteen

Elsa

August 1943. Berlin, Germany.
Nazi Courts.

Vogt appeared in the doorway. Elsa barely had time to sit up before an armed guard yanked her to her feet. His grip was hard, unforgiving, as he dragged her out into the hallway. Vogt gave her one hard glare, then, without saying a word, led the way down the corridor.

Where was he taking her, and why was he in such a hurry? Elsa was forced to break into a trot to keep up. The guard, still gripping her arm, cared little for her discomfort. He half pulled, half dragged her in Vogt's wake. At one point, she stumbled, fell forward and was immediately wrenched to an upright position. The shackles dug into her wrists.

"Where are you taking me?"

She received no response.

They entered a room with a long table crowded with men in SS uniforms. The one in the middle wore a robe over a dark gray suit. The Salzburg prosecutor, Reinhold Becker. Elsa knew him as a patron of the opera and one of Wilhelm's closest friends. She thought him also a fan of hers. The look on his face told a different tale.

There were no questions. No chance for Elsa to speak in her defense. In a tone riddled with profound distaste, *Herr* Becker read the official indictment:

"On this seventeenth day of August 1943, Elsa Hoffmann, also known as Elsa Mayer-Braun or Elsie Marie Westaway, a Misch-linge *of the second degree, is indicted for the willful act of treason against the Third Reich. With malice and misjudgment, and with mutinous intent, she did herein so provide escort for thirty-seven Jews, seven Communists and eighteen political dissidents out of Germany. It is also known that she did knowingly and willingly work in tandem with the British government and conscientiously provided false paperwork and stolen property to the enemy. The* Volksgerichtshof *will conduct the trial in Berlin."*

Elsa was sent to Germany later that night and scheduled to go before the *Volksgerichtshof* on the day after her arrival. She knew enough about the *Sondergericht*, the special court established by Adolf Hitler in 1933 when he was still the Reich Chancellor, to know that there was no chance of a fair trial. The court had jurisdiction over a broad array of political offenses, as determined by the Nazi leadership, and thus operated outside the constitutional framework of the law.

Treason against the Third Reich was considered the worst of all possible offenses.

There would be no presumption of innocence for Elsa. Nor would she be allowed to represent herself adequately. Upon arrival in Berlin, when she asked if she could consult with counsel, she was told her attorney was not yet assigned by the courts and wouldn't be determined until an hour before her trial.

He arrived minutes before she was due in court.

A small man with nondescript features and a perpetual frown, his ears stuck out and his face was soft as doughy bread. He wore a suit of expensive gray wool and, as he stood before her, staring, he did not give his name. He did, however, chastise her with his eyes. "I am to serve as your defense attorney."

The announcement, swollen with judgment, gave her no peace.

"*Frau* Hoffmann," he said in that same condemning tone, "you have been accused of a most horrific crime. The crime of treason. You will answer for this offense. We will meet again in the Great Hall of the Berlin Chamber Court, where your case will be tried."

He left without another word.

So, Elsa was to stand before the imposing building without a single ally.

Matters could not get worse. But then, they did.

She was given no chance to make herself presentable, but rather forced to wear the same clothes from the night of her arrest. The layers of creamy white lace that made up the costume she'd worn in the first act of *Don Giovanni* had turned a grayish brown. The sleeves were in tatters, and the tear at her waist was now a gaping hole that revealed too much skin.

Another armed guard dragged her from her cell, down a long corridor and out into the bold sunshine so bright it nearly blinded her. She shut her eyes and shivered despite the August heat. The crowd outside the building was large and vocal, shouting slurs at her, all of them ugly and swollen with contempt. *Verräterin!* Traitor! The word followed her into the core of the angry mob, where she was met with elbows and shoves. Spit and vitriol. The guard did not protect her. He may have even thrown an elbow or two himself.

Verräterin!

More shouts pummeled her, more shoves, until at last she entered the Great Hall adorned with giant swastikas. This was no ordinary trial, Elsa realized, looking around at the hostile faces.

Fear consumed her, skittering up her throat and clogging it. Her feet refused to cooperate. When the guard saw she wasn't moving, he shoved her forward with his open palm. She barely felt the push, she was too busy looking around, calculating the number of spectators, at least three hundred, possibly more.

On her way to the prisoner's dock, she passed the table of attorneys. They looked through her, as if she weren't worthy of their notice. Three judges stood at the front of the room, each in matching glossy black mournful robes, white pleated jabots and plain velvet skullcaps. SS soldiers flanked their table strewn with random stacks of books and papers.

The judge in the middle shot out his hand. The men beside him also produced the same Nazi salute. *"Heil Hitler,"* they shouted, and the room exploded with corresponding cheers for their revered leader.

Elsa did not give her allegiance.

The presiding judge invited everyone to take a seat. He then read the charge against Elsa. Setting the paper aside, he called her forward for her so-called examination.

Another explosion of words erupted in the room, angry, accusatory. The judge did not request silence. He seemed to enjoy the chaos. She swung her gaze around, to the right, the left, catching the eye of a man, a woman, another woman, younger than the first, not much younger than Elsa had been when she'd begun her rescue missions.

The girl's milky white skin, cornflower-blue eyes and pale

blond hair marked her as an Aryan. The scowl she threw at Elsa told of Nazi indoctrination. An enemy, then. Like all the rest in this room. Here to watch Hitler's favorite opera singer's fall from grace.

Breaking eye contact, Elsa moved to stand before the men ready to pass judgment on her. On the wall behind them hung the Nazi flag. In front of that was a bronze bust of Hitler. The Führer's head was three times the size of a normal man's. A reminder of who was really in charge. The same man who'd cried over Elsa's rendition of Wagner's "Liebestod" from *Tristan and Isolde.*

There'd been a time when he merely wanted the Jews out of his country, exiled to England, America or, at one point, Madagascar. How was helping him meet that goal treason? That would be the question she would ask, a plain and honest defense.

She had not been brought forward to speak but to bear the judge's condemnation. He began with, "Why did you not give the Nazi salute?"

"My hands are bound."

"Your mouth is not."

She looked away.

Her knees began to shake, and she felt the terror of what was to come. A quick death. In what form? A rope? A firing squad?

Although there was a prosecutor in the room, the judge asked the questions. However, as was the case during *Kriminaldirektor* Vogt's interrogation, the questions were not questions. He berated Elsa for standing before him in shabby clothing and never gave her a chance to explain.

The insults and condemnations continued, spittle forming at the edge of his mouth. He heaped loud and violent abuse on her and her very existence. *"Du bist ein fauler Hund."* You are a foul dog. *"Ein dreckiger Judenliebhaber."* A dirty Jew-lover.

She opened her mouth. He cut her off.

How was this possible? This thing that was happening to her, this gross miscarriage of justice? "Elsa Hoffmann, are you a Jew?"

His silence indicated he expected a response. "I was raised in the Christian church."

"Do you carry Jewish blood in your veins?" He consulted the paper beneath his hand. "Are you a *Mischlinge* of the second degree, a woman with one Jewish grandparent?"

"Yes."

"The examination is concluded." He smiled smugly. "Return to the prisoner's dock."

Elsa was dragged back into place by the same guard who'd led her into the building.

The judge addressed her attorney next. "Do you have any statements or questions?"

The man—she still didn't know his name—merely shook his head.

"Do you have a statement, *Frau* Hoffmann?"

She opened her mouth, but the judge spoke over her. "I am prepared to render my verdict."

He wanted her to be afraid, to be terrified. And, dear God, she was. She felt sick, and the world spun at her feet. She'd been given no chance to give a defense.

She saw the verdict in the judge's eyes before he made his pronouncement. "I find the defendant guilty."

Applause filled the cavernous hall, so different from the sort she heard in an auditorium from her devoted fans. The judge waited for the roar to die down before announcing her sentence. "You will serve thirty-seven years of hard labor at the Bergen-Belsen concentration camp."

He continued speaking, but Elsa could no longer hear past the drumming in her ears. She'd been given a death sentence, after all. Not a quick one. Slow and painful. And Wilhelm would never know what happened to her. Or would he? Was he here? She tried to look, but her eyes were filled with tears.

Her husband had made her believe she could trust him. He'd made her believe every terrible alliance he made was to protect her. How wrong she'd been.

And still, she loved him.

She would not regret marrying him. He'd been a different man then. She'd been so sure of him, of them, especially when he'd looked into her eyes and made his promise to love and honor her, always. He'd said those vows before God and three hundred witnesses, as many as stood in this courtroom today, cheering her demise.

Somewhere along the way, her husband had turned against her, and Elsa would never know why. She would go to her grave with the question forever unasked and unanswered.

Chapter Twenty

Hattie

February 1936. London, England.
The Roundel-Liston Gallery.

As the day of her first exhibit approached, dozens of details demanded Hattie's attention, including the age-old problem of what to wear. "I cannot think about dresses and proper foot-wear," she told Vera, "when my stomach is swarming with spastic butterflies and my mind is full of all the things that could go wrong."

Most notably, the possibility that no one would show. Or, worse, that they did show and hated her work. Bad reviews. Utter failure. These were the things that plagued her mind.

"Leave your clothing situation to Malvina and me," Vera told her. "We will find the perfect dress for your debut into the art world."

Malvina lived with them now, though only temporarily. At

least she was safe and had become one of Vera's closest friends and confidantes.

The two women often stayed up late into the night brainstorming Vera's next story, or simply talking about life, politics, even religion. Their conversations were lively, but never heated. Hattie had grown used to the low buzz of their voices providing a soothing background hum while she painted. Which she did at a feverish pace. She would not let Oliver down.

Vera and Malvina happily scoured the finest shops in London in search of the perfect dress for Hattie. They succeeded beyond her wildest expectations, choosing a sleeveless, long column of midnight-blue silk with a high collar. The silver, strappy shoes matched the ridiculously small evening bag that held a tube of red lipstick and very little else.

Hattie knew she looked rather nice and was grateful for the mink stole Malvina loaned her to complete the look. The February evening air was cold and the streets icy beneath the afternoon's light dusting of snow. Oliver's gallery wasn't much warmer than outside but would eventually heat up as more people arrived.

One of them would be Elsa. She'd come to London to perform the starring role in *Tosca* at Albert Hall and, of course, reunite with her aunt. Hattie had insisted Oliver set the date for her first exhibit to correspond with her friend's visit. He'd considered her request for an entire minute, then smiled. "Brilliant idea. We'll promote the exhibit to the opera crowd and choose a night for the opening when Elsa won't be singing. She is, after all, a major part of your show."

He'd been referring to Hattie's showpiece from Puccini's *Madama Butterfly*. She'd told Oliver the painting's history, about Malvina's lecture and how hearing Elsa's voice had transformed her art. Having the diva at the exhibit would bring it all full circle.

Now, minutes away from the official opening, Hattie wandered through the gallery alone, looking, assessing. Worrying.

Smiling.

Worrying a bit more.

She wondered whether, if she kept to the shadows, she could go unnoticed by the milling staff. And Oliver. The man made her nervous.

Stepping into the main hall, she paused. Oliver and his staff had decorated the room minimally so as not to take away from the art. Fragrant white lilies shared space with other white flowers. Hattie couldn't recall their name, but she knew their pleasing scent from her childhood. It was as if her mother were standing beside her, and that settled her nerves. She could hear the faint strains of chamber music, instrumental, coming from…somewhere.

As Oliver had promised, *Cio-Cio-San*—Butterfly—was, indeed, the centerpiece of the exhibit. The painting hung alone on a wall that could be seen from every angle. Cast under a single beam of light, the effect perfectly showcased the burst of inspiration that was the foundation for the rest of Hattie's work. Oliver had suggested a simple wood frame, nothing too ornate, and that had been the right decision.

Everything about this night had been the right decision.

Hattie's mind wanted to wander to the man who'd brought her dream to life. The man she now thought of simply as *Oliver*. He'd insisted they dispense with formalities that first afternoon in her flat. Since that day, he'd been attentive, patient, respectful. And fully invested in her success. He was already making plans for her next showings in Austria, Germany, Sweden, France. Hattie understood her success meant his success.

A glance at her watch told her it was nearly seven.

Soon, Oliver would open the gallery to the public, or rather, the carefully chosen list of invited guests. From the start, he'd been very hands-on, coordinating every detail with his highly efficient staff. Although, no detail was decided until Hattie gave her final approval. By including her in the process, he'd made her feel as though he cared not only about her art, but about her.

And there he was, striding toward her. He looked almost feline, all that boneless grace and those lazy movements. She swallowed down the ripple of pleasure until it was nothing but a slight flutter in her throat.

He stopped beside her and skimmed his eyes over her in appreciation. His smile turned the flutter into a flash of nerves. "Magnificent. You belong in one of your paintings."

How smoothly he said the words. Heart hammering against her ribs, Hattie turned her head to study his attire. He was dressed in a tuxedo that fit him so perfectly it had surely been tailored specifically for his lean, masculine frame. "Hello, Oliver." She heard the squeak in her voice and tried not to cringe.

He must have heard it, too, because his eyes ran across her face. "You're nervous."

"Nervous?" She laughed a little. How wrong he was. "I'm absolutely terrified."

"Hattie, dear, beautiful, sweet, sweet girl." Oliver took her hand, shifting her around so they stood face-to-face. "You have nothing to worry about. Your talent is undeniable. Don't for one minute doubt yourself or me. I'm very wise about these matters."

"Maybe you just know what I need to hear."

"Maybe I'm right." He squeezed her hand gently. "This is your night, Hattie. Your moment to shine. Enjoy every minute."

She watched him watch her and felt that startling flutter in her throat again. "So much could go wrong."

"So much could go right."

The man had a silver tongue. "You are very good with your words."

She wasn't sure she liked that about him. Or maybe, she liked it too much. And his smile. It could charm the spots off a leopard. "I'm going to take that as a compliment."

"It was meant as one." But not really. Why did the man make her so feel so clumsy?

"Henrietta Featherstone, you are a very pretty liar." Laughing softly, he motioned to one of the staff. A single head bob in the man's direction, and the doors were unlocked. To Hattie, Oliver said, "Ready to become the darling of the international art world?"

"As ready as I'll ever be."

His smile went tender, just for her, and Hattie thought her heart might beat out of her chest. "That's the spirit."

Within minutes of opening the doors, patrons began streaming into the gallery. Mostly couples, a few loners. The latter were probably art critics, and Hattie felt her nerves rise again. Oliver roped his arm around her waist and bent down to whisper in her ear. "Tonight belongs to you." Bold words.

And yet, she couldn't relax among all these people whose opinions would inform the rest of her life. As the night progressed, her doubts vanished. It seemed everyone had only compliments to give. "I… I can hardly breathe," she said. "I must remember to breathe."

Oliver craned his head to study her. "You truly have no idea how talented you are."

"It's hard to be objective about my own work."

"Let's mingle." The man knew how to work a crowd. He charmed with a look, a few words, and never stopped to speak with any one person for long. He kept Hattie moving from compliment to compliment and, for that, she was grateful.

When he pointed her toward the entrance, Hattie saw Vera

in the doorway. "Your sister has arrived," he said, unnecessarily. "And she's looking even more nervous than you. What do you say? Shall we liberate her?"

"Let's."

He kept a hand at the small of her back as they wound their way through the crowd. It felt strange, Hattie thought, to have this man bring her so much comfort when she'd only known him for a handful of months. There were times she thought him an open book. At others, he seemed as distant and unknown as the shoreline of some undiscovered island.

The mystery of Sir Oliver Roundel wanted solving and Hattie wanted to be the woman to do it, which both frightened and excited her. She'd never been this taken by a man, not even at school. She wasn't sure what to do about her complicated feelings except feel them.

Vera was as happy to see Hattie as she was to see her older sister. They grabbed each other's hands like lifelines. Vera's eyes shone with tears of wonder. She had much to say to Hattie, that was evident. However, her first words were for her companion. "Sir Oliver, thank you for taking such good care of my sister's dreams."

"The pleasure has been and will continue to be all mine. And please, Miss Featherstone, call me Oliver." He bent over her hand and brushed a kiss over her gloved knuckles.

"Yes, well. All right." Flustered, Vera took a large gulp of air. "At any rate, I must look around and see for myself how you've displayed her art."

She was off before Hattie could offer to join her, slipping through the crowd at a hurried pace. Oliver chuckled. "Was it something I said?"

"Vera is a little shy around men."

"I like her. I like your sister very much." A quiet smile slipped across his lips. "Although, not as much as I like you."

Hattie had to remind herself to breathe. There was that look in his eyes again, that knowing expression he gave her when they were alone. He touched her cheek, then quickly let his hand drop. "It surprises me how often I think of you, Hattie."

"Oh, I..." *Breathe*, she told herself again. It was difficult. One sentence. He'd uttered one sentence, and she'd lost the ability to take a decent pull of air. A simple collection of words should not make her this dizzy. "Is that good or bad?"

"Time will tell. Ah, look." He hitched his chin toward the opposite side of the room. "Elsa has arrived, and she has her aunt with her."

Not her husband. Hattie wondered at that, then set the thought aside to watch Elsa weave her way through the room, elegant as a queen in a gown of soft blue silk. She caused a terrific sensation as she traveled from person to person, cluster to cluster. A smile here, a touch of the arm there, an offered cheek. Always the right amount of attention given, the right words spoken.

Elsa and Oliver could have been fashioned from the same cloth.

Malvina was clearly happy to be in her niece's company. The same could be said of Elsa. Both women were clinging to each other. Hattie could only imagine how difficult the separation had been. Elsa appeared more relaxed now that her aunt was off the Continent.

Only recently had Hattie learned of Oliver's role in securing Malvina's entry into England. By means of his birthright and exclusive education, he had contacts in all sorts of places. Hattie had only been mildly surprised to learn that his brother, a man she'd yet to meet, worked in the Foreign Office serving King and country, as he'd done during the Great War.

Hattie watched Malvina separate from Elsa and move to speak with Vera. The two bent their heads and began, what

Hattie assumed, was one of their deep discussions. Elsa came directly to Hattie, smiled at Oliver and said, quite boldly, "I'm stealing my friend."

"She's all yours." He spoke without taking his eyes off Hattie's face. "For now."

Heat rose to her cheeks.

"Careful with that one," Elsa whispered once they were alone. "He's already halfway in love with you."

Hattie felt that heat in her cheeks grow warmer. "Nonsense. He sees me only as a protégée."

"Oh, Hattie." Elsa gave a delighted laugh. "How do you think Wilhelm and I began?"

She didn't know how to respond to that, except to remark on the man's absence. "I see your husband didn't come with you tonight."

A veil seemed to lower itself over Elsa's eyes. "He sends his regrets. The weather has given him a slight cough."

"And you came without him." Her presence was a tremendous gift. "Thank you, Elsa. It means a lot having you here. I couldn't have done any of this without you."

"And I couldn't have rested easy if you hadn't taken my aunt into your home. We have helped one another. Now, tell me, how is it going with Malvina? I want to know the truth."

"Wonderful, actually."

"Are you not cramped?"

"Not at all. She's an easy housemate and exceptional company, especially for Vera. My sister claims she and Malvina would keep talking all night if not for bedtime taking precedence."

Elsa smiled. "So, you see, we have given each other a gift. That is the way of friends. There are quite a lot of people here. It's a promising first step in what will prove a long and brilliant career. And...oh, Hattie." Elsa paused before one of the paintings. A scene from *The Marriage of Figaro*. "I knew you were talented. I *knew* it. And yet, I can't find my breath. This, it is… I don't have the English word. So very good. *Spektakulär*."

Elsa spoke in a voice that reminded Hattie of Vera that first morning in their flat. Touched, she blinked a few times, waiting for her pulse to settle. No use. "Let me show you where it all began."

As if sensing something big was about to happen, a break in the crowd opened up, a hush fell and Hattie guided her friend to the lone painting on the western wall. Elsa stood before Butterfly, gazing in complete silence, her expression stunned. "It's as if I'm looking at myself, my true self, but with someone else's memories."

I must breathe now. I must remember to breathe.

Hattie heard a click from behind them. Then, a burst of light. A flash.

The photograph appeared in the most important London papers the next morning. The caption read *Salzburg Songbird Meets Alter Ego*. The article went on to proclaim Hattie a budding superstar in the art world and predicted a meteoric rise much like Elsa's in the opera community.

Oliver rang Hattie to tell her more good news. She'd sold seven paintings, with three more in negotiations. She was, as he put it, a smashing success.

Was it Elsa's appearance at the opening? The photograph in the newspapers? Oliver's planning and execution of the exhibit? Or simply the art itself that had catapulted Hattie into overnight success? She would never know.

It was, however, a lovely way to start her career as a professional artist.

Chapter Twenty-One

Elsa

March 1936. London, England.

Elsa enjoyed her time in London. She spent every spare moment with Malvina, having no idea when they'd meet again: there'd been talk of her moving to America. Hattie and Vera joined them often and that only added pleasure to the various outings they enjoyed together. Malvina seemed settled in her position at the university. It was only an assistant professorship, but it paid well enough, and she seemed to like the work. But her housing situation was still unsettled. Although they never complained, the Featherstone sisters' home was small and not nearly large enough for three people.

The solution came from Hattie. She pulled Elsa aside one afternoon as they circled around the Albert Memorial. "Vera and I have officially signed the lease for a larger flat. It has four bedrooms, one for us each. Another will serve as my studio, and we're hoping Malvina will take the other. Do you think she would agree to live with us?"

"You should ask her. But, Hattie, thank you. It's a kind offer."

"Kind? Not at all, it's rather selfish on our part. Vera and I adore Malvina. Her presence in our home has made our lives all the richer."

"She feels the same."

"Excellent. We'll approach her with the offer later this evening."

The matter was quickly settled, but another problem arose the next morning when Elsa met her aunt for lunch at the Savoy. "Do you remember Zara Rosenberg?" Malvina asked.

"Of course I remember her." The woman had been Elsa's first vocal coach. Strict, yet kind, Rosenberg had imparted the piece of wisdom that had changed the course of her life forever. Without the insistence she focus solely on her singing, over all other pursuits, Elsa might never have made a career in opera. She owed much to the woman. "Has something happened to her?"

"Like so many of us, she lost her job at the conservatory of music in Munich," said Malvina, her expression one of anguish.

This was not pleasant news. Elsa did a quick mental calculation, coming away feeling even worse. "She must be nearing eighty by now."

"Zara turned seventy-seven last month and is not in the best of health."

What horrors must her former teacher be facing, an elderly, unemployed Jewish woman living in Munich, Germany? "What can be done?"

Malvina sighed. "Vera and I have a meeting with a local

refugee committee. I will see about getting their support for her escape."

"If it is a matter of money—"

"That is only one of the issues, Elsa."

"Of course." She knew the process of moving a Jewish refugee out of Europe was complicated. Proper paperwork needed filing, documentary proof had to be given—and those were the easiest steps. Even if all went smoothly, it would take time, a commodity a seventy-seven-year-old woman in ill health simply didn't have. "If there is anything I can do, *Tante* Malvina, please let me know. Money, a word in the ear of a diplomat, whatever you need."

Her aunt patted her arm. "You're a good girl."

"You will keep me apprised of the situation?"

"Every step of the way," Malvina agreed.

Three days later, with no definitive answer concerning Zara's immigration status, Elsa's London engagement ended with an invitation from a distant relative connected to her father.

Lady Sarah Westaway seemed to think it a lark to be related to a famous opera singer. Unfortunately, Elsa failed to live up to the woman's expectations of what that meant. She'd been hoping to discover a stereotypical diva who put on airs and adopted peculiarities. Elsa's overall lack of melodrama came as a massive disappointment to her distant relative.

Naturally, Elsa assumed she'd seen the last of Lady Sarah. Not so. She read the letter again, then set it on the table beside her tea, a treat she allowed herself now that she'd sung her last performance for the week. "Wilhelm, darling. I have received a rather unusual request from my father's second cousin, once removed." Or was it his first cousin, twice removed? The mathematics escaped her.

Wilhelm peered over his morning paper. "What is her request?"

"She wants me to sing at a private recital in Bath." Elsa rarely agreed to these types of events. They required a level of intimacy she found uncomfortable.

"You should accept the invitation." With a snap, her husband disappeared behind his paper.

Elsa stared at the flimsy wall of newsprint, confused. Wilhelm was no more a fan of private events than she. Perhaps he wanted to tour the famous English city named after its Roman-built baths. "You will come with me?"

"I have another obligation."

Again, Elsa stared at the barrier her husband had erected between them. What obligation? Was this his attempt to make additional *proper alliances*? A faintly sick sensation tumbled in her stomach at the prospect of her husband creating friends in opposing political arenas. What sort of game was he playing?

Frowning, Elsa drew the tip of her finger along the rim of her teacup. She and Wilhelm had found their rhythm again, a tentative truce of sorts that had brought considerable warmth back into their marriage. Enough that she hoped they were on the path to true intimacy that went beyond the physical. "That settles it. I shall send my regrets to Lady Sarah."

"This is not an invitation you should decline," he said from behind the paper. "Your father's cousin has many powerful friends, Elsa, both in England and on the Continent."

Something heavy filled her heart. Her husband was entirely too intentional when it came to their friends. "I'll ask Malvina to accompany me."

"That'll be fine."

"Truly?" Elsa couldn't keep the surprise out of her voice. "You have no objection?"

"This is England," he said, setting aside the paper finally, and looking at her as if that explained everything. Elsa supposed it did. There were no prohibitive racial laws in England, no anti-Jewish discriminating policies, save for their strict immigration rules.

"I'll ask her this afternoon." Elsa would enjoy spending the extra time with her aunt. It would also give her a chance to discover what progress Malvina had made concerning Zara Rosenberg's escape from Munich.

Unfortunately, her aunt had no resolution. She did, however, have another two appointments with Jewish organizations willing to hear Zara's case, which meant she could not attend the musical party with Elsa. Vera Featherstone would attend the meetings with Malvina, as she had all the others. Elsa would prefer to join them, but she'd already accepted Lady Sarah's invitation. She really, really didn't want to travel to Bath alone.

She approached Hattie next, issuing the same invitation she'd given Malvina. "Oh, Elsa, with the utmost regret, I must decline."

"I understand," Elsa said, her heart dropping. "You are busy with your art."

"It's not that. I would love to make the trip with you, but it simply isn't done."

What an odd choice of words. "I don't understand."

Hattie started to sigh, then seemed to pull herself together. "The Bath House musical parties are one of the few affairs still reserved for the most elite of British society. They are frequently attended by lords and ladies and, on occasion, even royalty."

Elsa didn't see the problem. "I have sung before all manner of audiences, even royalty."

Her friend wasn't the tiniest bit swayed, quite the opposite. "Events at Bath House maintain a degree of formality and exclusivity that precludes my being allowed in the door. Simply put, I have not been invited, nor will an invitation be forthcoming. I am a former civil servant."

"But that is not a problem." Elsa gave a quick flick of her wrist. "You will come as my personal secretary. It's the perfect solution, is it not? You will carry my music, bring me a glass of water, that sort of thing. I simply cannot sing without my music and water."

Hattie laughed, clearly delighted. "When you put it that way, then yes. I will gladly accompany you to Bath as your personal secretary."

They left the next day. The moment they disembarked from the train in the largest city in the county of Somerset— Elsa had done her research—she drew in her first full breath of fresh air in weeks and realized how much she needed this reprieve. For months, she'd been living on raw nerves, at a fever pitch. Now, with Hattie, she could be herself.

Her friend proved the perfect companion, or rather secretary, seeing to Elsa's needs without hovering. For the event, Elsa wore black tulle, very understated, very elegant and formal. She added the pendant Wilhelm gifted her at their wedding, a silent homage to their marriage and her secret desire to restore peace in their home. Long black gloves completed her look.

Hattie looked very sophisticated in a green velvet gown. The rich color complemented her matching jade jewelry. "What a beautiful necklace."

Touching the rope of beads, Hattie gave a self-conscious sort of laugh. "I suspect these will be the only Woolworth beads that ever attended a Bath House musical party."

It took Elsa a moment to understand her meaning, then Elsa gave her own happy laugh. "Oh, Hattie, I adore you." She gave her a brief hug. "Your outfit is missing one thing."

Hattie looked down, then twisted around to gaze at the backside of her dress. "I can't think what."

"Your prop." Elsa handed her a stack of sheet music.

During the concert, Hattie stayed in Elsa's improvised dressing room. "It would be inappropriate for your secretary to sit among the invited guests."

There was no changing her mind.

Later, when Elsa finished singing and had made the rounds among the important people of Bath, the two were able to explore the ancient artifacts in the building and the collection of coins on display. They even sipped water from the hot spring. Hattie made a face. "It's bitter."

"It's the minerals, I'm told."

"Ah."

Laughing, they retired to Elsa's hotel suite, where each went their separate ways to change into more comfortable attire. Over hot cocoa, they revisited the evening, Elsa commandeering the bulk of the conversation. "I wasn't in full voice tonight. My 'Habanera' was quite flat. You must have noticed."

"I am the wrong person to ask. I know little about full voice or octaves or flat versus sharp. I only know how your singing makes me feel."

Something in her friend's eyes told her she would not like what she heard, yet she could not resist asking, "How did my singing make you feel?"

Hattie picked up her mug and formed her reply above the rim. "Do you want honesty or reassurance?"

"Honesty, please." Elsa took a sip of her own cocoa. The too-sweet liquid turned sour on her tongue. "I would have not asked, otherwise."

"I felt..." Hattie set down her cup with exaggerated care. "Sad. A bit angry. Worried and uneasy."

Sadness, anger, worry. Strange, "Habanera" was supposed to be flirtatious. "You felt all that from one song?"

Hattie untucked her legs and moved to sit next to Elsa. Taking her hand, she asked, "What's troubling you, Elsa? No, don't deny it. I heard the pain in your voice. If you are worried about your aunt—"

"No, no. Well, yes. I suppose I am always worried about Malvina. She has lost so much, but she is safe and happy in London, and I'm grateful for all you've done to see to her comfort."

"She makes it easy to be kind to her."

Elsa smiled at the truth in her friend's words. "She does."

"We can't forget Oliver's involvement in her rescue," Hattie reminded her. "Or Vera's."

"Yes, you. Oliver. Vera." There was a name missing from the list. Wilhelm. "It was a well-coordinated effort."

Instead of giving her hope, Elsa's heart sank. One success did not mean there would be another. What if Malvina and Vera couldn't secure assistance from the Jewish organizations? What would become of Zara Rosenberg? She was not a young woman. Time was against her.

"Yes, Elsa." Hattie reached out and squeezed her hand. "We make a great team."

We make a great team. Could that be the answer? Could they coordinate another rescue in the same manner as the one before? For Zara and, dare she dream, others?

No, no. She was getting ahead of herself. Or was she? "There's more work to be done," she ventured, clutching her friend's hand. "Malvina is not the only one to lose a job, a business, a home. There are people who don't have the connections or means to flee or a place to go even if they could leave Germany."

"Vera said the same thing after she and Malvina met with religious leaders in our community."

Elsa pulled her hand free and leaned back into the cushions. "What do you know of these groups? Are only Jews concerned with the refugee problem in Europe?"

"There are others. Christian organizations, individual churches, ladies' auxiliaries. They do what they can, but there are policies in place that make the process difficult."

"Such as?"

"Well, for starters, refugees must prove they won't be a burden on England's resources."

"So it's about money."

"Partly," Hattie agreed. "But also, a refugee may only enter England on a temporary basis, unless there is proof of a job. Or a British family can sponsor their stay. A student visa would suffice. A child can be brought over, provided a British citizen will adopt him or her until the age of eighteen."

"What about a refugee too old and frail to work?"

"As I am given to understand, in the case of anyone over sixty the financial guarantee must be made, quite literally, for life. Why all these questions, Elsa?" Hattie shifted, leaning closer. "Is it simple curiosity, or is there something more personal going on here?"

Elsa explained about Zara Rosenberg, then said, "I'm afraid her situation is dire."

"Then, we must get her out of Germany as soon as possible."

We. How often Elsa had heard that word, from Wilhelm, Hattie, Malvina. Each of them used the term with very different meanings. "You would join me in this effort to save a woman you've never met?"

"Oh, Elsa, I am your most committed of friends. If Zara Rosenberg is important to you, she is important to me."

Hattie Featherstone was one of the kindest people Elsa knew. She smothered the other woman in a fierce hug. "Thank you, Hattie."

"Yes, well…" Hattie patted her back. "You would do the same for me."

"I would. I really, really would."

They pulled apart, laughing. "Now, let's talk logistics. We'll want to enlist Oliver's help," Hattie said, her mood thoughtful. "To secure travel documents and such. We'll need someone to sign the official guarantee form. That's easy enough. My signature will suffice. There is the matter of finances."

"I will supply the money," Elsa offered. "For however long she lives."

Hattie clutched her hand. "May it be many, many years."

Indeed. "I'll send her to England via first class, as I did with Malvina."

"We'll meet Zara at the train station, as we did with Malvina. Although," Hattie paused, her brow creasing in concentration, "does your friend speak English?"

"I don't know."

"That could be a problem. What if…" she paused a second time, looked down, looked up again "…what if Vera and I personally escorted your friend into England?"

"How would that work?"

"We would play the devoted opera fans who simply must attend one of your performances in—" she angled her head "—where did you say Zara lived?"

"Munich."

"Munich. Hmm." Hattie tapped her chin. "Are you scheduled to sing in Munich anytime soon?"

She thought a moment, shook her head. "I head to Stockholm from here, then Lisbon, and Paris after that. I won't be back in Germany until June for the Wagner festival in Bayreuth."

"June. That's three months from now. It could take that long to organize all the paperwork." Hattie fell into thought again. "How far is Bayreuth from Munich?"

"About a two-hour train ride, but that shouldn't be a problem. Many of the musicians scheduled to perform at the festival call Munich home. One of them could bring Zara to me."

"There you go. Vera and I shall be in the audience for opening night, seated next to your friend, who will find us so utterly charming that she will agree to accompany us back to England for a short holiday."

It was an astonishingly good idea. "It could work."

They both grew silent, each lost in thought.

A moment passed, and Elsa realized the rather large flaw in their plan. "I wonder," she began. "While transporting Zara out of Germany isn't illegal, precisely, the border patrol could become suspicious if you and Vera enter Germany, just the two of you, then leave with an elderly Jewish friend in tow."

"I see your point." Hattie stood and paced around the room. "We could enter one way and leave another."

"That could work."

"Of course it could. And, Elsa, if we're successful with this rescue, there could be more in the future. Oliver is already talking about showing my art in Europe. Why not—"

"—coordinate my singing schedule with your exhibits."

Hattie came to stand before her, eyes lit with the same enthusiasm she felt herself. "In between trips, Vera and I could coordinate financial offerings from friends, organizations, maybe even set up a refugee fund. A shilling a week from one person, a pound note donation from another would add up over time to a sizable amount. Oh, Elsa, with your help from inside Europe, we could rescue more than Malvina and your friend. We could save dozens."

Elsa pushed to the edge of her chair, bounced a little. "We could."

The planning began in earnest from there, through the rest of the night and into the morning. By the time they boarded the train back to London, Elsa was committed. If she and Hattie pulled off their plan, at least one life would be saved, possibly more. She would not tell Wilhelm what she meant to do. He would only try to stop her, and that Elsa would never allow.

Chapter Twenty-Two

Hattie

March 1936. London, England.

Hattie returned to London with her head full of details and her heart full of purpose. She wanted to rescue not only Zara Rosenberg but as many refugees as possible. She would not sit silently on a train and do nothing in the face of injustice again. She would not remain passive.

She would make a stand. She would act. One step at a time, one refugee at a time.

Before sharing her thoughts with Vera and Malvina, Hattie approached Oliver. He'd been instrumental in Malvina's escape. Surely, he would wish to do the same for Elsa's vocal coach.

He was immediately on board. In fact, without a single prompt from Hattie, he, too, came to the idea of expanding beyond this one rescue. He even offered to be their official contact with the Foreign Office, Whitehall and other government agencies should the need arise. Hattie became instantly suspicious. "You have an awful lot of connections."

"I attended Eton and Cambridge and graduated at the top of my class at both." He seemed to think that explained everything. And perhaps it did. It stood to reason that a man who'd attended the most prestigious schools in the country would have friends high up in the government. "I will assist you in this, Hattie. Under one condition."

"Only one?"

This earned her a dry, masculine chuckle. "You must continue providing me with new artwork. For every piece I sell, I expect another in its place within a reasonable period of time."

It was the answer to every dream Hattie had ever had for herself. "We have a deal."

He smiled. She smiled. His head lowered toward hers. She lifted up on her toes. They hovered like that for several seconds, each suspended in a moment of indecision. Then, Oliver stepped back, and Hattie stopped smiling. The awkward silence that followed had a new edge to it. They both said goodbye, and she headed back to her flat, where she brought Vera and Malvina into her confidence.

Both agreed to do their part. "I'll meet you at Paddington Station," Malvina suggested. "Zara will appreciate the friendly face upon her arrival in a foreign country."

Things moved quickly from there.

While Hattie and Malvina focused their efforts on Zara Rosenberg, Vera concentrated on building up their refugee fund. As she said, "Nothing will happen without a good supply of money driving our efforts."

She wrote letters, spoke at church gatherings, met with vicars and paid calls to anyone interested in hearing about their cause. Malvina did the same with the Jewish leaders in their community. They asked nothing of others they weren't willing to do themselves. Their own money was laid out as carefully as in their leanest years. Every pound saved mattered.

Hattie continued selling her art and met with Oliver often about her upcoming exhibits in Europe. Vera enjoyed her own brand of success. Her latest serial drew interest from two publishers wishing to turn it into a novel. She chose Mills & Boon because, as she told Hattie and Malvina the night after she'd met with the publisher, "Mr. Boon gave a sensational pitch."

He also gave her a two-book deal.

Hattie and Vera enjoyed financial success beyond all reason. They no longer had to economize. They chose to do so anyway. Apart from the extravagance of their new home, they continued their frugal lifestyle. It was no hardship to live as they'd always done. Vera said it best. "Who are we, that the mere fact we have a little extra money we would not spare the excess for others in need?"

"You sound like Mama."

"I do, don't I?"

By June, Zara's immigration paperwork was in order and her escape imminent. Hattie and Vera traveled third class to Bayreuth, Germany, for Elsa's performance in the festival dedicated solely to music composed by Richard Wagner. Elsa met them at the train station.

Greetings were rushed as she ushered them into her hired car and drove away from the curb. "I must warn you," she said rather breathlessly. "We have a problem."

"Already?"

"Word has spread of our little rescue mission." She looked over her shoulder, switched lanes and pressed her foot to the gas pedal. "Zara told her neighbors about us, who told their relatives, who told *their* neighbors, who then told their relatives. I also contacted a few people, and now, well, there are a few hopeful refugees seeking our aid in their escape from Germany."

A few was an understatement, as Hattie learned when she and Vera followed Elsa into the safe house she'd secured, which was really the home of a local woman and her Jewish daughter-in-law. The two-story home looked like many others on the street. A slanted roof of red ceramic tiles. White stucco on the first floor's exterior. Dark brown boards placed in a vertical pattern on the second.

The three entered through the back door that spilled into the kitchen. The noise hit Hattie first, and then she caught sight of the crowd. So many, huddled in small groups, a few alone and looking scared. They clutched their papers, determined to show themselves worthy of earning a chance to escape Germany. Some wore fine clothes and expensive jewelry. Others were in tattered suits and faded dresses with frayed hems.

But when Hattie looked at their faces, there seemed to be no real distinction in their expressions. She saw only the desperate wish for escape.

"Some of these people have been waiting for days," Elsa said as they pushed to the front of the line and up the stairs to a sparsely furnished room. She introduced them to the others she'd recruited to help. Max, an assistant conductor with the Vienna Philharmonic; Ursula, a pianist; Inga, the woman who owned the house; and her daughter-in-law, Hannah.

Where was Inga's son, Hattie wondered? "Sachsenhausen concentration camp," she was told in a whisper. "Sent there for refusing to offer the Nazi salute to an SS officer."

Hattie and Vera took their places behind a long table set up for the day's interviews. Elsa took the chair next to Hattie's, and their work began. Zara was their first interview, her rescue already guaranteed. The rest would have to state their case, and hard decisions would have to be made. Hattie was not looking forward to the task.

As it turned out, Elsa's former vocal coach was fluent in English and happily lent her language skills to the process. With Hattie's German not nearly as good as Zara's English, she welcomed the older woman's help. "Please, sit by me."

Zara moved slowly to take her place, each step indicating stiff, painful joints. Now that she was up close, Hattie could see her more clearly. She was as short as she was round, with a jowly face. Above her ruddy nose were a pair of sad brown eyes that had seen too many of the world's horrors.

Despite Zara's assistance, each story took its toll, both on the teller and the hearer, personal accounts of desperation and lost jobs, of seized businesses and lost hope. These were the human casualties of the Nazi anti-Jewish racial laws and their policy of discrimination. Many of the interviewees were practicing Jews, some were not. All were targeted for their race. All were drowning in despair. Most were afraid, and some were literally starving.

As Hattie heard tale after tale of brutality and injustice, revulsion moved through her. She had to get out. She needed to walk away, if only for a few moments, from the scent of sweat and desperation.

"I need a break." She used the stairs to make her getaway.

Elsa followed her outside, looking equally overwhelmed, furious and revolted.

"How do we save them all?" Hattie asked.

"We can't save them all. That is the reality we must accept."

Hattie wanted to howl in frustration. She thought the cost of this venture would be small inconveniences. Letter writing, a bit of money. How naive she'd been. It was only the first day of interviews, and she saw the mountain that stood before them. "Every one of these people has a story to tell, a sorrow to overcome. How do we choose which of them to help, Elsa? How do we decide the cost of one life over another?"

"I don't know."

They fell silent, each caught in their own horrified understanding that their failures would outweigh their successes.

"We must make a rule, right now," Elsa said, her eyes filled with resolve. "We will hear every story. We will listen and remember them all and refuse no one a chance to tell their tale."

"Agreed."

They returned and dedicated themselves to the interview process. As Hattie listened and heard, truly *heard*, each story, she became aware of another problem. Gradually, they would exhaust their own resources and those of their immediate circle. "We'll need better funding," she said to Elsa when they stopped for the day.

"We'll need better *everything*."

And with additional resources would come more responsibility. More successes. And more failures. Now, Hattie decided, would be a good time to pray. She lifted her gaze to heaven. *Dear God, please. This is bigger than us. We need Your help.*

Chapter Twenty-Three

Elsa

June 1936. Bayreuth, Germany.
Bayreuth Festspielhaus.

Elsa stood just inside the entryway of the safe house, her hands shaking, her heart heavy with the burden of so many counting on her. Hattie and Vera were still upstairs, gathering their belongings. Outside, a thick blanket of clouds covered the sky, giving the air a dark and chilly tinge despite the summer heat leaching through the seams of the shut door. It had been a long, difficult day and, for her, only the beginning. She still had to perform tonight.

The sound of approaching footsteps had her glancing over her shoulder. Zara appeared, her movements stiff and slow, her breathing labored. As her former teacher drew near, looking ill and unhappy, everything stood still and quiet in Elsa's heart. This woman's time was running out, and Elsa mourned the loss of her already, even as she smiled and took the old woman's hands in hers.

There were so many things she wanted to say, but as she studied Zara's pale features, worn with time and pain, one thing became clear. "I will miss you when you go to England."

Zara held her gaze, the look of steel in her eyes reminiscent of the woman Elsa had known in her youth. "I'm not going to England." The tenor of the woman's voice was firm, decided.

"You must. It's settled. There is nothing left for you in Germany." *Save persecution, despair and death.*

"No, Elsa. You're mistaken. There is much for me here." She spoke with the certainty of a decision made.

"There is life in England, hope, a future."

Zara brushed this off with a sniff. "What do I care of those things when my own people suffer daily? I have lived a long, full life, Elsa. I do not wish to spend what is left of it among strangers, when I can remain and help others in need, as I did today."

"How will you survive? You have no job, no money."

"I have friends, among them Inga. She and I have come to an arrangement. I will live here in her house, and together, we will continue helping refugees to fill out their paperwork and build their cases for immigration."

A throbbing began behind Elsa's eyelids and in the back of her throat. She couldn't bear the idea of this woman losing more and more liberties with the stroke of a Nazi pen.

"Do not be sad for me. This is my decision. And know that you," Zara said, cupping Elsa's cheek, "*you* have given me a gift far greater than a life in England. You have given me a purpose."

Elsa didn't want her gratitude. She wanted her safe. "I cannot convince you to leave Germany?"

Zara dropped her hand. "You cannot."

Elsa tried to control her grief. She looked away from Zara and immediately caught sight of Hattie and Vera. Elsa wasn't sure when they'd come into the entryway, but there they were, standing very still, their expressions equal parts sadness and resignation.

They'd heard everything or, rather, enough to understand the situation.

There was nothing more to do than say goodbye. Her lower lip shook as she said the words. Pulling her former mentor close, she made a promise in the old woman's ear. "You will never want for money as long as I draw breath."

In that, at least, Elsa could provide her mentor some semblance of normality.

After dropping the Featherstone sisters at their hotel, she drove in silence to the Bayreuth *Festspielhaus*. Her mind was full of the stories she'd heard, not fictional but real, heartbreaking. The depths of so many broken spirits, such desolation, such anguish. She'd listened, as she'd promised, and knew the true horror of the Nazi regime, a government bent on erasing an entire people. Their laws took away jobs and businesses and homes, leaving families unable to feed themselves. Their children.

It was the plight of the children that appalled her most. Elsa was moved to revolt against the injustice of their predicament. Perhaps it was because she'd never had a child herself. *We can't save them all.* She'd said the words herself and hated that they were true, even for the children. Mind wrapped in thought, she hardly noticed arriving at the theater, climbing out of her car, entering her dressing room.

She went through her preparations automatically. Off came her clothes, on went her robe, and then she was sitting at her makeup table, peering at her reflection in the mirror. She saw a woman with a guilty conscience. A fraud. Her passport claimed she was Elsa Hoffmann. A good, solid Austrian name, no hint of her Russian Jewish heritage.

Hands shaking, she stripped off the day's grime and began applying the first layer of stage makeup. A welcome mask. A kind of numbness set in, a queasy sort of dizziness, and she forced herself to stand, to empty her mind and begin her warm-up exercises.

The room was quiet but for her voice and filled with pools of late-afternoon sun, tinged pink as dusk hit its nightly cue. She wanted coffee, needed the caffeine, but no. She drank water, then continued her vocal exercises. Her voice seesawed up and down the scales, curving over the notes, under them, while anxiety churned in her stomach.

Wilhelm stepped into the room. No announcement. His presence intruded on her concentration, and Elsa tried not to resent him coming to her now, when she'd needed him earlier in the day, at the safe house, when Zara had made her intentions clear. But that would have required a confession on her part and a belief in him that escaped her. As her voice projected in the space between them, she ticked off all his failings in her head. His short-fused temper of late, his possessiveness, the way he made plans and created *alliances*—how she hated that word—without consulting her.

She sang. He watched—his eyes soft, entranced. A look she knew well. He'd come to cajole her into doing his bidding. She wanted to rail at him.

But then, other memories formed. The curve of his lips when he smiled just for her, his attentiveness, his protectiveness. Her own complicity to keep secrets from him. For months, she'd lied and concealed and withheld. Her guilt returned, shifted into her voice, a stark reminder that she'd played a role in their strained marriage.

Her voice faltered, and she paused in the middle of an octave. Wilhelm moved to stand before her, his eyes riveted on her face, his hands reaching to her. She was suddenly exhausted. Physically and mentally. She'd lost count of how many times she'd died or killed someone or suffered unimaginable grief on the stage.

Great love. Brutal death. Two sides of the same coin. Oh, yes. Opera was a dramatic, bloody business. The music tunneled into the very depths of the human heart and wrenched out every beautiful and ugly emotion. And now, Elsa was experiencing the same emotions off the stage, too real to be ignored.

Her career was soaring, while people were starving.

She wanted to go home. To Salzburg. She was tired of traveling. So very, very tired. Even she had her limits. Wilhelm took her hands. Why wasn't he speaking?

Why wasn't she?

Seconds ticked by with only the sound of their joined breathing. Conflicting emotions tangled inside one another, threatening to overwhelm her. Elsa adored singing opera, especially Wagner's *Tristan and Isolde* because of the way the composer had created musical tension by exposing the audience to a series of prolonged unfinished cadences. Musical resolution didn't come until the very end of the opera, coinciding, not by accident, with death.

Elsa closed her eyes, breathed deeply, opened them again. When she looked at Wilhelm, it wasn't censure she saw in his eyes, it was concern. "Something happened," he said. "Tell me."

She opened her mouth, nearly brought up Zara, then thought better of it. Her former vocal coach was in good hands. That was all that mattered. "There is nothing to tell."

"You were gone all afternoon."

"I was out walking." So easily the lies came.

He pulled her closer, very close, and releasing her hands, took hold of her chin, staring into her eyes, holding her gaze as if he was trying to see into her soul. Elsa attempted to brazen it out, to hold his stare, but her confidence wavered, and she looked away.

"You're lying." His grip tightened. "You were seen at the train station."

He'd had her followed. No, that couldn't be right. Their relationship was strained, true, but matters couldn't have gone that far. "I went to meet the Featherstone sisters. They have come for the festival to hear me sing. It's a long way from London, and I... I felt it important to spend time with them upon their arrival." She'd overexplained.

Never a wise thing.

He said nothing for a long moment, then slowly, with exaggerated movements, he dropped his hand. "You were with the Featherstone sisters." His face twisted with disapproval. "These British girls, they are not the friends you should be making."

Suddenly, with those words humming between them, Elsa was no longer feeling guilt but anger, rage. Wilhelm was her husband. Her mentor. Her business manager. He directed her career and organized her calendar. He kept her from having a child, always saying *Not yet*, which had driven a wedge between them.

Yes, her husband had done these things, and Elsa had allowed it all. Out of loyalty. Well, no more. Wilhelm would not dictate her every move. "Hattie and Vera are good people, Wilhelm. It is never wrong to make friends with good people."

People who traveled to Germany to rescue a woman who meant something to Elsa, merely because she'd asked it of them. They'd taken seats in a third-class train car so there would be extra money to give to refugees seeking asylum in their country. Good did not begin to describe their natures.

"You're right, Elsa."

Wilhelm's solicitude took her by surprise. "I… I am?"

"The Featherstone sisters have been kind to you."

"And Malvina."

"Especially Malvina." He met her gaze, and for the first time in months, she saw the man she'd married, not the regimented, implacable maestro who organized every piece of her life, but Wilhelm. Her husband. "You are under a lot of pressure. It's been a grueling season."

"Very."

"You are tired."

"*Very.*" She swallowed, then added, "I want to go home." *And start anew.* It wasn't too late to save her marriage. There was still love between her and Wilhelm. Elsa vowed to find a way to put warmth back into their home.

"If that is what you want." He hesitated only a moment. "We will leave once I make the arrangements."

We. That word. Used so freely now. By Wilhelm. By her. No longer two, but one. It took her a moment to realize he was doing it again. Making plans without asking her input. This time, she welcomed his machinations. "Thank you."

Now that it was in her mind, she wanted to leave. Today. Now. This very minute. There was still work to be done, both on and off the stage. Opera at night, interviews during the day.

"Yes. We will go home. However, before we do…" Wilhelm looked at her, deep into her eyes, and she saw something cross his face, a calculation, a purposeful intent that she was beginning to dread. "We will add an additional day to our journey. A slight detour, that is all."

Elsa felt a moment of trepidation. Wilhelm's tone, it was… He sounded pleased. "What sort of detour?"

He went to stand by the window, clasped his hands behind his back. "There is to be a private dinner party in Linz for a very powerful man in Germany. He's an Austrian by birth and an opera fan. You will sing for him at this party. The host made this request of me, personally."

Who did they know in Linz? No one Elsa could think of, which meant this person was another of Wilhelm's *alliances*. "The man giving the party is your friend?"

"An acquaintance, with close ties to top German leadership."

An Austrian with loyalty to Germany. She disliked him already.

"Elsa, it's important we make these alliances."

How she'd come to hate that word. She took a breath, blew it out slowly. What sort of dangerous game was her husband playing? To court the enemy like this, to move within such circles. A terrible, awful thought appeared. "Who is this honored guest I am to sing for?"

"Adolf Hitler."

Elsa gasped and, again, she thought she might be sick. Wilhelm wanted her to sing for a man who hated anyone with Jewish blood. Malvina, Zara, Elsa herself.

"You will do this, Elsa. You will come with me to Ernst Kaltenbrunner's home and sing for the Führer."

Ernst Kaltenbrunner. She did not know this name. "This man, this friend of Adolf Hitler, he is a Nazi? You expect me to sing in the home of a Nazi?"

"That's exactly what I expect."

Elsa gaped at her husband. How deep within the Nazi organization did his connections go? How far would he take these ill-conceived *connections* of his? How far had he already taken them? "Are you a member of the Nazi Party?"

Unclasping his hands, he made his way to the door. "I will leave you to your exercises."

"Wilhelm, I asked you a question. Are you a member of the Nazi Party?"

He stopped in the doorway and looked at her over his shoulder. "I am not." He made to turn away, then paused a second time, his expression unbending. "The Führer wishes to hear you sing in a more intimate setting than a theater. He is a man you do not want to offend."

The night would be unbearable, agony itself. She started to argue.

He spoke over her. "You will do this, Elsa. It is not a request."

Something inside her snapped. "And if I don't? If I come down with a cold that night, as you did in England before Hattie's art exhibit? What will you do, then, Wilhelm? What?"

"The Führer prefers works by Richard Wagner. You will sing the final aria from *Tristan and Isolde*."

He wanted her to sing "Liebestod," Love-Death. The song was beautiful and passionate and resolved the opera's musical contradictions at a haunting, steady pace.

No, Elsa would not sing such a perfect aria for Adolf Hitler. She would think of another. For now, she nodded and said through clenched teeth, her eyes burning, "Yes, Wilhelm."

"Very good." He wrenched open the door. *"Toi, toi, toi."*

A perfect farewell, yet empty, and full of Wilhelm's trademark calculation, and now the tears could not be held at bay. Elsa waited until the door clicked behind him to let them fall. She cried for herself, for her marriage, but mostly, she cried for the people she'd met today and her own hypocrisy. She'd sat before them and listened to their tragic stories and promised she would help, knowing she would fail most of them. Knowing, now, that she would head to Linz in three days and sing for a man who wanted them eliminated.

Chapter Twenty-Four

Hattie

June 1936. Bayreuth, Germany.
Bayreuth Festspielhaus.

After Elsa made her final curtain call, an emotionally exhausted Hattie and an equally somber Vera went backstage to congratulate her on another stellar performance. It had been a long day for Elsa. For all of them. Worse for Elsa because her former vocal coach had refused her help, for noble reasons. But still. The older woman's decision had to weigh heavily on her friend.

Once they exchanged greetings, it was clear to Hattie that Elsa was indeed feeling a sense of defeat. On impulse, she pulled her friend into a fierce hug and said simply, "You tried your best. That's what matters."

Elsa sighed into her arms. "I pray you are right."

They had more interviews planned tomorrow, but now that

they understood what they were up against, perhaps they could expedite the process without compromising the need for compassion. "Yes, well." Hattie stepped back and gave her friend a shaky smile. "We won't keep you any longer. Get some rest."

"You do the same."

Vera offered her own words of encouragement, hugged Elsa goodbye, then fell into step beside Hattie as they made their way toward the exit. "Hattie, look. Over there." Vera pointed to a spot near a collection of cables. "Is that Oliver?"

Hattie glanced to where Vera indicated, and, yes, there he was, standing beneath the rigging, speaking to an older gentleman she recognized from the orchestra, a violinist. "What's Oliver doing in Bayreuth?" she wondered aloud.

As far as Hattie knew, he didn't have a gallery in the tiny German town.

"I suppose we'll know soon enough," Vera said. "He's coming our way. And, if I'm not mistaken, he seems to have eyes only for you."

Vera was right. Oliver's gaze was locked on Hattie. A feeling of expectation curled in her throat. There were so many things she wanted to ask. *What are you doing in Bayreuth? Why didn't you tell me you were attending the festival?*

Stopping a polite distance away, he nodded at Hattie first in a gesture that seemed overly polite, as if they were strangers, or as if he wanted other people to think they were strangers. But then, he shifted his stance, and his entire demeanor changed, and he was smiling. *At Vera.*

That boyish tilt of lips wiped years from his face, making him appear so...very...approachable. "Vera," he said, taking her hand. "Always a pleasure."

"Yes, quite."

Releasing Vera's hand, he reached out to take Hattie's. Even through her gloves she felt the heat of his palm. She pulled her hand free. "My sister and I were just leaving." It was difficult to read his response, but the slight twitch of his lips suggested she'd amused him. Hattie didn't like the idea of him laughing at her. "If you'll excuse us."

"Let me walk you to your hotel."

"That won't be necessary."

"I insist."

"Oliver—"

"It's three blocks," he said, cutting her off, "and I have something I want to discuss with you both."

"Thank you, Oliver. We accept." Vera hooked her arm through his and carried on a long-winded, one-sided conversation about the opera as they exited the building. "What a tragic tale of love won and then lost."

Oliver easily kept pace, both with the conversation and Vera's unusually quick strides. Occasionally, he cast a glance at Hattie, who pretended not to notice. Outside their hotel, Vera disengaged her arm, then made a grand show of patting away a nonexistent yawn. An actress Vera was not. "It's been a long day. I think I'll head up to the room." She smiled at Oliver. "Thank you for the escort."

He nodded.

Hattie's stomach fluttered with a slice of panic. It wasn't that she was afraid to be alone with Oliver. Problem was she wasn't afraid. In fact, in that moment, she wanted the man all to herself. And now, she *was* afraid. Of herself. Her feelings. "Vera, you can't head up yet. Oliver said he wanted to speak with us both."

"He will say it to you, and you will, in turn, tell me. I'm sure Oliver understands." She turned to gaze at the man himself. "Don't you, Oliver?"

He sketched a bow. "Perfectly."

"There, you see?" Vera gave Hattie a satisfied smile. "All settled."

She waved goodbye.

Hattie was still watching her sister walk away when Oliver's voice fell over her. "Have a late dinner with me, Hattie. There's a restaurant one block over that boasts a traditional German menu. The potato soup is considered the best in the region."

She hesitated.

"I really do have something to say, and I don't want to say it in the middle of a crowded sidewalk where anyone can hear us."

A crowded restaurant would pose the same problem. Nevertheless, she said, "All right."

"Excellent." He placed his hand at the small of her back and led her in the direction they'd just come. Out of the corner of her eye, Hattie slid a glance in his direction. His strides were confident, each step light, quick, methodical. A military walk.

Just as she mulled over that, he turned his head and smiled down at her. It was not the smile of a stranger or a friend. It was the smile of man admiring a woman. She fumbled for a topic, found herself telling him about Zara's decision to stay in Germany. He listened without comment, then nodded when she finished. "Good enough."

"Why are you here, Oliver?"

"You know why."

"I, no, I..." She sighed at her own slow-wittedness, feeling a strange emotion, something very close to disappointment. Of course. *Of course.* "The interviews."

He gave another, briefer nod.

The gesture, given so casually, made Hattie wonder if there was something more to his trip. "Why didn't you tell me you would be at the…" she glanced around, noted the many people on the sidewalk "…festival?"

"I didn't know myself until yesterday."

Hattie was baffled all over again. For months, she and Elsa had been planning to interview Zara in Bayreuth during the festival. They'd known there would be others, though not as many as had shown up. Oliver had been part of the process from the start. So why did he only decide to come here yesterday? What wasn't he telling her?

They arrived at the restaurant before she could ask him to explain his sudden appearance.

The place was, as expected, crowded with festival attendees. Hattie spotted an empty table along a column of windows overlooking the theater. Once again surprising her, Oliver spoke to the maître d' in fluent, perfectly accented German, and as they were shown to the seats, Hattie kept her eyes focused straight ahead, refusing to speculate. There would be time to ask him whatever she wished, in the vaguest of terms in case the wrong people were listening.

Oliver pulled out her chair and waited until she was settled before rounding to his seat. Hattie removed her gloves, set them on the table and made eye contact with her dinner companion. There was something very masculine about him, an aura that exuded confidence. "Do you trust me to order for you?"

She should say no.

She should say she was quite capable of ordering for herself. Except, she didn't know much about German food, and Oliver was a man who spoke the language like a native. She abandoned her menu. "I do."

"Excellent," he murmured. "I won't let you down."

The waiter appeared and Oliver ordered two dishes of spaetzle. When they were alone again, he relaxed back in his chair and watched her with lazy, half-lowered eyelids. "How did the interviews go today?"

Something in his nonthreatening posture instilled a sense of safety, and the truth slipped out of her mouth in a single word. "Hard." She picked up her fork, set it back down, plucked at the tines. "Devastating. So many in need. It came as somewhat of a surprise."

Though, now she wondered why she hadn't been more prepared. The German government stole their rights and, in theory, wanted them to leave, but without their possessions or money or means to make a living in their adopted country. The worst part? The very worst part? Hattie's own government put up barriers and made the process unnecessarily complicated.

"You and Elsa, your sister, even Malvina, you've taken on a lot."

"It's painful, Oliver, knowing success could mean only helping a handful at a time." She closed her eyes, pictured the faces of the people she'd met today, remembering each of their stories. "It would be easier not to get involved."

Mortified at what she'd just revealed, she whipped open her eyes. Why had she said that? What must he think of her? No worse than she thought of herself.

Smiling sympathetically, Oliver reached out and placed his hand over hers. "Hattie, it's all right to be overwhelmed."

Mesmerized by his warm touch, she rotated her wrist until their palms met. Safe. Even with that frustrating aura of mystery that surrounded him, or perhaps because of it, Oliver Roundel made her feel incredibly safe. Guilt quickly followed.

Hattie was safe, while so many were not.

"It'll get easier," he said. "You'll find your rhythm and do what you can and go to bed each night knowing it was enough, because, Hattie, even one life saved is enough."

He was wrong.

One life wasn't enough. How many, she wondered, would be enough? A hundred? A thousand? Even then, not enough. She wanted to help them all, every one of them, the people she'd met and the ones she hadn't.

"I'm not going to quit."

"No, you're not."

Their food arrived and as they each picked up their forks, Hattie studied the oddly shaped little clumps of noodles covered in gravy. She took a bite and nearly sighed over the savory blend of flavors. "It's very good."

"I'm glad you like it." Oliver turned the conversation to lighter subjects. Hattie appreciated the effort, and something clutched around her heart, something wonderful.

The feeling became stronger on the walk back to the hotel. Hattie hadn't known how badly she'd needed Oliver's presence, until he'd shown up at the theater.

At her hotel, he took her hand and asked her to walk with him in the garden behind the building. They stood under a pretty trellis blooming with flowers, the bold scent perfuming the air. It was very romantic. She thought he might kiss her.

Hattie tilted her head just as the clouds covered the moon, casting them both in shadow.

Oliver moved another step closer but didn't take her in his arms. He was close now. She could feel his heat, the way it mixed with the humid night air and cloaked her in warmth.

She wanted him to kiss her. And he would. The inevitability of it had been coming on for months. He placed his hands on her shoulders. "Hattie."

The way he said her name, so soft, so full of affection. "Oliver."

He cupped her face, his head lowering. Her arms went around him. Inevitable. Him. Her. *Them*. The kiss started light, a brush of lips, and then there was more heat. One of them sighed, probably her, and then his hands were on her shoulders, and he was gently pushing her away, out of his arms. He said something. She didn't know what.

He said it again, and she realized he was apologizing, and she thought her heart might break in two. "Please, don't regret kissing me."

He shoved a hand through his hair, muttered something under his breath, and then, she was back in his arms. This time, his kiss was made of promises and passion, and yet also had a finality she didn't fully understand. This time, he didn't apologize as he set her away from him. He gave no soft words, either. Nor did he tell her to go away. He simply took her arm and gently guided her back to the hotel's entrance. "Good night, Hattie."

"Good night." She took the required steps to enter the building on her own.

When she looked back over her shoulder, he was gone, vanished into the night as silent as mist over the moors.

Chapter Twenty-Five

Elsa

August 1943. Lower Saxony, Northern Germany.
Bergen-Belsen Concentration Camp.

Elsa came awake slowly, and for a long moment she had no idea where she was. The room was poorly lit. She heard harsh, erratic breathing. Wheezing. Hers, but also belonging to others in the cavernous room.

It all came back to her then. She'd arrived at the camp after dusk, just as the sky had gone black. Other than the driver and the armed guard, she'd been the lone passenger in the car.

This, she sensed, was not the typical means for prisoner transportation. Her so-called escorts had grumbled their displeasure. "She is found guilty of treason. A traitor against the Third Reich, yet they treat her as prisoner of war."

More cursing of her name, her very existence. "If the Führer had known she carried the blood of Jews in her veins, he would not have been so quick to favor her. He would have..."

Elsa struggled to hear the rest, but she'd been denied food and water for hours, possibly days, and there was a buzzing in her ears. She waded in and out of consciousness, catching only snatches of their conversation.

The car hit a bump, and her eyes flew open, fully awake now. It was the sporadic horror of Vogt's interrogation all over again.

"She should have been hanged in a public square for others to know what becomes of a Jew-loving traitor." The complaint came from the guard. "Instead, they send her to Bergen-Belsen."

Though she knew there were many concentration camps in Germany, Elsa had never heard of this one.

"Why there?" the driver said.

"She has value." The guard spat the words. "This is what they claim. They sentence her to what's considered a holding camp with the potential for rescue if the British want to pay her ransom. Or exchange her for one of our own heroes captured by the enemy."

There was possibility of escape?

A shiver racked her entire body. Darkness encroached, grabbing at her with its tentacles. Elsa gave in to the bliss of nothingness. A slap to her face had her coming awake again. They'd stopped moving, and she was forced out of the back seat by the armed guard, the driver watching from his warm cocoon inside the vehicle.

An entire battalion of SS soldiers swarmed her then, their eyes harder than the men who'd marched into the theater the night of her arrest. These men were meaner, their angry faces twisted in disgust at her, at life. She had no baggage for them to rummage through, no jewelry to seize, and this seemed to infuriate them. They shouted at her, slapped her. Called her vile names. Tossed her to the ground.

When she finally gained her feet, she felt the sting of a rod at the back of her knees. She went down hard, the wind slapping her face. The air carried a chill unusual for this time of year.

They'd brought her north.

A hand clasped around her arm and yanked her to her feet. The grip was brutal, no doubt adding more bruises to ones that had come before. From Vogt, and others. Too many to count.

Elsa was dragged before a man who wore the Iron Cross at his neck. His collar held the SS runes on one side, bars and round buttons on the other, denoting his rank: *Hauptsturmführer*. Elsa had learned to recognize these things. This midlevel officer seemed to peer right through her, and like so many who wore the same uniform, his face held a permanent expression of hate.

"Where do you want her, *Kommandant* Haas?"

Haas looked at her. Their eyes met, and Elsa saw the intent in his gaze. She went still, mute with shock. He would hurt her. In the worst possible way that a man could hurt a woman. The humiliation began in front of his men. He took his time examining her, checking the muscles in her arms, her legs. He stuffed his fingers in her mouth and forced open her jaw to inspect her teeth. Things could not get worse. But then the nightmare escalated.

"Wait here," Haas told his men.

"Jawohl."

Haas took her inside the building, to a small room with a cot, and proceeded to prove he had a soul black as sin. He treated her like an animal, showing no mercy. Elsa closed her eyes and endured. When her humiliation was complete, he dragged her back into the brutal wind, shivering from her shame.

Her mind went to her husband. Why had Wilhelm not tried to save her?

Haas shoved her toward the collection of hard-faced guards. "She is fit to work. Take her to quarantine and begin processing."

The first stop was the delousing facility. Elsa was stripped and given an ice-cold shower. Still dripping, next her head and body were shaved, and then she was dragged to the clothing office. She received a pair of trousers and a jacket made of blue-and-white striped cotton canvas. Both hung on her petite frame. She was also provided a shirt that fell past her knees, a pair of underpants, a cap and two wooden shoes that didn't fit.

Again, her mind went to her husband. Why had Wilhelm abandoned her in such a terrible manner?

The harsh breathing, her own, brought her back to the moment and the foul-smelling room where she now lay on a bed made of wood, no blanket, no pillow. Barracks, she reminded herself. The soldiers had called this cavernous room with rows of wooden bunk beds a *barracks*.

She remembered the guard's complaint in the car. *She is found guilty of treason. A traitor against the Third Reich, yet they treat her as prisoner of war.*

She heard a soft sobbing. Not hers, someone else's. Yet the bubbling of despair rose in her own throat. Elsa didn't sleep again that night, too terrified over what new horrors awaited her in the morning.

When dawn came, she learned the camp had been divided into subsections. Designated a prisoner with exchange value, Elsa was made to work in what they called the shoe commando where she was tasked with salvaging pieces of leather from shoes collected from other concentration camps. Shoes that had once belonged to Jews, political rivals and other enemies of the state.

The woman working beside her looked familiar. Elsa discovered she'd been a Shakespearean actress, also of Russian heritage. Natasha had been at the camp for three months.

"You are a Communist?"

"Worse." She leaned in, her voice barely audible. "I am a Jew *and* a Communist. And you are an opera singer. I saw you perform once. In Munich."

"Is it true?" Elsa whispered back, clinging to hope. "Are we to be exchanged for German prisoners of war?"

"Yes." Natasha nodded. "And so, we are treated better. In other sections of the camp, many die of disease, starvation, exhaustion, lack of medical attention. The list goes on."

Elsa's stomach pitched at the thought. It roiled and threatened to release the rotted food they'd been given to eat. There was something comforting in knowing she could be saved, and something horrific as well. She was to enjoy special treatment, while people who had lived good, moral lives were treated like animals in cages.

"I didn't do enough," she whispered. Too many innocent people had perished, people she could have, should have, saved. People who were quite possibly in another part of this very camp.

That night, she fell asleep with guilt gnawing at what was left of her soul.

The next day, a male inmate in the food line came to her. He was elderly, or so he seemed, wrinkled and skeleton-thin, his hair absent on his head but for a few random gray patches. There was something familiar about him, around the eyes, though his face was sunken, and his shirt hung on his bony frame. He took her hand. His grip a mere whisper of a touch.

"You rescued my wife and daughter." He spoke with a cultured Austrian accent, a sign of his education and the status stolen from him by the Nazis. "You were able to send them to England before the war."

"Their names?"

"My wife, Miriam, and our daughter, Leah."

Elsa remembered them. Hattie had found a domestic position for the wife, who'd been allowed to bring her twelve-year-old daughter with the understanding she would help with chores when she wasn't in school. They'd struggled to find a position for the husband, this man standing before her. There, Oliver had come through, the paperwork nearly completed, when he'd been deported to… They hadn't known where.

Until now.

He touched her arm, tears in his eyes. "You saved the lives of the people I love."

But not him. Elsa had not been able to save his life. As a result, he lingered in perpetual danger, hovering in the shadow of death. She meant to apologize, to tell him she should have done better, worked faster, harder, been more committed. But the line shifted, and Elsa lost him in the shuffle of too many shockingly thin people wearing identical clothing.

Chapter Twenty-Six

Hattie

June 1936. Bayreuth, Germany.
Bayreuth Festival.

Hattie didn't tell Vera that Oliver had kissed her or that she'd kissed him back or that, given the chance, she'd happily do it again, even though *he* clearly had regrets. The first time, anyway. He'd been a rather enthusiastic participant the next go-round. Until suddenly, he was pulling back, setting her away, hustling her to the door of her hotel, and then *poof.* Gone. Vanished into the night. Like he'd never been there at all.

Oliver was stealthy, Hattie would give him that. He presented an intriguing challenge to all she knew about men. She'd like to discuss her confusing feelings with Vera. But having the conversation this morning, when they had a full day of interviews ahead of them, wasn't the right time. That didn't mean Hattie put the man out of her mind completely.

Looking back over their relationship, she saw the signs of his interest all along, beginning the moment their eyes had met backstage at the Salzburg Festival. Hattie had been instantly captured by his handsome face, those clever eyes and that attractive air of mystery. She had half a sketch pad of drawings to prove her fascination.

"Hattie?" Vera stood at the door of their hotel room, eyeing her closely. "Are you sure you're up for more interviews? Yesterday was difficult. This morning won't be any easier."

"I know. But we're in this together." She picked up her hat, set it on her head, secured it into place with a pin. "Besides, Elsa can't do the interviews alone. There're too many of them."

"Then, we don't want to be late."

Elsa was already sitting at the kitchen table with Inga, Zara and two other women Hattie didn't recognize. The newcomers were overdressed, looking as if they'd come for a party, and at least two decades separated them in age. Mother and daughter, Hattie guessed and discovered she'd missed the mark when Elsa introduced them as Margarete, the older of the two, and Greta, her daughter-in-law. "Married to my only son," Margarete told them.

Looking past their well-made garments, Hattie saw their unhappy story in the slump of Margarete's shoulders and the darting of Greta's eyes. The younger of the two was tall and extremely beautiful, with a long, slightly haughty face. Her coal-black hair had been twisted atop her head in a complicated knot that set off her strong features.

"Can we get on with this?"

Hattie winced at Greta's autocratic tone, the way her forceful enunciation of each vowel turned the question into a command. Put off by the condescension, Hattie looked to Elsa, who gave her a small, imperceptible shake of her head, as if to say, *We promised to hear every story.*

In the ensuing silence, Margarete whispered something to her daughter-in-law. Hattie didn't catch what she said, but she saw Greta's gaze flick towards Elsa, then Hattie. Vera next. She said nothing more, seemingly subdued, if not completely contrite. This was a woman unacquainted with want, a woman who'd never experienced the need for economy. But she was here, sitting at this table, and that meant she was in serious trouble.

Unlike her daughter-in-law, Margarete gave the impression of someone holding herself together with great effort, someone who might snap at any moment. "Thank you for agreeing to meet with us this morning."

She spoke in low, hushed tones, as if the walls had ears, and, yes, Hattie thought, this woman understood her situation far better than her daughter-in-law. "My husband and son have been taken."

She did not need to say more.

Elsa began asking questions. Hattie could not decipher the words, only the urgent tones. Later, after they were gone, Elsa relayed the sad tale. "The Gestapo took their husbands six months ago, after seizing their successful jewelry business. The women are left with their home, but that, too, will soon be seized now that their husbands have been arrested. They—" Elsa broke off, shook her head. "They will be forced out of their home with nothing but the clothes on their back."

Hattie thought about those clothes and the many jewels they'd worn. A small fortune that would fund a new life in England.

Vera came to the same conclusion. "The question is how to get their valuables out of Germany."

The border patrol was known for seizing personal belongings from Jewish passengers. But there was a way. If they were willing to become smugglers. "Vera and I will dispense of our

Woolworth beads and wear the jewelry ourselves," she said, then, realizing how ridiculous they would look, how suspicious, she added, "We'll wear only a few pieces and place a few in our valises. We'll sew the rest into the lining of our own garments."

Vera objected, vehemently. "We cannot. It's illegal and far too risky. The border patrol could recognize us and notice our sudden wealth."

A fair point. "We'll change our route home, possibly leave through Amsterdam." Oliver would help them make the arrangements. "We'll present ourselves as rather overdressed English girls with a love of opera and a taste for too much jewelry."

"It could work," Vera conceded, though with much reluctance.

After a long day of interviews, Elsa headed to the Bayreuth theater, while Vera and Hattie worked on the finer points of their plan. Rerouting their journey took a bit of organization, additional funds and a departure earlier than expected. On the morning they were to leave Germany, they checked out of their hotel. A heavy-lidded Elsa drove them to Margarete's home and would, after they'd retrieved the jewelry, drop them off at the train station.

Surveying Hattie wearing her perfectly matched pearls, Greta announced, "I don't like this." She turned to Elsa. "Are you certain we can trust these British girls?"

Margarete answered her daughter-in-law's concern. "That's enough, Greta. The Featherstone sisters are risking their lives to ensure we can support ourselves once we arrive in England. We will show them gratitude, not suspicion."

Greta folded her arms and looked from Hattie to Vera and back to her mother-in-law. "Must we leave?"

"We cannot stay. It's no longer safe."

A tortured sob tore past the young woman's lips. "What if Jonah returns and we are gone?"

"He's not coming back, Greta."

Hattie shivered at the finality in Margarete's tone. All at once, she had an urge to hug this defeated woman, to press her close and make promises she could not fulfill. Vera's hand touched her arm. "The train leaves shortly. We should get to work."

With Elsa watching them, her eyes wide and fascinated, they opened their cases and began systematically pulling out pieces of clothing. They ripped out seams, stuffed jewelry inside the linings, sewed in little secret pockets in the cases themselves, then restored the garments to their original spots.

The process took nearly an hour, which left them little time to catch their train.

Margarete thanked them. Greta did not. She turned on her heel and left the room. The door slammed behind her, loud in the somber room, and then there was a gust of sighs from the remaining women left behind. "I apologize," said Margarete. "This is hard on her."

Thanks to Elsa's expert driving and knowledge of the streets, Hattie and Vera arrived at the train station in the nick of time. There were soldiers everywhere, in the depot, on the platform, many with large-toothed guard dogs restrained on leashes. "I feel ridiculous," Vera whispered, looking up and down the platform, her voice reedy with anxiety. "I've never worn this much jewelry."

"You look very regal." Actually, on second glance, she looked nothing of the sort. "Well, you *would* look regal if you would stop fidgeting and keep your eyes cast forward."

The train arrived.

They boarded the first-class compartment and found their seats with little trouble. They didn't want, or need, to travel in such luxury. Hattie sensed Oliver had had a hand in their elevated accommodations. Her suspicions were confirmed when she read the note left on one of the seats in their private compartment. *Safe travels.* There was no signature.

Hattie recognized the handwriting, as did Vera. "That man has a thing for you."

"He wrote the note to us both."

Vera rolled her eyes, but she said nothing more.

With a clank and a screech of metal on metal, the train began moving. Sunlight flooded their compartment with a suddenness that had Hattie slamming a hand to her brow. They sped through the German countryside without incident, and then they were at the border.

A guard appeared at the doorway of the compartment, hand outstretched, demanding their travel documents. Vera showed hers first. He took her passport, glanced over it, then switched his focus to Vera herself. He looked her up and down, and Hattie could see him appraising her, taking in the various necklaces with the multicolored jewels, and the plain navy-blue wool suit beneath. "What was the reason for your visit to Germany, *Fräulein?*"

"Opera," she squeaked. "We came for the Bayreuth Festival."

Her referred to the passport again. "You do this often?"

Hattie took over. "Very often." She was careful to avoid too much detail, something Oliver had taught her. Oliver. Could she not get away from him, even in the privacy of her own mind? "My sister and I are quite the devoted fans."

Hand out, he took Hattie's passport next.

This time, his inspection took twice as long.

At some point, another official joined him. He was young, dressed in a German military uniform, and had the look of a bully in his eyes. Without a word, or permission, he took up Vera's travel valise and waved it in the air as if it weighed nothing. "Who is the owner of this?"

Vera clutched at Hattie's hand, lifted her chin. "It belongs to me. I purchased it two years ago, when I was in Paris. I do love to shop in Paris." Her words were running into one another too quickly. Hattie squeezed her sister's hand, a silent reminder to give as little information as possible. Vera stopped talking, then added, "Anyway, yes. That's my valise."

The soldier snapped open the lid and began pawing through the contents. He took his time, pausing, looking up to glare at Vera, at Hattie, then returning to the case.

He studied Vera again, a longer look, his gaze running over her face, her coat, then did the same with Hattie. What did he see?

Attention back on the case, he dug around and then pulled his hand free. Two identical pieces of jewelry dangled from his fingertips. "These are yours?"

Hattie tried not to wince. He'd retrieved a pair of earrings that could not possibly belong to Vera. She did not have pierced ears. Hattie, however, did. "Those are mine."

"Yet they are in this woman's belongings."

With great presence of mind, Hattie shrugged. "We're sisters. We share everything, clothes and jewelry and inadvertently, it happens, we pick up what belongs to the other and stuff it into our own case."

Her answer only seemed to increase his suspicion. He eyed her closely, his gaze running over her face, down to her neck, up to ears, back to her neck. "Those are very good pearls."

Hattie immediately thought of their owner. She took a deep breath, pictured Greta at her most haughty, and with the feeling she was taking a large step off a cliff, sniffed inelegantly. "Of course, they are very good. And why not? Do I look shabby? Do I look as though I might not wear very good pearls?" She sauntered to the small mirror in the compartment, studied her image, saw the bit of wildness in her eyes, decided to use it, then spun around. "What is it about my appearance that gives you leave to insult me with such an accusation?"

"Nothing, nothing," the other official assured her. The older one. "The *Sturmmann* was being thorough."

"He was being rude."

The younger soldier blanched but did not bend.

Hattie and Vera exchanged a fleeting look, then Hattie focused on the soldier, pressing her role as offended woman of means. "There must be something," she insisted, drawing closer to man, noting his youth, holding his gaze, refusing to look away.

And there, a small chink showed in his eyes. A hesitation.

Hattie seized upon it. "Explain yourself, sir." She drew a step closer. "Do *you* wish to imply something sordid about me? Then, I suggest you do so. In fact, I insist upon it."

His face covered in confusion, the young soldier spun on his heel and retreated without another word. The porter followed in his wake. As quickly as it had started, the incident was over. The danger gone. Yet, Hattie and Vera didn't speak about what happened, not even when they were alone.

The rest of the trip was uneventful. Vera said very little, not even once they were back on English soil. Hattie was equally quiet, her mind full of all that happened in the past four days.

Had it only been four days?

Only once they were inside their flat did Vera begin shaking and hyperventilating.

Hattie set down her case and pulled her sister close. "It's done, Vera. We made it out, and now two more refugees will be able to escape Germany."

"Oh, Hattie. That was awful, just awful." She sobbed out

the words. "I was so scared, for you, for me, but mostly you. You were so brave, and I was so frightened."

Stepping back, she searched her sister's face, saw the fear. "I was frightened, too," she admitted. "But that soldier was a bully. And bullies are cowards."

"You couldn't have known he was a coward."

"I saw it in his eyes."

Vera lifted her head, her eyes narrowed, and she began to move through the room. To stomp, really. "That was my last trip into Germany."

"You can't mean that."

"I do. I absolutely do. And I insist this be your last trip, as well, Hattie. It's too dangerous for either of us to continue crossing the border in the current political climate."

"We can't quit. We've only just started. There are people expecting us to follow through with our commitment."

Vera lowered her head, and the big sister Hattie had always admired, the person she trusted above all others, now lived on the other side of an invisible wall she herself had erected. "We can still do our refugee work from the safety of England."

"Elsa needs us in Europe. You must realize this, Vera, after what we went through this week, the stories we heard. It's too much for one person to take on alone."

"You make it sound so simple, but I'm not brave like you, Hattie. I can't do it."

"I'm not brave." Not like Elsa. She made the contacts inside Germany. She set up the safe houses. She spread the word through enemy territory, risking herself in the process. "I can't abandon Elsa. I can't quit until she does. I won't."

Vera opened her mouth, and Hattie thought she was going to relent, to tell her she was right, but her sister turned around and went to the window. "You don't need me, Hattie."

It wasn't true. She would always need Vera. "Of course I

need you. We're the Featherstone sisters. We always travel together. Safety in numbers, and all that."

Vera turned from the window, and all expression was gone from her face. "I'm much more valuable here in England, working with Malvina, raising funds and securing sponsors."

"But the interviews. Your German is impeccable."

"Your German is nearly as good. Or rather, it's getting there. No, Hattie. I'm decided." Her voice was resigned. "No more trips into Europe."

"You're scared. I understand that. It was a harrowing experience what we went through today. You'll feel better in the morning after a good rest, and you'll see matters as they are."

"I see matters just fine. My decision is final. Now, if you'll excuse me, I have a book to finish writing and a deadline to meet." She went to her bedroom, wrenched open the door and paused, her hand trembling on the brass handle. "I beg you, Hattie, with all that I am, please, follow my lead and stay put in England until it's safe to return to the Continent."

Hattie stood breathless in the wake of her sister's suggestion, her heart beating so hard she was sure the neighbors could hear it. This was it, then. Her moment of truth. The moment when she placed her loyalty with Elsa and their cause over her sister. It had to be done. "I'm sorry, Vera. I can't do as you ask, and you know why."

"Then, we have nothing more to say." The click of her door as it shut behind her had a finality to it that left Hattie staring in stunned silence. She stayed put, breathing hard, until her frustration and sense of defeat were gone, quite gone, and nothing but her resolve remained.

Chapter Twenty-Seven

Elsa

June 1936. Linz, Austria.
Home of Ernst Kaltenbrunner.

Elsa and Wilhelm left Bayreuth the day after the final night
of the festival. They had a four-hour drive ahead of them
to Linz. To give Elsa time to dress and warm up her voice
they'd left midafternoon. Now, two hours into the journey,
a warm, sluggish breeze filtered through the open car windows. Elsa flipped haphazardly through a magazine while
Wilhelm drove too fast.

An uncomfortable silence hung between them.

Part of Elsa wanted to lash out at her husband, force him
to admit his motivation for forging friendships with evil men.
Another part, equally strong, was afraid to hear his response.

She looked at him. He noticed her looking and smiled. In
that moment, everything was right between them. Elsa knew

the peace would not continue, but for now, she accepted the small gift and looked back out the window at the trees, their full branches waving like large, green fans in the wind.

As they approached their destination, Elsa took in the sweeping three-story mansion made of marble and stone. She felt a sick, frightful feeling. The urge to ask Wilhelm the names on the guest list for tonight's party was strong. She stopped herself. It was another answer she did not want to hear.

They arrived ahead of schedule and Elsa was immediately shown to a room where she could dress for her performance. A maid was already waiting to help. The girl proved to have a wagging tongue, which came as something of a surprise, considering the nature of her employers' political leanings.

Hungry for information, Elsa let her talk and soon discovered tonight's guests were, as she'd feared, members of the Nazi Party. Not only did the men belong to the organization but so did their wives. The women weren't allowed to hold leadership positions or speak at the meetings, yet they still felt the need to join. Because, as the maid told her in a voice that held quiet contempt, "They believe their cause is noble."

There was no responding to that.

There was no responding to any of it, not without revealing her own political leanings. So Elsa thanked the girl, sent her on her way, and went in search of her husband. She found him back in the marble entryway, speaking to an elegantly clad couple that had not been there when they'd first arrived. The man was around Wilhelm's same age, the woman possibly a bit older.

"Ah, Elsa." Wilhelm reached out to her. "Come and meet our esteemed host and his lovely wife."

Ernst Kaltenbrunner took her hand, murmured the usual polite platitudes with very little sincerity. Her fellow Austrian was tall and lanky, with a thin face, pointy chin and large, prominent nose. Not a handsome man. The scars on the left side of his face gave him an air of sinister intimidation. "*Frau* Hoffmann, this is my wife, Lisl."

Lisl Kaltenbrunner was even less welcoming than her husband, and no more pleasing to the eye. She was a fortyish woman with a sallow complexion. Her evening gown of silvery plum was stylish, but all wrong for her skin tone. She wore her dark hair pulled back in a tight bun that added a pinched look to her already-scowling face. She attempted no small talk or comforting chatter as she showed Elsa to the music room.

"You will sing at precisely eight o'clock, thirty minutes before we dine." She looked down her nose. "Two songs."

"Only two?"

"Two," the woman repeated, her chin going hard, her eyes clouding with condescension. "No more, no less. My husband and I are not opera fans. Our honored guest seems to enjoy the morbid music, so you will sing for him. The orchestra, as you will notice," she said as she jerked her chin toward the other side of the room, "has already arrived."

Seven musicians did not qualify as an orchestra, but Elsa thought it best to leave the unpleasant woman in her ignorance. Much to her relief, she knew each of the musicians. They were members of the Vienna Philharmonic. She greeted them by name. Some she'd known since the beginning of her career, others she'd met along the way. All were welcome faces in what she now considered a hostile environment.

The conductor, a former violinist at the Vienna State Opera, was in his early thirties. He had floppy light brown hair and an earnest expression as he approached her and kissed both her cheeks. "Good evening, Elsa."

"Good evening, Isaiah," she said, smiling. Did Ernst and Lisl Kaltenbrunner know they'd allowed a Jew into their home?

"I understand you are singing 'Liebestod,' followed by 'Dich, teure Halle.'"

"Yes," she agreed. "And no."

He lifted a brow.

She told him she would sing "Liebestod" as planned, but that she wished to substitute Wagner's piece from *Tannhäuser* with an aria composed by Mozart.

"He will not like it."

Before she could ask which *he* Isaiah meant, his sharp intake of air and the sound of heels striking marble—like hammers to nails—told her others had entered the room.

The hair on the back of her neck prickled. She suddenly remembered Hitler's words in his autobiography, *Mein Kampf*, and a cold, deadening sensation filled her lungs. The way he'd identified Jews as inferior and Aryans racially superior had horrified her. The writing itself had been incoherent in places, grammatically incorrect in others. And none of his claims had been substantiated. Still, people—mainly Germans and Austrians—flocked to him.

Elsa gripped her hands tightly together at her waist. She felt the man's evil presence in the roll of her stomach, in the kick of antagonism that hit her square in the heart. Her hands gripped tighter still. She was squeezing too hard, scorching the blood from her knuckles until they were white as bone. She couldn't help herself. Pain, sharp and unexpected, was her only lifeline in the sea of her fury. Her fear.

Wilhelm came to stand beside her. She turned to look at him, seeing nothing but her own emotions in his eyes. A trick of the light, or real? He secured his fingers around her arm, his hold light but firm, his eyes filled with understanding and something she'd seen before. A warning. "Do not embarrass yourself or me."

She said nothing, only forced her fingers to relax as she

turned. The man that stood before her was not the frenetic public speaker she'd seen on the newsreels. He was small and uninspiring, with a dead, impersonal stare empty of humanity.

Calling on every bit of her training, Elsa drew an invisible shield around herself and took slow, careful breaths. She couldn't stand looking into those large, empty eyes, or that characterless face. Yet she didn't dare look away.

Adolf Hitler was unremarkable in person, she realized. Below average in height with a receding hairline and thin lips. He was speaking now, taking her hand, bowing his head, praising her talent. Elsa did not want his admiration. This was the man who'd eliminated many of his rivals in a single night of terror and had gone on to institute hundreds of laws restricting Jews in every aspect of German life.

What next? Banishment? Death? Elsa could not bear his presence a moment longer. "If you will excuse me, I must prepare for the concert."

She turned without waiting for a response, feeling immediately unmoored. But then, Wilhelm leaned over her and whispered in her ear, *"Toi, toi, toi."*

The words only added to her misery. She shut her eyes. For a minute, unsure if she would cry or howl in frustration. She settled for a light squeeze to her husband's arm, a small recognition she'd heard him.

Twenty minutes later, she made her entrance to underwhelming applause. Not wholly unexpected, given the room held less than twenty guests. Hitler sat in the front row. A man she recognized as Albert Speer sat on his right and their host on his left. Wilhelm had been seated in the second row beside *Frau* Kaltenbrunner.

Elsa sought and found her husband's eyes. He gave her a small, encouraging nod.

She opened her mouth to sing, then saw her: Frieda Klein.

In the audience, sitting beside a man wearing an SS uniform. The smug smile she gave Elsa made her skin crawl, as did the way the mezzo-soprano clung to her escort. Elsa looked away and launched into the first of the two arias she was here to sing.

Upon reflection, she'd chosen to follow Wilhelm's suggestion for her first song. "Liebestod" was one of Richard Wagner's most intense compositions.

Elsa was in a very intense mood.

The melody began with a short, two-bar phrase and grew in fervor as the aria continued. There was immediate opposition in the music, exactly the reason she'd gone with the piece. She thought of the people she'd met in the safe house and sang for them.

As the aria continued, the orchestra took up the chaotic theme. Elsa sang each note, reaching for the climax, and when she hit it, she experienced a feeling of tremendous achievement, of soaring. She reached the final notes, which required an entire octave leap. The oboe played with her. The rest of the instruments joined in, and the music resolved on a pure B major chord.

It was done.

The audience applauded, several called out "Brava!" Frieda was not one of them. Elsa smiled, nodded, smiled. She'd been acceptable but not great, certainly not up to her personal standard. Only Wilhelm seemed to notice. She saw the disappointment in his eyes.

His displeasure was about to get worse.

She nodded to Isaiah. The opening bars began. Wilhelm's eyes widened, then narrowed. Too late. Elsa launched into the Queen of the Night's famous song of vengeance and impossible demands. She gave pieces of herself to the music.

Something was happening inside her. She saw that others felt it, too, saw it in the way Isaiah caught her rhythm with his baton and sent the orchestra flying through the notes with her, saw it in the way the audience sat straighter in their seats, the way they leaned forward. The way Hitler's right hand clutched at his left.

Elsa sang on.

Louder, more impassioned, pulling every ugly emotion from the pit of her angry, bitter soul. Fierce. Vengeful. Vicious in her delivery. She mimicked the Queen's placing a knife in the hand of her daughter Pamina, goading her to assassinate Sarastro, her bitter rival.

The guest of honor watched from the front row, his body perfectly still. Distant and aloof, his eyes shifting over her face.

She sang on, sliding up and down each bar. Her voice rose through the octaves, ascending, descending, ascending again. Nerves tried to intrude, to blunt her edge, to make her miss the pitch. But no. Elsa was in control now, careering toward resolution.

Her hand slashed the air, fast and frenetic, holding an invisible dagger, its hilt shoved into the palm of the Queen's invisible daughter. The Queen—Elsa—would have her vengeance.

She sang the final note.

Then…silence. But for her breathing and the beat of her heart surging in her ears. The audience jumped to their feet, all but Frieda, who glared at Elsa with absolute disgust in her eyes while the rest of the room shouted, "Brava! Brava! Brava!"

The loudest applause came from the guest of honor. He'd missed the point.

But so had Wilhelm. The pride on his face told her she was forgiven for choosing to sing Mozart instead of Wagner, an Austrian over a German. Her defiance had been for nothing. Or had it? Her vision cleared, and she saw her own power in this room of cheering Nazis. She saw her position as a Hitler favorite and what the future of an ugly alliance could mean. A shield. A tool. Doors opened. Lives saved.

It could be done.

Gaze empty, Hitler approached her. "I shall never forget tonight." The look on his face was impersonal, belying his praise. "Next time, you will stick to singing Wagner."

Elsa accepted the verbal slap with a nod, knowing she'd pulled off a small rebellion. The first of many to come. That was her silent promise to herself, to the many people she'd met in the safe house this week.

For the next few minutes, she went through the motions of accepting praise from the other guests while Hitler melted into the background, then out the door, then to his waiting car idling outside. Elsa was only too happy to see the back of him.

Frau Kaltenbrunner was the last to congratulate her, the woman's entire demeanor transformed into one of complete approval.

"My dear," she cooed, sending a side-eye to where her husband stood, watching them. "I had no idea you were so talented. We must have tea next week and you will teach me about opera."

Dinner was announced, and the woman walked away, leaving Elsa to stand alone in the room. She hesitated, unsure of her role. Was she a guest, or simply the entertainment? Frieda had no such qualms and marched beside her escort, once again with that superior smile on her face. The woman was courting danger and aligning herself with the wrong sort of men. Elsa could tell the mezzo-soprano this. But Frieda would not welcome the warning.

Wilhelm materialized beside Elsa and linked their arms, and they were soon entering the dining room. The table was set with blue and gold china and sparkling crystal goblets.

Their host sat at the head of the table. To her surprise, Elsa was put at his right hand. She quickly learned he was not interested in what she had to say. He was not interested in what anyone had to say. He completely, absolutely controlled the conversation. Clearly in his element as the center of attention before an admiring audience, he orated rather than engaged in discussion.

The first course was served, then the second. The food went untouched on his plate. He spoke rapidly, on and on, gesticulating with both hands, an explosion of nervous energy in every move. He was working himself into a frenzy. "A thousand years hence, Austrians and Germans alike will look to our conduct and see an example of limitless strength and courage."

He went back to denigrating inferior races and religions. His hands flew around his head. Elsa would have dismissed his rant as that of a madman. Which was nothing short of the truth. But the real insanity swam in the eyes of the other people in the room. Their shared fanaticism was terrifying. An entire nation of mad men and women rising to power.

The Nazis' criminal maliciousness that had infested Germany had bled across the border.

Her beloved Austria was doomed.

Chapter Twenty-Eight

Hattie

March 1937. Munich, Germany.
The Roundel-Liston Gallery.

The months following Hattie's first art show proved to be the busiest of her life. She honored her agreement with Oliver. For every painting he sold on her behalf, she provided him with another to put in its place. Meanwhile, England had gone through a bit of unexpected political turmoil when King Edward VIII abdicated the throne so he could marry the American divorcée Wallis Simpson. The country was still reeling from the scandal.

Nevertheless, life went on, and people were even more in need of rescue. Vera published books, three to be exact, and the sisters, together with Malvina, expanded their refugee work. Elsa played an integral role by setting up safe houses in the cities where she performed. She built up a network of trusted allies within Germany and Austria.

True to his word, Oliver tapped into his connections inside the British government, although Hattie had yet to meet even one of his so-called chums or even his brother. If this continued, she was going to suspect the man did not exist. Nevertheless, their coordinated efforts resulted in sanctuary for dozens of displaced Jews.

The need became greater every day. While Neville Chamberlain preached appeasement, Adolf Hitler's racial discrimination policies grew more prohibitive. Jewish men, women and children in Germany were literally starving.

Hattie wanted to save them all. When her frustration was too much to bear, she sketched their faces, vowing to remember them, and prayed to God for their rescue. She shared the drawings with no one, preferring them to remain her own private reminders.

On a personal level, her friendship with Oliver was stronger than ever, though there were no more kisses. Always the perfect gentleman, he kept Hattie carefully at a distance, often disappearing from her life for weeks at a time, sometimes a full month, but returning always, faithfully, when they needed to plan her next exhibit. With his guidance and the capability of his efficient staff, he introduced her to the European art community. She'd had exhibits in Salzburg, Vienna and, just last month, Stockholm, where Elsa had performed the role of Countess Rosina Almaviva in *The Marriage of Figaro*.

Tonight, Hattie stood in Oliver's Munich gallery. The crowd was large. She was surprised—and appalled—by the German military uniforms in the room, as upsetting as the Nazi flags hanging outside every building. It felt hypocritical to peddle her art to these people.

Oliver came to stand beside her. "Stop scowling, Hattie.

Remember, you want to be here. You want to show your art to this crowd. It's your dream."

This wasn't her dream. It made her ill to think of these people looking at her art, possibly buying a piece or two, hanging them in their homes, homes they'd possibly appropriated from a Jewish family now in exile.

"Remember," he said again, leaning in close and lowering his voice to a husky baritone, "this is part of the charade."

The part she hated most. The part where she moved among people who thought themselves members of a superior race, and she was supposed to be like them.

Her throat tightened with indignity, and her face went hot, but she forced her lips to curve in a smile as Oliver suggested.

He chuckled. "A little too much teeth, darling. Yes, there. That's better. Lovely, see that man over there, across the room?" He hitched his chin to a spot over her right shoulder. "The thin, sickly-looking fellow with the large forehead."

"I see him."

"That's Joseph Goebbels, head of the German Ministry of Propaganda."

She knew him by name and reputation. Goebbels was one of Hitler's closest and most devoted sycophants. As propaganda minister he exerted control over the news media, information within Germany and every aspect of the arts. His extreme, virulent anti-Semitism was well-known and, to Hattie, beyond frightening.

She wanted to flee the gallery.

From where he stood in the shadows, observing her art, Goebbels looked dark and sneering, not a single patch of stubble on his clean-shaven face. A fastidious man, like so many other Germans.

"This is good news, Hattie. Your art has caught Goebbels's interest. If all goes well, the Führer will be next."

"Adolf Hitler?" she croaked.

"Don't look so horrified."

How else was she to look? She *was* horrified. As if the hideous little man stood before her now, she crossed her arms over her chest, trying to make herself smaller, invisible, wishing she'd never embarked on the rescue missions. That wasn't true. What she wished was that there had been no need for the rescue missions in the first place.

Vera had warned her, in one of their many quarrels. *You are playing a dangerous game, Hattie.* Her sister was right. She was also very, very wrong. This was no game.

Some people will see your entrance into German society with little favor, Vera had argued. *They will label you a sympathizer.*

Sympathizer. An ugly, ugly word. But necessary, if she wished to continue her work with Elsa. "Relax, Hattie."

How could she? A top-ranking Nazi was inspecting her art. Not just any piece, either. Butterfly. Hattie felt instantly defiled, having a man such as Joseph Goebbels enraptured by a painting that represented so much of who she was as an artist, a woman.

And now, the man was turning and heading their way, and Oliver told her, "Smile, Hattie. This is exactly what we'd hoped would happen."

Was this their goal?

Couldn't she work with Elsa regardless of her own success? Hattie didn't have to sell her art. She only needed to interview potential refugees and coordinate their escape. And then find the funding. Resources that the sale of her art provided.

Oliver took her hand, bringing it up in a sweep to his lips. Holding her gaze, he seemed to say, *Trust me.* Then, again in a low tone, said, "Follow my lead."

What choice did she have? It was either continue this ruse or pull her hand away and leave the gallery. Stay, retreat.

Sink or swim.

Hattie was a very, very good swimmer. Something to remember. "*Herr* Goebbels," Oliver said in his flawless German accent. "It is a great pleasure to have you in my gallery."

The men exchanged a series of pleasantries before Oliver introduced Hattie.

"Ah," Goebbels said, admiration in his eyes. "The artist is as beautiful as her paintings."

Hattie blinked, wondering how her hand had found its way into his. She watched the way his predatory eyes washed over her in a head-to-toe appraisal. Her stomach tilted toward her knees. She would have slipped to the ground had Oliver not roped his arm around her waist and pulled her against him.

"You are very good at painting, *Fräulein*. I am particularly taken with your interpretation of Madama Butterfly." Spoken in his guttural German accent, the compliment sounded more like an offense. "Her despair is very real, very painful to see, and yet I find myself unable to look away."

It was surreal, standing amid her artwork, having this conversation with such a man as this. Every image hanging on the walls carried a bit of her soul, and here she stood smiling, accepting simpering praise from an unconscionable anti-Semite. The moment required every bit of the manners her mother had instilled in her as a young child.

"I wish to buy the painting."

"It's not for sale." The words came out of her mouth before she could censure herself. There were tactful ways to say *no*.

Goebbels's eyes narrowed. "Everything is for sale, *Fräulein*." He snapped out the comment with a flick of steel. "One way or another, I mean to have the painting."

Oliver attempted to discourage the man. His words were far more diplomatic than Hattie's had been as he offered alternative paintings. Goebbels would not be swayed. He ultimately left with the painting. He did not ask the price. He did not offer to pay a single mark.

He simply lifted the painting off the wall and exited the gallery.

No one stopped him. No one even tried. Not even Oliver.

Stricken, Hattie muddled through the rest of the evening. Unable to look at Oliver, knowing he'd let this happen, she walked through the gallery in a semidazed state. She was aware of the rise and fall of voices around her, but she didn't engage in conversation herself.

At midnight, Oliver ushered out the final guest, dismissed his staff, then closed the gallery doors, leaving only the two of them.

Hattie stood in the shadows, waiting for him to come to her, to explain himself, to promise her he would get the painting back. His face was weary as he reached for a half-full wine bottle and poured the ruby liquid into a glass. He drained the entire contents in one gulp. "That didn't go precisely as we planned."

"No?" she asked defiantly. "What *was* the plan, Oliver? Explain to me how a man walked out of this art gallery with the one painting I wished never to part with. You knew this. It was my one stipulation."

He set down the glass, very slowly, very deliberately, then turned to face her. "You were only to meet Goebbels, gain his interest in your art, have him pass on your name to Hitler."

The way he said the words, so cold and calculating, Hattie knew she was staring at a stranger. Her breathing slowed in her lungs, becoming even and featherlight, and she remembered the times Oliver had stepped in whenever one of her rescues hit a snag. She remembered how he never failed to secure the proper contact in whatever government agency held up the process. She remembered his extended absences, his utter and total silence for weeks at a time, until he showed up again. All smiles and hellos and zero explanations.

"Who *are* you?"

She saw the shutter come down over his face. There was a kind of wary reserve behind the blank mask. "I'm not who you think."

That much she understood.

He came to her, reached for her hand. She batted him away. "Is your name really Oliver Roundel?"

"Yes."

"And the title is real or false?"

"Real."

This didn't reassure her, quite the contrary. "What about your brother in the Foreign Office?"

"Also real."

Hattie wanted to stop there, but she couldn't. She knew too much and yet not nearly enough at the same time. "Who are you?"

What are you? Liar, thief, spy?

"My brother does, indeed, work in the Foreign Office." There was no hint of subterfuge in his tone. "I also work for the government. But my role is more, shall we say, clandestine."

All the pieces began to fall into place. The ease in which Oliver moved through Europe: the galleries were his cover. All this time, Hattie had thought Oliver's connections came through his brother. Now she knew the truth. "In what capacity do you serve the British government?"

"I'm in the economic division of MI6."

She shook her head in a kind of mute misery. This man standing before her was not who she'd thought him to be. *Liar, thief, spy.* Their friendship, the budding romance, were those also lies?

She thought of their dinners together, his kisses last year, the way he'd suddenly pulled back, as if he'd crossed some invisible line.

"The British government has been keeping an eye on Hitler for years," Oliver told her. "Ever since the Beer Hall Putsch."

"What does any of that have to do with the art world?"

"He has a passion for art, as do I. That's real, Hattie, and it has opened doors previously closed via other routes."

Hattie stared at him, feeling humiliated, profoundly stupid and used, wishing the ground would swallow her up. Why, *why* had she let him find his way into her heart? "And my role in all of this?"

"Your connection to Elsa has proven more valuable than we'd expected."

Her mouth fell open before she could shut it. "You've exploited our friendship, pushed us together, coordinated all of it to—what? Gain access to Hitler's inner circle?"

He didn't deny it.

"Your assistance with our refugee efforts, was that your idea, or was it a directive from your...your..." she searched for the word "...superiors?"

"Actually, I was told to shut the operation down."

She'd thought he couldn't surprise her again, but he had. "And yet, you didn't. You continued helping us. Or... No! Is that what you're doing now? Are you confessing as the first step in shutting us down?"

"The directive came down twelve months ago."

"What?" Twelve months ago? "You denied a direct order?"

"I argued the merits of the program."

"You mean you found a way to exploit our efforts for your own purposes." Her tone was bitter. It couldn't be helped, and nothing compared to the feeling in her heart.

"While I wouldn't put it that way, exactly, yes. In a manner of speaking, the program is important to you both, it keeps you working together and motivated to meet regularly."

For a minute Hattie couldn't comprehend the meaning behind his words. And then she saw it, the way he'd come into her life, backstage after one of Elsa's performances, his interest in her art, the catapult to success. *The kisses.* "Was any of it real?"

"Hattie, come now." He stepped toward her, stopped. "Don't look at me like that. I never meant to hurt you. My feelings for you were real. They *are* real. Never doubt that."

Oh, but she did. "You targeted me, for…this." She swept her hand in a wide arc to include the entire gallery. "I was part of some secret government plan to gain the notice of high-ranking Nazis."

"You knew this was the goal. You agreed."

Had she? She thought back to the night with Elsa in Bath. Their scheme had seemed so righteous, so noble. They'd been so naive. Each of them had discovered that. Now, Elsa, the Salzburg Songbird, carried the label of Hitler's favorite opera singer. And, if the British government had its way, Hattie was heading in the same direction, as one of his favorite artists.

At home in England, she would carry other labels. *Opportunist. Nazi sympathizer. Traitor.* "I never wanted to gain the notice of Adolf Hitler. Never that."

"What did you think success would look like, Hattie? When you and Elsa began your secret network, what did you think it would take to save lives?"

"We thought, I thought… Not this." She looked down at her evening gown made from the finest silk and then up to her elegant surroundings, her paintings, her sketches—on display in a German city ruled by Nazis.

This had not been the goal, only the means. Their efforts were never meant to be secretive, or even dangerous. They'd only wanted to provide safe passage to people in need of escape. "I only wanted to help refugees find a way into England."

"What you do, Hattie, it's important work. You must continue."

His words, they seemed to hold unspoken agendas in them. Agendas that included more than the rescue missions provided. *You are playing a dangerous game, Hattie.*

"The day you came to my flat and saw my art for the first time beyond that initial sketch. The things you said about the paintings. Was that part of your plan to gain my trust?"

"I meant every word."

It wasn't an answer, but a deflection. "My first showing in London." She swallowed as an awful thought occurred to her. "Did the government buy my paintings?"

"Only three out of the ten."

"Of course," she said, ignoring the prick of tears at the back of her eyes. "The photograph of Elsa and me in the papers? Did you or someone in the British government orchestrate that?"

"Both."

How completely, utterly wrong she'd been about this man. He was nothing but a liar. "And us? The kiss we shared in Bayreuth? Just another ploy to gain my trust?"

"I can honestly say, without reservation, that everything between us was real."

Hattie wanted to burst into tears. She would not do so here, not in front of this man. This stranger. "I need to think." She spun around, glanced to her left, her right, seeing nothing, nothing but Oliver's deception. "I have to go."

"I'll walk you to your hotel."

"No."

"Hattie, it's late. It's raining. This is Germany. You can't be out alone and—"

"No, Oliver. Just…no."

"All right." He lifted his hands in a show of surrender. "I won't accompany you."

But, of course, he lied. He stayed a half block behind her, but Hattie knew he was there, a dark presence against the silver shimmers of the rain falling, watching over her, keeping her safe as she walked through the empty streets of Munich. Neither bothered with an umbrella. It was as if the sky were weeping for what might have been.

No, that was Hattie weeping.

She let the tears come. Oliver would never know, even if he attempted to gain her attention; he would not see her tears. The rain washed them away as soon as they appeared on her cheeks. This should have been such a romantic moment. The cool spring rain, the two of them alone in the night, speaking of art and right winning over wrong.

If only Oliver was truly concerned for her safety and wasn't watching over her because it was his duty. A duty. That's all she was to him. An asset that required protecting.

At her hotel, she paused in the entryway. As she'd done in Bayreuth, she glanced back. Oliver was there, in the shadows, and Hattie felt a wave of irritation. "Go away," she said.

He remained unmoving.

She spent the rest of the night in her hotel room, staring up at the ceiling, her heart filled with nothing but memories, regrets. Her eyes remained dry. Then, just as dawn spread its rosy light into the room, Hattie curled into a ball and, with the covers clutched in her hot fists, indulged herself in a good, hard cry.

Chapter Twenty-Nine

Elsa

January 1938. Salzburg, Austria.
Home of Wilhelm and Elsa Hoffmann.

"Elsa?" Wilhelm's call was loud and easily heard from her bedroom, but she didn't reply.

She continued her toilette, putting the final touches to her makeup. She applied a coat of red lipstick, added a strip of black kohl to her eyes. She was ahead of schedule, barely, assuming the woman from Munich who'd shown interest in Elsa's refugee work arrived on time. They were at the delicate phase of their partnership, where Elsa had yet to judge the woman's sincerity.

"Elsa," Wilhelm called again, appearing on the doorway. "You are going somewhere?"

"Tea with a friend," she said, putting on her gloves, checking the fit, wriggling her fingers until they were perfectly snug. "I won't be gone long."

His eyes narrowed. "Who is this friend?"

"Does it matter?"

"You know it does."

She felt a twinge of guilt because he was right. It did matter. If Brigitte Reinking proved to be sympathetic to the Nazi cause, as she claimed publicly, and was not sickened, as she'd whispered to Elsa in secret, then everything she and Hattie had worked to achieve would be compromised. Lives would be put in danger. "I met Brigitte through Lisl Kaltenbrunner." True. "She is in Salzburg to tour Mozart's birthplace and take tea with me."

Also true.

"Ah." Wilhelm came into the room and put his arms around her waist. "If she comes recommended by *Frau* Kaltenbrunner, then you should pursue this friendship."

Something twisted inside Elsa's heart, a pain that felt as real as a physical blow. Of course, Wilhelm would push her to make friends with Brigitte now that he knew she was closely connected to a top-ranking member of the Austrian Nazi Party.

"It pleases me," he began, "to know you finally understand the current political situation and what it can mean for us." His lips went on a familiar quest for her ear, the side of her neck, finally resting on her mouth.

Elsa let her husband kiss her, but inside a small part of her rebelled. When he pulled away, she found herself asking, "Why do you insist on aligning yourself with *Herr* Kaltenbrunner? He is an Austrian, yet he makes no apologies for his loyalty to Germany."

Or, she thought bitterly, for his hatred of Jews.

"He is a powerful man. We are fortunate that he and his wife show us favor."

Elsa could not agree. "They invite Adolf Hitler into their home, a man who has risen to power on an agenda of hate." Hate for people like Malvina, Isaiah and so many others, including herself. "Do you not agree this is wrong, Wilhelm?"

Her husband said nothing for so long Elsa feared he hadn't heard her. But she knew he had. They were standing three feet apart, looking into each other's eyes. "It would not be wise to say such things outside this home."

"That is not an answer."

"I do not choose sides, Elsa. You know this about me."

There would come a time when he would be forced to do so. "Surely, you have an opinion about Hitler's policies."

"The Führer has brought stability to Germany, a nation that was under great economic duress before he took power. Austria could use some of that stability."

Elsa's hand flew to her mouth. "I thought you were against annexation."

A smile flickered across his face for a fraction of a second before it disappeared behind a veil of inscrutability. "You are missing the point."

"Perhaps you should enlighten me."

"If Adolf Hitler wants to annex Austria, it will be done."

It was her greatest fear. "And if that happens? If Austria is absorbed into Germany?"

"Then, we will have made a powerful alliance. The Führer is a great lover of opera and of you. He was recently quoted as saying you are his favorite singer."

She'd read the quote, Wilhelm had shown it to her himself, and Elsa had felt the same rush of repulsion that she did now.

"This is a good thing, Elsa, for your career, for us, our marriage, our future together. As Germany's power expands, so will ours."

It was a shock, listening to her husband speak of such matters openly. To recognize his agenda fully. The very thing Elsa had spent so long fearing had come to pass. Had Wilhelm always been a sycophant? Had she failed to see his true nature?

What did that say about her?

That she'd been blinded by love. Well, now she saw her husband with the eyes of a woman who'd sent her beloved aunt to another country to keep her safe.

Wilhelm's loyalty was to himself. He had no allegiance to Austria or Germany or even to her. He didn't care about the greater good, or a monster's perverse ideology; he only cared about himself, and that made him dangerous.

More dangerous than Elsa had understood.

What, she wondered, would he do to save himself?

She made a sound deep in her throat, then pulled herself together. "I need to finish dressing for tea with *Frau* Reinking."

"I'll leave you to it."

She checked her appearance and headed down to the first floor. At the same moment she finished her descent, Wilhelm was stepping aside to let a man enter their home. Elsa did not recognize his face. He wore black on black on black. A wolf in a business suit and a wool overcoat. Something about him...

Elsa suppressed a shiver.

Another man stepped across the threshold. Elsa did not know him, either. This one was dressed in the uniform of the German SS. Neither of the men took off their hats.

Introductions were not made.

With Wilhelm leading the way, the trio walked right past Elsa, and she instantly knew she would be late for tea with Brigitte. She paced in the parlor outside Wilhelm's private office, checking the time, checking it again.

What was happening inside that room?

She thought back over her conversation with her husband about annexation and what it would mean to them. The Austrian Nazi Party had gained many supporters, especially the people most affected by economic hardship. Just like the German people, they needed an enemy they could blame for their difficulties.

Adolf Hitler had given them one in the Jewish people.

Elsa had a sudden urge to follow Malvina to England. *Who would provide help to the refugees?* No, she could not leave Austria, not yet.

At least Wilhelm didn't know what she did in secret. He would never know, not so long as he kept company with men who wore the SS runes, as if they were a badge of honor.

More like the mark of evil.

Elsa took another circuit around the room. Another handful of minutes passed, and the door remained firmly shut. Time was running out for her. She would have to leave for the restaurant very soon. Ten minutes. She would give it ten more minutes, no more.

She paced.

She worried.

Looking around the parlor, she took a cursory inventory of the room. She'd attempted to make this home her own, but it lacked a certain amount of clutter to be considered comfortable. Wilhelm preferred his environment neat. Rigidly ordered. Unpretentious. Much like himself.

He was not flamboyant.

He was brilliant, methodical.

And an opportunist.

She could not get the horrible realization out of her mind that her husband cared only for himself. And possibly Elsa, in as much as he was able to care for another person.

The door to the office swept open, and she swung around.

All three men exited the room, one after the other, Wilhelm bringing up the rear. Satisfaction vibrated off him, and Elsa knew: he'd made a deal with the enemy.

She did not join her husband as he escorted them to the door but instead waited for him to return to the parlor. He did almost immediately, looking very pleased. "Our future is secure."

"What have you done?" She tried to sound haughty, but her voice held a hollow edge. Her world had just been shaken off its foundations, and she had no idea how to set it right again.

"I have been appointed director of the Vienna State Opera."

Not Berlin. Vienna. So, it wasn't as bad as she feared. She should congratulate him. She couldn't bring herself to do it.

"I have done this for you, Elsa. For us."

She tried to speak, could even feel her jaw working, but words eluded her. Swallowing, she tried again. "Let me see if I have this straight. You have secured your future—"

"—our future."

"*Our* future, by aligning yourself with Nazis. Do I have it right?" She paused, waiting, praying, hoping Wilhelm would redeem himself.

"Do not be naive, Elsa. You know what is coming."

Who was this man? Surely not the one she'd married. The ticking of the mantel clock mocked her. *Tick, tick, tick* went the pendulum. *No, no, no* went her heart. Wrapping her dignity around her like a shield of armor, she set her chin and said, "Do not take this job."

"It's already done."

Elsa stared at her husband. Wisps of memories from their courtship flitted across her mind. She thought of the man who'd cut down whole gardens of flowers for her. The man who'd taken long walks with her late at night when the streets were theirs alone. It had all seemed so wonderful and idyllic. But that man had been a lie.

The man who'd married her, the man who stood before her now, was the true Wilhelm Hoffmann. He aligned himself—and her—with the enemy rather than do what was right.

Wilhelm wasn't a bad man, she realized. Just a weak one.

She took a deep breath. And accepted the truth. She'd lost her husband. No, she thought, she couldn't lose something she'd never had. "Congratulations on your appointment."

It isn't over, she told herself, feeling calmer now. Hopeful. *He could still come around.*

Now she was telling herself lies.

"This is a good thing, Elsa. You'll see." He took her in his arms, set his chin atop her head. "I love you, *Liebling*. That's why I make these alliances, why I took this job. Say that you know this."

She knew he believed it. She knew he spoke his truth, and so she said, "Yes, Wilhelm, I know this." She forced a smile. "And I am late for tea."

She fled their home, the first time in her marriage she was afraid of what she would find when she returned. The sense of loss was there, drumming in her head, in the chambers of her heart, but too much hung on the emotion, so she pasted on a smile and entered the restaurant a full thirty minutes late.

Brigitte Reinking sat at a table, looking the picture of patience. Elsa would not allow herself to be impressed. The woman was not her friend. She was not her ally, possibly never would be. Because unlike Wilhelm, Elsa was careful with the people she brought into her life.

Chapter Thirty

Hattie

April 1938. London, England.

Hattie had always considered winter a time of death, of cold and frost, and waiting for the weather to break. The first hint of spring usually occurred sometime in mid-March. However, this year, the promise of new beginnings did not arrive. On the thirteenth day of March, a day after German troops entered Vienna, Hitler annexed Austria and immediately applied his anti-Semitic decrees.

Malvina worried for Elsa. Hattie did, too, and was more determined than ever to exhibit her art in Salzburg as previously planned, despite the political unrest. Vera begged her not to go. Malvina encouraged her to do so, for Elsa's sake.

Oliver was the deciding vote.

He'd remained in Hattie's life, showcasing her art in his galleries throughout Europe, and eventually they became friendly again, if not friends. They never spoke of their rift or its cause. They were both great pretenders. He coordinated Hattie's exhibits with Elsa's performances, while also continuing his direct role in their refugee efforts. And, with much internal conflict, Hattie continued making nice with art patrons in Germany.

There'd been some awkward moments in the initial weeks after she discovered the depths of Oliver's duplicity. But their work was too important to allow personal feelings to get in the way of saving lives. So Hattie put on a brave face whenever she had to interact with the man, and ensured, above all else, that she was never alone with him.

The situation was tolerable, if not ideal.

A telegram arrived the day before she was to leave for Salzburg. The very sound of the boy's motorbike was not new and always brought apprehension. When she discovered the messenger brought word from Salzburg, her worry turned to terror. Hattie took the telegram, hand shaking, knowing she would never again be able to hear a motorbike approaching without a grave sense of alarm.

She scanned the message. "It's from Elsa."

Malvina rushed to her. "What does she say?"

"Georg not home," Hattie read. *"Maria helpless."*

Malvina collapsed on a ladder-back chair. Hattie let out her own breath of air. Although Elsa wasn't in danger, as they'd feared, the news was not good. *Georg* and *Maria* weren't real people. The use of these specific names was code for a husband seized, and his wife, even with Elsa's help, had exhausted all means of saving him from the camps.

There had been a time when Jewish men were sent to the work camps, then returned home. Those days were long over. Hattie looked at the message in her hand. This was the kind of telegram she dreaded most, now that Germany had annexed Austria.

Austrian Jews were no safer than German Jews, and the rest of Europe looked away. There'd been little international resistance to the *Anschluss*. Some of the London newspapers even called it a natural union of German-speaking countries.

Frowning, Hattie passed the telegram to Vera. "Don't make the trip, Hattie."

"You know I must."

"We've saved dozens of lives."

Hattie shook her head. "And have failed twenty times that many."

"When will it be enough?"

That her sister had to ask only showed how little Vera knew the woman Hattie had become. "It will be enough when men, women and children are no longer persecuted for their race or religion."

Vera launched into the same argument she'd thrown at Hattie since they'd been harassed on the train ride out of Bayreuth. "This is not your fight, Hattie, not anymore."

"Tell that to the woman whose husband has disappeared."

Vera held firm. "The Nazis will arrest you if you are caught helping her."

That wasn't entirely true: possible, but not a given. The Nazis wanted Jewish people to leave their country. They'd adopted a policy of forced emigration, while providing no means for the refugees to escape. They seized their property and their money and closed off all means for acquiring the necessary paperwork to enter another country.

What Hattie and Elsa were doing didn't break any German laws, but they skirted along the edges of many. She wouldn't think about the smuggling. "I will not be caught," Hattie said, as she often did when the topic arose. "And, thus, I will avoid arrest."

"What can I say to change your mind?" Vera's voice turned desperate. "Tell me, and I will say it."

"I'm going into Austria. With or without your blessing."

She and Vera argued deep into the night, all the way to the moment Hattie exited the flat, her bags packed and her travel papers in order. Never had Hattie left an argument unsettled between her and her sister. Their mother had often paraphrased one of her favorite Bible verses. *Do not let the sun go down on your anger.*

Hattie crossed the border without incident, and although thoughts of the angry words she'd exchanged with Vera played in her mind, she refused to let her sister's fear repeat itself in her own heart. Easier said than done, Hattie realized, as she exited one train and joined the queue to show her passport and state her business at the checkpoint before boarding the next.

Austria had transformed into a carbon copy of Germany. Barely three weeks since the *Anschluss*, and the countries looked identical. Nazi flags hung from every rooftop. Men in SS uniforms patrolled the train platforms, armed with guns and vicious-looking dogs. Hate lived in their eyes. The entire world, at least this part of Europe, felt as though it were sinking.

Everyone had known annexation was coming—Hitler had been clear about his intentions—and still, the British government preached appeasement. Did they not know what was happening? They knew. They had to know.

Anger flared. As if sensing her reaction, one of the soldiers gave her a cold, malicious glare. Hattie looked away. Her face was stiff, but she was careful not to show her fear. She glanced down the tracks to see a train coming. It sounded its horn, and she jumped.

Vera's warnings filled Hattie's mind. Her sister was right. Germany's power was growing stronger, their aggression more dangerous, and the British government's hands-off approach more profoundly disappointing.

Rescuing refugees would be more difficult now, more perilous, and Hattie didn't like the direction of her thoughts. It would seem Vera's fear had infected her.

Hattie rarely prayed for the Lord to be with her on these trips. Not that she didn't believe in the Almighty's willingness to intercede. It was that He had other, more urgent matters to attend to. But now, here, alone on this platform full of strangers, and armed soldiers all around, Hattie shut her eyes and prayed for God's presence.

Peace that transcended all understanding filled her.

By the time her train arrived in Salzburg, it was midmorning, and a fluffy, late-season snow had begun to fall. The streets stood flat and silent, and the still, quiet air rushed in Hattie's ears, the echo of sound from a long-forgotten dream.

There was no time to stop at her hotel. Keeping off the main streets, Hattie went straight to the safe house to meet Elsa, luggage in hand. By now, her seventh visit to Salzburg, she knew the route by heart. Snow fell harder, fat and wet, obscuring the house's wooden slats, gabled roof and shuttered windows. The Nazi flag that hung over the front door was a foul addition to the exterior, marring the house's charm, but Hattie understood the rationale. Hide in plain sight.

She hurried inside, set her bags in the makeshift office off the kitchen. Voices drifted from the interview room. Hattie mounted the stairs and listened. Elsa was speaking with another woman, who sounded very positive, self-possessed and terribly young. Calm though the stranger came off, it didn't take Hattie long to realize it was a ruse. She entered the room and practically felt the wave of high-pitch nerves rolling off the young woman.

"Ah, Hattie, here you are. Come meet Misha."

Hattie took in the woman who was indeed quite young, not yet twenty. Petite and thin, almost gangly, Misha had curly black hair and bright green eyes.

Elsa encouraged Misha to tell her story.

As Hattie listened, it became clear the young woman was prepared to do whatever it took to save herself and her younger sister, a girl of thirteen, five years Misha's junior. "Our parents are gone." She didn't need to say where. "My sister has only me. Will you help us get to England? I will do any work, live at any level, no matter how low. The barest necessities, food and a place to lay our heads, that is all we need."

It was difficult to know what cases to pick for rescue, Hattie knew. Each had a complete and miserable story attached to it, but this one had a relatively easy solution. Misha's commitment to her sister, their five-year age difference, these things made Hattie think of Vera and the sacrifices she'd made. "We will get a student's visa in your case, Misha. You and your sister will come to England and live with me until we can find you permanent housing."

This was not unprecedented. The flat she shared with Vera and Malvina had become something of a clearing house for refugees and the central point for their work. The separate suite served as temporary accommodations for people they brought into England. Originally, Hattie had hoped to use the extra room as an art studio. Vera confessed she'd hoped to use the space to write her books. A worthy sacrifice, they both agreed.

"How well do you speak English?"

Misha shook her head. "Poorly, I'm afraid."

Hattie had expected this. "We'll enroll you in an English-language class immediately. When you finish that, we will find a way to extend your studies and your stay."

"There. You see, Misha?" Elsa clapped her hands together and moved to take the young woman's hands in a very Elsa-like manner. "You now have a reason to request a passport and temporary visa."

The young woman's eyes widened. "Only temporary?"

"It's how these things work," Hattie explained. "The question of final emigration need not be raised at this point."

"Thank you." Misha left crying happy tears.

Alone with Elsa, Hattie asked about the other case, the one that had initiated the telegram. There was something in the intensity of her gaze that made Hattie look closer at her friend. Elsa had lost weight, and she looked more defeated than usual. "The assistant conductor and choir repetiteur at the Vienna State Opera disappeared five nights ago," she said, her voice mournful. "His wife is frantic. They have a small daughter, an infant, and she can't leave the child to go out looking for him."

The despair in Elsa's voice told Hattie what she needed to know. This case was personal. The assistant conductor was a friend. "He's Jewish?"

"Not only is Isaiah Jewish, he is also Polish."

"Oh." Hattie better understood Elsa's dismay. For some reason, the Nazis especially hated Polish Jews. Wherever they'd taken Isaiah, he was not coming back. "Will his wife leave Austria without her husband?"

"Not until she knows what became of him."

These types of matters were out of their purview. Elsa knew it. Hattie knew it. There was, of course, someone who had the proper contacts to make the necessary inquiries. Hattie had hoped never to cross that line with Oliver. But this case—this man—mattered to Elsa. And so he mattered to Hattie. "I'll approach Oliver when we meet tonight to discuss my exhibit."

Decision made, she and Elsa prepared the argument she would present. They'd barely begun when it was time to begin the other interviews. "We'll finish this later," Elsa promised. "Come to my dressing room after the performance tonight."

"I can't. Oliver is taking me out to a late dinner." At Elsa's raised eyebrows, she added, "To discuss plans for the opening of my exhibit tomorrow tonight."

"So you said."

"It bears repeating. We're business associates, Elsa. Nothing more."

"Keep telling yourself that, Hattie."

She held her friend's stare, wondering why after all this time Elsa still chose to believe there was something between Hattie and Oliver. She'd told her friend about that night in Munich and his confession and the full nature of his duplicity. When she'd finished, Elsa had looked at her oddly. "You never guessed he worked for the British government?"

The casual comment had made Hattie think, really think, and she realized how naive she'd been. "I don't understand why he withheld the truth for so long."

That question beat at her. There'd been plenty of opportunities for him to explain his situation, and yet he hadn't.

"My guess," Elsa said slowly, eyeing her with the look of a much older woman, "is that he didn't want you to see him in a bad light. He likes you, Hattie. Rather a lot."

Hattie felt her cheeks flaming as she realized what Elsa meant, but her own humiliation wouldn't abate. If anything, it grew stronger. "Do you want to know what I think?" She hadn't waited for Elsa to nod but pressed on. "I think he is an accomplished liar."

Elsa nodded, but slowly, with a great amount of weariness. "We are all three accomplished liars, Hattie."

The words were shocking, spoken aloud like that and with

such anguish on her friend's face despite the conviction in her tone. Hattie wanted to argue. She wanted to tell her friend the lies they told saved lives, while Oliver's lies and deceit...

Also saved lives.

"Come to my dressing room before the show, and we'll decide what you will say on Isaiah's behalf. Then, maybe..." Elsa paused for a long moment, and when she spoke again, so softly that Hattie had to lean in, she wasn't sure she heard her friend correctly "...I can bring a level of peace to at least one Austrian wife."

Chapter Thirty-One

Elsa

April 1938. Salzburg, Austria.
Felsenreitschule *Theater*.

When she'd begun her career, Elsa's life had been remarkably simple. She'd swept from stage to stage and one tragedy to the next. She'd loved every dramatic, heart-wrenching moment. The passion, the emotion… She'd always—*always*—wept for her doomed heroines.

Now, she wept for real people who found themselves deprived of their basic human rights. She'd been right to send Malvina to England. Her aunt lived a good, rich life with the Featherstone sisters. But what of the others?

Their faces haunted her.

For every life saved, many were lost. She sat at her dressing table, alone, watching her reflection through narrowed eyes, seeing only her failures.

War was coming, and her beloved Austria would be on the wrong side. She could escape. She could run to England. America. Anywhere. She could leave her husband, her marriage. It would not be easy. Divorce went against everything she believed as a woman raised in the Christian faith. What would be her reason?

Wilhelm wasn't always forthright with her, he'd lied about his application to the Nazi Party and he pandered to evil men, but he'd never raised his hand to Elsa. He'd never been openly cruel. That didn't mean their marriage was secure.

He would arrive at the theater soon. Elsa didn't want to see him, not here in her dressing room or out in the auditorium, plying his will over her from behind the baton.

The expected knock at the door came.

She swiveled in her chair. "Come in."

Hinges creaked, a soft breeze shifted the still air, and then Wilhelm was in the doorway, his face flooded with complicated emotions. He stood there, watching her, with the intense stare that never failed to steal her breath. Why, she wondered, after all she knew about him, did her heart still flutter at the sight of him?

Why could her love not have faded along with her respect?

Holding his gaze, she stood and made her way across the room, letting happy memories fill her. Memories of what life had been like when the charming maestro had pursued her for his wife. Elsa had believed their love story would have a happy ending.

It's not too late. Please, let it be so.

She drank in the sight of him dressed in his traditional black tie and tails. She tried to see past the cracks in their marriage and straight to the man she loved still. It was not so hard. Wilhelm was tall and leanly muscled, his face aristocratic with a strong cut of cheekbones under those pale deep-set blue eyes.

Even the stark white of his shirt set off his handsome features. "Hello, Wilhelm."

"Darling." He shut the door with a jab of his elbow and then lifted a single eyebrow at her. "I missed you this afternoon. You didn't come home after meeting your friend for tea."

This was it, her chance to tell him why she'd been late. To confess the work she and Hattie did on behalf of the persecuted, some of whom Wilhelm knew personally. Then she remembered his application to the Nazi Party, and she knew she could not trust him with the truth. "Her train was late. I telephoned you. Did you not get the message?" She'd left a detailed explanation with their recently hired housekeeper. A sour-faced box of a woman Elsa didn't trust any more than she did her husband.

"I received it." He drew closer. "You know how I feel about your friendship with that British woman. She is beneath you."

Elsa didn't want to rehash the same old argument. Nevertheless, she found herself defending her friend. "Hattie has become a successful artist. Her work has caught the eye of important people in the Third Reich. Even Joseph Goebbels has one of her paintings."

Much to Hattie's horror.

Wilhelm raised an eyebrow. "This is your defense? That she has garnered interest in her art from high-ranking Nazis? She's British, Elsa. You must keep your distance."

Elsa thought she saw a flicker of something different in Wilhelm's eyes, something dark. A shiver iced across her skin. "Hattie is not a threat to me."

He gave a short, mirthless laugh. "Let us drop these pretenses. You are keeping secrets from me, Elsa, and I don't like it."

"I have my secrets, Wilhelm, and you have yours."

This, she realized, was the wrong tactic. He closed the distance between them in two angry strides. "I know about that house you go to when she is in Salzburg. I know you conduct interviews with Jews." With each word his voice grew softer, lower, more menacing. "I know what you are doing, Elsa. I know. I know it all."

His words staggered her, and she found she had to clutch the side of her makeup table to steady herself. For a minute, she couldn't speak, could only stare, gasping, and then suddenly one word slipped past her lips. "How?"

"I have my sources."

She stared at him, trying to process those four words. *I have my sources.* No, he had one source. The new housekeeper. "You had her follow me."

"For your own good."

A defense wrapped inside an answer. How very like Wilhelm. Elsa could do nothing but blink.

"You must stop this dangerous work. You must." He was no longer the confident maestro but a desperate man worried about his wife's clandestine activities. The thought brought her no comfort, because she knew he wasn't concerned about her, only what her actions meant for him.

She pressed her lips together to keep from sobbing.

"How many Jews have you helped escape?"

Her mournful thoughts disappeared. She'd prepared for this conversation, knew the answer she would give, the lie she would tell. "Only one family."

"It is more."

The blood drained from her face. "Many lives have been saved."

It was all she would give him.

"How many?"

"Not enough." *Not nearly enough.*

"You will stop this secret work." He took her by the shoulders, shook her hard. "You will stop it at once."

An impossible demand. What was happening in her homeland was shameful. Within days of the *Anschluss*, the rights of Austrian Jews had been stripped away completely. They could not take employment. They could not enter a restaurant or café. Nor the theater, a church or synagogue, or any public place. They couldn't sit on a public bench. Their children could not play in the parks. If they wanted to sell their possessions, they were allowed to do so at a price determined by the government, a twentieth of any genuine value.

Like their counterparts in Germany, Austrian Jews had only two routes left to them. They might starve or, if they had the resources, turn on the gas.

How could Elsa quit her work, when so many needed her help?

"I will not see you arrested."

"Are you worried about my safety, Wilhelm? Or yours?"

His grip turned merciless. "I will not have you endanger what we have built."

She shoved away from him. "You're an opportunist. A common sycophant. That's what they say about you, the Nazis, the British."

His face turned hard. "If you think your words insult me, you've missed the point."

"Oh, I know the point, Wilhelm. I know you make alliances to protect yourself. I know you write to Hitler, suggesting you become the artistic director of an alliance between the Munich and Vienna State Operas. I know you pander to men like Kaltenbrunner to secure your position with the Nazis, and that you befriend men like Oliver Roundel in case you need to flee to England." She lowered her eyes and very carefully, very slowly used his own words against him. "I know what you are doing, Wilhelm. I know. I know it all."

He clasped his hands behind his back, straightened to his full height and drew in a long breath. His stance was full of unchecked pride. He stood tall, chin lifted, head erect. That, too, was so very Wilhelm. "You will stop this nonsense, or I will take matters into my own hands. The choice is yours."

How could he think he offered her a choice? "I would like you to leave me now."

"Elsa, listen to me. I make this demand because I love you."

His eyes pleaded with her to believe him, and to her shame she wanted to do just that. Hadn't she known Wilhelm's love in the past? Hadn't she known his feelings had been as real as hers had been? Even now, a part of her loved him still. He was her husband. They shared a life, a home, a bed. How had they come to this?

The room was suddenly hot, so hot she feared she would faint. Dry eyes were her only defense. And, sadly, more lies. "Yes, Wilhelm. I will do as you ask."

A fresh range of emotions crossed his face, more subtle, and much harder to read. "I have your word?"

"You have my word."

He nodded. "Very well. We won't speak of this again."

A knot twisted in her stomach as she watched him walk away without wishing her the customary *Toi, toi, toi.* Perhaps he would return, tell her he was wrong, and that he was proud of her. She waited for his return, saw the shadow moving under the door. She held her breath and prayed for…what? What did she want? More time? A moment of inspiration? Wilhelm to be a different man when he returned?

And then it came. The prayed-for knock at her door. A tangle of emotions lodged in her throat. She called out, "Enter."

Hattie appeared in the doorway. One look at Elsa's face, and she was across the room. "What's happened? Did he hurt you?"

He. She meant Wilhelm. How much did Hattie know about the decay of her marriage? "I'm fine."

"You don't have to put on a brave face for me." How well this woman could read her, better than her own husband.

Elsa went to her friend and pulled her into a fierce hug. They were so similar, and, oh, how she wanted to unburden her heart. But now was not the time. They had a precious few minutes before she had to take the stage. Stepping back, she wiped at the edges of her eyes where tears had formed. "It is too much to share at the moment."

"Give me the finer points, then."

Where to begin? Her thoughts whirled in her head like a small tornado. "There are so many who need our help."

"Too many. It's overwhelming at times."

This was a thought they'd shared in a thousand conversations at a thousand moments like this. "The sense of failure is always with me. It keeps me up at night."

"It's the same for me." There was a kind of sadness in her friend's eyes that Elsa saw every day in her own mirror. She tried to smile, to reassure her, even as she felt her own heart cracking. "I have something for you, and I need to ask a favor."

"All right."

Elsa went to her travel case. She worked open the lid, dug her hand inside. When her fingers grazed over the small lump, she pulled back the lining and produced a small cylinder that looked like a lipstick tube. "Give this to Oliver, but wait until you're in England."

"What is it?"

She looked around. Her husband could have spies listening at the door, through the wall. "The less you know, the better."

"Consider it done." Hattie tucked the tube into her purse.

"Now for the favor." Elsa reached back into the valise and pulled out the brooch she'd accepted two nights ago from a woman close to starvation. "This belongs to a friend, an older woman, a former soprano with the Berlin State Opera. She has health issues and was denied entry into England because of rheumatism of the knee." And thus, no visa. No work permit.

The brooch represented monetary support for her life in England once they found a way to get her there. Which, of course, they would. It was what they did.

"I understand."

"I knew you would." Elsa pinned the piece of jewelry to Hattie's dress, trusting she would not only wear the brooch out of Austria, but would ensure the owner received it back when she arrived in England. "You are a good friend, Hattie."

"Always. Never forget it." Smiling softly, Hattie wiped a tear from Elsa's cheek, then she said the words Wilhelm had not. *"Toi, toi, toi."*

Chapter Thirty-Two

Hattie

April 1938. Salzburg, Austria.

Hattie left Elsa's dressing room feeling out of sorts and unsettled. Her friend had not been herself. Her face had been leached of color, and there was a kind of fear in her eyes that hadn't been there earlier. Something had put her in that gloomy mood.

Or someone.

Hattie had passed a scowling Wilhelm in the corridor on her way to Elsa's dressing room. The disagreeable man hadn't seen her, and she hadn't made herself known.

She'd never fully trusted him. Now was not the time to begin, nor was it the time to dwell on her concerns for her friend. Hattie had more pressing concerns. Namely the piece of jewelry she wore pinned to her dress. When Elsa had presented the brooch, she'd been appalled by its sheer size. A great, oblong monstrosity of blazing diamonds worth a small ransom. The sort of thing she'd seen on only the richest of art patrons.

She'd never owned, much less worn, anything so outrageously large and ostentatious. Fortunately, tonight, Hattie's jacquard dress had an understated print and glass buttons down the front panel. The brooch looked as if it belonged where Elsa had pinned it. Hattie was confident no one would say a word.

Her friend's somber mood was not so easily dismissed.

Something was amiss. It was a thought she couldn't dispel as she entered the auditorium and settled in her seat. As always, Elsa's singing was perfection. She poured her emotions into each aria, every note raw, painful and very, very believable. Hattie sensed Elsa was only half acting tonight. The soprano shared Carmen's heartbreak and grief.

Hattie left the theater feeling her friend's pain as if it were her own. She needed release and wanted to sequester herself in her hotel room so she could sketch the scenes that played in her head. It was a luxury she couldn't afford. There was still work to be done, information to gather, a woman and her infant child to help. And a late dinner with a British MI6 agent to start the process rolling.

Oliver waited for Hattie in the lobby of her hotel. Didn't he look handsome, she thought, all tall and perfectly self-confident. His face smoothly shaven. The sigh that tickled her throat made her feel young and foolish. She took a moment to settle her nerves, reminding herself this wasn't a date. It was dinner, and not the first one since their falling out.

"I made a reservation at a restaurant two blocks away." He was being so terribly polite, but so was she.

She nodded and smiled, needing him to think she'd moved past the hurt he'd inflicted on her heart. She was not a woman who held a grudge. No, no. Hattie Featherstone was mature and responsible, and if her artist's soul wanted to howl in frustration or beg the man to grovel for her forgiveness, well, she would channel that into her art later tonight.

They walked at a reasonable pace. The evening air was heavy with the scent of the late snowfall. Fat, languid flakes floated softly around them, creating a surreal, wistful feel to everything. Hattie wanted to enjoy the moment.

She could not.

How could a sovereign God create such beauty in a city, a world, where so much ugliness lived? What had once hidden in shadows now moved in the light.

By silent agreement, neither she nor Oliver spoke until they were seated at the table and their orders had been placed. Their eyes met across the table, consideration in his, a question in hers. The moment passed, and Oliver leaned back in his chair. "Let's talk about tomorrow night's showing."

They discussed the exhibit, which was really a matter of form at this point, now that she'd shown her work to great success in Oliver's other galleries.

"It's official," he said, looking pleased. "You're the talk of the international art world. Enthusiasts and collectors are clamoring for a Henrietta Featherstone original."

He'd just uttered the words Hattie had spent most of her life waiting to hear. Where was her elation? Her hand went to the brooch that wasn't hers, while her mind thought of its owner, a woman denied entry into England because she had bad knees. "It feels wrong," she said, "that I should accomplish my dreams at a time when so many have lost everything."

"You have the means to live a better life, Hattie. One of comfort." He placed his hand over hers, pulled it away just as quickly. "And still, you economize and go without for the sake of funding the rescue of one more soul."

He made her sound better than she was.

Hattie gave out of plenty. Others made far greater sacrifices. One of Vera's coworkers forwent public transportation. Every day, she walked three miles to work and gave the saved fares to their refugee fund. "It's no hardship to arrange my life as I always have."

"We both know it's more than that."

She shrugged. "One day, the horror will be over, and then there will be time to make different choices."

"You are a wealthy woman now. You could afford your own flat, with a studio for your art, and still give loads of money to the cause."

"Why would I do that?" The home she'd made with Vera, and now Malvina, was large enough to accommodate her needs and still act as a clearing house for refugees in transit, often serving as their first haven.

"You would have the peace and quiet to create more art that I would then be able to sell. More shows means more sales and more resources."

"If I may be permitted to be sentimental for a moment..." She glanced around them, lowering her voice for his ears only. "The visitors who stay temporarily in our home are happy to be there. Their joy fills the space while they are with us and leaves a faint trace after they are gone. That feeling feeds my soul, Oliver. Which is good for my art."

Despite the increasing danger that came with her trips into Europe, the moments of brightness with the refugees were not to be taken for granted. That was something Malvina had taught her and something Hattie held on to in her darkest moments.

"You're a good person, Hattie." There was a look in his eyes, a soft, admiring glint that contrasted with the blandness of his tone. *My feelings are real. Never doubt that.*

She wanted to lean into the memory. This was not the time. "I need to ask you a favor."

Her words didn't seem to surprise him. However, her timing clearly did. "Not here."

"That goes without saying."

She waited until they were heading back to her hotel. Oliver directed her to sit on a stone bench in the hotel gardens. She did. And was instantly trapped inside the memory of another time, in another garden. They'd been here before, in this moment, if not this specific garden, and she wondered if he also remembered.

"Go on, Hattie. Make your request."

In the most general of terms, she told him about the missing assistant conductor and his wife's desperation. "She won't travel until she knows what's become of him."

"You want me to find out what I can and relay the information to...you?"

"Elsa."

He nodded. "Is that all?"

"No." She explained about the owner of the brooch and the reason for her difficulty acquiring a visa or work permit, careful to keep her words vague in case anyone were listening. Someone was always listening.

"It's possible to secure what you need. For a cost."

"How much?"

The sum he quoted was shockingly high, and yet a small price for a life. "I will pay it myself."

"How did I know you were going to say that?" He stood before she could respond. "It's late. Let's get you back to your hotel." He offered his arm. "Shall we?"

She quickly regained her feet, confused by the tenderness in his gaze. And yet, he couldn't seem to get out of her company fast enough. The man was an enigma. Tonight, she didn't have the mental energy to sort it all out, so she simply hooked her arm through his, and off they went.

From beneath her lashes, she took in his broad shoulders, the firm set of his lips. And oh, his eyes. Such an unusual color, and so clear, as if they could see past the clouds and straight into the light.

Have a care, Hattie. The man is not what he seems.

People strolled past them. Some dropped smiles in their direction, not quite making eye contact but not quite ignoring them, either. It was an odd sort of cool cordiality, as if nothing sordid were happening in their country. "Why don't they do anything?"

She'd meant the question rhetorically, but Oliver responded anyway. "People don't like to interfere in matters that make them uncomfortable," he said with a note of bitterness. "They want to pretend they don't see what's right in front of their face."

Hattie's heart hurt for the people not allowed on this street or in the restaurant where she and Oliver had dined. She wanted to howl at the situation, to yank at her hair. Mostly, Hattie wanted justice.

Blood rushed in her ears as she and Oliver walked on, past men and women they didn't know, some of whom would appear at the exhibit tomorrow night. Where Hattie would smile and mingle and sell them her art, all while wearing an enormous diamond brooch that belonged to a former opera diva with bad knees.

Hattie's star was rising, while another woman's faded.

Where was the justice in that?

Chapter Thirty-Three

Elsa

August 1943. Lower Saxony, Northern Germany.
Bergen-Belsen Concentration Camp.

A new inmate arrived in the middle of the night. Another so-called important detainee, Elsa guessed. She'd heard the familiar sound of the state car rumbling past the gates. She would never forget the growl of that engine or the way it bounced over the divots in the road.

She didn't want to know the identity of the person—man or woman. No, Elsa only wanted to find a moment of peace in another fitful sleep. There were many hours before dawn. She needed the rest, if for no other reason than to restore some measure of her sanity.

Peace did not come.

Her mind raced over what the new arrival would endure at the hands of the commandant and his soulless guards. She wished she could turn off her thoughts, ignore her curiosity, her fear, and let the stifling air close in around her. Wished she could ignore the ants marching single file in her mind, their faces hard and ruthless, identical to her SS jailers and the soldiers who'd stormed the *Felsenreitschule*.

Lying perfectly still, feeling panicky, she realized the sense of isolation was strong tonight. Even knowing she was up for exchange—Haas had told her this during one of his summonses—the waking nightmare of her incarceration remained. And still the dark, muddled question of her betrayer's identity plagued her. Elsa thought she knew, then she thought she didn't. And always, always she wondered what had happened to Wilhelm after their eyes had met that one final time.

Kriminaldirektor Vogt had laughed at her when she'd asked about her husband. He'd laughed at her a lot. The memories of his cackle wouldn't stop stabbing at her. His face red and blotchy, shouting at her, spitting out his words, then going wildly calm, eerily so; then the laughter would erupt from his thin, sneering lips, and the pattern would begin again.

Would she ever forget?

She thought she heard it now. The cackle. Not Vogt's. This one belonged to *Kommandant* Haas. She knew it well. The new arrival was a woman. Haas would not leave the comfort of his bed for a man. Who was she?

Elsa's eyes kept glancing to the corner of the room, where the door stood unopened. The shadows stretched the longest in that part of the barracks, hiding the broken bodies of once-vibrant women trying to hold on to the last scraps of their dignity. Each of them was slowly dying, rotting away in this forgotten hole in northern Germany, and Elsa was among their ranks.

Her hair had begun to grow back in unruly patches. Her skin had a sickly gray-green tint, giving her the look of death.

Life was very small and contained in this room, full of the quiet, still fear that threaded through every woman, every breath, every heartbeat. Any day, despite negotiations on her behalf, Elsa could be deemed unworthy of exchange and sent to the other part of the camp where hope would be exterminated.

In Germany and even Austria, Elsa had dismissed the imminent danger as a necessary part of her work. That had been her mistake. Hattie had tried to warn her, as had others. Even, in her own way, Frieda.

Elsa shivered, glanced back at the door. It opened at last, and she saw movement in the shadows. A ghostly figure emerged from the gloom. Had she followed Elsa to this place from another life? Her *other* life? The woman wore the clothing of an inmate. A stone-faced soldier stood beside her in his SS uniform, holding her arm in his huge fist. A picture flashed before Elsa's eyes, a scene she'd seen in her nightmares and had tried to forget but could not.

The sight of this woman outside the interrogation room in Salzburg, their eyes meeting, the truth of her guilt impossible to deny. She wore the same look now. Fear. Guilt. Shame. And Elsa knew, without a single shadow of a doubt, that she stared at the face of her betrayer. She shut her eyes, put her own face in her hands and tried to scrub the image away, but when she opened them again, the woman was still there.

Elsa blinked, repulsed, a little dizzy.

Unpleasant memories assailed her. She let them come. Let them remind her of all the times she'd reached out and had been rebuffed. A sigh escaped past her tight lips.

The guard shoved the woman forward and exited the building. She fell to her knees, then crawled forward, moving into the weak moonbeam that limped through the dirt-smeared windowpanes. She slowly came to her feet, looked around somewhat dazedly and caught Elsa's eye. Her back stiffened. Her eyes filled.

Elsa turned away, unable to bear the sight of the woman she'd let into her life. The one she wanted to hate but couldn't quite get there. She appeared older, so terribly old. Her gray eyes, the color of morning fog, were red and swollen. She made little whimpering noises in her throat as she shuffled across the room, her progress slow and clearly painful.

She continued until she stood before Elsa. Swaying, she made a sound deep in her throat, a low, flat moan that wasn't human. It stripped away her anger and a portion of her bitterness, but not all. No, not all.

"Elsa."

Turning away, she lowered herself back on the bed made of wood, but not before she told her betrayer, "Go away. I have nothing to say to you."

Chapter Thirty-Four

Hattie

3 September 1939. London, England.

"Hattie, come quick," Vera cried from the sitting room. "Hurry!"

Setting down her paintbrush, Hattie stepped away from the image of Carmen singing "Habanera." The face wasn't right. There was dejection in the eyes that should not be there.

Hattie had given the image her own emotions. She'd fix it. She must. She would somehow set aside thoughts of refugees needing asylum, families split apart, missing husbands.

"Hattie." Vera's voice held impatience. "The prime minister is on the wireless."

"Yes, yes, I'm coming." She entered the living room, squinting against the change in light. It was late Sunday morning, and the room was too bright. Her eyes needed a moment to adjust. When they did, her heart seemed to stop in her chest.

Vera and Malvina were huddled together, their arms wrapped around one another, worry on their faces.

"What is it?"

Vera pointed to the wireless.

Before she could think what had put them in such a state, Neville Chamberlain's voice filled the room. "I am speaking to you from the cabinet room at 10 Downing Street. This morning the British ambassador in Berlin handed the German government a final note stating that unless we heard from them by eleven o'clock that they were prepared at once to withdraw their troops from Poland, a state of war would exist between us. I have to tell you now that no such undertaking has been received, and that consequently this country is at war with Germany..."

Vera's choked gasp drowned out Malvina's sob.

Chamberlain continued. "You can imagine what a bitter blow it is to me that all my long struggle to win peace has failed..."

Hattie's eyes widened, her hand flying to her mouth.

"Up to the very last it would have been quite possible to have arranged a peaceful and honorable settlement between Germany and Poland. But Hitler would not have it..."

The words continued coming from the wireless. Hattie stared, thinking not of herself but of Elsa and the refugees waiting for paperwork that would not be coming now that their countries were at war. She'd known this day was coming, they all had, but now that it was here, all she could think was *How do we continue our work?*

They hadn't put together a proper plan.

Her next thought was of Oliver. Would he be called into service? He was already in service. Only now did she understand what that meant. Her legs were suddenly weak, and she had to sit.

"His action shows convincingly that there is no chance of expecting that this man will ever give up his practice of using force to gain his will. He can only be stopped by force..."

Hattie could feel the sobs rising to the back of her throat, but there was no release forthcoming. She was too stunned to cry. Malvina had no such problem.

Her soft weeping cut to the marrow as she said one word, a name, over and over. "Elsa."

Elsa. Her friend and now, overnight, her enemy. Their countries were at war. They were stuck on opposite sides, unable to communicate. Unable to show each other support.

Her friend had known this terrible day was coming, hence the list of names and addresses she continually passed off to Hattie each time they met. Always in the same manner, inside a cylinder made to look like a lipstick tube.

The prime minister continued his address to the British people. The only sounds in the room were his disembodied voice and Malvina's sobs.

Hattie pressed her fingertips to her temples. She'd been a child during the last war with Germany. She couldn't recall the announcement being this formal. But she did remember when the fighting was over and the men had come home. They'd been asked to do horrific things and had returned shattered of mind and body.

How much worse had it been for the losers?

Hattie knew, of course. Hate had grown in their hearts. And now, they wanted vengeance. Lives would be lost on both sides. The innocent would die alongside the guilty.

All too soon, the prime minister finished his speech. It had been alarmingly short, no more than five minutes. Another voice took over. "All places of entertainment are to close with immediate effect..."

People were discouraged from crowding together unless it

was to attend church. Hattie lifted up a prayer to God. She prayed that right would win over wrong, that good would overcome evil, that lives would not be lost.

Words continued spilling out of the wireless. She only half listened to the details of the air-raid warning. "Tube stations are not to be used as shelters..."

The rest of the instructions sounded like a buzz in her ear. Where else were they to go if not underground? Surely, she'd misheard. The voice rattled on and on, and not ten minutes after mentioning an attack, an air-raid siren sounded.

Could Germany have been that prepared to send their bombers in the air so soon? "Surely, it's a test."

"We can't take that chance," Vera told her.

All three of them rushed outside. Chaos reigned on the streets. Caught up in the crowd, Hattie snatched glances to her right, her left. The fear in her fellow Londoners' eyes was too great, too much like her own. She looked to the sky, expecting bombs to rain down any minute.

None came.

Not then, not ten minutes later, not thirty, not two hours after Hattie and Vera and Malvina returned to their flat and huddled around the wireless, desperate for news. Eventually, the report came that the warning had been a false alarm.

The next one, Hattie feared, would not be so lucky.

With the news of war, the shock of it, the impossible finality, she attempted to pull herself together. She stood, quietly clutching her hands at her waist. Her mind kept returning to one terrible thought. There would be no stopping Hitler now. No checking his behavior. He would target the Jewish people without conscience, without regard to human life.

There had to be a way to save them, or at least a few. One, even one life would make a difference. Oliver had said that. Hattie worked on the problem for weeks. She enlisted the help of Vera, who, surprisingly, didn't immediately claim the situation was impossible. Unfortunately, her sister signed another publishing contract for three more books with tight deadlines. According to her editor, the British people needed to escape in stories with happy endings.

The government agreed, in theory. Many businesses were shut down or given strict operating hours. However, pubs and nightclubs were to stay open so that young people could have a place to congregate deep into the night.

Hattie wasn't interested in congregating. She wasn't interested in escaping into stories with happy endings. She was interested in saving lives. Unfortunately, all routes in and out of Germany, and German-occupied countries, were closed. Communication was impossible.

The worst was that she couldn't get word to Elsa or know her fate.

It was horrible, but oddly enough, life went on through the rest of 1939 and well into 1940, as if war had not been declared. There was some minor action at sea, but very little activity on land or in the air. Both sides seemed content to stay behind their defenses.

The British people were calling it the Phoney War.

The government was not so complacent. They braced for all-out warfare, especially in the air. Precautions were put into place and rigorously imposed. By February and into March of 1940, the feared aerial attacks never materialized.

Hattie couldn't bear living in ignorance as to what was happening on the Continent and specifically with Elsa. She had a resource: they'd kept in touch, barely, and quite infrequently now that war had been declared. The making and selling of art was no longer a priority for either of them. Oliver worked exclusively in the War Office or, to be precise, a branch of military intelligence. Hattie wasn't sure which one or what new duties he'd been given. She knew only that he no longer served in the economic division of MI6.

Much to Hattie's relief, Oliver agreed to meet her at his art gallery. She didn't want to see him in his office at Whitehall. The change in his position would be too real, and her fear for him would increase a hundredfold.

She chose to walk the ten blocks, despite the sound of thunder rolling in the distance. There was a tremendous crack in the air, and a shard of lightning sliced across the sky. The sound sent her feet rushing across the ground. She was nearly to the gallery when the clouds opened up. She was instantly soaked through, the fabric of her dress slapping against her calves. Inside the gallery, she stood on the threshold, dripping wet, her clothes and hair hanging limp.

The clerk recognized her immediately and, handing her a towel, nodded toward the back of the building. "He's waiting for you in his office."

His door was open, but his head was down, his eyes scanning a document beneath his hand. Hattie stumbled back a step. It shocked her to see Oliver wearing an army uniform, minus the hat. He'd speared his fingers through the thick waves of his hair, a bit too long to meet regulation, and leaving the ends to stick out at some places.

The scent of cigars filled the air.

Hattie watched him a moment longer, feeling the weight of his burdens. The rain pounded outside, its watery gloom giving the room a gray tint. That, Hattie realized, was how everything appeared now that they were at war. Gray and shadowy.

Shoring up her courage, she knocked twice on the doorjamb and waited for him to look at her before saying, "Hello, Oliver."

"Hattie."

Ever the gentleman, he rose and met her halfway across the

room. Taking her hand, he held on. Neither of them moved, both caught inside an unspoken agreement that by remaining still they might stop the world from falling apart around them.

He eventually let her go, and she felt an instant chill without the warmth of his palm pressing against hers. "What can I do for you?"

"Have you heard any news from Elsa?"

"She's...safe."

His tone suggested there was more to the situation. "What aren't you telling me, Oliver? Please, I have to know what's become of my friend."

He didn't answer straightaway; instead, he raked his fingers through his already-mussed hair. "She has inserted herself deeper within Germany society and grows closer to the Nazi leadership."

This was not good news. "How close?"

"She reserves the best seats in the house for high-ranking SS officers and their wives or, more often than not, their current lovers. She sings at private parties in their homes. She does this, all while continuing her..." he thought a moment "...secret work for us."

Hattie felt a surge of confusion. "How can that be? She and I haven't been in contact since war was declared. Our refugee work has come to a stop."

Oliver's face changed, and Hattie felt a sudden coldness drip through her like cyanide. "There are other ways for a woman such as Elsa to support the war effort, especially with her direct ties to the British government."

Hattie stared at him for several beats, his words not quite registering. She couldn't think what he meant. Then, realizing exactly what he meant, *who* he meant, her hands started to shake. "You mean you."

"And others."

His brother in the Foreign Office.

"Oh, Oliver." Hattie started to pace. But his office was small, and there was nowhere to go. She halted. Suddenly, her mind cleared, her resolve returned, and all those nights wooing Germans to buy her art, moving in their circles as if she belonged made a providential sort of sense now. She'd been preparing for this moment. "I wonder…" she said in a low voice.

She couldn't think how to say what was in her mind, to explain what she was thinking, or if her idea had any merit. The details were vague, without concrete shape. "Put me to work. Use me, as you use her."

"No." His voice was stony, unbending, decided.

Hattie thought about Elsa.

She thought about the time she'd served as her friend's secretary.

She thought about the Phoney War and how life had stayed relatively normal in England, and she knew the time to make a move was now. "Send me into Germany. Elsa and I will work side by side. We will—"

"No." His voice was hard, angry.

"Why not?"

He stood there, mutely, towering over her, looking fierce and inflexible. "I won't put you in harm's way. I won't."

"But you will put Elsa at risk?"

There was a long silence, but then he swallowed, the muscles moving in his throat. "She made that choice on her own."

He was angry, very angry. At her, or Elsa? Did it even matter? "Well, this is *my* choice, Oliver. If you were me, would you not make the same decision?"

"I'm not you. I'm me, and I won't send you into Germany. I can't. Please don't ask this of me, Hattie. Please."

His words shocked her in ways she couldn't define. The

confusion in her head, her heart, was strong, making it hard to know what to think, what to say. But then, she did know what to say. "Oliver, I'm not afraid to do my part."

"You think I don't know that?" He swung around, strode, heavy-footed, around his desk and sat. "You think I don't know what I have to do, regardless of how I feel about you?"

Regardless of how I feel about you.

He cared for her, deeply. She felt the same, and that made her intolerably sad. How many days had she lost with him because her pride had been hurt? She'd waited too long to tell him what was in her heart. England was at war, and she had to do her part, as Elsa did hers.

As Oliver did his.

She moved to stand in front of him, the desk a physical barrier between them. There was an inevitability to the moment, this meeting here and now, and she knew everything between her and Oliver, their work with the refugees, their time spent hobnobbing with art patrons on the Continent, had brought her to a place where her personal feelings simply didn't matter.

"Sit down, Hattie."

She did.

"I can't send you into Germany," he began. "You aren't trained."

"Then, train me."

"There isn't time and—" he lifted a hand in the air, palm facing her "—before you interrupt, or try to make your case, there's another way for you to help the war effort."

In the softly piercing light, Hattie could see a vein pulsing in Oliver's neck as quickly as her own heart was beating. "What do you have in mind?"

He cleared his throat, the sound unbearably loud in the small, confining space. "Sweden is determined to remain neutral."

"What does that mean?"

"People from both sides of this war, Germans and Brits, Italians and Russians, may come and go across the Swedish borders. All that is required is the proper paperwork and a reason."

Hattie's heart picked up speed. "There is a grand theater in Stockholm."

"As coincidence would have it, Elsa will be singing at the Royal Swedish Opera on three separate occasions before the end of the year, with twice as many performances in the next."

"I've always wanted to visit Stockholm again. It's a lovely city."

Oliver laid out his plan. Hattie would take on the role of courier for information Elsa gathered from inside the Third Reich. "It will be dangerous," he warned. "And there will be no heroics on your part. You simply need to be yourself, Elsa's friend and devoted fan."

"How will I get the information out? Won't they search my belongings at that border?"

"It's a possibility, but if they do, they won't find anything."

He seemed awfully certain of this. And then she remembered the tiny cylinders Elsa had been passing off to her for years. Hattie couldn't help but feel Providence unraveling.

There were many pieces to the puzzle, with everybody holding different fragments, not always knowing who had what. And maybe, while passing valuable information, there was a way to rescue Jews.

Something to think about.

"When do I leave for Sweden?"

"Next month." He rattled off the dates, looking slightly ill. "I'll coordinate your travel and ensure your papers are in order. Until then, continue living your life as before. Make art, Hattie. The world needs your art."

She thanked him, stood, turned to go.

"Hattie. Wait." He came around his desk again, placed his hands on her shoulders. "I need to say something, so, please, let me say it."

"I'm not sure this is a good idea."

"Probably not, but I have left it too long, and for that I'm sorry."

He was going to apologize, and she wasn't sure how she felt about it. She could marshal her resentments, tick them off one by one and toss them in his face. She could bring up his many lies. She didn't. A part of her had been waiting for him to explain his actions since that horrible night in Munich.

"I admit, originally, I pursued you because of your connection to Elsa. She was already in our sights as a person of interest. Friend or foe, we hadn't yet determined. Then, as a friendship bloomed between the two of you, we saw our way to uncover her true loyalties."

Elsa had been his target, Hattie his pawn. A kind of dizzying heat washed over her. "If you're trying to justify your behavior, this is not the way to do it."

"I'm not finished."

"By all means." She wound her wrist in the air. "Continue."

"It was a bonus that your art was good, better than good, exquisite. Breathtaking." He spoke with great detachment, but his eyes told a different story. "Then, I began spending time with you, and I found myself thinking about you when we weren't together. I fell for your talent first, then your goodness. Then, Hattie, I simply fell for you. All of you, while I was only able to give you a small part of me."

In those early days, her relationship with Oliver had seemed a perfectly straight road. But then twists and turns had brought to light hidden agendas and lies, and what had seemed so easy was nothing of the sort. Yet, here they stood, his hands on her shoulders, and Hattie heard his sincerity. His regret.

She wanted to tell him what was in her heart, the love, the hope.

Something held her back. And she knew what. "I don't think I can trust you again."

For one heart-stopping moment, he seemed to accept her words. He even dropped his hands. But then, he nodded, as if coming to a decision and, squaring his shoulders, became a man quite determined. "Let me win back your trust. Give me a chance, Hattie. One chance. That's all I ask."

"It will take time, but all right. I will give you a chance, Oliver. One chance. That's all you get."

Chapter Thirty-Five

❧

Elsa

March 1941. Stockholm, Sweden.
The Royal Swedish Opera House.

The journey into Sweden left Elsa exhausted. She'd lost track of how many times she'd made the trip since the war began, at least a dozen. Having remained neutral, Sweden was a hotbed for spies. Many of them German expats, or so they claimed. Elsa had her doubts and made it her business to know their names. She trusted none of them, especially now that the war had heated up. What had begun as a relatively peaceful conflict had become violent, especially in the air. Each side bombed the other, leaving death and destruction on the ground.

When would it end?

Not soon, Elsa feared. Hitler seemed unstoppable, and Wilhelm was pleased with the side he'd chosen, more so now that his wife had joined him in making powerful Nazi friends. He never asked why the change of heart, and Elsa never volunteered the information. Better her husband thought her an opportunist than a traitor.

Today was her twenty-eighth birthday, still young by most standards, especially for a soprano, and while her career had reached new heights, her body felt ancient. Her country was at war. Her marriage was a mockery, and another life required saving—the young Jewish woman posing as Elsa's personal secretary.

One at a time, Elsa told herself; that was all she and Hattie could rescue these days.

Wilhelm played his role, unknowingly. Each new unholy alliance put Elsa deeper in the heart of the Third Reich. At least her husband hadn't joined her on this trip to Sweden. He had his own responsibilities in Austria now that he was the artistic director of both the Munich and Vienna State Operas.

Elsa shook her head. Wilhelm and his social climbing.

With final rehearsals complete, she left the stage and made her way to her dressing room where her secretary, Sophie, mended the hem of one of Elsa's gowns that didn't need mending, all part of the ruse. She would miss Sophie when the young woman abandoned her for a position with Hattie. Hattie had a terrible habit of stealing Elsa's secretaries.

A slight smile crossed Elsa's lips as she made her way down the darkened corridor. A few more twists and turns, then suddenly she stopped. A movement had caught her eye. A sigh soon followed as Frieda came out of the shadows and positioned herself directly in Elsa's path.

The mezzo-soprano stood with the attitude of a woman whose high opinion of herself far outweighed her talent. That haughty stance, along with her questionable choice of escorts, had launched Frieda to new heights in the opera world within Germany.

Frieda had made her choices, and Elsa was done trying to speak reason into her former friend's ear. "You have something to say?"

"I wonder." Frieda's lips curled at an unattractive angle. "Tell me, Elsa, why is it you seem to go through secretaries so quickly and why they always resign when you're in Sweden?"

Elsa should have expected this question. Why hadn't she expected it? Because she'd been careful, ruthlessly so, intentionally singing in Swedish productions with differing casts, no repeats, not even in the chorus or orchestra. In fact, this was the first time Frieda had made the trip to Stockholm.

Which begged the question, Where had she gained her information?

Who was whispering in her ear?

"I believe that's none of your business," Elsa replied with stiff courtesy, choosing her words carefully, channeling Wilhelm at his most imperious.

Frieda let out a long, dramatic sigh that had a surprisingly musical quality. Clearly, the singer had been working on her voice control. "Of course, my mistake. The great Elsa Mayer-Braun must never be questioned, especially by the likes of me."

"I see you at last understand your place."

"My place?" Frieda let out an ugly snort. "Have a care, Elsa. You don't want to anger me. You see, I know what you're up to. One word in the right ear and *poof*—" she snapped her fingers "—you're gone."

Please, God, let her be bluffing. "Be careful what you say next, Frieda."

"Or what? You'll tell your British friend?" Frieda snorted. "She's here, isn't she? No, don't answer that. I saw her in the theater. Did you think I wouldn't recognize her? Or put the pieces together?"

Elsa stared at the singer, searching for what she wasn't saying, seeking to uncover how much she really knew. For a moment, Frieda looked sad, vulnerable. A trick of the light. There was nothing sad or vulnerable about her, not anymore. "We are in Sweden, a neutral country. There are no enemies within these borders."

"There are enemies everywhere. People are watching you, Elsa." She slanted her lips in a slow, meaningful smile. "Even inside your own home."

Elsa took in a slow, careful breath, but nothing could stop the ragged edges of despair moving through her. Was Frieda referring to Wilhelm or their housekeeper? "I don't know what you mean."

"Don't you?" Frieda placed a hand on Elsa's arm. The touch was surprisingly gentle, her gaze oddly forceful. "Sometimes the ones closest to us are the ones we can trust the least."

Elsa's mouth opened to give the other woman a setdown, but Frieda was already turning away. Elsa stared after her, her mind on the mezzo-soprano's warning.

On Wilhelm.

She'd made peace with her husband. She smiled and simpered and accompanied him into the homes of his Nazi friends where she heard things, all of which she passed along to the Allies via Hattie. Sometimes, Elsa learned about a raid on a home under suspicion for harboring a Jew. In those instances, she'd been able to get word to the family before the Gestapo arrived. Only once had she failed to send the message in time.

Elsa had cried herself to sleep that night. Wilhelm hadn't noticed, or maybe he simply hadn't cared. He still conducted some of the operas in which she sang, not as often as before. Whenever he insisted she perform at a private party thrown by one of his new friends, or requested she attend a special gathering or pander to the SS elite backstage after a performance, she never questioned the request. She simply went along.

She'd never intended to taint her legacy, to leave it twisted and tarnished. She would have to answer for her choices one day. Not now. Now, she had a precious life in her hands. Elsa found Sophie in her dressing room. "Thirty minutes to curtain," she said to the young woman. "Time to get me dressed."

Ten minutes later, Sophie circled her, taking in her appearance with an objective eye. She smoothed out a final wrinkle here, another there, and then declared, "Perfection."

Consulting the clock above Sophie's head, Elsa noticed Hattie was late. That wasn't like her. She looked to the door, sighed again.

Sophie followed the direction of her gaze. "You're worried about your friend."

Elsa couldn't help thinking something was about to go terribly, terribly wrong, and there was absolutely nothing she could do to stop it. "She'll be here. Soon. Any minute."

They both continued staring at the door. In the quiet moments that followed, Elsa grew even more convinced some nameless, unseen evil lurked in the night.

"Perhaps I should go look for her," Sophie suggested.

"How will you find her? You've never met."

"But we have. I attended her showing in Salzburg three years ago." She took a deep, steadying breath. "With my mother."

"I'm sorry."

Sophie didn't seem to hear her. "How innocent we were. Even then, when we'd already lost so much—our home, my father—we still thought, *This is the worst of it, it will go away soon, he will go away, the world powers will stop him*, but they didn't."

"No. They didn't." And here they were. Sophie's beautiful black hair was now dyed a yellowish color that resembled straw, and her doelike eyes held the horrors of what she'd been through, the losses she'd suffered. First her father, then her mother.

The expected knock sounded on the door, and they both jumped. A sudden draft swirled through the air, and Elsa caught a strong whiff of a damp, moldy scent that brought to mind death. She fought to stay calm.

"Come in," she called out.

A woman stepped into the room. The shadows threw her figure in silhouette, masking her features, but Elsa knew her. The cloaked image took another step, and Hattie stood before them. The sister of her heart.

"Oh, Hattie," Elsa breathed. "Praise the Lord. It's you."

"Of course it's me." Her friend burst into soft laughter so wonderful that it was impossible for Elsa not to join in.

She rushed in for a much-needed hug. A rustling noise interrupted, and Elsa held out her hand for Sophie to come forward. "This is my new secretary. Sophie, this is Henrietta Featherstone, Hattie to her friends, which now includes you. You will be sitting with her in the audience tonight."

After making the introductions, Elsa stepped back and Hattie moved forward, a symbolic gesture that signaled the transfer of the young woman's care.

There was no need to go over the plan. They'd done this type of exchange before.

This time Hattie altered the script. "You will come with us tonight for dinner, after the performance." She looked meaningfully into Elsa's eyes. "There's a pub near the train station that serves standard English fare. The food is ghastly, the weather worse, but the company is well worth the trip."

Elsa knew her friend spoke in code and understood Hattie wanted her to escape to London. She thought of Frieda's warning, and it shamed her that she wanted to go. But her work wasn't finished. Their network, though small and amateurish, preserved the lives of those who would otherwise be erased. "I can't join you for dinner. I leave for Salzburg to-night, right after my performance."

"Elsa—"

"No, Hattie. I am determined to make my train."

Hattie shut her eyes a moment, opened them again. She was trying not to show it, but she was worried and very determined to get Elsa to agree to her scheme. She turned away.

There. She could no longer see the plea in her friend's eyes.

All that remained was the relaying of the information she'd gleaned since their previous meeting. "Your lipstick has smudged."

Hattie and Sophie shared a look. That, too, Elsa ignored. She took a single breath and went to her valise, opened the lid with a determined flick. After a quick rummage around, she pulled out a gold tube of lipstick and passed the device to Hattie.

Knowing her role, her friend went to the mirror, opened the tube, glanced inside, then nodding she applied a coat of the bright red lacquer to her lips. She restored the lid and placed the tube into her own bag. The handoff was done. Inside the casing, Elsa had provided a list of homes in Salzburg harboring Jews. If anything happened to her, the British would have those names and addresses.

She said goodbye to Hattie, feeling that sense of doom again, the surety that this would be their final meeting. She set the sensation aside and hugged Sophie, then escorted both women out into the corridor.

Hattie grabbed her hand and, eyes locked with hers, said softly, *"Toi, toi, toi."*

Pulse beating wildly in her veins, Elsa kissed her friend's cheek. Out of the corner of her eye, she saw Frieda watching them from the shadows. Hattie swiveled her head and saw her, as well. The sight seemed to jolt her, and she stepped toward the singer.

Frieda melted back into the shadows.

"I don't trust that woman," Hattie whispered, her voice husky with dread. Then she pulled Elsa into her arms again, crushing her costume in the process. "Come to dinner with us tonight," she begged. "Please, for Malvina's sake, if not your own."

It was an underhanded ploy, but Elsa didn't fault Hattie for it. "Good-bye, my friend."

"Elsa, no, please. Listen to me, I need you to—"

She shut the door on Hattie midspeech, then went to the full-length mirror. What she saw made her wince. Tension showed in the fine lines around her mouth and eyes. Elsa blamed her recent conversation with Frieda and the seeds of doubt the singer had sown.

Had her words been a warning or part of some cruel game she played?

Hard to know.

Frieda was jealous and spiteful, but she could have spoken truth inside all that nastiness.

If Wilhelm *was* watching Elsa with the intent of turning her into the Gestapo, it was too late for her. Besides, such a thing was too ghastly to contemplate.

She spun away from the mirror and thought about Frieda again, her words, her warning. There had been a fleeting moment when she'd stared into the singer's eyes and had recognized an aching loneliness that called to her, one human being to another, two lost souls searching for their place in the world.

That couldn't be right. She'd misread the moment, and now she was running behind. The audience expected her best. Elsa always gave them what they wanted, always. She glided onto the stage, arms outstretched, and gave the performance of her life.

Chapter Thirty-Six

Hattie

March 1941. London, England.

Hattie delivered an exhausted Sophie into Vera's capable hands. The young woman had never been on a boat before, despite growing up near a river and, as Hattie told her sister, "The Channel crossing was especially bumpy."

"We'll get some broth in you." Vera steered the young woman deeper into the flat. "It's my special recipe. You'll feel right as rain in no time."

Sophie refused to continue another step. She dug in her heels, then spun around and rushed to Hattie, taking both her hands. "Thank you. Thank you for saving my life."

"Not me," she said, smiling gently at the haggard young woman. "I was just your travel companion. Elsa did the hard work."

At the sound of her niece's name, Malvina popped into

view. "Is she with you?" The older woman peered around Hattie. "Did you convince her to leave that wretched country?"

Defeat slumped Hattie's shoulders. "I'm afraid not."

Malvina collapsed in a nearby chair. Acceptance came much slower. "How was she? How did she look?"

Sunken, as defeated as I feel. Those were the words that came to Hattie's mind. However, out loud she said, "She is a strong woman, Malvina."

"Perhaps, I think, too strong."

"I'm sorry." More than Hattie could put into words. There'd been a moment backstage, when her eyes had met Frieda Klein's silhouette, a glimmer of shadow on shadow, that she'd thought, *That woman is dangerous.* Hattie had wanted to drag her friend away, kicking and screaming, if necessary, but Elsa had been firm. And Hattie had honored her wishes.

"I appreciate that you tried." Malvina sank deeper into the overstuffed cushions, her body bowing inward, as though she might disappear into the stuffing.

"I'm sorry, Malvina. I'm so very, very sorry I left her behind."

Malvina didn't answer. Not in words, but in a low sob. A groan. Then she was crying. No, that was Hattie, her eyes blurring with tears. Malvina sounded beside herself with grief. Hattie tried to come up with words that would soften the older woman's pain. But now that Frieda Klein was in her head, she had a terrible premonition that Elsa was in serious trouble.

Hattie needed to tell Oliver what she suspected. As soon as possible. She cleaned off the travel dust with a quick bath, changed into a clean dress, then moved to the front door as quietly as possible, careful not to disturb Sophie who slept soundly on the sofa, her head resting on Malvina's lap. Hattie wanted to fall into the oblivion of sleep.

Not yet. Not yet. She had a lipstick tube to deliver and a

debriefing to endure and, most of all, a warning to give that was founded only on gut instinct. Oliver would not like what she had to say. Hattie didn't like it, either. At least the first part of her mission had been successful.

Pausing at the door, she looked over her shoulder and sighed. Amid Sophie's soft snores, Hattie was sure she heard Malvina say, "Hush, now. You're safe."

Yes, Hattie thought, the young woman was safe.

Vera and Malvina would take over now. They would settle Sophie in their guest room temporarily, for however long it took them to secure a more permanent situation. Either they'd locate a job for her as a domestic with a willing family, or they would enroll her in school, or possibly Malvina would find her a job at the university.

Wherever Sophie ended up, it was far better than a concentration camp.

Closing the door quietly behind her, Hattie hurried out into the hallway, running now, toward the stairs, down the first flight, the second, then out the door.

She made the trip to the War Office in record time. Given the early-morning hour, the streets were relatively empty. There were few pedestrians and even fewer cars. The air was frigid for March, freezing her breath in a cloud around her head.

At the War Office, she gave her name to Oliver's clerk, a man dressed in an army uniform that carried the rank of corporal. "He'll be with you in a moment."

Hattie sat in the lone chair reserved for guests and waited patiently for Oliver to appear, her purse resting on her lap, her hands clasped together atop the bag. Her mind wandered back to the Royal Swedish Opera and Elsa's final words before she shut the door in her face. *Good-bye, my friend.* The finality in her tone hadn't struck Hattie at first. It did now.

"He's ready for you, Miss Featherstone."

The clerk escorted Hattie into the inner office, pulling the door behind him as he left her alone with Oliver.

He came around the massive desk, the wide surface filled with papers, documents and what appeared to be all sorts of ledgers and books. He, too, wore his army uniform, his rank much higher than his clerk's, that of captain.

Hattie took a long pull of air, released it slowly, desperate for Oliver's arms to come around her and for him to tell her the world was not falling apart around them. She considered herself a woman of great control, except when it came to this man. He always managed to slip past her defenses and make her crave his strength.

She schooled her features into a blank expression. Oliver wore a similar mask. They were each very good at pretending there were no romantic feelings shimmering under the surface.

What a pair they made.

"Welcome home, Hattie," he said softly, guiding her to one of the two chairs facing his desk before he took the other. "I trust your trip went well."

In response, she reached inside her handbag, pulled out the lipstick Elsa had given her. "I brought you a gift from Stockholm."

He accepted the small gold tube without a word, never taking his gaze off hers. The longer he looked at her like that, with such tenderness and concern, the harder it was to keep her composure. For a moment, she simply sat staring at him, happy to be near him.

Still holding her gaze, he set the lipstick on his desk, and before she realized what was happening, before she could stop him, he took her hand, pulled it to his lips. She shivered. "What's wrong? Did you have a problem with the other package?"

"No, it's nothing like that. Soph—" She cleared her throat. "That is to say, the other package is safely sleeping off a rather rough Channel crossing. It's... Oh, Oliver." His name came out of her mouth as a plea. "Frieda Klein is onto us."

His entire body stiffened. "Are you certain?"

"I am. She was lurking in the shadows, watching Elsa and Sophie and me, listening to our conversation. She didn't try to hide her interest. And I can't explain how I know this, but I think," she said and swallowed, "I think she'd been there for a while, waiting for us to appear."

He stood, dragging her with him. "No more trips into Sweden. It's not safe anymore."

"I'm not afraid for myself. But for Elsa..." Her words trailed off.

She didn't continue, understanding the danger her trips posed for her friend. Elsa had chosen to go back into German-occupied Austria. She'd chosen to live and work among the enemy. And Frieda was watching her every move. "I should have tried harder to make her come with me."

Oliver was saying something, but she didn't hear him. The air-raid warning signal screeched, the sound reverberating in the room, drowning out his words.

"To the basement." He took her arm and led her out into the darkened hallway and toward the stairwell that would take them to the large basement beneath the building.

Hattie had never got used to the sound of the sirens. Forcing back her panic, she sprinted down the steps. She thought of Vera and Malvina, and Sophie who'd only just arrived in London. She couldn't lose any of them to German bombs.

Stop it, she told herself. Vera and Malvina knew how to take care of themselves and their guest.

Heart pounding with each step, she cast a quick glance at Oliver. A shelf of ominous emotions cut a sharp swatch across his face. They arrived at the stairwell, and Hattie hesitated. Oliver pushed her through the door. Not gently but a proper shove that got her feet moving down the first flight, Oliver hard on her heels.

Others joined them in their descent to the basement, though the thought gave Hattie no comfort. Caught in their own sense of urgency, men and women, some in uniforms, some in regular clothing like her, rushed along with them, scrambling down the stairs.

Hattie stumbled, nearly lost her footing.

Oliver's hand steadied her. "Watch your step," he shouted above the wailing horns.

Instead of calming her, the sound of his gravelly voice, so strong and masculine, shot a wave of terror through her.

"It's all right," he said, drawing alongside her. "I have you."

She leaned in to him, letting him guide her the rest of the way, until they were on the threshold of the basement. "You first," he ordered.

"I—"

"Go, Hattie."

She went.

In her haste, she tripped again, on the bottom step, and fell forward, landing hard against the wall. She turned, flattened her back against the unforgiving brick and mortar and tried to settle her ragged breathing. She shifted slightly to her left and found Oliver beside her, reaching for her arm again.

A few seconds later, they were backing into a corner, out of the way of moving bodies. They huddled together in the dark, waiting, waiting. Oliver pivoted to face her, and she could just make out his features, his eyes. He probably didn't realize he gave her a glimpse into his soul. Such frustration, such fury. Not at her, at the situation. The enemy. The war itself. Without realizing what she was doing, she reached her hand to his face, cupped his cheek. Then...

Boom.

The bomb rattled the building. Oliver took her hand, pulled it to his heart, flattened his palm over hers. *Boom.*

Boom. Boom. Boom.

She trembled. Life could transform in an instant. With one bomb it could be over. It was important to remember that. To remember that the threat of death was real, even in London.

Hattie had lost friends to the air raids. The building where she and Vera had formerly lived had been leveled, killing several of its residents who hadn't heeded the sirens. Now, Hattie felt her own fury at the enemy. The war itself.

Oliver held on to her, staring at her without speaking, his eyes a maelstrom of emotions. She saw his feelings for her, the love.

"Hattie."

She nodded, giving him silent permission.

He kissed her, a brief brushing of his lips to hers, over before she had a chance to react. He pulled her close, rested his lips near her ear. "When this war is over, I'm going to court you properly."

Hattie swallowed. "That could be years yet."

"Good thing I'm a patient man."

Chapter Thirty-Seven

Elsa

August 1943. Salzburg, Austria.
Salzburg Festival.

Elsa arrived home from the theater weary and worn to the bone. At Wilhelm's insistence, she'd been in rehearsals all morning with a vocal coach. The small, nasty little German who'd taken Isaiah's position at the Vienna State Opera had pushed her hard, demanding she hit the high notes again and again and again, never satisfied when she gave him exactly what he asked, always wanting something different. Something more, something that wasn't in her.

How dare he? Her blood boiled with outrage. Wilhelm would hear about the behavior of his handpicked lackey. Rounding the corner, she saw the official state car parked at the curb outside their home. Her exasperation seeped into anger and then into quiet despair. There would be no private conversation with her husband this afternoon.

She heard the voices coming from Wilhelm's study the moment she stepped across the threshold. She didn't need to listen at the door to know the identity of her husband's visitor. She'd recognized the black automobile parked outside. A flash of fear passed through her. The sensation lasted only a second. Elsa was too exhausted for fear. It had been a long morning, and she'd chosen to walk home among the tourists and festival attendees enjoying her beloved city.

Moving as if she were walking through melting glass, she picked her way up the stairs to her bedroom on the second floor. No sign of the witch of a housekeeper. Good. Elsa wanted to be alone. She needed a bath, a cup of broth, then it would be time to return to the theater and tonight's final performance of the festival, her last ever. Her hand froze on the bannister.

Where had that thought come from?

Why this nagging sense of doom that had been with her since her last trip to Sweden, when Hattie had begged her to escape to England?

I should have gone.

Too late now.

An hour later, her head calmer and her thoughts less noisy in her head, she dressed in a lightweight, simple day dress made from blue muslin for her return to the theater. She still felt hot and sticky as humidity crept in through the narrow gaps around the window's edges.

At the window, she looked out and down and discovered the black Mercedes-Benz was still parked at the curb. The driver, tall, hollow-eyed, stood military-straight beside the state-sponsored vehicle. His earth-gray uniform carried not a single wrinkle to mar the excellent fit, and even from this distance, Elsa could see the runes on his black collar, the Iron Cross at his throat. A dark rage gripped her.

Wilhelm and his evil friendships, as shadowy and ominous as the thunderclouds that hung low in the sky. They would be the end of them both.

How could her husband not see he made friends with dangerous people?

The owner of that state-sponsored Mercedes-Benz, Ernst Kaltenbrunner, had risen quickly since she'd sung in his home. An unapologetic anti-Semite and fanatical Hitler loyalist, he'd been rewarded for his assistance in the *Anschluss* with command of the Austrian SS and police force. His power was absolute, and Wilhelm's friendship made Elsa's clandestine work harder, nearly impossible.

At least the British knew where most of the Jews left in the city were hiding, thanks to the lists she'd given Hattie. Elsa had done what she could to protect them. If anything happened to her now, they would be safe. Or at least have a chance at safety.

The clock marked the top of the hour, five distinct chimes. Time to leave for the theater. Exiting her room, a movement at the top of the stairs made her freeze. Wilhelm stood before her.

He appeared anxious, on edge. It was not a new look for him. He hadn't been himself for weeks. He gave her no greeting, other than a frown of displeasure. That wasn't new, either. "How long have you been home?"

His words were as much an accusation as a question.

"Not long," she said, afraid she might cry. Her husband was looking at her with such cold calculation. She was about to force out some response, a semblance of an apology, when he grabbed her arm.

"Come and greet our guest." He steered her toward the stairwell, down to the first floor. "Smile, Elsa." It was a command, as if she were a lowly assistant, not his wife. "I'll not have you offend *Herr* Kaltenbrunner with your scowls."

A sudden burst of energy, fused by fear and too much exhaustion, had her yanking her arm free of his grip. How glad she was they'd never had a child. To bring a baby into this cold marriage, this frigid home, was unthinkable. "I am capable of walking on my own."

He said nothing.

Outside, thunder rumbled. A storm was brewing, slowly moving toward Salzburg, but not yet there. There would be no respite from the crackling tension outside. Or, it would seem, in her home. "Elsa," Wilhelm began, as they stood at the bottom of the stairs, facing their odious guest.

Kaltenbrunner stood with the left side of his face visible for Elsa to see. The network of scars was underscored in the gray light, giving him an edge of cruelty.

"Elsa," Wilhelm repeated, "you know *Obergruppenführer* Kaltenbrunner."

"*Frau* Hoffmann," Kaltenbrunner greeted her, as her husband had not, with a smile and brief bow of his head. "My wife and I had the privilege of hearing you sing last evening. You were exquisite. A triumph."

The critics had agreed.

To think, Elsa's voice was at its best when so many others had been silenced. By this very man bending over her hand. She swallowed back the bile rising in her throat. "Thank you, *Herr Obergruppenführer.*"

"I am very proud of my wife." Wilhelm was doing a fine impression of a doting husband, but Elsa knew something wasn't right. The lies were still in his eyes. The strain that had become their marriage stiff in the air between them.

Elsa gritted her teeth. Wilhelm had been awful toward her lately, demanding, cold and distant, yet now, in front of his powerful friend, he was all compliments and conciliatory manner.

"My husband flatters me, when it is he who deserves the credit." She gave Wilhelm a very large, very false smile. "Had it not been for him, I would still be a struggling singer hunting for the parts that best suited my voice."

Not true: she'd already been a star the day they met. But Wilhelm preferred this version of their history over the truth.

"I only sped up the process. Your success was inevitable. You were my greatest achievement." *Were.* Past tense.

And there it was again, that strange expression in his eyes. Discomfort, something darker, uglier. Elsa felt as if she were picking her way through a minefield, trying to find the man she'd married, not this stranger who she suspected capable of terrible things.

She kept her smile in place and prayed for her suspicions to be false, for Wilhelm to be a good man. A crack of thunder split the air. Her cue. "I should be going, before the rain arrives."

"You will take my car." Kaltenbrunner made the offer without a smile, in a tone that brooked no argument.

"The theater is a short three blocks away. I can easily—"

"Elsa." Wilhelm took her arm, his grip hard and unforgiving, a physical reminder that she would not embarrass him in front of this powerful Nazi. It was a revelation, this meanness in the man she'd married almost a decade ago. "You will accept this generous offer from our friend."

"Thank you, *Herr Obergruppenführer.* You are too kind."

More pleasantries followed, each of them as false as the next. Wilhelm held her gaze a moment, *something there*, she thought again, and he was dismissing her with a flick of his wrist. "You may go now."

He did not escort her to the door.

A final glance over her shoulder revealed she'd already been forgotten. Her husband's head was bent in discussion with his foul guest. The sight filled Elsa with dread.

Outside, the sky overhead took on a dingy hue. The summer heat was oppressive. The driver, his eyes not quite meeting hers, stood at attention, hand on the open door.

Inside the car, Elsa leaned back against the cushions and released a long sigh. All she wanted to do was sit in her favorite chair, stare at a blank wall and review the disturbing events that had led her marriage to this point of utter failure. She needed perspective.

Her mind wandered back to Wilhelm, and she tried not to worry about the hard look she'd seen in his eyes, the way he'd gripped her arm.

He'd chosen to stay behind with his Nazi friend, instead of journeying with Elsa—his wife—to the theater. He'd already relinquished the baton to one of his assistant conductors for tonight's performance, instead of taking the platform in front of the orchestra.

Why?

Fear swept through Elsa's heart, stilling its beat. She shoved the sensation down with a hard swallow. She was not yet defeated. She'd gone to great lengths to keep Wilhelm in the dark.

If he uncovered the truth, would he betray her?

Could she be betrayed by someone she didn't trust?

She sat up, her breathing slow and heavy. The driver had chosen the same route to the theater she'd taken on foot a decade ago when she'd first met her husband. The sky had carried a similar threat, and she'd hurried along, straight into the theater. Into a life with Wilhelm. From that initial meeting, she'd found herself intensely drawn to him for reasons she hadn't understood. She'd thought it love, but now she wondered if it hadn't been the emptiness of her life, the loneliness and her need to seek something—someone—to fill that barren feeling.

A blinding headache burst behind her eyes, darkness crept over the edges of her vision, threatening to pull her into a deeper despair. She rubbed frantically at her temple, as if the gesture could banish her fear along with the pain.

The black Mercedes-Benz approached the *Felsenreitschule* theater at a steady pace, giving Elsa time to settle her nerves before stepping into the heavy August heat…

Chapter Thirty-Eight

Hattie

September 1943. London, England.

News of Elsa's arrest reached Hattie on a beautiful morning filled with chirpy birdsong and loads of sunshine. Not a single cloud in the sky, the temperatures unusually warm for mid-September London. The perfect weather was an insult, though Hattie hadn't known it at the time. It hadn't occurred to her how wrong the setting was for what she was about to learn.

All Hattie would remember of that day was that she'd felt a sudden change in the atmosphere. The sensation had been so strong, she'd looked out the window. That was when she'd seen him, his familiar form striding toward her flat. A flurry of terrible thoughts had swept through her mind. Her hands had begun to shake as she stepped away from the window and the easel she'd moved there to capture the morning light.

She'd been working on a new painting, the image from the opera, the opera...

Hattie couldn't remember.

She didn't much care. She was too busy bracing for the knock that would herald Oliver's appearance. When it came, that quick, bold staccato, she hurried out of her room.

Heart racing, she swung open the door. For several seconds she stood unmoving, her mind and body wooden as she took in her unexpected visitor. If Oliver had come to her home in the middle of the day, the news was not good. "Oliver, I..." She stopped: his expression, his face... She'd never seen him this upset. "I didn't expect to see you today."

He shifted, his eyes darting toward a spot over her shoulder, back to the doorjamb, then to her face. "Are you alone?"

"Yes."

He sighed, all weariness and distress, as if he'd hoped for a different answer and he could turn and walk away.

"Oliver?"

At last, he looked at her. She wished he hadn't. The instant their eyes met—she knew. "Something's happened to Elsa."

He ran his hand along his jawline, hidden under a day's worth of stubble, possibly two. "May I come in?"

Not if you have bad news. She wanted to screech the words at him in an effort to combat her mounting fear. Hattie thought of her beautiful, brave friend and closed her eyes against a wave of nausea. She had to toughen up. For Elsa's sake, she must be strong. She must listen and accept what Oliver had to tell her. "Of course. Please."

She stepped aside to let him pass.

Their hands brushed, and for a moment, just one, Hattie felt a sense of calm. It didn't last. "What is it, Oliver? What's happened to Elsa?"

"You should sit."

Hattie didn't want to sit. The next few seconds would surely bring great sorrow. She'd been here before, in this moment, in her childhood, when her father had told her and Vera of their mother's death. She'd relived that moment her in nightmares, and again after she and Elsa had begun their refugee work.

Oh, yes, Hattie had shivered with this same sense of imminent and terrible unraveling of life as she knew it. There were so many echoes of this scene in her head she couldn't remember if any of them had been real or just a terrible, awful dream.

She needed something to do with her hands. "I'll make tea."

Nodding, Oliver followed her into the bright, happy kitchen. Another insult.

Hattie went through the motions, seeing the kettle, the cups, through a cloud of misty tears. She hardly noticed the bare cupboards due to rationing, or even the lack of sugar for their tea. Her mind was on what Oliver had come to tell her, the words she didn't want to hear. No matter how hard she tried, Hattie couldn't stop her hands from shaking. She felt dizzy, her mouth dry.

At last, the tea was brewed and poured. Hattie handed Oliver one of the two cups and sat at the table she shared with Vera, Malvina and the many, many refugees they'd brought to England. But never Elsa. Hattie had never welcomed her friend inside this flat. Now she feared she never would.

Oliver joined her at the table and drank half the liquid in his cup with one swallow.

Hattie regarded her own tea. The watered-down milk had curdled, just like her heart. Her hands began to shake again. Oliver reached for her cup, took it gently out of her grasp and set it on the table.

Slumping in the chair, she studied her hands, clasped together on the smooth surface. "I'm ready now. Tell me your news."

"Elsa was arrested by the Gestapo four weeks ago. We still don't know what evidence they had against her, or how long they took to gather it, or who specifically provided it. Perhaps more than one person."

"What was she arrested for?"

"Treason against the Third Reich."

Treason. A death sentence.

Oliver gave more details. Hattie didn't want to hear them. She owed it to her friend to listen to every word. She sat paralyzed, trying to comprehend. Elsa arrested. For treason.

"The trial was a farce," he said. "She was found guilty and sent to the Bergen-Belsen concentration camp."

She shut her eyes.

"Bergen-Belsen, Hattie. This is a good thing."

"Elsa was sent to a concentration camp. How is that a good thing?"

"They didn't give her the death sentence," he reminded her. "She's still alive."

"I can't bear it," Hattie cried and couldn't seem to stop the tears. She battled her grief, trying not to make this harder on Oliver, whose own eyes were red-rimmed and glassy. Elsa had been his friend before hers. He suffered as much as Hattie.

The others must be told. Malvina. Vera. Hattie would have to let them know. Worse than hearing would be the task of telling. How had it come to this? Scrubbing her hand across her face, she said one word, a name. "Hoffmann." Her voice was hard, unforgiving, her grief momentarily turned to rage. "Was her husband behind her arrest?"

"It's unclear how the Gestapo gathered their information." His voice was hushed, restrained. "As I said, they could have tapped multiple sources."

"What does it matter who betrayed her, or how many? Elsa is as good as dead."

"Maybe not. There may still be a way to save her."

The air left Hattie's lungs, and she stumbled to her feet, sat back down, stood again. "How can you say such a thing?" She ground out the question through sheer force of will. "Elsa has been sent to a concentration camp, a *death* camp. There is no hope of rescue now."

"Hattie, sit down, and I will tell you the rest."

Slowly, she did as he requested.

"Elsa was sent to Bergen-Belsen."

Why did he keep emphasizing this? The name meant nothing to her. Somehow, she knew it should. "I don't understand."

"Originally, it was a holding camp for prisoners of war. Back in April of last year, part of the camp was taken over by the SS Economic and Administration Main Office and turned into an exchange camp. Hattie," Oliver said and placed his hand over hers, "Elsa has considerable worth in the eyes of the world. She also has powerful friends outside of Germany. The Nazis know this. It's why they didn't hang her and why we may be able to barter for her release in exchange for a high-value German prisoner of war."

Hattie let out a sound, a cross between a whimper and a sob. "Is this possible? This is something that's been done?"

"Yes." He stood. Straightened the jacket of his uniform with a snap. "I have a meeting later this morning with the American intelligence liaison to discuss Elsa's case."

"So there's hope."

"Yes, Hattie. There's hope."

By the time her racing thoughts sorted through what he was saying, they were standing face-to-face, smiling tentatively, and then she was in his arms, clinging to him, her knees no longer serving their purpose.

Hattie squeezed her eyes shut and thought of all that could go wrong.

But then, she realized, so much could go right. "Make it happen, Oliver."

"I'll do my best."

Chapter Thirty-Nine

Elsa

August 1943. Lower Saxony, Northern Germany.
Bergen-Belsen Concentration Camp.

"Elsa, I beg you." The new inmate lost her fragile sense of calm and began to sob softly, pitifully. "Hear me out."

Unable to bear the sight of her betrayer, weak and mournful but only marginally contrite, Elsa kept her head turned away. "You can have nothing to say to me, Frieda."

"I will stand here all night. If that's what it will take."

Frieda would, of course she would. She would stand over Elsa until she collapsed. She was stubborn like that. But Elsa could be just as stubborn. She didn't want to hear Frieda's confession. She simply wanted the woman gone. With great effort, she sat up. "All right, speak."

For a long moment, Frieda said nothing. Shadows played across her face, giving her the look of an old woman carved in stone. Then, she began speaking, and Elsa didn't see a statue. No, she could see nothing but the black tint of her own rage. "I turned you in to the Gestapo."

"I know."

"Can you forgive me?"

A burst of resentment stole Elsa's breath. Was it that easy for Frieda to say the words? Was it that simple to ask for forgiveness after what she'd done? She stared into the gaunt face, one word echoing in her mind, moving up her throat, screeching past her lips. "Why?"

"I resented you." She sounded like a petulant child rather than a woman full of remorse. A woman who'd had chance after chance to accept Elsa's offer of friendship.

"Why?" The word would not stop running through her mind, pushing past her lips. Each time Elsa uttered it was another shard to her heart. "I only ever wanted to see you succeed."

That made Frieda wince. "I think I hated you for that most of all."

Elsa stared at the other woman, beaten and full of simmering anger. Still, that savage light of bitterness lived behind her eyes, dwelled in her heart, even as she asked for forgiveness with her pinched, cracked lips.

In the darkened barracks, Elsa let her mind pass over all the times she'd gone to conductors, composers, theater administrators on Frieda's behalf, and she saw her own contribution to their mutual tragedy. A new lump formed in her throat. "I share a portion of the blame."

Silence hung between them.

Even in the stingy light, Elsa could see Frieda's face contort with surprise. The muscles in her neck shifted and tightened, and Elsa expected the other woman to launch into one of her furious tirades. The rant never came.

And then she knew: Frieda wasn't angry, she was broken. Everything in Elsa shattered into tiny, jagged little pieces. So much shared sorrow. Pain. Despair. The cause of which she would not wish on anyone, not even her betrayer. "What I don't understand is how you knew my secret."

"I overheard you arguing with *Herr* Hoffmann that day in your dressing room when he ordered you to stop. I was outside, listening at the door."

Elsa thought back to that day, tried to remember what theater they'd been in, what city, what opera she'd sung.

"It was the Salzburg Festival of '38."

Five years ago. Elsa remembered now. All this time, she'd thought Wilhelm was the one she needed to watch. Frieda had intimated the same. Now she knew why. "You were listening at the door."

"I could have turned you in then. Maybe I should have, but at the time, there was no point. You weren't doing anything illegal, not that I could tell. So I kept the knowledge to myself in the event I needed leverage against you in the future."

Frieda, always looking out for herself. How alike she was to Elsa's husband. No wonder Wilhelm had never liked her. He saw himself in the mezzo-soprano. Frieda swayed, stumbled. Elsa caught her, helped her sit beside her on the hard wood that served as her bed.

They sat there, in the shadows, silence wrapping around them. It suddenly became easy for Elsa to think of Frieda not as her betrayer but as a fellow inmate. Their shared tragedy, the dire reality of their circumstances, fashioned a bond that had been absent between them, despite all of Elsa's efforts to build a friendship.

Frieda began talking, doling out her story, piece by piece, and this time Elsa listened.

"*Herr* Schmidt, my latest paramour," she clarified, "thought

I was spying on him. He was right. I was spying on him. He kept important papers in his private office. He caught me looking through a stack of files on his desk. I tried to convince him I was looking for a pen to write down what I knew about Hitler's favorite opera singer."

It was hard to hear, but Elsa listened to Frieda's confession.

"I told him everything I knew. He made me write it all down. Then he used the information against me. After your arrest, after you were hauled out of the theater, I was next, the charge the same as yours. Treason."

At this, Elsa stopped her. "You weren't involved in my network."

"I was tried for collusion and for withholding the truth of your activities."

"Caught in your own trap." Elsa did not try to make her voice kind.

Nodding, Frieda kept talking. She told of her own crippling fear as the soldiers marched her out of the theater ten minutes behind Elsa. As she spoke, Elsa relived her own terror. "And so…" Frieda said and bowed her head "…here I am."

"Here we *both* are."

"Because of me."

"Yes." Elsa kept her voice free of emotion. "Because of you."

The sobs came then, big, loud, uncontrollable. They rocked Elsa to the core. "Forgive me, Elsa. Please…" Frieda's voice strangled on the rest of the words, making each one incomprehensible, not that it mattered what she said, how she said it.

Elsa knew her forgiveness would free them both. They were each trapped in their own waking nightmare. Yes, she needed to say the words.

They would not come.

"I want to forgive you," she said, her voice bleak, her heart bleaker still.

Forgiveness is only the first step. Elsa realized this and understood reconciliation would come harder. Take longer. She wiped her palms down her thighs and sought to take the first step, to offer grace, unearned on Frieda's part, freely given on hers. "I... I forgive you, Frieda."

"Thank you, Elsa. I... I know it's more than I deserve." Frieda sounded sincere and, finally, contrite.

Maybe, Elsa thought, they would find reconciliation in time. One step, then another. She spent the rest of the night telling Frieda about Bergen-Belsen. She spoke slowly, mapping out the layout of the barracks and other buildings. She told of the other inmates and shared their stories. She didn't mention the deaths or the prisoners sent to the other side of the camp, only the ones released for a ransom. The ones exchanged for a German prisoner of war.

She didn't mention her own possible release. Nothing was set in stone. Her words flowed in the dark, weaving over them, around them, creating a tighter bond, until Elsa no longer hoped she and Frieda would reconcile. She knew it would come to pass.

Chapter Forty

Hattie

February 1944. London, England.

Hattie fell into step behind Vera and Malvina as they picked their way through the rubble. She was only half-awake, a sleepwalker drifting this way and that. Her exhaustion wasn't wholly unexpected. The air raid had been an unusually long one, lasting deep into the night. The sirens had caught them by surprise. With Hitler fighting two fronts, the bombings had tapered off, though not completely, as evidenced by the damaged buildings the three of them passed. The all clear had come a half hour ago, mere minutes before dawn.

Shivering, Hattie huddled deeper inside her coat. Winter had its nasty grip on London this morning. The chill bit at her exposed cheeks. They rounded the final corner home, and it was with much relief to discover their neighborhood had been spared from the bombs. This time.

Next time...

Hattie wouldn't think about next time.

Vera increased her pace. Malvina matched her step for step. Hattie fell farther behind, watching them together. The two continued chattering softly. They never seemed to run out of topics to discuss, even while they took shelter below ground and bombs exploded above their heads. Hattie and Vera had once been that close, and if she were being honest, she couldn't blame the collapse of their relationship solely on her sister. Hattie had chosen to continue her refugee work, despite Vera asking—begging—her to stop.

The cooling off hadn't begun then; it had built slowly. A pair of earrings and a set of pearls had put the final wedge between them, but the start had been on the train from Cologne to Munich, when a young brother and sister had been harassed because they were Jewish.

Hattie had been changed that day and, given the same choices, she would do it all over again.

Today, however, she missed her older sister. As she watched Vera with Malvina, their heads bent, a sob worked its way up her throat, and she thought of the other woman she'd lost. It had been months since Oliver had given her the news of Elsa's arrest, and still her friend languished in that concentration camp. "The process is complicated," he'd told Hattie. "But we are making progress. There is much reason to hope."

She wasn't sure about that. All rescues were complicated, but this one mattered most. Because this one was personal. This one was Elsa. Entering the flat behind the other two women, Hattie closed the door softly behind them. A ferocious ache settled between her eyes. The prospect of returning to her room and the unfinished painting was nothing short of daunting. She would eat a quick breakfast first.

Then she would paint. She would put Elsa's face on Isolde

singing "Liebestod" and paint until she expired from exertion. Once Elsa was alive on the canvas, only then would Hattie sleep.

Another sob rumbled in her throat. She simply had no desire to eat or pick up a paintbrush or do anything but pace. So she paced. And worried. And paced.

This was getting her nowhere.

Hattie ordered herself to stop dawdling and get to work. She took the brush, stood before the blank canvas and applied herself to her art. She painted Elsa singing the final aria from Wagner's *Tristan and Isolde*. She painted the calm inside the chaos, putting a hint of hope inside the loss. She stepped back often and viewed the whole, then its parts, making small adjustments, until finally the image was complete, and Hattie knew a moment of joy. There was her friend, Elsa, at her most glorious. She needed to show Malvina.

Pivoting, she'd taken only a few steps when she heard someone at the door. Hattie recognized the three fast blows of fist to wood. Her heart skipped. Could it be? Was it possible? She rushed into the entryway, yanked open the door and connected her searching gaze with a beautiful pair of tiger eyes. "Oliver."

He smiled, a smile that crinkled the skin at the corner of those remarkable eyes and made him look...happy. "Good morning, Hattie."

An avalanche of emotion crowded inside her racing mind. She could hardly breathe, could hardly make sense of the moment. He should not be on her doorstep so soon after an air raid. He should be at the War Office doing whatever it was he did for King and country. But he was here, smiling at her, and she started to hope. "You have good news."

"Better." He took her hand in his, a kind of clasp, as if he were promising her something. His hands were ungloved, warm and strong over hers. "I have brought along a friend. Someone I know you'll want to see."

He let her go, stepped aside, and then a shadow moved inside the shadows of the landing, morphing into the beloved form of the woman she loved like a second sister.

"Elsa!" Restraint shattered. Calm evaporated. Welcoming speeches died on her tongue. The only emotion left was shock. Relief. Joy—complete, heartrending, breath-robbing joy. "Oh, Elsa! At last, at last, at last."

Hattie all but soared across the threshold into the hallway and, sobbing now, drew to a quick stop when her friend shrank back. She was so small, too thin and frail. *Oh, Elsa, what did they do to you?* The horrors she'd endured, all of them were in her hollow, flat gaze. Her eyes darted left, then right, left again, giving her the look of a wounded animal, cautious and afraid.

"Elsa." She reached out tentatively, her movements slow, hesitant, as she wrapped her arms around her friend's thin frame.

A small moan left Elsa's lips, and Hattie gentled her hold. "Shh. You're safe now."

Her shoulders heaved, and then she crumpled in Hattie's embrace, sighing softly between silent sobs. "Yes," Hattie whispered, closing her eyes and soothing her hand over Elsa's shorn hair, the feel of it stiff as hay. "Cry it out. There you go. There you go, now."

It took a while, but her friend's tears slowly dried. Her sobs turned to hiccuping sighs. Then her breathing slowed, and she began speaking softly, mumbling really, in heavily accented German, her voice belonging to a small child, and Hattie remembered they were standing in the hallway. This reunion was not for her neighbors' eyes, and Malvina was inside the flat unaware her beloved niece was free.

"Come inside," she said kindly, then glanced at Oliver. There was something about his intense gaze, the way it communicated he cared, utterly and completely, for Elsa.

And Hattie.

Some unacknowledged wall deep within her came tumbling down, and the empty crevices of her heart that had once held grief filled with a much happier emotion. "Come inside," she said again. "Both of you."

Oliver shook his head. "I'll leave you ladies to your reunion."

"No. Don't go," Hattie said, reaching to him. "Please, Oliver."

She tugged on his hand and, when she found no resistance, pulled him across the threshold. Inside the flat, Hattie took Elsa's shoulders gently in her hands. "Now, let's have a proper look at you."

Her breath caught. Suddenly, viciously, she wanted to hit every person that had ever touched her friend with malice in their heart. Hattie wiped her face free of all expression and placed a happy note in her voice. "Yes, well. We'll put you to right quickly enough."

Elsa opened her mouth, but the sound of shuffling feet heralded the entrance of another.

"I thought I heard voices. Oh! Oh!" Malvina's hand flew to her throat. "Elsa. My dear, dear, sweet child."

Weeping softly, the older woman opened her arms in quiet invitation. Elsa rushed to her aunt, who enveloped her in another embrace. They clung, both crying and speaking in rapid-fire German, and Hattie felt like an intruder.

This was a private moment meant only for family.

She looked away from the tender reunion with her mind in a muddle. She was unable to form a clear thought, save one. Oliver had done the impossible. He'd saved Elsa from the camps. She turned to him, caught him watching the reunion as she had, averting his eyes and shifting uncomfortably from one foot to the other.

She motioned for him to join her out in the hallway. They were nearly to the door when Vera rushed into the room, her eyes wild with happy shock. Instead of moving closer to Elsa and Malvina, she swerved around the two women, side-stepped Hattie and stopped directly in front of Oliver, finger pointing at his chest. "You did this," she declared. "*You* made this happen."

"There were many people involved."

"You humble, silly man. Come here and take your lumps." Vera framed his face with her hands and, lifting onto her toes, gave him a big, smacking kiss right on the lips.

His eyes widened.

"You're a good man, Oliver Roundel." She dropped her hands, grinned. "Now, do right by my sister, or we shall have a terrible row, you and I."

"Wouldn't want that." He looked rather pleased as he tugged Hattie into the hallway.

She felt her heart beating in her throat. After so much worry, so much waiting and praying, Elsa was alive. She was free. "I don't know how you did it, and yes, yes, I know you can't reveal details. So I'll simply say thank-you."

"You're welcome."

She was smiling now. He was smiling. The next thing she knew, she was in his arms, unsure which of them moved first and not really caring. Her cheek was pressed to his chest, her arms wrapped around his waist, and this was exactly where she wanted to be. She tightened her hold and whispered again, "Thank you."

They stood locked together for several long seconds. Hattie didn't want to let him go, feeling as if she'd found her place in the world, here in his arms. Two magnets that had found home, compelled by a force stronger than themselves.

Oliver brushed his lips over her hair. "I have to go."

"I know."

His hold loosened, and she lifted her eyes. The dim lighting in the hallway defined the angles of his face, the curve of his lips. She wanted to kiss him. But not here, not in the hallway.

Why not? He'd just pulled off something remarkable, and she loved him for it. She loved him.

He settled the issue, by placing a soft kiss to the tip of her nose. "We'll talk soon."

"All right." She expected him to leave. He stayed put, lowering his head again. The kiss to her lips was far too brief but so tender that Hattie sighed.

He lifted his head just as the door to the flat opened and Elsa shuffled over to him. "Please consider what I asked, Oliver."

Something came and went in his eyes. "You're certain this is what you want?"

She took a long, shaky breath. "It's important to me."

"I'll do my best." The same words he'd said to Hattie when she'd asked him to accomplish the impossible.

"Thank you."

Placing his hat on his head, he turned to go, then paused. "Welcome to England, Elsa. It's good to have you here."

For just a moment, the sadness lifted from her face. "It's good to be here."

They shared a smile, and then he was sprinting down the stairs, taking them two at a time.

"What was that about?" Hattie asked the moment he was out of sight.

Elsa moved to stand beside Hattie. She reached down, took her hand and squeezed gently. "I asked him to negotiate Frieda's release from the concentration camp."

"Frieda Klein was arrested?"

Elsa nodded, then swayed as if she might collapse right there on the spot.

"Let's get you back inside." Hattie guided her friend across the threshold and then deeper into their home, taking great care not to push her too fast or too hard. Her mind burned with curiosity, though she tried not to show it. There would be time for questions later.

Malvina hovered close. Vera, too. It took all three of them to convince Elsa to sit in the overstuffed chair and allow them to pamper her. There was a whisper of agitation, of impatience on her face. Only a softening around her eyes and then a gentle smile on her lips gave Hattie a sense of understanding. Elsa wasn't annoyed with them or their rushing around her seeing to her every need. She was frustrated with her own infirmity.

Hattie decided to get her mind off her limitations. "So, Frieda was arrested with you and sent to the same concentration camp."

"We were not arrested together, only at the same time."

A nonanswer, delivered with an odd tone of voice, and Hattie found herself sitting on the ottoman so she could be at the same height as Elsa. Their knees touched, and their eyes were on the same level. She didn't know what she was looking for in her friend's gaze. "Will you tell me about your arrest?"

Elsa pressed her lips together, thinking. Then, nodding, she motioned for Vera and Malvina to join them, and as she launched into her tale, the three of them held perfectly still. She told them about the argument with her husband before heading to the theater on the final day of the Salzburg Festival. She spoke of her sense of doom as she took the stage. Then the SS bursting into the building, her arrest right there on the stage. "I was taken to Gestapo headquarters and *interrogated*."

Her voice broke over the word, and Hattie took her hand. "Do you want to take a break?"

"No, I… I want to get it out. All of it, then I never want to speak of it again."

"Take your time, Elsa." This from Malvina, who made a valiant, unsuccessful attempt to keep from crying. Vera and Hattie lost a similar battle.

Head down, Elsa traced a seam on the chair with her fingernail. "I don't know how long I was in that room. Hours, possibly days. My memory isn't complete, there. Whenever I try to recall details, my mind closes, and I see only mist. I hear only weeping, my own."

Hattie dipped her head to hide her reaction. Not sadness, fury. Bone-deep rage. She wanted to find that evil man, the bully in the Gestapo uniform, and shake, shout at and hurt him the way he'd hurt her friend. She looked up to see Elsa watching her. There was a faint smile on her face, as if she knew exactly what Hattie was thinking.

She continued her story. "There was a trial." She didn't expand. "It lasted only a handful of minutes. I was found guilty and sent to the camp."

"Do you know who turned you in?" She spat out the words as though they were poison. "Do you know the name of the person who betrayed you?"

"It wasn't Wilhelm."

"But your marriage," Hattie said softly, "it was not a good one. And he was not a good husband."

The words were out before she could think them. She'd never liked Elsa's husband, never trusted him, but until this minute she hadn't realized how much she disliked him.

"No, he was not a good husband. But I was not a good wife, either. Wilhelm made his choices, and I made mine. When I look back, we were not nearly as happy as I thought or would have wished. My marriage grew worse over time." She shook her head. "The war changed us."

Hattie shared a look with the other women in the room. The war had changed them all. But whatever hardships they'd endured, Elsa had suffered worse.

"Where is Wilhelm now?" Malvina asked.

Elsa lifted a delicate shoulder. "Germany, I suppose. He has become very important in the Third Reich and has made friends with the most evil of men. I was certain he was the one who had betrayed me. I still have my doubts about his character, but no. He did not do this."

"Who, then," Vera asked, "was your betrayer? Do you know?"

She nodded, met Hattie's eyes and said, "Frieda Klein."

Hattie's breath clogged in her throat. All this time, she'd secretly believed Elsa's husband had informed on her. But, no, it had been a spiteful, jealous rival. Hattie thought of the last time she'd seen Frieda, a shadowy figure lurking backstage at the Royal Swedish Opera. "A friend turning on a friend," she said, unable to keep her hostility at bay. "It's unconscionable."

"It happens often in Nazi Germany. Friends betray friends, neighbors inform on neighbors. Frieda, like so many others who think only of their own safety, had been gathering information about me for years." With a surprisingly steady voice, Elsa told them about Frieda's confession, how she'd overheard an argument between her and her husband. "She saved the information until she needed it and was, ironically, arrested for withholding what she knew for so long."

Again, Hattie thought Elsa seemed so calm, so steady. And then, she remembered. "You asked Oliver to orchestrate Frieda's rescue."

"I asked him to save her, in the same way he saved me."

A collective gasp sounded in the room. Hattie closed her

eyes briefly and tried to think why Elsa would ask for such a thing. Why would she want to see Frieda released? A woman who had betrayed her in the worst possible way. A woman who was angry and duplicitous and full of resentment toward her. "It makes no sense," she said aloud.

"Hattie." Elsa's hands came to rest on her knees. There was great wisdom in her eyes, great tenderness, and none of the bitterness she herself felt. "You cannot understand what we endured together. We were treated better than most, but not well. We lived in constant fear and were given very little food. That bonded us in a way I cannot explain. I have forgiven Frieda, and I ask that each of you," she said, glancing from Hattie to Vera to Malvina, "do the same."

Her request made Hattie's brain become a tangle. She tried to untwist her thoughts, tried to stand and walk off her confusion, but Elsa's hands tightened on her knees. "Please, Hattie. Do this for me. Forgive Frieda, as I have forgiven her."

Malvina said the words Hattie was thinking. "Dear Elsa, you are too good for this world, but I am so very glad you're still in it."

It was that statement, that truth, that gave Hattie the courage to say, "If this is what you want, then yes, Elsa. I will find a way to forgive Frieda Klein." It would require much prayer.

"Thank you." Elsa's eyes began to droop.

"We've exhausted you," Malvina said, taking charge. "You will want a bath and rest."

"Yes, I would like that, but first, I want to look at something beautiful." She held out her hand to Hattie. "Will you show me your latest painting?"

"It would be my honor."

She took Elsa's hand, and together they stood before the painting of Elsa as she saw her. A woman of eternal beauty, with endless stores of strength. The very embodiment of grace.

Epilogue

August 1945. Salzburg, Austria.
Salzburg Festival.

American troops took control of Salzburg on the fourth of May in 1945. Three days later, the war officially came to an end when top-ranking representatives from the Allied and German forces signed surrender documents in northern France. To celebrate, a decision was made to revive the Salzburg Festival that same year.

The festival opened in mid-August. Two-thirds of the attendees were American soldiers. The remaining tickets were distributed among Austrians, a few dignitaries and two British sisters who'd made the trip to witness their favorite singer's return to the stage.

Hattie took her seat in the third row of the *Felsenreitschule* and placed a plain cardboard box on her lap. Vera and Malvina sat on her left, Oliver on her right. He took her left hand, kissed her palm, then turned it over so he could survey her wedding ring with uxorious satisfaction. He did that a lot, as if needing to remind himself Hattie was truly, finally, forever his. She could have told him she had always been his. From the first moment their eyes met backstage in this very theater all those years ago.

Lifting his head, he leaned in close to her ear and whispered, "I love you, Henrietta Featherstone Roundel."

"I love you, too," she whispered back, meaning it with all her heart. Oliver was the blessing that had come out of the chaos.

This was their first trip together as husband and wife, and so far, every minute had been complete and utter perfection. They were staying in the Hôtel de l'Europe in the honeymoon suite, while Vera bunked at Elsa's house in a room next to Malvina's overlooking the Salzach River.

Hattie was so proud of her sister. Vera had recently signed another contract with her publisher, Mills & Boon, and was cheerfully writing book two of the six romance novels they'd acquired. Even before the war ended, with Elsa healing in their home, her aunt never far from her side, Hattie and Vera often discussed the refugees they'd saved. They honored the ones they'd lost by remembering their names and retelling their stories to anyone who would listen.

Sometimes it was only Elsa and Malvina in the room, sharing their stories as well. Sometimes a lectern and large crowds were involved. Other times it was just the two of them, sisters with a common goal yet very different means. The conversations brought them to a new understanding and always had a melancholy tone. Respecting the lives lost dictated a certain amount of solemnity.

The lights in the auditorium blinked, once, twice, a third time, then dimmed.

Still holding her hand, Oliver kissed Hattie's cheek before turning to face the stage. Tonight's performance was not a full opera but a concert, with a series of singers, all Austrian-born, making their return to the stage. The curtain rose, as it had so many times through the years, and Elsa glided into view. She was alone, her steps full of liquid grace.

An explosion of applause guided her to center stage, where she stopped and gave the full brilliance of her smile to the conductor, a man Hattie didn't know, not Wilhelm Hoffmann. Elsa's husband had disappeared months ago. Oliver had information that suggested the maestro had escaped to South America. Because he'd done nothing illegal, that they knew of, Oliver was unable to pursue the lead in any official capacity.

"I'll do some digging on my own," he promised Hattie. But for now, he had other duties at the War Office. The weapons had been laid down, but the war effort wasn't fully over for him.

Elsa acknowledged the audience with a wide sweep of her arms. Every soul in the building, including the members of the orchestra, surged to their feet, their hands beating harder and harder, faster and faster. The noise was deafening.

Smiling, Elsa nodded to Hattie. She nodded back, feeling the burn of tears in her eyes. Her friend was still too thin, too fragile-looking. Hattie feared she would never return to the robust, happy woman she'd once been, not fully. There were moments when her pretty blue eyes turned distant and unspeakably sad, and she seemed to lose herself in some horrible memory.

Eventually her eyes would clear and she would return to herself, and Hattie would breathe a sigh of relief. The Nazis hadn't broken Elsa Mayer-Braun. Wilhelm Hoffmann hadn't broken her. They'd only made her stronger.

The applause died down, and the audience returned to their seats. Elsa pivoted slightly to her left and stretched out her arm to where a shadowy figure stood in the wings. Time seemed to stand still, and then Frieda Klein came into view, her arm outstretched in a similar fashion to Elsa's.

They joined hands and, as a single unit, turned to face the audience. Frieda's first smile was not for the conductor but for Oliver, who'd done the impossible a second time and co-ordinated a prisoner exchange for her release. Frieda's silent acknowledgment of his unselfish act gave Hattie her first real reason to like the other woman.

The music began, soft and tranquil, full of sweetness and innocence. Hattie immediately recognized the aria from Léo Delibes's *Lakmé*. "The Flower Duet" was one of the most famous duets written for a soprano and mezzo-soprano.

Elsa sang the opening stanza alone. Frieda responded with the next, also alone, and then their voices joined in the same manner as their hands, separate but intertwined, pressed tightly together, blending in perfect harmony. Hattie had never heard anything so beautiful, or two voices so absolutely in sync.

The music turned almost dreamlike, otherworldly.

Hattie was certain she'd been given a glimpse into eternity, into the true nature of God's grace that played out between the two women on stage. She would paint this scene and never, ever put the piece up for sale or hang it on a wall at an exhibit. The performance ended all too soon. The audience surged to their feet again, this time with cries of "Brava!"

Backstage after the concert, the cardboard box tucked under one arm, Hattie and Oliver congratulated both singers. Then, while her husband spoke softly with Frieda about her life since her release, Hattie asked for a word in private with Elsa.

"We'll talk in my dressing room."

She followed her friend, shutting the door behind them. She waited for Elsa to sit on the small settee beside the dressing screen before placing the box on her friend's lap. The plain brown wrapping gave no clue as to what was inside. "For you," she said simply.

Confusion teased across Elsa's face. "You didn't need to bring me a gift. Your being here tonight is enough."

It was such a sweet, kind, Elsa thing to say.

Heart in her throat, Hattie lowered onto the settee beside her friend and flattened her hand on the lid. She'd waited until tonight for this moment, wanting Elsa to be back to herself again, or nearly there. "Go on. Open it. You'll understand once you do."

With her bottom lip clamped between her teeth, Elsa tugged on one end of the string. The knot released, and she removed the lid. A thin layer of tissue covered the contents. She looked up. Hattie nodded. Another smile, then Elsa shoved the paper aside.

"Are these..." she dragged her fingertip across the edge of the box "...are these," she repeated, almost reverently, "what I think they are?"

After a brief hesitation, where Hattie had to swallow several times to gain control of her voice, she nodded and said, "You and I learned very early on that our failures would far exceed our successes. So I decided, out of a need to remember the good we were doing, to keep a small something or other from each of the refugees we helped."

"Oh, Hattie." Elsa's hand flew to her mouth, then slowly, with great care, she began sorting through the contents. There were letters and handwritten notes. Telegrams from America. Photographs. Buttons off jackets, small pieces of string from a child's toy, some fringe from a sweater.

Tears sprang to Elsa's eyes. She dashed them away with an impatient swipe and continued digging through the box. Every now and again, she would pause over an item, shake her head and then, sighing, continue her inspection.

"Whenever you wonder if we made a difference or wonder if what you suffered was worth it, I pray these keepsakes will remind you of the good you did. And the lives you saved."

"*We* saved," she corrected, lifting her head. "The lives *we* saved, Hattie."

"The lives we saved," Hattie agreed. "And this," she said as she picked up the tube of lipstick that had traveled from Austria to Sweden with Elsa, and from Sweden to England with Hattie. "*This* will remind you of how brave you are."

Tears streamed freely down her cheeks now. "Thank you, Hattie. Thank you. I will treasure each item until my last dying breath."

Hattie blinked hard, holding her own tears at bay. If she let herself cry, she feared she wouldn't be able to stop. "May that be many, many, many years from now."

"I wish the same for you."

They shared a soft, watery smile.

"You have given me something else, dear friend, something of equal value as these keepsakes. You have given me hope that, despite my failures and mistakes, despite the loss of my marriage, I did what I could, and it was enough."

Hattie's vision blurred again. This time, she let the tears fall. And as she stood and pulled her friend into her arms, she said, "Yes, Elsa. It was enough."

★ ★ ★ ★ ★

Author's Note

I'm often asked, "Where do you get your ideas?" This seemingly simple question comes with a complicated answer. To put it bluntly, I really don't know. My stories come from somewhere, nowhere, everywhere. A snippet in a news story, a friend's personal triumph, a tragic moment in my own life or the life of someone I love. Mostly, though, the journey begins in the library or on a website dedicated to historical events. My research process is never straightforward. I tend to wander around haphazardly and have been known to fall down all kinds of rabbit holes.

One such path led me to the original inspiration for this novel. In my research about British immigration policy during the interwar years, I stumbled upon the daring Cook sisters, Ida and Louise, who orchestrated the rescue of twenty-nine Jews from Nazi Germany in the 1930s. What drew me to their story was my indirect connection to the younger sister.

Between 1936 and 1985, Ida wrote 112 romance novels as Mary Burchell for Mills & Boon, many of which were later reissued by my publisher, Harlequin. Like the fictional Hattie and Vera, the Cook sisters were civil servants with a strong passion for opera. In fact, they first learned of the persecution of Jews through their association with the Austrian conductor Clemens Krauss and his wife, Viorica Ursuleac. As I dug deeper into their incredible story, I continually asked myself, *What if?* (an author's favorite question) and soon began reimagining their brave feats into what ultimately became *The Secret Society of Salzburg.*

While I borrowed details from certain people and events, each of my main characters are a composite of their real-life counterparts and other extraordinary people who risked their lives to save Jews from Nazi persecution. If you're interested in finding out more about Ida and Louise Cook, I highly recommend Ida's autobiography, *We Followed Our Stars*, which was reedited and expanded in 2008 as *Safe Passage.*

Another particularly twisty path down a rabbit hole landed me at the gates of the Bergen-Belsen concentration camp. Located in northern Germany in the town of Bergen near Celle, the facility began its life as a prisoner of war camp during World War II. The official opening date is somewhat in question. However, in 1943, a portion of the facility became an exchange camp, where valuable Jewish inmates were held with the intention of exchanging them for German POWs. Most estimates claim that some 2,500 Jews were released or exchanged between the summer of 1943 and December 1944, though it may have been more. By March of 1944, a portion of the facility was designated as a recovery camp, and inmates too sick to work were brought there from other camps. With them came innumerable diseases. In November of that same year a section was dedicated solely to women and, sometime in the spring of 1945, both Margot and Anne Frank died at Bergen-Belsen.

While I took some creative license concerning Elsa and her case, my research did reveal that high-value inmates were treated less harshly. They were fed better and worked in the shoe commando where they salvaged scraps of leather from other concentration camps. Any errors are solely my own. I should also point out that the Salzburg Festival in 1935 ended at the beginning of September. For plot purposes, I pushed that date to later in the month.

On a happier note, the Salzburg Festival did reopen after the Allied victory in Europe. On May 4, 1945, two days before the war was officially over, American troops took control of Salzburg. Almost immediately, a decision was made to revive the festival. The event opened in August amid grand speeches and several concerts. Two-thirds of the attendees were members of the Allied armed forces, mostly American GIs, while the rest of the tickets were distributed among Austrians.

Confession time. I wasn't much of an opera fan before I wrote this book. After spending hours watching video clips and full operas, I am now a true devotee. I highly recommend any version of the Queen of the Night's aria from the second act of Mozart's *The Magic Flute*. My personal favorite rendition is by Diana Damrau from her performance with the Royal Opera.

"The Flower Duet" from *Lakmé* by Delibes is another recently discovered gem. Check out Nicole Heaston and J'Nai Bridges's or Elīna Garanča and Olga Peretyatko's performances on YouTube.

I would be remiss not to mention the many people who made this book happen. My agent, Michelle Grajkowski of 3 Seas Literary Agency, has been both cheerleader and consummate business partner from the start of our relationship.

Without her belief in me, her encouragement and unending support, my pivot into historical fiction would never have taken place. Special thanks also to my editor, Melissa Endlich. She caught the vision of this story from the very start and gave me the confidence to take risks I otherwise would have avoided. I adore working with such a funny, generous, like-minded woman whose enthusiasm and dedication keeps me happily meeting deadlines. Cheers, Melissa!

I'm so incredibly blessed to have the best writer friends on the planet. A huge shout-out to my "Step into the Story" co-horts, Barbara Tanner Wallace and Donna Alward. You make navigating this unpredictable business worthwhile, and who doesn't love talking books? I also want to mention my fellow authors Donnell Ann Bell and Winnie Griggs, who never fail to pick up the phone when I call in a story-induced panic. Each in her own way has managed to pull me out of a major plot hole (or twenty). You ladies are Rock Stars!

Another shout-out goes to my twin sister, Robin, who understands me in ways no one else does. Her artistic talent inspired Hattie and helped me bring the character to life.

As always, I'm grateful for my husband, Mark, and my beautiful daughter, Hillary Anne, two of the kindest people with the biggest hearts I know. I love you both dearly. Life would not be worth living without you in this world. I'm proud to call you mine.

Last but never least, thank you to my loyal readers. Your constant support, insightful reviews and thoughtful messages inspire me to continue writing bigger and better stories. Huzzah!

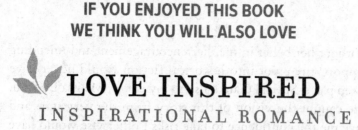
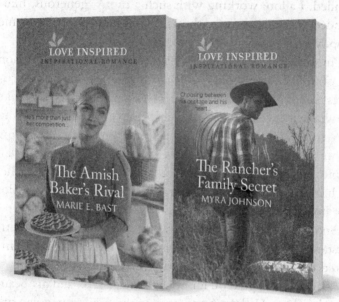